Letters of Mrs Gaske

Letters of
Mrs Gaskell's Daughters,
1856–1914

Edited by Irene Wiltshire

$\mathcal{HEB}$ ☼ Humanities-Ebooks

COPYRIGHT

First published by *Humanities-Ebooks, LLP,* Tirril Hall, Tirril, Penrith CA10 2JE

ISBN 978-1-84760-203-9 PDF
ISBN 978-1-84760-204-6 Paperback
ISBN 978-1-84760-205-3 Kindle

For Sarah Prince,
Mrs Gaskell's great-great-great granddaughter

On such a full sea are we now afloat

Julius Caesar, 4.3.221

Contents

ACKNOWLEDGMENTS

So seldom is anything worthwhile achieved by one person alone, that even a modest undertaking such as this incurs many debts, which I would like to acknowledge here. Jenny Uglow's footnotes to her *Elizabeth Gaskell: A Habit of Stories* first alerted me to the unpublished letters in the Houghton Library, Harvard University; and in the Wedgwood Archives, now at Barlaston. I am grateful to Jenny for this information and to both institutions for making it possible for me to transcribe documents held in their care. Staff at the John Rylands Library Manchester have been helpful in supplying me with unpublished letters for me to transcribe. Staff at Manchester Central Library, where Christine Lingard, even into retirement, helped to locate documents, proved once again just how valuable this institution is. During the time Central Library was closed for refurbishment, staff at Greater Manchester County Record Office retrieved documents from the Gaskell Collection, and from their own archives. Still in Manchester, staff at the Portico alerted me to the letter written by Meta following her father's death and supplied me with a photocopy. Emma Marigliano, Portico Librarian, has been helpful in locating rare out of print books and in suggesting English translations of Meta's and Marianne's Italian. I am also grateful for the opportunity to present a paper at the Portico in 2008 on letters sent by Marianne and Meta to the Norton family in North America. The British Library at St Pancras; Shropshire Archives in Shrewsbury; and the Brotherton, Leeds; all made me welcome and supplied me with manuscripts. The National Library of Scotland speedily sent me photocopies of letters when I was unable to undertake the journey to Edinburgh. Cambridge University Library has been helpful in locating a Darwin letter and sending me a photocopy. In my search for footnote material I have visited the British Library at Colindale where staff were helpful; and Birmingham City Library, where staff willingly brought up a trolley-load of nineteenth-century journals for me to peruse and helped me to photocopy selected articles. Knutsford Library provided me with access to the Stanton Whitfield Collection and newspapers held on micro-film.

Gaskell scholars who have been helpful in innumerable ways include Angus Easson, my former PhD supervisor; and Alan Shelston, co-editor with John Chapple of the *Further Letters*. Christine Lingard, retired librarian, has generously shared her specialist knowledge with me. Nancy Weyant, bibliographer and former university librarian, has helped with American idioms and customs. Dr Christine Joy, archivist at Manchester High School for Girls, where Meta Gaskell served as a governor for forty years, made me most welcome and allowed me to consult important material. Sarah Prince, Elizabeth Gaskell's great-great-great granddaughter, kindly consented to the publication of family letters. I very much appreciate Richard Gravil's willingness to publish this volume, especially given the difficulties faced by an unknown author. Friends who have expressed an interest in this work, as it has progressed from its infancy, are too numerous to mention individually; I hope their patience will be rewarded. Members of my family have been supportive, especially my husband Gerry. Any errors or other shortcomings in this volume are of course entirely my own.

Illustrations

The cover illustration is a portrait of Marianne, Meta and Flossie in 1845 by Charles Allen Duval. It is from a private collection.

The manuscript illustration on page 211 is reproduced by kind permission of the Portico Library and the engraving on page 241 by kind permission of Manchester Libraries.

Illustrations elsewhere have been used by the publisher in the belief that they are in the public domain: on receipt of information from copyright holders that this is not the case, appropriate action will be taken at the earliest possible moment.

INTRODUCTION

'These are my 4 children; for you must go on knowing them as they are, not their mere outsides, which are all you can see in pops'.[1] These words, in a letter written to her sister-in-law in 1851, indicate just how much Mrs Gaskell respected the inner lives and individual characters of her daughters. Nowhere do we gain a better insight into these aspects of her daughters' lives than in the content of their surviving letters. Not written to satisfy the demands of an English examining board, or any other critical authority, they provide today's reader with access to the spontaneous thoughts and feelings of Mrs Gaskell's daughters as they sat down to communicate with friends, family, or scholars associated with the publication of their mother's writing.

The letters cover a time-span of more than fifty years, starting in the middle years of the nineteenth century and concluding with Meta Gaskell's death in the second decade of the twentieth century. All periods of history are eventful and these years were no exception. Events overseas that impinged on the lives of these women include the Indian Mutiny (1857); the American Civil War (1861–65); the Franco–Prussian War (1870–1871); the Boer Wars (1880–81 and 1899–1902); and the Irish struggle for independence. At home they witnessed at first-hand some of the consequences of the American Civil War; were made aware of Fenian activities on British soil; followed the demands for electoral reform; and engaged in many of the debates current at that time. The connection by marriage between the Gaskell family and Charles Darwin promoted an interest in the changing attitudes that followed the publication of Darwin's research. All of these events and topics feature in this correspondence.

Mrs Gaskell's daughters were very privileged, in that they were never compelled from financial necessity to perform tasks they detested. Unlike Charlotte Brontë and her sisters, they did not work outside their own home as governesses, nor did they undertake any other paid work. Charitable work performed in Manchester was done from a sense of duty, but never from necessity. They enjoyed com-

---

1 *Gaskell Letters*, p. 61. In this context 'pops' refers to brief visits.

plete financial security but this did not lead to indolence or selfishness. They inherited from both their parents a sense of social responsibility and from their mother sociability and sympathy towards all who knew them.

As the girls were growing up in Manchester, Marianne and Meta, as the two older daughters, enjoyed privileges denied to Florence and Julia. The holiday in Italy in 1857, when they were joined by Charles Norton, proved to be a pivotal event for the Gaskell family. Marianne and Meta accompanied their mother on this adventure but Florence and Julia were considered to be too young to benefit from the trip. This means that the two older daughters formed relationships, notably with the Nortons and Storys, from which Florence and Julia were largely excluded.[1] In one of her letters Meta even refers to Julia as 'the child of the family'. The structure and hierarchy of the family changed considerably after Marianne and Florence married, especially as both made their marital homes in London, leaving their unmarried sisters behind in Manchester. Although there was an age gap of nine years between Meta and Julia, they became close companions, sharing many, though not all, interests and friendships. They were known for their hospitality at Plymouth Grove and honoured for their public duties.

As so often happens in families of several children there is one upon whose shoulders specific responsibilities fall. In this case it was Meta to whom publishers and editors turned, especially during the run-up to the Gaskell Centenary in 1910, when her mother's books were being reprinted. Meta appears to have accepted this responsibility at least initially with enthusiasm, taking pride in her mother's achievements and willingly protecting her reputation. Unfortunately, some of the demands made on her at this time proved to be intrusive and burdensome at a time when her health and strength and – one suspects – her memory were fading.[2] To make matters worse for her, she lost two sources of emotional support in one year: her sister Julia and her friend of fifty years, Charles Norton, both died in 1908.

---

1 The two letters in this volume from Florence to Charles Norton arise from only a brief meeting in England, after Norton and the older members of the Gaskell family had returned from the holiday in Italy.
2 Born in 1837, Meta was aged seventy-three by the time of the Gaskell Centenary.

If a certain amount of querulousness creeps into her later letters it is easily understood. Julia and Meta performed many public duties, some of which were associated with their father's ministry at Cross Street Chapel and the Sunday School at Lower Mosley Street. They helped to relieve distress in the city as their mother had done, following on from her example. They felt the loss of their father in 1884 keenly, yet there is some indication that from this time on they felt able to develop the hospitality for which Plymouth Grove became renowned.

Though only a small number of letters from Julia have survived, they offer valuable insights into her mode of thinking and her interest in public events of her time. One letter in particular demonstrates a certain mental toughness and agility as she grapples with the complex issues of Fenianism as she struggles to express these complexities. Overseas travel was important to both women for as long as they were able to undertake the journeys. One suspects that Meta may have taken delight in introducing her younger sister to sights she herself had first seen with her mother and Norton in 1857. A recurring motif in the letters, especially those from the unmarried daughters, is their sense of loss without their mother. A major source of consolation for Meta was a sharing of this sorrow with Charles Norton since he had known and admired Mrs Gaskell so well. For Julia it was the sharing of thoughts with her sisters, especially Meta, that provided consolation. During their later years, letters and notes are increasingly written from Silverdale where many family holidays had been spent with their parents. There is never any suggestion in their letters that either Meta or Julia felt less than happy in their unmarried state or in their place of abode. Manchester, with all its disagreeable aspects, provided them with ample opportunities for fulfilment.

In many ways life was kinder to Meta and Julia than it was to Marianne and Florence. Marianne, who was so thrilled with her engagement to Thurstan Holland, may indeed have enjoyed a happy marriage, but suffered blow after blow as her children were born. Not only did she suffer the loss of at least one infant, a common enough occurrence during her lifetime, but at least two of her children were born profoundly deaf, a tragedy made topical by the post-

Darwinian challenge to the custom of cousin marriages. After the death of William Gaskell in 1884, Meta and Julia still had each other for companionship, but in that same year Marianne became a widow following the death of her husband Thurstan. In spite of all these sorrows she was the longest surviving daughter, living on until 1920. Unfortunately, her extant letters peter out shortly after her marriage, either because no more have been found, or because pressures of family life prevented her from writing more. It is through Meta's letters that we learn of Marianne's marital joys and disappointments.

Florence, the first daughter to marry, enjoyed considerable material comfort and social position in her marriage, writing from a grander address near Hyde Park than Marianne's in Wimbledon. Although her mother had once written despairingly of Florence's lack of ability, she clearly inherited her mother's talent for socializing and, with more time at her disposal than her mother, was able to entertain some of the London literati of that time. Though childless, it was a full and happy life until her untimely death in 1881 when she was still in her thirties.[1] We may surmise that this early death impacted most severely on Marianne, since it robbed her of the one family tie available to her in London. Three years later, following the death of her husband, she removed to Alfrick in Worcestershire; from where some of Meta's later letters were sent, apparently visiting her older sister.

Though each decade of the time span, 1856–1914, is represented here, there are many tantalizing gaps in this correspondence. It seems likely that Meta and Julia would have kept up correspondence with their married sisters 'down south', but whatever was sent from Manchester or Silverdale has not yet surfaced, and may indeed have been destroyed. Any letters sent to Plymouth Grove were almost certainly destroyed as Meta was particularly sensitive to any kind of intrusion into family affairs. Apart from family correspondence, there was undoubtedly an exchange of letters between Meta, acting as her mother's literary executor, and Adolphus Ward during the time he was preparing the Knutsford Edition of *The Works of Mrs Gaskell*, but this is also yet to be found. Another exchange of letters not yet

---

1   The official death certificate recorded an accidental overdose as cause of death. I am grateful to Christine Lingard for this information.

found relates to the commissioning of the Gaskell Memorial Tower in Knutsford in March 1907. All we have are newspaper reports of the event, which include apologies from the Miss Gaskells who were abroad, albeit on medical advice.[1] Their feelings about this project remain obscured, though some of the surviving letters do indicate a rather ambivalent relationship between Mrs Gaskell's daughters and Knutsford people. Other gaps relate to subject matter. Meta and Julia were interested in the visual arts and especially newly commissioned works by the Pre-Raphaelites, yet there is no reference to Ford Maddox Brown's murals commissioned by Manchester Town Hall. This is especially surprising since Brown moved to Manchester at this time even becoming a near neighbour of the Gaskells as he took up residence in Victoria Park. If this volume leads to discoveries of letters tucked away in family archives some of these gaps may be filled in the fullness of time.

The lives of these four women, especially those who lived into old age, ran parallel with the lives of women who pioneered higher education and entry into the professions for women, including Millicent Fawcett and others. Meta's letters, especially, show an awareness of these developments but there is no indication that she or her sisters wished to participate in these opportunities themselves, or that they wished to campaign for them on the behalf of other women. Any involvement in formal education appears to be restricted to Meta's activities as governor of Manchester High School for Girls. Perhaps this is the more typical attitude of middle-class women of their generation; the more forward attitude of others being the exception. Activities of suffragettes and the more moderate suffragists find no mention in these letters.

In addition to insights into the thoughts and feelings of Mrs. Gaskell's daughters, these letters also provide insights into the world of the nineteenth-century urban bourgeoisie, non-conformist in religious persuasion and Liberal in political allegiance. Social contacts are principally with other Unitarians, including the Wedgwood family, the Darwins, the Greens and of course the Norton family in

---

1   *Knutsford Guardian*, 27 March 1907, p. 2, cols. 3-6 and *Manchester Guardian*, 25 March 1907, p. 5, cols. 2-3.

North America. All are very comfortably off, but their income is not derived from land. Generally speaking they are people who enjoyed their privileges but not without a sense of social responsibility. As the last surviving daughter, Marianne would have witnessed major social reforms of the first decades of the twentieth century. What were her thoughts on the introduction of the old age state pension, or national insurance? Since her marriage in 1866 Marianne had kept herself isolated from urban misery, visiting her old home in Manchester infrequently. Julia and Meta died in 1908 and 1913, peacefully, in the city which had claimed their allegiance throughout their lifetimes.

Elizabeth Gaskell, the writer, has left a legacy that has been well nurtured and which is widely appreciated. But Mrs Gaskell was also a mother who gave the world four quite exceptional human beings. Only one of her daughters, Marianne, contributed to an ongoing line of descent, a line that continues to this day. All four daughters have bequeathed to us in their letters their thoughts and feelings as they engaged with significant issues of their times. Mrs Gaskell's early death when her youngest daughter was only nineteen meant that she was spared the sorrow of one daughter's untimely death and the agony of witnessing another daughter's struggle to come to terms with the plight of her disabled children. If she had been spared another twenty years, reaching her mid-seventies, as two of her daughters did and many people do today, she would certainly have been proud of her four children, for their noble thoughts and feelings and for their courageous attitudes to life.

EDITORIAL POLICY AND NOTE ON THE TEXT

It is only when reading manuscript letters, such as these, that one has the opportunity to capture the thought processes and feelings of the writer. For these reasons every effort has been made to remain faithful to the original manuscripts, reproducing all the hesitations, second thoughts, and deletions that are characteristic of spontaneous writing. To indicate the author's deletion I have used { }; for an author's insertion I have used \ /. For an editorial insertion I have used [ ]; where a word is illegible I have placed a question mark in brackets [?]; where there is uncertainty I have placed a question mark in front of the doubtful word in brackets, for example [?word]. Manuscript gaps are indicated by < >. All four authors of these letters have made regular use of the dash where we would use commas or other forms of punctuation. The varying length of these dashes has been standardized in this volume by using the en dash – . Idiosyncratic spelling and punctuation have both been reproduced here, with *sic* used only sparingly. Titles of publications are given here in the same form as in the original letters, with full details in the footnotes. Where underline has been used in the manuscripts, usually to indicate emphasis, this appears in italics in my transcription. Paragraphing has posed a particular problem, not only for its lack of consistency in the original scripts, but because of the habit of 'cross' writing towards the end of the letter. While trying to remain true to the original divisions in the letters, I have standardized the indentations in order to achieve a neat and attractive layout. The date the letter was written, wherever it appears on the manuscripts, is given here at the top right-hand of the letter, after the sender's address.

The letters are presented in four groups, beginning with the oldest daughter and concluding with the youngest. Within each group, letters are presented in chronological order. Most have been dated, either by the author; an archivist; or by myself, picking up clues from the content of the letter or from the postmark when that is present. Unfortunately, a few have to remain undated. Every effort has been made to produce comprehensive footnotes, but some references have remained stubbornly elusive.

Whenever possible I have examined the original script. Where this has not been possible, either because of travel distance, or because material is kept on microfilm, I have transcribed photocopies. Unless stated otherwise, all transcriptions are my own, as are any inadvertent departures from accuracy, of which I hope there are none, or at least very few.

ABBREVIATIONS AND SHORT TITLES

Bartholomew   A.T. Bartholomew, *A Bibliography and Memoir of Sir Adolphus William Ward 1837–1924* (Cambridge, 1926)

BHW   Barbara and Hensleigh Wedgwood, *The Wedgwood Circle, 1730–1897* (London, 1980)

Brill   Barbara Brill, *William Gaskell 1805–84: A Portrait* (Manchester, 1984)

BPM   Brontë Parsonage Museum

Catton   Bruce Catton, *This Hallowed Ground*, Wordsworth Edition, (Chatham, 1998)

Chadwick   Ellis H. Chadwick, *Mrs Gaskell: Haunts, Homes, and Stories* (London, 1910, revised 1913)

Colloms   Brenda Colloms, *Charles Kingsley: The Lion of Eversley* (London, 1975)

Companion to Dickens   *Oxford Reader's Companion to Dickens*, ed. by Paul Schlicke (Oxford, 2000)

CSS   Confederate Steam Ship

Darwin: Life and Letters   *The Life and Letters of Charles Darwin, Including an Autobiographical Chapter*, ed. by his son, Francis Darwin, 3 vols (London, 1887), in *The Complete Works of Charles Darwin Online*

David Peter   David Peter, *In and Around Silverdale* (Silverdale, 1984 and 1994)

Davies   Norman Davies, *Europe: A History* (Oxford, 1996)

Davis and Ginsborg   John A. Davis and Paul Ginsborg, *Society and Politics in the Age of the Risorgimento: Essays in Honour of Denis Mack Smith* (Cambridge, 1991)

DNB   *Dictionary of National Biography* (London and Oxford, 1882–1990)

Domestic Mission   *Annual Reports of Manchester Domestic Mission to the Poor* (Manchester)

Early Years   J. A. V. Chapple, *Elizabeth Gaskell: The Early Years* (Manchester, 1997)

Further Letters   *Further Letters of Mrs Gaskell,* ed. John Chapple and Alan Shelston (Manchester, 2000)

Gaddums Revisited   *Gaddums Revisited: A Family's History*, rev. by Anthony H Gaddum (Macclesfield, 2005)

Gaskell Letters   *The Letters of Mrs. Gaskell,* ed. J. A. V. Chapple and Arthur Pollard (Manchester, 1966)

Grove   *The New Grove Dictionary of Music and Musicians*, ed. by Stanley Sadie and John Tyrrell, 2nd edn, 29 vols (London, 2001)

GSJ   *Gaskell Society Journal*

Hall   Vernon Hall, *A Scrapbook of Snowdonia* (Ilfracombe, 1982)

Hewison   Robert Hewison, Ian Warrell and Stephen Wildman, *Ruskin, Turner and the Pre-Raphaelites* (London, 2000)

Hyde   F. E. Hyde, *Blue Funnel: A History of Alfred Holt and Company of Liverpool from 1865 to 1914* (Liverpool, 1956)

Jump   *Women's Writing of the Romantic Period, 1789–1836: An Anthology*, ed. Harriet Devine Jump (Edinburgh, 1997)

Henry James Letters   *Henry James Letters*, ed. by Leon Edel, 2 vols (Camb. Mass., 1975)

Keegan   *The American Civil War: A Military History* (London2009)

Kuper   *Incest and Influence: The Private Life of Bourgeois England* (Harvard and London, 2009)

Letters of Charlotte Brontë   *The Letters of Charlotte Brontë*, ed. by Margaret Smith, 3 vols (Oxford, 1995–2004)

Lohrli   *Household Words: A Weekly Journal 1850–1859 Conducted by Charles Dickens; Table of Contents, List of Contributors and their Contributions*; compiled by Anne Lohrli (Toronto, 1973)

Manchester Martyrs   Paul Rose, *The Manchester Martyrs: The Story of a Fenian Tragedy* (London 1970)

Messinger   Gary S. Messinger, *Manchester in the Victorian Age: The Half-Known City* (Manchester, 1986)

Milward   Richard Milward, *Wimbledon Past* (London, 1998)

Norton Letters   *Letters of Charles Eliot Norton, with Biographical Comment by His Daughter Sara Norton and M. A. De Wolfe Howe*, Illustrated, 2 vols (Boston and New York, 1913)

OCEL   *Oxford Companion to English Literature*, ed. by Margaret Drabble 6th edn (Oxford, 2000)

ODBH   *Oxford Dictionary of British History*, ed. John Cannon (Oxford, 2001)

ODNB   *Oxford Dictionary of National Biography*

Parry   His Honour Sir Edward Parry, *My Own Way: An Autobiography* (London, 1932)

Payne   The Revd George Payne, *Mrs Gaskell and Knutsford*, 2nd edn (Manchester and London, 1905)

Piper   David Piper, *The Illustrated History of Art* (London, 1991)

Portrait   J. A. V. Chapple and John Geoffrey Sharps, *Elizabeth Gaskell: A Portrait in Letters* (Manchester, 1980)

Ruskin Norton Letters   *The Correspondence of John Ruskin and Charles Eliot Norton*, ed. by John Lewis Bradley and Ian Ousby (Cambridge, 1987)

Sharps   John Geoffrey Sharps, *Mrs. Gaskell's Observation and Invention: A Study of Her Non-Biographic Works* (Fontwell, 1970)

Uglow   Jenny Uglow, *Elizabeth Gaskell: A Habit of Stories* (London, 1993)

Vanderbilt   Kermit Vanderbilt, *Charles Eliot Norton: Apostle of Culture in a Democracy*, (Cambridge, Mass., 1959)

Wellesley   *The Wellesley Index to Victorian Periodicals 1824–1900*, ed. by Walter E. Houghton and others (Toronto, 1966–89)

Whitehill   *Letters of Mrs. Gaskell and Charles Eliot Norton 1855–1865*, ed. with an Introduction by Jane Whitehill (1932), (Hildesheim and New York, 1973)

Wik.   *Wikipedia*

MARIANNE GASKELL

1834–1920

Elizabeth and William Gaskell's oldest surviving daughter,
'practical and humorous' (*Gaskell Letters*, p. 537).
Family names included 'Minnie' and 'Polly'.

Marianne may have been the first daughter to form an attachment, but she was the second to marry. A year after her mother's death, after a long courtship, she married her second cousin Edward Thurstan Holland, grandson of Swinton Holland. Marianne and Thurstan set up home in Wimbledon, South of the Thames, at 1, Sunnyside. In 1884, following the death of her husband, Marianne removed, with her children, to Alfrick Court, Alfrick, Worcestershire, where she spent most of the remainder of her life.

As one of the two older daughters, she accompanied her mother and sister to Italy in the spring of 1857, thus meeting Charles Eliot Norton, the young American who became a lifelong friend of the Gaskell family.

CHARLES ELIOT NORTON

43 Via di San Isidoro –
[Rome 1857]

Dear Mr Norton

You need not ask if we are tired of seeing your hand-writing without it being necessary to ask you the same question. The Vittura man has been here and agreed to take us to Sienna [*sic*] for 65 Scudi, and now the question to be settled is whether to start on Tuesday or Wednesday, which would you like best – If we start on Tuesday Mr Story[1] and he thought it best to leave at 10 o'clock in the morning. Déjeuner at [?], sleep at Ronciglione – The next day Déjeuner at Viterbo, sleep at San Lorenzo – The next day Déjeuner at [?Contino] or [?], sleep at San Quirico and by noon of the following day reach Sienna, leave by the ½ past 3 train for Florence and arrive at 7. I suppose the same arrangements would hold good if we started on Wednesday, always wishing for your consent to it. What do you think of those stopping places? and what do you think of waiting till Wednesday, and so having one quiet day after all the confusion of Easter. Many thanks for your invitation to lunch, it would have been very "jolly" only we were hearing Palestrina's Mass[2] which I privately speaking don't admire – Tomorrow we go to see the Benediction & to the English Church in the afternoon. I am sorry we have not been able to see you today.

Written in the name of all the Gaskells by the hand of yours
Very truly
Marianne Gaskell.

I don't know why ladies write on the third page except when no blotting paper is in the way.

Address: Charles E. Norton Esq 3 Piazza di Spagna

Houghton Library, Harvard University. MS Am 1088 3485.

---

1 William Wetmore Story, an American sculptor who, with his wife Emelyn, provided hospitality to the Gaskells at 43 Via di Sant' Isidoro, during their holiday in Rome (Uglow, p. 417).

2 Giovanni Palestrina, sixteenth century composer of madrigals and masses, he composed more than one hundred masses (*Grove*).

CHARLES ELIOT NORTON

43 Via di San Isidoro
Thursday Evening.
[Rome 1857]

Dear Mr Norton

Mama wishes me to write and tell you that much as we should like to take four days between here and Florence, she thinks we cannot manage to give more than three, without cutting either Florence or Venice short of a day. You see we are obliged to be in Manchester by a certain day[1] and therefore have no extra time to spend in small places. We should very much like to see Sienna, but that seems impossible. Will you tell François[2] please that we should be glad to go in three days from here to Florence and then we leave the stopping places to his decision as he will know much better than we do which will be the best.

I am sorry I did not know when I spoke to you this afternoon that three days was the time Mama wished to go in as it may inconvenience François, but I hope not. We shall see you early tomorrow I hope.

Believe me to remain
Very truly yours
Marianne Gaskell.

Address: Charles. E. Norton Esq 3 Piazza di Spagna

Houghton Library, Harvard University. MS Am 1088 3486.

CHARLES ELIOT NORTON

June 26th [1857]
Plymouth Grove

My dear Mr Norton,

We are so glad you are coming to us next Tuesday only we very much hope that you will not think of going away on Wednesday. You

---

1 A likely reference to the Manchester Art Treasures Exhibition, which opened in May 1857.

2 François was Norton's courier (Whitehill, p. 2, n.1).

must really not treat us so shabbily or we shall for the future disbelieve in poetical licence[.] I think that Mr Lowell's line "I only know [s]he came and went" is much too sober earnest.[1] Mama says that she quite expects & very much hopes that you will stay longer; if you really cannot next week, you must come again before you sail. This evening with your letter, came one from Mrs Story written from their villa at Sienna [*sic*] – They have taken a lease of six years, of a wing of the Barberini palace, the part that used to be inhabited by Lady Coventry.[2] They are going to furnish it for themselves – The next time we go to Rome I suppose it will be there.

Beau-beau has had his curls all cut off, much to Mrs Story's regret as you may imagine. Mr Wild[3] has gone to Venice with Mrs [?Tapham], but he goes to the Storys in September. Don't you envy every one at Venice? All our Italian tour seems like a very vivid dream, more than a reality, we have so completely settled down into our home life again, though to be sure not quite as it used to be for the Exhibition makes us not as quiet as usual. You will [be] sorry Hearn[4] has been very unwell; she is at present at the sea-side – but she comes back tomorrow.

Did you see Dr Cruickshank in Rome, one of the noble band of Catholics, he has been in Liverpool lately, so the Roman colony both Catholic & Protestant seems now quite broken-up. In the frivolity line, I must tell you that Mrs Story got the Scarabic ornaments for Mrs Sturgis,[5] and entrusts them to Mr Waters to bring to England. Mama sends you a ticket to inspect a private collection of Pre-Raphaelite pictures, that Rosetti sent her & that she has no use for. Good bye till Tuesday do try and stay as long as you can, we shall have so much to talk to you and to tell you about.

---

1   James Russell Lowell, 'She Came and Went', *Poems of James Russell Lowell* (London: Oxford University Press, 1912), p. 125.

2   Possibly wife of George, 6th Earl of Coventry (1722–1809); for the Barberini Palace, see *Baedeker Rome*, p. 80.

3   Hamilton Wild, painter and friend of Charles Norton; he was a member of the group of friends with whom the Gaskells kept company during their Roman holiday (Uglow, p. 420).

4   Ann Hearn, family servant, and friend, for more than fifty years (Uglow, p. 150).

5   Mrs Russell Sturgis, American acquaintance of Mrs Gaskell; see *Further Letters*, p. 166 and 168, n.11.

Yours most truly
Marianne Gaskell.

CHARLES ELIOT NORTON

42 Plymouth Grove
Thursday July 9[th.] [1857]

My dear Mr Norton

Thank you very much for your note and all the things contained in the parcels. Mama thanks you very much indeed for the fan which is just the kind she likes so much. As for the "Guida di Venezia"[1] in its binding no one would recognize the old friend though the inside[,] the important part of a friend, is just like itself. The gondola does so carry one back to Venice and those happy days there. We had a long letter from Mr Story the other night so "picturesquely" written, you know his charming way of talking and his writing is just like it. How I do envy Mr Wild & Mr & Mrs Field,[2] where are they at Venice at [?Danielli's]? We were not particularly loyal when the Queen came, by we I mean Mama, Meta and I, but all the rest of the household went and waved handkerchiefs and shouted and did everything loyal. You ask if we celebrated the 4th of July? Why should we? We are true Britishers, and don't keep your American festivals. Send me word what July 4th is really. When you write to Mr. Field please send my kindest regards to him and his wife, indeed we all send our kindest regards to them. Mama sends you her very kindest regards and says we shall be delighted to see you next week whenever you like to come.

Mr Ruskin lectures tomorrow and Monday. Did you say you were going to hear him at Oxford.[3] I enclose a note to you from Meta telling you of her engagement.[4] I don't know if it will surprise you.

---

1   *Guide to Venice.*
2   John W. Field and his wife, friends of Norton (*Norton Letters*, I, 127–28, 159; and Uglow, pp. 422–23).
3   Ruskin spent time in Oxford in July 1857 working on the lectures he was to deliver in Manchester that month (*Norton Letters*, I, 173).
4   Meta Gaskell became engaged to Captain Charles Hill, a British army officer in the Madras Engineers (Uglow, pp. 416 and 437). The engagement was subse-

We are very glad to see her so happy, though at present owing to Indian news it is very anxious work. He & his sister and little boy are coming tomorrow and will be with us next week when you come. We shall have a bed to offer you & *quite* at your service all week so please don't fancy because the Hills are with us that it will be any inconvenience for indeed it will [?] only a great pleasure. We were so much disappointed that you could not come last week. I have never either been to Oxford or Cambridge so that I have a great pleasure in store yet. Mama joins me in best remembrances

Ever yours faithfully
Marianne Gaskell

Houghton Library, Harvard University. MS Am 1088 3495.

CHARLES ELIOT NORTON

{Plymouth G}
Knutsford
September 8th. [1857]

My dear Mr Norton.

I am taking advantage of what you said one day that you hoped the correspondence begun in Rome should not stop. I am very anxious you should hear something about us, and our doings and in return that we should hear about you and yours. Captain Hill left us for India last Monday week. The parting was very trying for Meta of course. She tried too much a great deal to control herself and so afterwards had to pay the penalty and for a few days she was very unwell. However now she is much better again. Indeed quite well. Mama I am sorry to say is very far from strong. I think all the anxiety she has gone through has been too much for her, and after keeping up for so long the reaction has now come. Papa too has been very unwell. He went with his brother to the Lakes for some time and the complete change and freedom did him a great deal of good. The Indian news has depressed us all very much. Our friends the Ewarts have lost a brother, his wife and child in the massacre at Cawnpore[1] and what

---
quently terminated.
1 A reference to the Siege of Cawnpore, during the Indian Mutiny, in which all

makes it much worse for them is that they have heard no definite account, and are only feeling quite certain they are killed from hearing that every one at Cawnpore is massacred. It seems to me strange that a person holding as high a position as Colonel Ewart did should never have been mentioned by name in any account or list of names that has been published. I still feel as certain as they do that there is no hope of his escape and all one can now wish for them is that they may have been killed at once – instead of suffering any of the atrocious tortures so many have. It seems a very heavy price to pay for keeping India. All this dreadful bloodshed and murder. [?An acquaintance] I was talking to the other day said, that all this was a strong medicine which was quite necessary and that India would after it be in a better state than it had ever yet been and Europeans would have a greater prestige there than they ever yet have had. Do you think it can be so? It is a great comfort that the Madras Presidency remains quiet and people seem to think it will continue so. The Sepoys there are allowed to have their wives and children with them, whereas in Bengal they are separated from them. Since you left we have had a pretty constant succession of visitors. Among others Captain Hill's little boy. A charming manly little fellow. Julia was most anxious that he should call her "aunt" but Dudley could not understand why Julia so little older than himself should be dignified with such a title, so his answer was "If you will call me Uncle Dudley I will call you Aunt Julia". So that was the agreement made, but broken on both sides. staid with us six weeks and now has gone back to school. I feel quite proud of "my nephew". I wish you could see him. We have been very constant in our visits to the Exhibition and I think now we are pretty thoroughly acquainted with it. The old pictures grow upon [one] the more one sees of them. The Giottos particularly. I found out the other day what seemed to me a little gem, a Titian in the clock gallery where the [?] are[.] I wonder if you saw it. It is a Madonna and child.

Meta had a letter yesterday from Mrs. Story; they are still at Sienna and expecting Mr[?s] Wild to come and spend a month with them.

---

members of a British garrison were murdered (*ODBH.*). Colonel Ewart was in command of 1st Native Infantry at Cawnpore; his brother was William Ewart (1798–1869), M. P. , of Broad Leas, Devises, Wiltshire (*Gaskell Letters*, pp. 468 and 474).

Was it before you came or while you were with us Mr Waters "turned up" (forgive the slang!) as I remember while you were with us. Since then the only Roman friend we have seen has been Lord Feilding.[1] He spent his evenings with us and one morning at the Exhibition he looked particularly at the Turners and the early water colours, and compared them together. François sent Mama the most charming French letter the other day. Just like himself. He gave a little criticism of Mary Barton which was very good. Oh! and who do you think I saw the other day at the Exhibition? [?Speracus] He was with the Queen of Spain's son. Poor fellow, he does not like his employment at all. He says the son [?"est coucen un vrai diable"]. Now for him to use such strong language one feels sure things must be very bad. He enquired a great deal after you and Mrs Field. I was very glad indeed to see him. What a charming master he was. Papa was very much obliged to you indeed for the hymn books you sent him, and I am very much obliged to you for Sir I. Inglebley. I pronounce the name to the great admiration of my family who cannot manage it.

I came here (alias Knutsford) yesterday to stay with some very old friends of ours. Knutsford you know is Cranford, only the people here don't at all approve of its being called Cranford. I might be also going to a regular Cranfordian party of old ladies and hardly any gentlemen and the Sedan Chair and lantern will be in requisition.

How are Mrs Norton and your sisters[?] I wish I might send them some message for I feel to know them through your account of them. Please if I may will you give them some message.

 And believe me –
 Affectionately yours
 Marianne Gaskell.

Houghton Library, Harvard University. MS Am 1088 3488.

---

1   Possible reference to the seventh Earl of Denbigh, father of Lady Mary Feilding (*ODNB*); *Gaskell Letters*, p. 334 and *Further Letters*, pp. 182–84 and n.1.

CHARLES ELIOT NORTON

Plymouth Grove
January 25th. 1858.

My dear Mr Norton

Thank you very much indeed for your letter which came abut ½ an hour ago when we four Miss Gaskells were having lunch off a true English piece of roast beef. Mama I am sorry to say \is/ not well at all. All this year's anxiety is telling upon her. You knew her enough to know how anxious she makes herself & that continued anxiety must tell upon her in time. She is very weak and is not allowed to see any one; otherwise she has not much the matter, still it makes me very anxious when I see her lying quite helpless and not having energy enough to talk. Still I hope long before this letter reaches you she will be quite herself again. I have read your letter which she enjoyed hearing very much indeed. I am very sorry indeed for your loss, it is of a most provoking nature, because you cannot have the satisfaction of feeling that the things so precious to you will be valued by the person who has got them – I am particularly sorry the Albert Durer's[1] are lost; indeed I am sorry for all[.] I don't know which thing could best have been spared.

Today is our Princess Royal's Wedding Day, and every loyal subject feels doubly loyal today[.][2] I, as being one of her Majesty's most devoted subjects, feel great interest and rejoicing for her. You Americans though you may have some wonders we poor Englanders have not, are very badly off in not having a Queen such as we have. Dukes I *could* dispense with if there was a great necessity for doing so, but our Kings and Queens never[.] However as there is the Atlantic between us, instead of the width of a gondola I don't mean to quarrel because we could not shake hands and make peace as the children say.

Meta's auroral hours are very much altered. She finds bed these cold mornings irresistible and cannot understand how even to see

---

1   A likely reference to Albrecht Dürer (1471–1528), German painter and engraver, whose work was admired by Norton and his friend John Ruskin (*Ruskin Norton Letters*, p. 180, n.1).

2   Queen Victoria's eldest daughter, Victoria Adelaide (1840–1901), married Frederick III, German Emperor and King of Prussia, in 1858 (*ODNB*).

friends off you can have managed being down to breakfast at 7. Mr
Field's letter the part you quoted takes one back almost painfully
to Rome. It seems to me so unlikely that I shall ever go there again
that to have it brought as vividly before me as he does is as I say
almost pain – February 24th was the day you made vain attempts to
catch Meta's bonbons. It seems so long and yet so short a time since
then – There is such a complete alteration in our future since that
visit owing to Meta's engagement. The days seem slipping away
so fast that she is to be with us. I dread this year more than I can
tell you, the anxiety for Mamma & Papa will be most trying to see
– However there is no good being gloomy so long beforehand[.] I
am sorry though as you say not very much surprised at Mr Story's
want of success in obtaining orders, while I suppose there is no
real cause for them to be anxious about money matters is true[.] It
seems to me Mr Wild must be a good artist in the end. I hope he has
plenty of orders. It would be most discouraging to go working on
and filling your studio with your own works and no one coming to
buy them. I remember so well the particular \Knutsford/ story that
took Mr Wild's fancy, but I am sure we must have told it you about
'Scrattling'? Some cousins of Mamma's very often had an old lady
staying with them who was inquisitive and if the cousins went out
of the room or were away from her for some time, on their return
this old lady would make a point of saying "Well Mary, and what
have you been doing". Mary told her, but in time this grew very tiresome, so they determined to invent a word which was to mean anything they chose. So the next time the old lady asked the everlasting
question of "Well Mary and what have you been doing" ["]Oh["]
said Mary, ["]I have been 'Scrattling'["] The old lady never liked
to betray her ignorance of this word so she said "Oh Scrattling have
you and a very nice employment it is for you". Mr Wild was particularly charmed with this word and if anyone enquired too much
into his day's employment "Scrattling" was his constant answer.

We are so very much obliged to you for telling us the writers
in the Atlantic,[1] it adds very much to the interest knowing who

1   *Atlantic Monthly* founded in Boston, U.S.A., in 1857. Early contributors included
    H. B. Stowe, R. W. Emerson, H. W. Longfellow and Charles Norton (*Norton*

they are by. Mamaul is capital so very bright & sparkling. I have
not read it all yet, but little bits here and there. I think Theodosia
Comfort Green's begging letter in it is inimitable. "The two imbe-
cile children of various denominations" beyond measure good.[1] Did
you ever read Mr De Vere's poem called the Waldenses.[2] I met the
other day with an extract from it, in some American lectures on
English Literature, which was most beautifully. It was some lines
on Sorrow. Just like him. I have found out who "Philip my King"
is by.[3] It is by Miss Mulock the authoress of John Halifax etc. Mr
Henry Bright told me,[4] he had seen it in a book of autographs in her
hand writing and was told by the owner of the book that it was by
her – I have just lately been staying at the Brights and had such a
"good time". Harriette Bright is one of the noblest most conscien-
tious girls I have ever met with.[5] In her own home no girl can do
more than she does, and all done so quietly and naturally. Mr Henry
Bright is coming to us today. There is the Annual Examination of
the Home Missionary Students and Mr Bright has offered a prize
for theology[.] He is going to examine them and stays here when
he is not examining. My pens are so bad, I wish your pen that,
I left at Padua, do you remember?, was here instead of this quill
that will go every way but the one you want it to go. Did you ever
hear that an idle workman always complains of his tools, but I am
not idle – Meta says anything that you ask her to do she will have
the greatest pleasure in doing, only she is very curious and wants
very much to know what it can be. Hearn and the children have

---

Letters, i, 169 and 186; and Vanderbilt, pp. 68–69). Articles appeared unattributed in the *Atlantic*.

1 'Mamoul. Through the Cossitollah Kaleidoscope', *Atlantic Monthly*, 1 (1858),
336–43.
2 Aubrey Thomas de Vere (1814–1902), Irish born poet and author of *The
Waldenses, or the Fall of Rora: A Lyrical Sketch: with Other Poems* (Oxford,
1842); Waldenses were an early Protestant movement originating in Europe
(*OCEL*).
3 First published in Dinah Mulock, *Poems* (1859); see *Further Letters*, p. 183 and
p. 184, n. 3.
4 Henry Arthur Bright (1830–1884), a Liverpool Unitarian and friend of the Gaskell
family (*Further Letters*, p. 302).
5 Harriette Bright (1836–1916), younger sister of H. A. Bright (*Further Letters*, p.
302).

been spending their Christmas holidays with some cousins of ours both in Worcestershire and Gloucestershire. They came home on Friday and settled down again to lessons on Thursday. I have never thanked you in the name of the 4 Miss Gaskells for "Nothing to Wear["].[1] It is a clever little satire on the prevailing folly of dressing so extravagantly. My copy is so much superior, having illustrations which no English one has, that it is very seldom at home.

Baird Smith[2] has acted most nobly. I fancied that article on the Revolt must be by you because of the insertion of his letter. The Miss Ewarts[3] are always so glad to hear anything of him. I must go upstairs and see how Mama is, I have banished her from the drawing room as some friends are coming to stay here and I have forbidden her seeing them, as the medical man says so much about keeping her quiet. This letter dear Mr Norton has been a fortnight in my desk, for some unaccountable reason, I meant always to send it off directly and why I did not is one of the mysteries as great as where all the pens in this world go to. Mama is so much obliged to you for sending us the names of the writers in the Atlantic, you sent us all for January. May we always, if not very troublesome, have a list of the writers. Don't please take this as a specimen of my calligraphy, but my hands are perishing with cold. How winter makes one long for Italy. Should not you like to be there again? Mama since I began this letter has improved very much, indeed she is very nearly herself again, and in much better spirits than before her illness.

Did you ever \hear/ that Annie Austin is engaged to be married since you were here to a Mr Jenkins an old friend of ours & a very nice person indeed.[4] He has been staying with us lately and has taken

---

1 William Allen Butler, 'Nothing to Wear: An Episode of City Life', first published anonymously in *Harper's Weekly,* 7 February 1857, with illustrations by Augustus Hoppin.

2 Richard Baird Smith (1818–61) was a British Engineering Officer involved in the defeat of the Indian Mutiny (*ODNB*).

3 Agnes and Mary Ewart, friends of the Gaskell family, who lived in Manchester (*Gaskell Letters*, pp. 67 and 224–25).

4 Annie Austin was a Knutsford friend of Meta's. Henry Charles Fleeming Jenkin (1833–85), who was introduced to the Austin family by Mrs Gaskell, became a distinguished engineer, involved in cable laying across the Atlantic Ocean and, subsequently, taking the Chair of Engineering at Edinburgh University in 1868 (*ODNB*).

a very nice likeness of Meta. Going to Rome has made me so discontented with England. I do so wish now the year is nearly come round again since our setting out last year that I was going again. How soon do you think you shall be coming to England?

We had a long letter from Captain Hill on Sunday and had very good accounts, he seems quietly settled down in his new quarters at Dowlaiswaram[1] and is making great improvements in the station, from building a Roman Catholic Chapel, like the church at Ambleside, to a billiard room like a Swiss Chalet. Is Mr Black[2] come to England yet, because do you remember telling me once that you had asked him to bring some Italian songs for us, and I have never heard either of him or them. Also Mama would be most grateful to you if you would send her any American receipts that you know of. In return for them I will send you a bunch of daisies, & Mama a pot of raspberry preserve as we think America does not produce such sensible fruits. Our dear little Queen we won't send you. You would not appreciate her as she ought to be appreciated[.] Every member of our family from Papa to Lion[3] sends you their love.

> Believe me to remain
> Yours affectionately
> Marianne Gaskell.

Houghton Library, Harvard University. MS Am 1088 3489.

EFFIE WEDGWOOD

[London]
[22 April 1858]

My dearest Effie

To begin with dont be angry with Snowie[4] for reading me your letter but I wanted to hear about Monday. You horridly discontented girl why if I had a dance with Messrs Stirling & Wedgwood and sat

1   Dowlaiswaram, then an army station, is situated in south east India.
2   Charles Black, an English friend of Norton's, friend of Robert Browning the poet, and enthusiastic traveller in Italy (*Norton Letters*, I, 73 and 144–45).
3   Lion was the name of the Gaskell family pet dog (Whitehill, p. 20, n.1).
4   Frances Julia Wedgwood, known as Snow (1833–1913), older sister of Katherine Euphemia, better known as Effie (BHW).

out every other I should consider myself happy for a month[.] Mr
Reiss escaped my entirely. You never say what your [?dear] friends in
the next carriage said or did. Nothing has happened in these parts[.]
Snow & Meta did the article all yesterday morning and when I could
stand it no longer I took refuge in going to the school[;] fancy what a
pitch they must have reached to make *that* preferable. No more chapters for you.

     Your very affecte
     Minnie Gaskell.

Envelope: Miss Euphemia Wedgwood A J Scott Esq. Halliwell Lane Cheetham Hill
Manchester.

Postmarks: (back of envelope), Cheetham Hill AP 22 1858; Manchester AP 22
1858 and London.

By Courtesy of the Wedgwood Museum, Staffordshire; W/M 375.

CHARLES ELIOT NORTON

Silverdale
Monday July 5th [1858]

My dear Mr Norton

   Ever since a letter Mama sent to you some three months ago I have
been planning a letter to you but as you see it has never been accom-
plished. I was so very much ashamed of a shabby scrap I sent to you as
a kind of private letter of introduction, introducing my cousin to you.
The scrap above named was written in a country house which was as
full as it could hold of young people who entered a crusade against
letter-writers therefore I just escaped any serious harm by promising
to be a very short time writing; that explains why I wrote so shortly.
Why I have never written since I do not know, it has certainly not been
from want of inclination, {of} or from want of things to say, but partly
from want of time & partly from want of energy. This morning I got up
firmly determined that nothing should prevent me from sitting down
for a good long letter and to help on my resolution came your last
letter to Mama. Do you know writing a letter that has to go all the way
to America is a serious undertaking, one feels it ought to be so sensible
& grammatical, I am afraid I never do as I ought for sense & gram-

mar are not attainable. I have been to London for a month this spring. I went to see a dentist who kept me constantly dancing attendance on him for three weeks and the other week of the month in London I spent at Brighton. There's news for you – I did not see very much during my stay. I went twice to the Royal Academy which seemed to me poor. I never profess to know artistically what is good, but I know what pleases or displeases me and I think my Italian tour has helped me to like and dislike with some small degree of discrimination. The colouring of modern pictures after the old Italians, the very early Italian paintings I mean, seems very gaudy and no rest is given to the eye. Wallis the painter of Chatterton's death bed had a picture that I liked about as much as any in the Academy. It was a dead stone cutter.[1] The man has fallen back at the end of his day's work, quite wearied out with life, the heap of stones he has been cutting, or rather breaking is in front of him, he has been sitting in a little dell surrounded with grey rocks, and bushes everywhere but at one place through which opening you have a distant view and the moon light which falls on the man's face. A weasel is stealthily coming out of his hole on the dark side of the picture, that gives you a great feeling of the loneliness of the place. I liked it very much. I heard people objecting to the colouring as too grey, but it did not strike me in that way at all.

There was a picture of the Derby day by Frith[2] which was always crowded with people and was quite considered *the* picture of the Exhibition. To me it was very vulgar and unpleasant. There were no Millais, & no Hunts, indeed very few P. R. pictures, and those that there were, were not good. When I say not good, please remember I am speaking of pictures as they seemed to me, and by no means trying to pass a judgment upon them. Another thing that I did in London was going to see Kean's representation of the Merchant of Venice.[3] He said in his book of the play that he had been very care-

---

1　Henry Wallis (1830–1916), *The Stone Breaker*, 1857, first exhibited Royal Academy 1858, now at Birmingham Museums and Art Gallery.

2　William Powell Frith (1819–1909), *The Derby Day*, 1856–58, first exhibited Royal Academy 1858, now at Tate Britain.

3　Edmund Kean achieved fame in 1814 as Shylock in *The Merchant of Venice*; his son Charles (1811–68), also an actor, was manager of the Princess's theatre, 1851–59 (*OCEL*).

ful in representing Venice as it was in the days of the Merchant. The scenery was very good. There was the Piazza of St Mark but much smaller than it [?] now is which altered it very much indeed. The gondolas were quite different to what they are now. Did not you say that gondolas never had changed since they were first made? The inside of the council chamber {quite} looked very like a Titian with the senators in the dark crimson robes.

This letter got put away the other day and now today I am determined to finish it that it may not miss tomorrow's mail. Yesterday came from Miss Carey[,][1] we conclude[,] that "Come into the Garden Maud" that she used to sing in Rome.[2] Most provokingly it has come when we are staying in the country and have no piano to try it on. We are staying at Silverdale near Lancaster. Knowing the Gaskell family as you do, you must I think have heard of Silverdale as our dear summer haunt. We were calculating the other day and it is actually 15 years since we first came here. It seems making us very old to be reckoning back so far. We are all here but Papa who is going to make a walking tour somewhere in the South of England we believe, but Papa never tells us his plans beforehand. He is wonderfully better than he was when you were with us last year. Indeed I think he is better than he has been for 7 years. I wish you could see him now. Mama too is *much* better than she was when I last wrote. Silverdale air and quiet has worked wonders. The children, only really they are hardly children any more, play out of doors and lately I am sorry to say indoors, as the weather has been very bad; and very much regret that half their holidays are over. We have three weeks longer here. Then we go home to Manchester.

There is a very tiny little talk of an expedition to Heidelberg this autumn but whether it will be carried out is very doubtful. Having been to Italy makes one rather disinclined to go anywhere else. Still Heidelberg always sounds very beautiful. Miss Kate Winkworth[3] is

---

1   See *Gaskell Letters*, p. 514, for Mrs Gaskell's reference to Miss Carey.
2   Tennyson's lyric from his poem *Maud*, published in 1855, set to music by Michael W. Balfe, a prolific composer best remembered today for *The Bohemian Girl*.
3   Member of the Winkworth family, originally Manchester friends of the Gaskells, though in 1850 they moved to Alderley in rural Cheshire. Catherine and her sisters took lessons from William Gaskell (*Further Letters* p. 308).

coming to stay with us tomorrow for a few days. Our employments here are very few. We get up rather late and after that we go and fetch our letters as we are too primitive to have a post man of our own, then comes answering them and taking them down to the post again before dinner. After dinner we take a siesta though we have done nothing to merit the luxury of a siesta. Then we all go out a long walk till late tea which meal we consider the chef d'oeuvre of the day. After that we are almost ready for bed. Unfortunately the last week has been almost constant rain so that our employments have had to be indoors. One day this week we made an excursion some miles off we went partly by train partly by walking. When we arrived at Grange the place we were going a tremendous shower came on and instead of walking about the place we had to sit in the little tea parlour looking out at a cloud of rain straight in front of us. We could not get home till the train chose to start. It was rather amusing though quite differ-ent from what we planned. Annie Austin has been spending two days with us. She was here when your letter to Mama came, and begged when I wrote to be very kindly remembered to you Harriette Bright also has been here, so that our party has been much as last year, only we missed you among us – When will you come back to England, to Plymouth Grove rather. We will give you such a welcome if you only will come, & really as you try to make out to us crossing the Atlantic is nothing, and to you who have crossed so often it must be less than nothing. I saw Miss Emma Weston[1] in London. But I think you did not know her in Rome. Mr De Vere also I passed in the street, but I was driving and he was walking and not alone [so] that I did not like to stop. I am so very much disappointed that we have neither seen or heard anything of him except through you since we were in Rome. I had hoped he had cared enough about us not quite to let one most pleasant acquaintance with him drop. I suppose he never came to the Exhibition last year, or surely he would have come to see us. Mama had a charming note from Mr Wild the other day accompanying a book of sketches of the people at the Story's fancy ball this year. Do you remember last year when we were in Rome planning for all the Roman colony to meet in Scotland this summer. The Storys and Mr

1   A friend of Mrs Gaskell's since 1855 (*Gaskell Letters*, p. 352).

Wild seemed quite to think they should be in England this summer instead of which one set are at Sienna [*sic*] the other in Spain Do the Fields come home after this year? I must send this letter with a petition for forgiveness for my long silence and a promise of amendment. Mama and Meta send their love, they have a letter in contemplation to be written very soon.

Believe me to remain affect'ly yr
Marianne Gaskell.

Houghton Library, Harvard University. MS Am 1088 3494.

CHARLES ELIOT NORTON

Boughton House[1]
Worcester
Oct.13 59.

My dear Mr. Norton,

I hardly know how to begin a letter to you I have been so long in writing. Don't you know how when one puts off writing very long one is ashamed to begin. Today however I was determined no feeling of shame should prevent me from setting to. I sent you a message by my cousin Thurstan Holland in the spring to thank you so much for the Italian songs you told us long ago you had asked Mr Black to get for me. Owing to some mistake I only received them this year. They are excessively pretty for two months after I got them I could only sing them in my head as we were without a piano both in London and in Scotland. But before I begin with such late events as our summer excursion I must tell you as much as I can of our doings since I last wrote. It is actually nearly a year since I sent you a letter. I know you received it when Thurstan was with you. Mama, Meta & Florence came home from Heidelberg the day before Christmas Day, so that we were all together on that day. Soon after that I went for a short time to stay with the Brights in Liverpool. They are all very well and

---

1   Boughton House belonged to the Holland family. Marianne's mother frequently stayed at this address, especially when she needed rest or peace and quiet for her writing (*Portrait*, pp. 68, 92 and 94), but on this occasion she was at Plymouth Grove (*Gaskell Letters*, pp. 578–79).

going on just the same as ever. In May or rather the end of April to be quite accurate Thurstan came to spend a few days with us and to tell us his American experiences. He seemed most thoroughly to have enjoyed his trip. I was very glad he had seen so much of you, but it was very strange that you who secured *one* property should be quietly appropriated by him – We tried to convince him that he must not claim what did not belong to him – As soon as he left our house began to be painted & papered so we were obliged to leave it. Florence I forgot to mention had gone to school at Christmas to some old friends living at Knutsford (alias Cranford) who had just begun a school.[1] So she was there[,] Julia went as a boarder to her day school, Papa was quartered on different friends & Mama Meta and I set out together on our wanderings. First we went to stay with some cousins living in Derbyshire[.] But we were only five days together. When we separated Mama & Meta went to Oxford and I to London. In a week Mama & Meta came up to London and we went to Canterbury. Have you ever been there? The cathedral is I think one of the most beautiful English ones I have seen if not quite that. I used to be there hour after hour with Dr Stanleys "Memorials of Canterbury["],[2] and a handbook of Murrays.[3] I felt so much as if I were abroad again being in a cathedral and with a red Murray. Do you remember how in Italy you & Meta always arranged that I should have the red Murray thereby directly proclaiming myself to belong to the tribe of "forestieri", while you and she kept the black, red-leaved one. But I have gone away from Canterbury. I was a week there staying with one of Meta's old schoolfellows. After being separate for about a month, we joined forces & went into some lodgings up at Bayswater, where though we were a long way from every thing we had delicious air. We did all the pictures most thoroughly. The Royal Academy was not very good this year – Millais had two pictures about which there were

---

1 Henry Green (1827–73) was a Unitarian Minister at Knutsford; his daughters set up a school in the town (*Further Letters*, p. 305 and Uglow, p. 454).

2 Arthur P. Stanley (1815–81), *Historical Memorials of Canterbury* (London, 1855). Stanley was installed as Dean of Westminster in 1864; as leader of the Broad Church movement he promoted religious toleration (*ODNB* and *OCEL*).

3 John Murray published a series of travel guides, known as *Murray Handbooks*.

great differences of opinion. One was called "The Vale of Rest"[1] –
In the foreground were two nuns, one digging a grave and the other
sitting down with her face turned over her shoulder and looking out
of the picture – It was the time of day just after sunset when though
the lights are not as brilliant as at sunset there are most beautiful
coloured clouds, and a glow over every thing near them while the
rest is black. The nuns I did not particularly like, their faces were
very hard and their attitude did not seem to me good, but the background of small flowers between gravestones and shrubs relieved
through the branches of which the clouds were seen I thought capitally painted. The other picture "Spring Blossoms" I did not like.[2] In
the foreground were eight girls (I think) in a very awkward position,
you can imagine, lying, kneeling, & sitting, some playing with flowers & some eating something mysterious out of a bowl. They had all
brilliant coloured drapes, cheeks & hair so that there was no rest for
the eyes anywhere – Behind them was a low stone wall the bound-
ary to an orchard full of apple trees in full bloom. The flowers were
most carefully painted in point of colour & shape, but the size of
a girl's head considering the distance they were. Some people said
the grass underneath the trees was well done, to me it seemed too
blotchy – When I made the remark to Thurstan, he insulted me with
saying I was town-bred and could not tell what grass would look like
in Spring. We went to Rossetti's studio one afternoon and saw some
exquisite pictures, and also one he has done for you which we liked
very much. He is or rather was at that time at work on a picture of the
Magdalene when she first saw our Saviour. It is a most striking picture. Through the window of a house you see our Saviour sitting with
his disciples, I suppose hearing the noise outside he is looking out of
the window and his eye falls on the Magdalen who is outside with
her friends – She also is looking in at him & when their eyes meet,
it seems at once to bring before her the knowledge of her guilt. The
contrast of the holiness inside and the recklessness outside is most
beautifully given. And the Magdalen's look of anguish is too beauti-

---

1   *The Vale of Rest*, 1858–9 (Tate Britain).
2   *Spring (Apple Blossoms)*, 1859 (Lady Lever Art Gallery; National Museums
    Liverpool).

ful to be described – She is teasing the flowers out of her hair & you can fancy she is anxious at once to put away all recollections of the past except in so far that the remembrance may do her good. We only saw the sketch. I hope the picture will be a[s] well done.

From London we went straight up to Scotland where we spent a very pleasant month of complete solitude. There was no-one near us except some [?Maitland Kirwans] who strangely enough found us out and & claimed acquaintance for Rome's sake. They had met us the one evening we spent at Mrs Waters. You were not there but I think we told you about it. As soon as we saw him we remembered his face. We used to take long walks and read a great deal to make up for our two months dissipation. When we came home we had visitors directly, Mr & Mrs Brodie from Oxford and Sophie & Eunice Holland.[1] We worked hard at Manchester sight-seeing. Mr Brodie was particularly anxious to see the working of chemistry when applied to manufactures, so we dived into places we did not know existed before.[2] Meta & I went back with Sophie and Eunice to Dumbleton[3] where we spent ten days. We then came on here to stay with another set of cousins. Meta only staid four days & I have been a week longer than her but I go home on Saturday to be ready to receive Harriette Bright who comes to us on Monday. At the end of next week I hope Mama, & Meta will go to Whitby for a fortnight or so – Mama is much better than she has been for a long time but I want her not to be in Manchester during November if it can be helped. That month always tries her so very much. When we were at Dumbleton Thurstan gave us the likeness of Mrs Field that you sent Mama. You must think us the most ungrateful forgetful family going never to have written to thank you for all your kind remembrance of us, but in this case Thurstan is to blame & not us for we only got the parcel a fortnight ago – We are so sorry that Mrs Child[4] is obliged to go straight back

1   Sophie and Eunice were probably Thurstan Holland's sisters; he was one of twelve children (Uglow, p. 486).

2   Mr Brodie became Professor of Chemistry at Oxford in 1865 (*Further Letters*, p. 99, n. 1).

3   Dumbleton Hall in the Vale of Evesham belonged to a branch of the Holland family and was the home of Thurstan Holland before he married Marianne (Uglow, pp. 56 and 486).

4   Mother of Francis J. Child, scholar and friend of Norton, best remembered today

to America without coming to see us. Miss Sedgwick[1] sounds much worse and they seem anxious to get home as quickly as possible.

Have you seen "Ten Years of Preacher Life"? by a Mr Millburn[2] – There is a very interesting review of it in the Spectator of last week,[3] my cousin Mrs Isaac[4] wanted much to hear something about Mr Millburn so I said I was going to write and would ask you. All this time I have been writing a most egotistical letter about nothing but self. Please when you write will you do the same and tell me what you have been doing & how you are, and whether there is any chance of your coming to Europe soon – and when this may be. We heard from the Storys a short time ago – They and Mr Wild were at Sienna [*sic*] but talked of soon going back to Rome[.] They wanted Mama, Papa & Florence to go there this winter but they will not be able to manage it. I am afraid I must quite have tired you out with my long letter, but I hope for the future there will be no need to make it necessary to write such a long one, I mean I hope I may not be so lazy again.

Ever yours affectionately
Marianne Gaskell

Houghton Library, Harvard University. MS Am 1088 3490.

CHARLES ELIOT NORTON

42 Plymouth Grove
Friday Oct. 30ᵗʰ 1859.

My dear Mr Norton

I am not writing an answer to your charming letter received this week, that I shall do very soon. This letter is a business one for

for his *English and Scottish Popular Ballads*, 5 vols, 1882–98 (*Norton Letters*, I, 457, n.1 and *OCEL*).

1   Miss Sedgwick became F. J. Child's wife in August 1860, after a period of poor health (Whitehill, pp. 49 and 71).

2   William Henry Millburn (1823–1903) an American Methodist clergyman who lost his sight as a result of an accident in childhood (*Wik.*). Among his published works is his autobiography *Ten Years of Preacher-Life: Chapters from an Autobiography* (London: Sampson Low, 1859).

3   'Ten Years of Preacher-Life', *Spectator*, 32 (1859), 1040–41.

4   Mrs J. W. Isaac (née Charlotte Holland) (*Further Letters*, p. 180, n. 4).

Mama. Do you remember her telling you that she had undertaken to write a story for Harpers?[1] She finished it on Monday and sent it off to Sampson Low the American {book} publisher in London, he did not acknowledge the receipt of the parcel till this morning (Friday) I enclose his letter in which he says that Harper like the rest of the American world is suffering from money difficulties. Mama is very much afraid that Mr Low has delayed answering her letter that he might be able to send the story off tomorrow by the packet which sails then, without Mama's having the power to stop it. She says he has \done/ one or two "*dodgy*" things of the kind before. She is afraid that her story will be lost altogether, having got into Harper's hands. What she wants, is to know if you would be so very kind as to see a little about it, if you having all particulars think it necessary. She is afraid she is very troublesome but she knows you will be so kind as to help her out of her difficulty if you think there is likely to be any. The name of the story is "The Doom of the Griffiths"[.] It is about 53 folio pages. I am writing in great haste to catch the post. Tomorrow I mean to write you an answer to yours for which very many thanks.

Yours ever affectionately
Marianne Gaskell.
Everyone joins me in love to you.

Houghton Library, Harvard University. MS Am 1088 3491.

CHARLES ELIOT NORTON

46 Plymouth Grove
April 21[st.] 1862.

Dear Mr Norton.

I must write to you to tell you how glad I was to hear of your engagement to Miss Sedgwick[2] and how much happiness I wish you and her for your sake, though I hope sometime to be able to wish it to her for her own sake. The news came to us as a great surprise Mama came in and made us guess who was going to be married,

---

1 *Harper's Monthly Magazine.* For details of this particular transaction see Sharps, p. 267 and n.1.
2 See *Norton Letters*, I, 224–25.

Meta I think was the one who found it out the first. I hope so much that we may some time know Miss Sedgwick[.] Why should you not come over to England and to the Exhibition[1] for your wedding tour? It would be so pleasant to think we might see you so soon again. It is now nearly five years since you were here. I am sure you ought to be coming again, {and} if for no other reason that that it is your duty to make us acquainted with Miss Sedgwick. We want to hear a great deal about her; at least we want to hear as much as you like and will tell us, how old is she? is she tall or short? dark or fair? But do write a full description for her such as you gave us of your sisters; a description which seemed quite to place them before us. I do wish you most sincerely every happiness – I wish America were not so far off so that I might give you my wishes by word of mouth instead of on paper – I never can at all write what I want to say, and on reading over what I have said it does seem so unsatisfactory, and not to convey half what I meant to have said; but please put any want down to inability to express what I feel, not to any inability to feel most deeply Many hopes and wishes for your happiness.

I have a letter to thank you for; which I received about a fortnight or three weeks ago. It was very kind of you to have written so fully to me and I hardly know how to answer your letter; and yet I do not like not to answer it. Unitarianism does seem to me not fully to embrace all that the Bible teaches as we ought to believe, but as yet I cannot see what does seem the right belief, or whether Unitarianism really is wrong, and this unsettled state is as you may imagine most unsatisfactory – It seems to me that Unitarianism tests everything too much through Reason, and leaves nothing to Faith, while very possibly Catholicism may have too much Faith and too little Reason. Since I came home I have been reading with Papa, as yet only the reasons against, Catholicism not reasons for Unitarianism[.] It will be a long time before all the reasons for & against are gone into, and where one hears the endless {positions} arguments against, and knows that to each of these arguments Catholicism must have an answer which ought equally to be weighed, one almost despairs of ever arriving at

---

1 A reference to the Great London Exposition 1 May to 1 November 1862, South Kensington; now the site of the Natural History and Science Museums (*Wik.*).

any conclusion – I cannot believe that doctrine is of no importance, and that leading a holy Christian life is all that is necessary, though I do think most certainly that that is of the greatest importance, but as long as I believe doctrine at all a thing to be thought of I cannot rest satisfied with this indecision. I feel it so difficult so impossible to write on this subject, that I do not mean to attempt it. I doubt even if I could do it if I knew that the morning but one after this I could get an answer, but when I know that ten days must pass before you can receive it, and another ten before I could get any answer, I find it quite impossible even if I clearly knew what to say, which I really do not, all I can say, and that I do from my heart, is that I am most grateful to you for being enough my friend to write me the letter you did, and that {you}I know you will not misunderstand my not writing more fully, and not put it down to unwillingness to write, but to not knowing what to write – I felt particularly how kind it was of you to write when I heard of your engagement and thought how many other things you must have had to occupy your mind –

> Believe me to remain
> Yours most faithfully & truly
> Marianne Gaskell

Houghton Library, Harvard University. MS Am 1088 3492.

CHARLES ELIOT NORTON

Plymouth Grove
March 3rd. [1865]

My dear Mr Norton,

Thurstan has sent me on his letter as I very much wished to add my line to his to tell you of my, or our, great happiness. Before your letter to Mama came saying you had heard of our engagement from Henry Bright,[1] we had wished to write and tell you of our engagement. I particularly wished to tell you myself of it, because though I seldom write; I don't seldom think of you, and I always think of you among one of my dear friends; and therefore like that you should

---

1   See Norton's letter dated 16 Jan 1865 in Whitehill p. 115.

hear straight from {me} us of this happy news – We have now been engaged for more than 6 months but it was to have been kept secret as probably it will have to be long before we can marry as we have not money enough yet. I am very glad that you know Thurstan: I like you to be able to imagine us knowing both. I had no \idea/ two people could be so completely happy as we are, I fancy every two people think no other two as happy as themselves, but in our case I do believe it is no common share of happiness that has been given to us. My only hope is that I may prove worthy of the great prize I have gained in such a good true upright man's love. No one can tell as I can Thurstan's unusual goodness and nobleness – I am quite perfectly happy and I believe and hope that Thurstan shares my happiness to the full. I know you will be glad to hear because you will know how much it adds to our joy that Mama, Papa, and my sisters all love Thurstan, not only for my sake but for his own worth. We must wait I am afraid a long time before we are married as we cannot muster enough to set up even a most modest establishment. We are only waiting for prudence not for luxury – Dear Mr Norton you will let me have your good wishes I am sure, and don't please think because I have been so lazy about writing for so long that I am less than I used to be

    Your very affectionate

    Marianne Gaskell

  P. S. Meta sends her love and would have written had she had time[.] My love to Mrs Norton and kisses to the children.

Houghton Library, Harvard University. MS Am 1088 3493.

SUSAN NORTON

1. Sunnyside Wimbledon
Surrey. S.W
September 10th. [1867][1]

My dear Mrs Norton –

  I must thank you and Mr Norton very much indeed for the lovely

---

1 See Meta's letter to Norton, dated 13 January 1867, for the year of this letter.

broach you were both so kind as to send me as a wedding present. I admire it particularly and value it very much as coming from you both and I am very glad whenever I put it on & because it comes with kind greeting to me in my new life. I must tell you something about that new life. It is happier than I could have imagined possible. Each day shows me more and more how much cause I have for gratitude. We are now settled in our own house and have been some months. It is a semi detached house at Wimbledon, a suburb of London that Mrs Norton may know. Our house is small, but larger than when we came to it as we have added three rooms, and made one large one of two smaller ones. We have a tiny garden and next year it is to be very lovely, but this year we have not done anything to it because with the building going on work people would have trampled down and spoilt it; but this autumn it is to be replanned and prepared for next year's levelling.

The only drawback to our happiness this year has been that I have been an invalid for some months and not able to go about with Thurstan as I should have liked. First I had bronchitis in the spring, and since then I have been very much kept to my sofa, but I hope in a month's time from now to be set free and to have another blessing added to my life – I tell you this because though I have never seen you I cannot help feeling as if you were a well known friend because you are Mr Norton's wife, and so I trust to your friendship for caring to hear anything that interests me as much as the prospect of a new life springing up to make our home quite perfect. Letter-writing is and has been such a difficult matter to me months past that I think you will forgive me for sending you so short a letter, it is the longest I have written for some time. You would have heard much sooner how much I liked & valued your broach had it not been so difficult to write – but I did not like not writing to you as soon as I could – my husband wd. send kindest remembrances to Mr Norton were he at home but he is dining out tonight.

My love to Mr Norton –
Ever yours affect
Marianne Holland

ISABELLA GREEN

[?1870][1]

My dear Isabella

Your note has made me very sad. I do so feel for you all, & both Lucy & I do so wish we could do any thing to help you. But I am sure if there was any thing we cd do, you would let us know – as nothing wd gratify us more than to be of any use or comfort to you. Will you be so very kind as to send us word by your man in the morning how our dear friend is.

> Most affectionately yours
> M. Holland

Written on a scrap of paper, without date or address of sender.

Reproduced by courtesy of the University Librarian and Director, The John Rylands Library, The University of Manchester. Green Jamison Archive.

CLEMENT KING SHORTER

> Alfrick Court,[2]
> Worcester.
> Dec 10 [1914][3]

TELEGRAMS, ALFRICK.
PARCELS, KNIGHTWICK STATION, G.W.R.

Dear Mr. Shorter

I am afraid I cannot help you about my mothers brother John Stevenson All I can tell you that when I was about 10 years old my Mother told me that she could only just remember her brother that he went to sea I think she said when she was quite a young girl, that she remembered coming up to a visit to her father from Knutsford to wave her brother good bye. I think she must have been about twelve years old when she paid that visit – I wish I could help you more As regards any papers or documents relating to my Mother I have none.

---

1   See Florence Gaskell's letters to Isabella Green, dated 7th September and 9th December 1870 for the likely year of this letter.
2   Marianne moved to Alfrick Court, Worcester, following the death of her husband in 1884.
3   The year 1914 is attributed by the Brotherton.

My sister Meta left directions I believe that all her papers should be burned by her executors who were also her solicitors Messrs Worthington & Padmore

18 James Square

Manchester

They would probably be able to say whether there were any documents relating to my Mother among them. I do not think that there were any – I fancy that Sir A. Ward[1] had all there were when he was editing the Knutsford Edition of my Mother's works I wish I could help you more.

Yours very sincerely

MA Holland.

The Brotherton Collection, Leeds University Library. BC MS 19c Gaskell MS 16.

Venice, from *Fasciculus Temporum*,
(Venice 1480)

---

1   Adolphus Ward (1837–1924), Professor of History and English Literature Owens College Manchester and Principal 1890–97. He was involved in the foundation of Manchester Victoria University, of which he was Vice-Chancellor for two terms, 1886–90 and 1894–96, before taking up a position at Peterhouse Cambridge in 1900 (*ODNB*).

MARGARET EMILY GASKELL

1837–1913

Elizabeth and William Gaskell's second surviving daughter,
'a most pleasing, amiable, sympathetic woman'
(*Henry James Letters*, II, 159–60).
Universally known as 'Meta'.

Meta accompanied her mother and older sister Marianne on the Italian holiday in the spring of 1857, thus meeting Charles Eliot Norton. Perhaps because she remained unmarried throughout her life, Meta continued her correspondence with Norton until his death in 1908. As the older of the two unmarried daughters, living in Manchester, Meta accepted the responsibility of literary executor for her late mother, a role that is reflected in her later correspondence. Of the four Gaskell daughters, Meta's extant letters are the most numerous.

SNOW WEDGWOOD

42. Plymouth Grove.
Nov'r 8ᵗʰ· [1856]

My dear Snow,

\(*Don't please* show or read out a bit of this letter for it is silly & morbid.)/ I am so sorry I have been so long in writing to you, but indeed it has been want of time and not inclination that has prevented me. My interest in the "White Feather" is unflagging, but it has struck me that it was very selfish of me to beg as I did for an immediate answer to my last letter, when you must really be so anxious to devote every available moment for writing to your book.[1] However [?impatient] I am for letters from you for the future do not, dearest Snow, think it necessary to satisfy me – when you have safely dispatched your m.s. to the printers, then I hope you will often write to me – for it is such a great pleasure always for me to hear from you. At present however it is for *you* to complain of *me* for not writing, but what with Gaiety, & Greek, & a cold, & Brontë work[2] I have had hardly any time left for other things. We had a dance here on Wednesday – very jolly indeed, & on Thursday there was a splendid concert of Mr. Hallé's with Ernst & Piatti[3] – & last night we went to his house to meet a Lady Catherine Egerton,[4] & her brother – a young honourable who fiddled in grand style. Eating ices, [?] party people & hearing Mr. Hallé play made up a very pleasant evening – (Don't be shocked at my putting ices first. Effy would call me "sensous" but the truth was we sat in a circle round a blazing Lancashire fire, so that ice was acceptable. Mr. Hallé is so pleasant to people who

---

1   There is no record of this title by Snow Wedgwood having been published.

2   A reference to *The Life of Charlotte Brontë* (1857), which Elizabeth Gaskell was then working on, with the help of Marianne and Meta Gaskell and Snow Wedgwood (Uglow, p. 396).

3   Heinrich William Ernst (1814–65) was a Moravian violinist and composer who, by 1855, had settled in London (*Grove*). Alfredo Carlo Piatti (1822–1901), Italian born composer and cellist; from 1844 he was a regular performer in British concert halls (*Grove*).

4   Daughter of William Tatton, 1st baron Egerton of Tatton; in 1870 she married Hon Lionel Arthur Tollemache (*Cracrofts Peerage*). As the Hon. Beatrix Lucia Catherine Tollemache she developed a career as a writer, publishing in 1900 *Cranford Souvenirs, and Other Sketches.*

can get on with him, but unfortunately I am not one of those; & to me he seems fastidious, & satirical. He has always some story to tell against "a friend with whom he was dining last week", & one feels conscious that one's own foibles & gaucheries will be served up for future entertainment to other friends. I am rather in low spirits, Snow, today, for Miss Margaret Price[1] undertook to convince me last night that I was "morbid" – (a prerogative solely Mama's as I told you –) & in the next breath she assured me it was a thing she particularly disliked. Now is not that enough to upset one for a year?

Oh I wish I could see you, for I feel very wicked, & I could make you my Mother-Confessor more easily than any one else, I think.

I begin to think dancing & Gaiety was bad for one – for me, at any rate, for when one dance is over I can do nothing but reckon the days till the next, and regret passages in [?the] past and anticipate brighter \ones/ in {the} future ones. But how can I expect the Authoress of the "White Feather" to care for these confessions and regrets? Pray excuse them, dear Snow.

Margaret Price is staying here till after the Bachelors' Ball – you know her – don't you? She is strangely like Mrs. Price when you don't see them together –

I think she is really a nice girl, but there are some things in her manners very unprepossessing.

If Hillary C. is at home please give my love to her – and to Elinor. It was such a pleasure to me to see her in London – this Spring.

With much love to yourself & hoping you will forgive & forget this stupid letter wh. I only send in the faint hopes of its bringing what *I* have determined not to ask for.

I remain ever yours
Most aff'y M. E. Gaskell

Envelope: Miss K. E. Wedgwood 17 Cumberland Terrace Regent's Park London; containing two letters, including one from M. E. Gaskell. *Postmark*: NOV 11 56.

By Courtesy of the Wedgwood Museum, Staffordshire; W/M 324.

---

1 Margaret Price was daughter of Mr Bonamy Price, an economist and friend of Dr Arnold and the Gaskell family (*Further Letters*, p. 85, n.10). Marianne Gaskell was bridesmaid at Margaret Price's wedding in 1861 (*Gaskell Letters*, p. 646).

CHARLES ELIOT NORTON

Friday Evening. 11.30. p. m.
43. Via di Sant' Isidoro.
[Rome, 1857]

Dear Mr. Norton,

After a very long consultation it has been decided that it would be best for us not to go to Tivoli[1] tomorrow, even if the weather prove beautiful. Mr. and Mrs. Storey [*sic*] say that it would be a chance if we got home punctually by eight o'clock, which is the hour fixed for the torchlight proceedings at the Vatican; and {that} also that if we did accomplish that, most probably we should all be so terribly tired that we should have no energy left to enjoy the statues.

We are so very sorry to have [to] give up this expedition; but we must hope for many pleasant country-days with you en route to Florence, and I hope you will have strength enough to enjoy them.

Luigi has just told us of a vetturino, who is willing to take us to Siena in three days and a half, with four horse[s] and a good carriage that holds four people inside and two out, for 60 scudi. His name is Magherini, and perhaps François {?} could go and inspect the carriage at the enclosed address, if you thought that precaution necessary.

Mama is very tired tonight, so you must please excuse her not having written this herself.

I am so sorry about Tivoli. I cannot answer positively about the drive in the afternoon, as Mama has said nothing of it, and I do not like to trouble her for another decision, but I am sure we should all enjoy it, if it were possible.

Very truly yours
M.E. Gaskell.

Envelope: Charles E. Norton Esq. 3. Piazza di Spagna.

Houghton Library, Harvard University. MS Am 1088 2599.

---

1 Tivoli is a resort outside Rome. The journey of more than twelve miles would have been a long one by carriage.

CHARLES ELIOT NORTON

42, Plymouth Grove.
Manchester
January 27th. [1859][1]

My dear Mr Norton

As Mama's deputy I write to you to beg you to enquire if Messrs. Ticknor and Fields will buy the copyright of a story which she is now writing for the "Household Words"[2] and which she expects to be about the length of "Lady Ludlow". She has been very badly treated abt. the latter – *Mr. Sampson Lowe* must have behaved badly, she thinks. Without one [?letter] of application to her, either directly, or through Mr. Lowe, \at least none has ever reached her/, Messrs. Harper have republished Lady Ludlow; the authorship of which they can have learnt only through him, Mr. Lowe. Mama has written to Messrs. Harpers abt. this piracy, sending her letter through Mr. Curtis that attention may be paid to her complaint. Of course she has been unable to accept Messrs. Ticknor and Field's offer, the consequence of Messrs. Harpers having snatched at it \("Lady")/ so dishonorably; of course, too, it brings her dealings with the Harper firm to an end for ever. If Messrs. Ticknor and Field will give her a certain sum for this new story, and in addition to the price of the story enough more to pay for the copying of it, – (which she can get done by a poor lame cripple) – and if you will let Mama know by return of post, Mama will see that they have a copy of the story in time for them to have the start of any other American publisher with it. She is not quite sure whether the "Household Words" people will allow of its publication in America before its conclusion in their paper; but she will enquire. At any rate she supposes that its appearance as a whole story in America simultaneously with the publication of the last chapter in Household Words is allowable. Perhaps you know how this is –?

I hope you are pretty well now. We look forward much to seeing Thurstan Holland soon, and hearing a viva voce account of you all. Pray do not think I forget the portrait of Mama for which you asked.

---

1   See Sharps, p. 275, n.2, for confirmation of this date.
2   *Household Words: A Weekly Journal, 1850–1859*, conducted by Charles Dickens.

I am waiting till she will and can sit for a fresh one, in preference to copying the old one, as I hope I have improved sufficiently during the last three years in my drawing to be able to succeed better.

I have seen a great deal lately of your friends Lady Elgin and Lady Augusta Bruce. I never could speak of you to the latter without thinking of how we talked to you of her that dark snowy evening as we drove down the Appenines – Bologna-bound. They both desired their aff'c remembrances to you. Lady Elgin is now almost helpless, physically, but her eyes gleam and the expression of her face varies with all the old sweetness and intelligence. They say her memory and power of understanding are as good as ever but she cannot utter a word and seems often in sad distress from wanting the power of expression which occasionally she replaces with terrible cries like those of an animal in pain. Lady Augusta's marvellous patience, you, who know her, may guess – but it is far beyond description.

Mama is very well just now, I hope not merely for just now, though. So is Papa –.

> With our united affectionate remembrances,
> Believe me; my dear Mr. Norton,
> Most truly yours
> Meta Emily Gaskell.

Houghton Library, Harvard University. MS Am 1088 2644.

CHARLES ELIOT NORTON

> Ashbourne Hall.
> Derbyshire
> May the ninth 1859.

Dear Mr. Norton,

I am staying here alone with some cousins of mine. Mama went home this morning for two days. Before she went she left it in charge to me to write and thank you very much indeed for your kindness in enquiring about the price that she could get for a tale in America.

She hopes you will not regret your trouble, but forgive her having caused it you; when you hear that it {is} \has been/ useless. The offer that Messrs. Ticknor and Fields make is so *very* small in comparison with what she gains here that she does not think it worth accepting. Mr. Sampson Lowe has just offered her £1000 for a tale but little longer than the one Messrs. T. and F. bid for.

Privately speaking I am so glad that she should thus give up the resolution she formed in 1857 of publishing for the future in America. It always pained me, when she mentioned it. Her abandoning her natural and wanted *publishing field* for a new and foreign one, would, I thought seem like an attempt to renege on the English reading-public (who have so warmly received and appreciated her works) the sorrow caused her by a small party – or rather by two families – in consequence of the publication of her last book. C.B. I dare say that I am mistaken; and see it in to narrow a light; but I cannot help feeling glad at this termination to the negotiations which you have so very kindly conducted. I should so like to know what you think about it, but pray do not mention the *unofficial* part of what I have written in your next letter; for any allusion to what happened in 1857 about the Life of C.B. seems to open the old wound.[1]

Thurstan Holland stayed with us for a few days in Easter week; and had to stand a great deal of catechizing about Shady Hill and its inhabitants.[2] I was very sorry to hear from him how ill Mr. Child's Miss Sedgwick is.[3] I hope that by this time she may be better. Mama is a great deal stronger than she has been lately. Country air and hours always suit her; and she has gained a great deal from her week here It is an old rambling house; standing at the end of *the* street of the little town, with a large terrace like garden, and beyond fields and wood rising up into prettily-moulded hills. The house is haunted: by a Madam Cockaine, who every night drives up the avenue in a coach and six – the spectral coachman and horses all *headless*.

---

1   The first three paragraphs, written for her mother, may also be found in *Further Letters*, p. 197.

2   The Norton family home in Massachusetts.

3   A reference to Francis J Child, American scholar and friend of the Norton family. Charles Norton married Miss Susan Sedgwick, and her sister married a son of Charles Darwin. It is not clear which member of the Sedgwick family is referred to here.

The village has been in a tremendous state of excitement about the S. Derbyshire Election. Capt. Holland, the cousin with whom I am staying, was Chairman of the Committee in Ashbourne for the Election of a young Liberal Member, instead of Mr Mundy, an old Tory of 70. But unfortunately the veteran has won the day; and what is most aggravating, by the very smallest possible majority – by *one* sole vote – and that *his own*: for, it seems candidates have votes, as well as other men; but of this the Liberal Candidate had neglected to take advantage.

The Mundy-ites spared no pains to gain votes. They went to fetch one labouring man to the poll in a "one-horse shay", into which he indignantly refused to step, as Dick, his neighbour had been just carried off in a carriage & *pair* to the booth of the other party. The gentlemen, \who were/ determined to lose no vote for want of perseverance and energy, hastened back to Ashbourne to procure a second horse; and when his \wounded/ vanity was thus appeased, the man kindly consented to give his vote to Mundy. Another poor farmer was willing to go and vote as requested, but said that he daredn't for shame to shew his face, he was so dirty with his field-work, (and, apparently too lazy to remedy the defect); which, however, the two gentlemen sent to bring him to the booth did, {?}, by acting as valets, and literally with their own hands scrubbing, shaving, and re-dressing him!

We hear great things of Tennyson's new poem on the Morte d'Arthur. Mrs. Norton, in a note to Mama, described it as most beautiful. She had heard the Canto "Queen Guenever, or Penitence" read aloud by Tennyson – I wish I cd. remember her exact words. She says there is in it a song "most solemn, most sad", beginning "Too late, too late: – you cannot enter in "of the Bridegroom in Scripture" (?the foolish virgins?).[1]

Hunt's great picture is almost finished; the papers say. I saw it when he was half through with it, last spring. It is our Saviour being led away by his mother, after he has been found teaching in the Temple. It is small – exquisitely finished – having all the detail without any

---

1   The lines Meta tried to recall may have been as follows: 'Too late, too late: ye cannot enter now. | Have we not heard the bridegroom is so sweet? | O let us in, that we might find the light! | O let us in, tho' late, to kiss his feet! | No, no, too late ! Ye cannot enter now' (Tennyson, *Guinevere*, ll. 176–79).

of the stiffness of the Pre-Raphaelite School – and *full* of symbolism.
For instance: the floor is of polished marble, red-veined; and the figures are so disposed, that only where our Lord stands, does it receive
any reflection to counteract this bloody hue – but where his image is
mirrored, \there/ the stain is wiped out. The architecture of the background is full of interest. Mr. Hunt looked the subject up in Josephus
a little; but found out nothing more than that the general style was
light and gilded. So his imagination; unshackled, set to work, and
has {?} \conceived/ a most graceful structure. In some vineyards in
Egypt he saw {?} vine-poles stacked together, and bound with tough,
ribbon-like reeds or grasses; and from these he has taken the idea of
pillars; the capitals are grapes and vine leaves. The Virgin's face is
most heavenly – one hardly likes to think from whose it is painted – a
Miss {?}, a worn-out London belle, who has been coaxed & flattered
to her face by those, who behind her back have spread wicked stories to her discredit; leaving her with an aching sore heart, & feeling
of friendlessness, & disbelief in sincerity. However, either the fact
of sitting \as model/ for the "Blessed Virgin" drove all but peaceful
thoughts out of her face; or else the painter supplied the fitting look
of holy calm (just *tinged* with a shadow of reproach, for the three
days & nights wandering, and despairing search) – for there it is. The
Child is lovely; with red-gold hair forming a sort of natural halo to
the pale face – the deep, purple eyes casting a longing, lingering look
back on the circle of doctors; who, with eager faces, are still argu-
ing on, or else marvelling at the words of the child, just snatched
from them. They are mostly portraits. There is one *very* old man;
little glazed eyes (like the scapegoat's): – the \original/ was one of a
very select tribe now living in Jerusalem abt. which the tradition is
that it ought never to outnumber 12; and Mr. Hunt said that directly
a little baby was born in it, making a 13th, the oldest member felt it
his duty to die, and usually contrived to do so very soon by the mere
force of will. This man looked as if a baby wd. be the signal for a
very welcome release. These doctors are mostly dressed in white.
Mr. Hunt said he thought the phrase "whited sepulchres" had a sort
of half-punning \allusion/ (if one may say so without irreverence) to
the white drapes of the Pharisees. – I hope{d} I have not bored you

with this long, rambling account, dear Mr. Norton? You must forgive me, if I have. When next you write, please mention whether you have heard anything of the Storys or not. We half hoped that one of the few good effects of this terrible war might be to drive them England-wards; but we have heard nothing from them to justify the hope.

When are you coming again to England?

Ever yours very truly

M. E. Gaskell.

Papa and Julia are in Manchester – very well. Minnie is at Canterbury.

Houghton Library, Harvard University. MS Am 1088 2600.

CHARLES ELIOT NORTON

46. Plymouth Grove
Thursday Evening.
September 20[th.] 1860.

My dear Mr. Norton,

I feel quite sorry to think that I troubled you uselessly abt. letters for Mr. [?]. I do not mean 'uselessly' as regards the result; but because, after all, I got more than sufficient for him from other friends, who heard of his wanting Paris introductions. It made me feel ashamed of having troubled you, but we often \think first of/ applying to you for help, when we might obtain it much nearer home – and in consequence of my great haste, I acted on this first thought. I think that the proverb "give an inch and take an ell" is so true; and I am almost glad it is, and that people learn trust in future, through gratitude for past kindness. – Thank you so much for your first letter.

Who do you think shared the pleasure of hearing about you from it? Mr. and Mrs. Field!! One morning Mama received a note from the latter, dated Coniston, saying that they must sleep at Manchester one night, as they passed through en route to Paris, and might they spend the evening with us. Of course we jumped at the chance of getting them here; and most happily they could spare us six days. I wish they could know how much pleasure their visit gave us. How charming

Mr. Field is. I used often, when with him, to think of what you said at Venice: – that all sympathetic people were \always/ more or less variable and inconsistent. I think that he has warmer, tenderer sympathy than *almost* any one I ever met; and yet how perfectly true and truly consistent he is throughout. Do remember that beautiful sermon of Robertson's[1] in which he speaks of the reconciliation of two apparently contradictory truths in a deeper one, which seems to contain both? and so Mr. Field's character seems to blend perfect sympathy, and perfect truthful consistency, and makes me feel that I must never \{again}/ quote your saying again in palliation of want of the latter, for that it is not a necessary consequence of great powers of sympathy. I Cicerone'd Mr. Field abt. Manchester and in our long walks it was so pretty to see that he hardly ever passed a little crying child, or weary, sad-looking grown-up person, without some word of comfort or greeting; and he even answered the cabmen quite civilly when they volunteered their services when we passed with a "No, I thank you, not today", instead of with a gruff grunt of refusal as I always give. He is so loving and warm-hearted throughout. Mr. Wild rightly called him "Champs {?} Elysees".

(Sunday Evening. Sept. 22[nd.]) The only drawback to their visit was that Minnie was away and her \absence/ made me feel almost selfish as if I had her share of the pleasure as well as my own. Effie Wedgewood, a great friend of mine, was staying here while they were and I think she and Mrs. Field "colloned"[2] together very much as we say in Lancashire; (and of which expression Mr. Child must give you the derivation, as I believe it is of Anglo-Saxon and not as you would suppose factory origin.) Mrs. Field asked her and me to go over and spend the winter of 1861–2 with them and we used to have such great fun planning {?} \our visit/ with them, entering into it all the more eagerly, I fancy, because we knew that it was only in imagination we ever shd. go. But we [?liked] to talk quite knowingly about "clam bakes" and the "cars".[3]

1   Possibly Frederick William Robertson (1816–53) Church of England clergyman, friend of Ruskin and admirer of Wordsworth's poetry (*ODNB*).'
2   Possibly a regional variation of 'collogue', for which Wright's *English Dialect Dictionary* gives 'to conspire'; 'talk confidentially'; or 'talk over'.
3   Clam bakes are meals consisting of baked fish, often eaten by the shore where

{?} Mrs. Field has left us the legacy of her hearty "oh my", as a household exclamation. Effie always uses it now – Minnie comes home from Kreuznach today and she has gone to the Brights of Liverpool for two or three days. What she has gone through of the 'Kure' [?almost] seems to [?have] done her very much so that it reconciles us to see her continue the dreary regime. We are happy all at home and wish you would come and see us. It would be a very different visit to the one you paid before. Papa and Mama are now so *much* better than they have been for years. And our only sorrow, that of losing the \last/ child of the household thro' Julia's rapid development, is quite made up for by her turning into the sweetest dearest little companion imaginable. I am sure this is the happiest part of my life; and at length I understand that home is better than Rome; even tho' the former is in that *black* 'Metropolis of the North'.

I have not read the 5th vol. 'Modern Painters' yet: for a very delightful reason. – When I came home I was always trudging into town to the Library to try to get it there and always rather wondering at Mama's evident want of sympathy for my disappointment, when one morning "by the cars"[1] comes a huge brown paper parcel for me; of which I cut the strings as if I had never read Miss Edgeworth and lo and behold! there were the five fat green volumes and all for "my very own" as children say, from Mama. So as I had read none but the 3rd steadily I then began at the beginning and am going to work straight through. I can only therefore speak as to the beauty of the plates \of the 5th/ and as to the pleasure with which Mrs. Field and I cut our way to a certain footnote of which we had heard relating to your book. What a wonderful book {it} \the Modern Painters/ is and [?] not quite an original type of book? Or is it only my ignorance that makes me think so? What wonderful collateral research and knowledge he brings to bear on the subject. And do you not think that it does one *as* much good morally, nay even religiously, as in raising one's appreciation [and] love of art in the way he sees God in everything [?] [?] should point us always to his laws.

---

the fish was caught. 'Cars' refer to railroad mail cars. I am grateful to Professor Nancy Weyant for this information and for directing me to appropriate websites.

1   Railroad mail.

[?] I *cannot* bear to hear people abusing Ruskin. If they choose not to like & love his books, that [?is] for them; but when they begin to attack him personally, to call him arrogant; affected; intolerant; etc., it *does* make me feel so angry. Worst of all, when they call him egotistical; because he is so *full* of any cause he may be advocating as if \it were more than/ every champion ought not to be, absorbed & enthusiastic. I am fresh from a 4 months long fight, for Miss Darwin could not bear him or his writing. How generous of him {?} to send you that 2ⁿᵈ Rossetti and what a beauty {?} it must be, if *you* think it a worthy representation of that most exquisite scene. You do not say what is the subject of the 1ˢᵗ; the unsatisfactory one –? Well – Effie & I shall come and find out for ourselves some morning. – Do you remember Annie Austin? She came and spent two days with me when I was alone, and asked after you, and said she so often thought some conversation you and she had had waiting for a train, and how she tried to make you not see that {?} one was ready that the conversation might not be cut short. Her husband who is an engineer has just gone to the Mediterranean to pick up a broken telegraph cable. He did so once before and said that it was so curious to see [?] {wound} \hauled/ up out of the sea where it had been \lying/ a thousand fathom deep; and how the coral with which it was encrusted flew off like sparks from an anvil, as the sailors wound it rapidly on to the windlass –

Have you read Ruskin's "Unto this Last" in the Cornhill?[1] If not, do. Flossy – (how I am jumping about;) has left school, you know; and come to live at home. She is exceedingly pretty & very caring. And I suppose Edie Story[2] too is grown up. Thank you so very much for sending another report of your speech on Garibaldi.[3] Have you to wait long for the mails that bring you news of the land across the Atlantic? Papa reads us out the telegrams abt. him in the daily paper.

1 John Ruskin, *Unto this Last*, four essays attacking the science of Political Economy, first published in the *Cornhill* in 1860, subsequently in book form in 1862. See *Unto this Last and Other Writings by John Ruskin*, edited by Clive Wilmer (Harmondsworth, 1985).
2 Edith Marion Story, 1844–1907, daughter of William Wetmore Story (Uglow, p. 417).
3 Giuseppe Garibaldi (1807–1882), Italian national hero who helped to bring about the unification of Italy (*Wik.*).

What [?] is [?] pointed out [?]; as reputedly [?] a lady who has just been touring there met a little son of Garibaldi's at [?] abt. a fortnight ago; and says the boy said so simply "Papa does not write to him often just now; you know he is *very busy*." There has been a most trashy, [?] badly written life of him published in England, purporting to be an autobiography, but I hope it isn't, or that if it \is,/ it has changed its character in the hands of the Editor – Dumas. I found it unreadable & you may fancy what it is to be that in these days of his glory.

I hope you are better than when you wrote first – : I am so sorry you had to return instead of going on to Lake Sarawak; tho' when I said that to the Fields, they said you were not to be pitied, as you had Miss Norton with you, for that you and she always had "such a good time," when you were together alone, that you wd. not \either of you/ much regret giving up anything for that.

Lion is [?] flourishing and as naughty as ever. We take him out sometimes with us; but he behaves so badly that it is not till the recollection of his misdeed has gone, or has faded, that we venture to do so again. He jumps at horses, at their heels or [?noses] and I am even more afraid of his frightening them & so causing some serious accident than of his getting a deadly kick.

Goodbye, dear Mr. Norton; and thank you so much for writing abt. the introductions for Mr. [?] so quickly.

> Ever yours truly
> Meta Gaskell

Houghton Library, Harvard University. MS Am 1088 2601.

CHARLES ELIOT NORTON

> 46. Plymouth Grove.
> Friday : April 19th. [1861]

My dear Mr. Norton,

It seems such a long, long time since we heard from you; but I believe it is our own fault for not having written to you – \for/ I am afraid such virtue does not exist in this world as to continue a *one-*

sided correspondence; if that is not a contradiction in terms. Mama, who I know has just written to you,[1] will have told you everything \ that we have been doing/ so graphically and well, that there is only one little thing I can add, without fear of troubling you with a twic-etold tale; and that is what *very great* pleasure I had in reading your "Travel and Study in Italy"[2] – I read it last December, and it was really quite a Christmas treat, and one which I have often recurred to since without finding out of season. It only made me wish that I had read it before being in Italy : I should like to have known all that was in it on the spot. It is so much better than most tourists' books, which give you only ravings about the places, {?} causing a sort of useless 'schusucht' to return : it is so full of facts and history and life. The account of the building of the Cathedral at Orvieto I liked best of all – it seemed such a work of faith and love, and all the people joining with one heart & hand to carry it forwards. Papa was telling us the other day about the building of a chapel at Todmorden; which is a little out of the world place on the borderland of Yorkshire & Lancashire; where there are only rough stone cottages, built in long grey rows on the hill-side, near the two or three factories which have "made" the village or town. There had been a Unitn. Missionary there for some years, and he worked so successfully amongst the people that at length he began to hope for a chapel. Directly it was proposed they came forwards, (*all* men and women working in the factories) with what one would call, tho' happily it is not merely so, a Medieval spirit of self-sacrificing readiness to accomplish the building of it: many set aside a week's wages, some a month's, and those who {?} could not afford to give money, came after their factory hours, & spent their evenings in carrying the stones from the quarry to the site. Many women & girls did this. I thought of Orvieto when I heard of this. But the whole book is so very interesting : thank you for it.

Mama will have told you everything about ourselves; so goodbye.

Ever yr. most truly

Meta E. Gaskell.

---

1 Mrs Gaskell wrote a long detailed letter to Norton on 16 April 1861 (*Gaskell Letters*, pp. 645-51).

2 *Notes of Travel and Study in Italy*, published in book form in Boston, 1859 (Vanderbilt, p. 243).

P. S. I saw Thurstan Holland in London: he inquired after you a gt. deal.

Houghton Library, Harvard University. MS Am 1088 2640.

CHARLES ELIOT NORTON

46 Plymouth Grove.
Tuesday, August 28[th.] 1861.

My dear Mr. Norton

We are all so very, very sorry for the anxiety and suspense which this war must be to you.[1] I know one ought to feel glad that it is being fought; as on your side you are fighting not only against what Mr. Curtis[2] calls the "principle of monstrous anarchy" but against slavery; but still it is terrible to think of a civil war in these days of rapid communication, when people's friendships & sympathies are so widespread and strong[.] You cannot think how we hope and long for speedy success for you. – There was a very good article in the Cornhill[3] for last month on American affairs: that formed a supplement as it were to your letter – It seemed very just and clear; & so much calmer in tone & feeling than most things that have been published in England on the subject. Marianne said that she believes it was considered very good by people in London.

You cannot think how beautiful Mama's new story promises to be.[4] She herself is hopeful and pleased about it. We had such a happy visit at Silverdale this year. We wished for you to share our pleasure often. There was only one drawback – & that was to find what inroads the touring world had made during the three years which have passed since our last visit there. Is it very selfish to dislike such invasion? I always feel as if there were no larger amount of pleasure given; for surely each visitor feels less when the country is less still & quiet &

1   The American Civil War commenced in 1861.
2   George William Curtis (1824–92), one of Norton's American friends, supporter of the Northern cause, related to Robert Gould Shaw by marriage and, from 1863, political editor of *Harper's Weekly* (*Norton Letters*, I, 226–28).
3   'The Dissolution of the Union' *Cornhill*, 4 (1861), 153–56; *Wellesley* attributes the article to James Fitzjames Stephen.
4   A likely reference to *Sylvia's Lovers* (1860–63); see Uglow, p. 504.

peaceful. All the little paths that we knew so well, and that formerly we tracked by the broken fern & crushed grass, were now distinct, bald, [?] walks; and sometimes we met a perambulator; in them! But there is one good thing – the people are not spoilt, and are just as simple and kind as ever. We had some such pleasant afternoons sitting on the edge of the [?] looking on to the sands below, stretching for 20 miles till they ended in the glittering sea-line, with the wing-like shadows of the clouds coming swiftly towards us over them, & then passing onto the purple crescent of hills behind us. We used to wish so much to live at Silverdale; but I think it would be too peaceful a life, and we should forget all the struggles & pain of many people's lives, that strike one so sharply on returning to a town.

Dr. Thompson's sister was staying with us for a month at Silverdale.[1] She told me that in one of his letters he said that you had been the kindest to him of any of the people he had had an introduction to; and that he had had such great pleasure in being with you at Boston.[2] How very terrible Mrs. Longfellow's death was[3]. Effie Wedgwood told me that poor Mrs Macintosh[4] had been quite "prostrated" by grief; but that Mrs. Mosley[5] had been so very good and kind to her.

Ever, dear Mr. Norton,

Yours most truly

Meta G[askell]

P. S. You once said you would send me yr. edition of Mr. Clough's poems,[6] and I believe I never thanked you for the promise – but I shall like them exceedingly – if they are all like the three I know. Thank you very much.

---

1   For an account of this holiday see *Gaskell Letters*, p. 657.

2   For Dr Thompson's meeting with Norton see *Gaskell Letters*, pp. 661–62 and p. 673.

3   Second wife of the poet, H. W. Longfellow; she died from burns sustained in a domestic accident (Whitehill, p. 88).

4   The Wedgwoods were related to the Mackintosh family through marriage. Robert Mackintosh (1806–64) married a wealthy American Molly Appleton, whose sister Fanny became the second Mrs Longfellow in 1843 (BHW, pp. 248–49).

5   Josiah Wedgwood's grandson Frank had married a member of the Mosley family in 1832 (BHW, p. 217); it is not clear which Mrs Mosley is referred to here.

6   Arthur Hugh Clough (1819–61) English poet and friend of Norton, with whom he corresponded throughout his life (*Norton Letters*, I, *passim*).

Envelope: Charles Eliot Norton, Shady Hill, *Cambridge*, Newport, Massachusetts.

Postmark: AU 27 MANCHESTER 1861

This letter is a continuation of one started by Mrs Gaskell (See *Letters*, pp. 664–67).

Houghton Library, Harvard University. MS Am 1088 2602.

EFFIE WEDGWOOD

46. Plymouth Grove.
Jan. 7th. [1862]

My own darling Effie,

There has not been a day during the past fortnight in which I have not planned beforehand to write to you; but which has not proved too full when it came. We have been very gay; and tremendously busy. – Thank *you*, darling, for *your* letter. I am sure it fully repaid any – & every letter I ever wrote to you. I do love you with such perfect loyalty that our friendship would be my greatest delight, if it were not dimmed by a terror lest someday or other the 'entente' between us shld. be different from what it is now. Not that I ever feel that my love for you cd. change; so why I am polite enough to suspect you of inconstancy I don't know? (I am rather writing agst. time now: and know I shall not say half I wished.) –

Why has the Sat'y fallen foul of Mr. Hughes?[1] I am so sorry – All that Working Men's College set, acting on the gt. principle of there being 2 sides to every question take up violently the unpopular, unrecognized one; till – though perhaps they put the question in right balance in the eyes of the world – they get themselves the character of morbid fanatics. But now the Sat'y is hitting friends and foes alike!

We are going to an Assembly tonight, and our dresses are not yet come from Marshall & Snelgrove's;[2] and when they come they will have to be made up – so we have a sort of strange hurried feeling, most impropitious to letter writing; tho' as I have just been stripped for the martyrdom of having a "body" tried on, I hope for a little present respite.

---

1   *Saturday Review* (1855 to 1938); Thomas Hughes (1822–96) was associated with F. D. Maurice and the working men's movement (*OCEL*).
2   A popular Manchester department store.

The Hallés'[1] dance was such a success last Friday; though I went thro' 5 minutes of mortal terror – for while the musicians were at supper Minnie came to me & threw herself at my feet to play. I know no dance music of any kind, & shld. have had to plunge into what the men might have left; and there was Mr. Hallé, Hecht,[2] Capt Harmett (notoriously " the best amateur player in England" in those parts) and a background of 180 Manchester swells. It was very silly & vain to mind; but I must say I walked up to the piano with the feelings of an [?]. Fortunately I did my "virtue cheap" – for just as I reached the altar, another victim seated himself.

How I do admire you for the way you tolerated my presence in the drawingroom, and that of my fingers on the keys of yr. piano, whilst you were in the thick of yr. Hallé lessons! Why did you not turn me out of the room oftener, instead of so meekly asking me half an hour before he came, if you might have 5 minutes practice? If yr. friendship cd. stand that test . . .

Edith [?Grey] is coming here on Thursday (I dread having an utterly unknown beauty billeted on me!) & Fred Holland,[3] both to stay till Sat'y –

I have not written to Catherine[4] since [?Ingston]!

Goodbye, my own very dearest Effie. Do forgive this scrawl.

Yr. own M.E.G.

P. S. We have capital news fr. Minnie, & conclude she must be much stronger for she went through 24 hrs of midnight masses (excuse the Irishism of that) on Christmas Eve; tiring out 4 parties of people, who served as escorts.

I am so sorry abt. Mrs. Langton.[5] You *know* that I wd. rather hear yr. own home news & doings than anything.

---

1   Charles Hallé and his wife were friends of the Gaskell family. Hallé (1819–95) established a successful orchestra and series of concerts in Manchester (Uglow, p. 305 and *Further Letters*, p. 80, n.3).

2   Edward Hecht (1832–87), English chorus master and pianist of German birth; from 1875 he taught music at Owens College, Manchester (*Grove*).

3   Thurstan Holland's brother (Uglow, p. 501).

4   A likely reference to Catherine Darwin (BHW, pp. 272–73).

5   Charlotte Langton (1797–1862), née Wedgwood, Effie's aunt, died in January 1862. The following year her widowed husband married Catherine Darwin (BHW, p. 272).

Envelope: Miss Effie Wedgwood. 1. Cumberland Terrace. Regent's Park. London. S. W.

Postmark: Manchester JA 7 62

By Courtesy of the Wedgwood Museum, Staffordshire; W/M 408.

EFFIE WEDGWOOD

> X. Street Chapel Vestry.
> Sunday. Noon.
> Jan.19. [1862]

My own dearest Effie,

Please believe me when I tell you that I should have written \(you know one never writes London letters on a Saturday)/ to you today, whether I had heard from you or not. I only learnt Mrs. Langton's death yesterday, (through a letter from Cousin Mary),[1] and I was quite meaning to write to you today to tell you how sorry I was abt. it, (for all your sakes – not less, after what you have said), and how afraid I was that my \last/ letter must have *jarred* very much upon you if you were all anxious about her just then. I feel just as one does, when some person has chaffed, or slightly sneered at one, not knowing that one was suffering from hidden pain, and one makes a resolve never to speak for the future in that way without se*cur*ity that the person one is speaking to is quite happy and at ease. Now I know that my letter was full of frivolity & vanity, and if you were "waiting for Death" to come to some one you loved very much it must have worried you, to say the least[.] I feel very sorry for Mr. Langton. I hope that his son will be a real comfort to him? I know one or two people like you describe Miss Wedgwood, who really seem superhuman – and as if mortal trials did not ever *pierce* them –

Cousin Susan (Dane)[2] is an example, I think. I did so enjoy yr. long musical confessions. I wish one did not lose one's appreciation of music that one knows quite well; and yet how one wd. hate only to

---

1   Probably Mary Holland, Knutsford cousin who corresponded with the Gaskells and with whom Meta sometimes stayed (*Further Letters*, pp. 209, 225 and 261).

2   Possibly meant to be Susan Darwin (1805–66), related to Effie and to Meta. There are numerous references to Meta's time spent with Miss Darwin, one of Charles Darwin's sisters, in *Gaskell Letters* and in *Further Letters*.

learn non-classical music! Sometimes I think that it is rather a case of action & reaction with one's love for a particular piece of music. The first time one hears it, one cannot care for it properly: then comes the happiest state of all when one has heard it 3 or 4 times, and though each lovely bit *startles* one into recollection, yet it is reawakening a memory; then comes *surfeit* – and then I think one begins again to care for it & to see something beyond & within – & to look at it more as a whole. But nothing comes up to the first freshness, when one only just knows it thro' – (Do you not think that it is much the same with personal acquaintance? & that one is never secure of one's feeling towards anyone till one has passed through shyness, through undue attraction to what one finds \afterwards/ is merely varnish or else an index of \(variable,/ uncertain charms or goodness, for \one has/ got through to the real nature?) – With Op. 7. of Beethoven, the Sonata (in E b,) which I have just been learning with Mr. Hallé, I felt so very much the top of my first rapture with its loveliness. There are some phrases of melody in the 1st. movement that almost draw tears to one's eyes at first, & it seems sacrilege to practice them over & over merely to attain a mechanical accuracy in playing them : but by degrees how flat, & stale they become – and I think that from Mr. Hallé's playing \of them/ it is the same with {them} him – a familiarity that breeds indifference. I am enjoying my music lessons quite maniacly – I mean that I am so apt to let one thing absorb me too much, which *is* mania after all. I have to put moral handcuffs on myself daily, or I shld. practice far too long; but I cannot help my thoughts running on the disappt.mt. or success of my last & the chances of my next lesson. I am learning the Pastoral Sonata now. I cannot think why Mr. H. has given it me for there is no practise in it hardly – at least of what one is apt to call practice – though [?] are not sure whether this paradox is not true – that easy things are {?} the most difficult to play. In gt. roaring, rushing passages, one is so over-whelmed by the mere music, \that/ the means & art are pretty nearly hidden; but nothing can disguise the faults in playing a simple scale. {?} I think Mr. Hallé's chief excellence in teaching is his insisting so much on perfect clearness – "the note the whole note, & nothing but the note." Do you think that it wd. be *very* presumptuous to ask to learn Op. III. \CXI/ of Beethoven? I have played it over, & found it not an impossibility; but then it is considered rather a 'crux', & so one wd. be laying oneself out for a good snub for one's conceit. Will you tell me before next Saturday, queen? I am killing two birds with one stone, for I shall get my doubt on this head settled, & still better a letter from you, if you accede to my request. Abt. yr. singing lessons.

– – Tuesday Evg. Post-time,

I have no time – –

I will not keep this any longer, but will write again in a day or two.

Very best love.

Envelope: Miss Effie Wedgwood. 1. Cumberland Place. Regent's Park. London. N.W. *Postmark*: Manchester JA 21 1862

By Courtesy of the Wedgwood Museum, Staffordshire; W/M 408.

EFFIE WEDGWOOD

Sat'y Jan. 25th. [1862]

My own darling Effie,

I was so disapp[']ted when this morning's post brought me no letter from you; as I had quite hoped it would. I don't need to know about "the hundred and eleventh", for I find that this next Hallé lesson is to be my last, so I am saved from the pitfall of presumption into which I had so nearly fallen. – I was so sorry to send off such a fragment of a letter to you: but I wanted to shew you how I had been writing to you – and I did not foresee where I shld. have time to finish it. I began it in a queer place – the Cross Street Chapel vestry, where I dine in a picknicking fashion on Sunday now – to take the affn. school, without returning home: Did I ever tell you of what was such a *real* sorrow to me this autumn? banishment from my dear Ragged School, because of certain representations that Mama had made in confidence to the Surgeon abt. the amount of scrofula in the school, and the inadequate food, as to quality not quantity.[1] This good stupid man went

---

1   Ragged Schools were a feature of the poorest districts in Manchester during the second half of the nineteenth century, some surviving well into the twentieth century. Between 1861 and 1865 the work of the Ragged Schools extended to provide free meals, not only for schoolchildren, but also for poor and destitute adults.

& laid the letter before the Committee of the School, and we were
expelled with flaming swords of wrath & indignation & another case
was added to my experience that "innocence was no consolation",
which it was one of Arthur Darbishire's[1] compliments not to be surprised at, "because I shld. doubt, Meta, whether you ever *had*; the
consciousness of innocence".

Abt. yr. singing. *I* think you sing perfectly – you know I committed the unpardonable heresy of thinking you sang better than Mrs.
Senior. If you want anything, it is a certain dramatic aplomb, but that
comes with such much better taste from married ladies than from
girls that I think the omission is rather a must for after all, almost
all songs are love songs, & to sing them with expression is not quite
pretty for a Miss. Do you remember what Robertson says abt. reti-
cence with regard to religious feeling that applies to sacred music. In
an oratorio one likes the people, singers, I mean, to forget {their own}
themselves in the presence of such hundreds in the face of such an
opportunity of wakening people's religious feeling, and to really pour
forth their hearts; but somehow it is very different with a yg. lady on
a Sunday evening in a drawing-room, when half the people in the
room are whispering gossip, or glancing at yesterday's "Saturday".
Do, do learn from Garcia[2] again. I am sure he is the best master. I
fancy from what Minnie told me that you did not lay yourself at his
feet enough. All those great masters do get so fawned upon, that they
construe mere passive dignity into antagonism – I am sure one can
see *that* from the way in which pupils here treat Mr. Hallé. There
is one of them, a very nice girl indeed too, who the other night at a
small "tea-spree" there, was seen to put her arm round Mr. Hallé's
neck, and they keep saying such honeyed things, & "going on" so –
generally – I *cannot* understand how they do it. I am sure that Garcia
requires people to be very "sub" to him, as Mme. Mohl[3] says – If you

---

1 A member of the Dukinfield-Darbishire family, long-standing Manchester friends
   of the Gaskells (*Further Letters*, p. 303 and *Gaskell Letters*, p. 84).
2 A reference to Manuel Patricio Rodriguez Garcia (1805–1906), singing master
   who established a singing school in London with Jenny Lind among his pupils.
   He also joined the staff of the Royal Academy of Music in London where he
   taught from 1858 to 1895 (*Grove* and *Further Letters*, p. 149, n.4).
3 Mary Mohl, née Clarke (1793–1883), a long-standing friend of Mrs Gaskell
   (*Further Letters*, p. 306).

cd. ingratiate *yr.*self personally with him, I think that then he wd. be the very best man for you; for certainly you want nothing but finish in the highest sense. Yr. asking me to be egotistical encourages me to lay before you at weary length {before you} a statement of difficulties with wh. otherwise I shld. never have troubled you. I shall care for yr. advice much more than for anyone else's I cd. get. You know I have completely given up singing – & was rather revelling lately in the success of my [?H]. lessons, & meaning never again so completely to drop my practicing as I have done for years and years. Well, *yesterday*, Mama was speaking of the (odious) necessity of giving a party here soon; & she said that she shld. not like to do it for want of home-made music – as Minnie was away – how we missed her singing – how she did wish that I had gone on with mine etc. Those were not her words exactly; but she implied that were there ever so desperate a gap in the entertainment, I cd. never spring into the breach, as I did not *sing*; completely ignoring playing, & shewing – what after all, Effie, *is* the truth – that the piano is worth *nothing* as a means of pleasure-giving except to yourself, unless you are a Mr. Hallé, or at best nothing, nothing, nothing compared to singing. You cannot think what a slight this has thrown over me. Do not think for one moment that Mama said it inconsiderately – of course she didn't – she is far too full of sweet consideration for me, in comparison to what I am for her – but out of the fulness of the heart the mouth speaketh. Ever since I have been wondering whether I ought not to take up singing again. You see my singing cd. never be worth anything except as a substitute for the absent Marianne's – but then I know I shld. constantly be dragged forward *after* her . . . fancy! But yet Mama evidently wishes it : shld. not that be final? – & the piano is mere selfishness – & merest fifth-rate warbling enchants 99 out of a 100 unmusical people. Oh Effie – *now* am I not as egotistical as any one cd. wish? What shall I do? I have such a false shame abt. singing. I feel so perfectly selfconscious always when I sing : & what is perhaps of more consequence considerably – I have a *very, very* medium voice, with the despicable range of from [?] – che [?] – Do answer me, will you, dearest queen?

These are such black days, of death & distress just at present, that one feels it very wrong – (Sunday) to let one's thoughts dwell so self-ishly on a purely personal matter – a mere matter of accomplishment too. However, does not the word *accomplishment*, a little explain one's restless desire? It is an ambition to *accomplish* an end – to achieve success, which after all, though \it may be/ purely selfish, is the key to half one's dissatisfaction in life. I *am* so sorry that there is no letter from you again this morning. I only hope that I said nothing in my last that vext you.

Abt. the Thompsons – I think it is so strange. I fancy I may be partly the cause, by raising a sort of [?Aristedes] – the just feeling abt. you. Whenever Isabel[1] speaks of any of you, and does *not* come up to the proper enthusiasm-pitch (which it wd. be so difficult for her to do in my eyes, that it is merciless to expect it), I turn upon her with such indignation & indifference – (indignation that her opinion is not as enthusiastic as mine, indifferent in as far as it cannot touch mine) – that no wonder she owes you a grudge. But the [?], Isabel specially, have such a perpetual background of pain & anxiety in one way or another, that you *must* not judge hardly of anything they do. I do not mean that their sorrow blinds them to your past as a [??], but that it shld. suffice to earn their forgiveness for any aberrations of impolite-ness. The loss is *theirs* : if yrs. too.

Do you know, Effie, I shld. so dearly like to come to you this spring; but I do not know at all whether I ought – you see, to be open with you; Major Hill,[2] as he is now, is in London, & will be thro' the summer, & so I have a very strong feeling agst. going up – but at the same time – *you* are too powerful a loadstone for me to resist placidly – & I *know*, against my reason, & almost my *will*, that it will end in my coming if you really mean you wd. like me. Catherine gave gen-eral & special invitations to us Gaskells most kindly when here; so I wrote on Friday to bring one into effect for Florence, whose vague ambition it is to "stay in London", but no answer has come today. I am so sorry abt. poor Mr Philip [?]. (I am afraid he never cd. venture on a scd. engagement.[ )] I am sorry for yr. cousin too. It is so much

---

1 Marianne's and Meta's friend whose uncle, General Perronet Thompson, advised Mrs Gaskell on aspects of *Sylvia's Lovers* (Uglow, p. 485).
2 Formerly Captain Hill, to whom Meta had been engaged to be married.

worse to break off where there is no discovery of bad choice to justify the loss & quench all feeling of wrong on the gentleman's part. I think Catherine might have spared her reproaches for there must have been necessary pains enough – but I can fancy with what gusto she poured them forth. Now I am going again to ask for a letter [?] a first time, & do send me darling a line – It is this time to ask *how* you pay Mr. Hallé, à la Physician, or asking for an "account". Will you let me know before Wed., till when I have deferred my last lesson. You can never accuse me of not writing egotistically after this letter which will serve for egotism, for a year or so.

Your own most loving & faithful

M. E. G.

Envelope: Miss Effie Wedgwood. 1. Cumberland Place. Regent's Park. London.

Postmark: Manchester JA 26 1862

By Courtesy of the Wedgwood Museum, Staffordshire; W/M 408.

EFFIE WEDGWOOD

46. Plymouth Grove.

Jan. 28th. [1862]

Tuesday Morn'g

My own darling Effie,

You were very nearly having a second letter from me on Sunday; – wd. have had one yesterday, if I had not passed the day chez the dentist, and shopping, & then writing a foreign business letter for Mama – for both she and I *do* so want you to come here, *at once*. I go to Edinbro' on the 15th. or 17th. for 3 {months} weeks, or a month – possibly; but if you thought it worthwhile to come to us for the interval, we shld. be so delighted. Only I must prepare you that it wd. be such a dull visit. There wd. be no Jacks – and all our visiting is over completely, except a party, nature unknown, at the Scotts' next Friday.[1] There are Mr. Hallé's weekly concerts; but I am ashamed to

---

1   A possible reference to Professor Scott, principal of Owen's College, and his wife (*Further Letters*, p. 75, n.6). Owen's College, founded by a Manchester textile merchant, was the forerunner of Manchester Victoria University.

say we don't subscribe.[1] However we constantly have tickets sent us, & you of course shld. & wd. always have the first. There is a Concert at the Concert Hall *when Stephen Heller*[2] *plays*on the 12th./; & for that we *have* tickets; and there is an Assembly on the 18th., to which *Mama and Florence* wd. be proud to take you. Mrs. Stern,[3] the great Manchester "lioness", is giving a private Ball in the Assembly Rooms on the 14th.; and tho' as it is {our} her first invitation to us, Mama is doubtful how far she cd. ask to take you, yet I do hope she might, if she had an opportunity of doing so viva voce, with wreathed smiles etc –

Incomplete and unsigned

Envelope: Miss K. E. Wedgwood. 1. Cumberland Place. Regent's Park. London. N.W. *Postmark*: Manchester JA 29 1862

By Courtesy of the Wedgwood Museum, Staffordshire; W/M 408.

CHARLES ELIOT NORTON

Dusk.
Sunday Evening.
April 20th. [1862]

My dearest Mr. Norton,

You might have been quite sure of our great sympathy in your engagement,[4] whenever we had learnt it; but just now, when you have given us such help and sympathy in our anxiety, you are doubly sure of the latter from us.[5] Please accept my *very, very* best wishes for your happiness; and may I send my love to Miss Sedgwick? I am sure from your account of her, and from knowing that you have chosen

1   See Uglow, p. 305, for subscriptions taken out 'as an indulgence' for a previous season.
2   Heller was a French composer and pianist. A friend of Charles Hallé and Robert Browning, in 1838 he settled in Paris where he also made friends with Berlioz (*Grove*).
3   Possibly the wife of Sigismund J. Stern, who lived nearby in fashionable Victoria Park, Manchester (*Gaskell Letters*, pp. 644 and 1005).
4   Following a brief engagement, Norton married Susan Ridley Sedgwick on 21 May 1862 (*Norton Letters*, I, 224).
5   A possible reference to British concern regarding the American Civil War (Whitehill, pp. 95–96).

her, that I should love her, if ever we met; or, rather let me say, *shall* love her, *when* we meet –

Do send us her photograph – soon – and tell us your plans. When you are to be married; and whether you cannot take Manchester on your wedding tour.

I do trust that nothing will ever dim your present joy – It is so pleasant to think of yr. happiness.

Ever yrs. aff. M.E.G.

Houghton Library, Harvard University. MS Am 1088 2603.

CHARLES ELIOT NORTON

46, Plymouth Grove.
Monday, Octr. 21st [1862]

My dear Mr. Norton,

You do not know how very sorry I am that you should have been so long without a letter from any one of us. A month ago, when your kind long letter came, I felt that even then the pause in our writing to you had been far, far too great; and I began, and wrote three sheets of, a letter to you, which, as ill-fate would have it, I lost instead of finishing and dispatching. You see our silence (thank God) has not been caused by any sorrow; and I am sure you will believe me when I say that it has not arisen from any forgetfulness nor from our most affectionate interest in you and yours having flagged. We never hear of any American news without thinking how it has first fallen on your ear : and if it is good news for the North, we rejoice with you; and grieve so for you if it is bad. Mama and I are staunch Northerners, and fight for you in words whenever we hear Southern sympathy expressed.

I do hope now that the tide of war has turned, and that success will remain on your side till the South has learnt to repent humbly of its treacherous rebellion. It does seem to us so very terrible. The bitter enmity between North and South cannot surely be healed for generations – and whatever is the issue of the war – there will always remain to you terrible memories of these years of horror and of the death of so many dear ones. We do so hope that Mrs. Shaw may not lose her son. Mr. Sturgis, whom we saw lately, said that he thought anxiety for his safety and despair about the war were killing her by inches.[1]

To tell you of what we have been ding all summer will make a very peaceful chronicle – and will seem in strong contrast to your year. I believe that you have not heard from any of us since Minnie came back from Rome : but yet I think that we can *hardly* have left you unthanked for your most kind letter to her. Our fears about her have almost past. I suppose that it was Dr. Manning's[2] personal influence that worked the mischief, and when that ceased and she re-entered her {natural} home-life, the excitement died a natural death; and now I really believe that her thoughts hardly ever revert to Roman Catholicism.

You were so very good and kind in giving us such helpful sympathy, dear Mr. Norton.

October 30[th.] or 31[st.]

Again, another delay! and ten days (for it is just midnight) added to a silence already far too long. But we are leading an unusually busy life just now, owing to the great distress prevailing in Manchester for want of cotton; and to alleviate which classes for the factory people out of work have been established, in which we all try and help. [3] It is not the actual work in attendance at these sewing schools that makes us so busy; but the trying, at other times to do something for the poor creatures with whom we have thus come in contact. And all this is not in*stead* of, but over and above our ordinary occupations; which we have always hitherto considered 'sufficient for the day'. It is very sad to see so much distress, but I think \that/ it leads to as much blessing as sorrow. The spirit of the poor people is so patient and brave – they can turn from their misery and want to think with heartfelt pity of the

---

1 Mrs Shaw's son, Robert Gould Shaw, died commanding a black regiment in 1863 on the Northern side of the conflict (*Further Letters*, p. 168, n.11 and Uglow, pp. 603–604). Russell Sturgis was Mrs Shaw's brother and known to Elizabeth Gaskell (*Further Letters*, pp. 166 and 168, n.11).

2 Henry Manning, a convert to Roman Catholicism, exerted a powerful influence on Marianne, which upset her parents greatly. See Uglow, pp. 421 and 500.

3 See *Domestic Mission*, 1862.

sufferers in the American War, though they feel that that is the chief cause of their own distress and one never hears a murmur of distrust against their masters, only gratitude and blessings for those who have tried to help them. I think that the Times is very much to blame for its reports from the manufacturing districts, for certainly it is a gross misrepresentation to paint the masters as indifferent to the distress of their men. However I should think it rather unnecessary to warn an *American* against the inaccuracies of the Times. In many cases that we know of, where a manufacturer's name appears in no subscription list thereby exposing him to the denunciations of the Times correspondent, it is because every penny that he can spare is employed in continuing the work in his mill, at an immense loss to himself, because he feels that this is the best way of giving relief.

I was to tell you something of our year's doings – Mama and I have crossed the Channel, and had a very pleasant week in Paris and ten days in Brittany and Normandy, making a pilgrimage to Mme. de Sévigné's château;[1] but we are the only two who have been abroad. All June we \(all but Papa, who made two flying visits, himself)/ spent in lodgings in London, *doing* the Exhibition, which is a massive failure – except for the picture galleries, and those I hardly ever left – how you would have enjoyed them! You would hear of Mr. Story's sudden bound into fame, through his Cleopatra and Sybil. Did you remember how he used to talk of the former, when we were in Rome? I think he has a little clay model of what she was to be. There were a few, a very few, people who did not join in the chorus of admiration, but Woolner[2] was the only one amongst them, whose unfavourable opinion was worthy to shake one's judgment in their favour. Woolner's own sculpture was beyond praise; but unfortunately he suffered through the very ardour of the praise given him in an official catalogue by his friend Mr. Palpan, at the cost of all the other sculptors; and a very bitter correspondence between Mr. Palpan

---

1 In May 1862 Meta, with her friend Isabel Thompson, accompanied her mother on a tour of Normandy to collect material for a memoir of Madame Sévigné (1626–96), on which Mrs Gaskell was working but did not complete (Uglow, p. 499).

2 Thomas Woolner (1825–1892), sculptor and founding member of the Pre-Raphaelite Brotherhood (*OCEL*).

& "Jacob Omniam",[1] which perhaps you saw, in consequence of this over-partial criticism {?} linked these special pieces of his work {?} with very unpleasant associations.

It was so charming day after day to go the these galleries, and single out one's great favourites for a short morning greeting, before settling steadily to work on some fresh field. Several of the foreign pictures were very fine – (two Isräels, a Belgian, almost the finest pictures there) – and very interesting to see how foreign schools have either caught from England the best part of the pre Raffaelite {?} tendency or else are influenced by a reaction in themselves producing such results.

After June, we all came flocking home, one by one; and since then we have been steadily here, with the exception of short absences on Marianne and Papa's part, one long visit that Florence paid "Down South", and a month when Mama and I went to Eastbourne for sea air. Somewhere at Eastbourne, blown into the sea, I should think – is my unfortunate letter to you that should have reached you so long since.

I have just been reading Trollope with great delight.[2] It is the spirit, perhaps more than the letter, of his book, that shows such hearty sympathy with us all. I *hope* you feel it as I am sure it is meant. I think his book gives one a great idea of how America may come forth purified from this terrific strife – of "the advantages of defeat".

We talk of going abroad in the spring, when we hope (vaguely) that the distress may be lessening. Mama's book; is to come out in February. She always likes to fly the reviews, and she thinks of first going to [?] with Minnie, a fortunate combination of a visit to some friends of Minnie's there with a tour through Germany making that plan very satisfactory – and then she, that is Mama, Florence, Julia, Hearn, and I (rather a Cranfordian party!) mean and hope to go to Florence for a 6-weeks stay. If you and Mrs. Charles Norton *would* but join us there! Of all people, you would be the best guide there

---

1   Matthew James Higgins (1810–1868), Irish born writer who wrote under the name Jacob Omnium, best known for his letters to *The Times* and contributions to the *Cornhill* (*OCEL*).

2   A possible reference to *Framley Parsonage*, serialized in the *Cornhill* January 1860 to April 1861 and much admired by Mrs Gaskell (*Further Letters*, p. 214 and n.2).

– but I think that I would rather take you and the pleasure of seeing your wife, separated, from Florence; for the two together would be too extravagant a treat, and enough to spread over more than six weeks. – I forgot to say that we saw the Storys in London, and again at the Sturgises, where we stopped two nights as their friends. He is as warm and quiet and affectionate as ever, she so kind, too. Edie is quite fledged, but rather a riddle, tho' very noble in all she says and *looks*. The two boys most 'carino'. Oh dear old Rome – and poor America. We do so hope for you – If you see either of the Mr. Hales, that is either Mr. Edwd. Everett Hale, or his brother, Mr. Chas. Hale,[1] do give them our most affect. remembrances. – May I send my love to Mrs. Chas Norton?

> Ever yrs. aff.
> Meta E. Gaskell.

You must not think that because I only write that Mama has forgotten you. It looks quite silly to put such an idea into writing, but she is overwhelmed with business.

> M.E.G.

Envelope: Charles Eliot Norton Esq, Shady Hill. Cambridge. Massachusetts. United States of America. p. p. d

Postmark: Manchester OCT 31 62

Back of envelope: 'Thank you for the lovely photograph'.

Houghton Library, Harvard University. MS Am 1088 2604.

EFFIE WEDGWOOD

> 46 Plymouth Grove.
> Nov. 7. [1862]

Dearest Effie

I must write today to send you my birthday greetings, as you cannot receive them through the post on the day itself. I quite meant to have made you, or drawn you, something; but have not had time – or have lost it somehow – God help you, dearest darling Effie. You know how

---

1   Edward Everett Hale (1822–1909) was a Boston Unitarian Minister and friend of the Gaskell family; Charles Hale was his brother (*Further Letters*, pp. xvii and 230, n.1).

very dearly I love you, and you must measure the warmth of my real wish for your number of happy birthdays by my love. Something more, too, than *happiness* I wish you – the 'peace' which I think you have nearly earned –

Today is the grimmest, blackest November day possible – and inwardly, as well as outwardly, we are all most sad – Of course our one thought & object of talk is the Distress – and the different modes of relief. Yet still individually \one/ feels to be doing so little, and to be spending such a large percentage of one's time in alternations of rest and weary *collapse*. I dare say that you have heard that Miss Thornton is going to have a factory girl; a sweet gentle, dimpled little orphan. Miss Henrietta Lynot sends a *most* welcome order for work, too. Thank you so very, very much for the bundles of clothes. They will be most welcome, dearest Effie. I am afraid that I acknowledged {them} \yr. offer of them/ very abruptly. Vernon Lushington[1] was here the other day, & brought us such a capital account of our dear orphan girls – who certainly were charming. One of them has advanced in household service enough to deserve promotion to another place; but had declined leaving the [?l.s]! Please tell Snow this: she was so good in helping abt. their clothes, & start – I will not beg you to write to me for two reasons – firstly, because you know how much I like & long for yr. letters, & secondly, because begging is perfectly useless! Miss Effie.

Ever yr. own most loving

M. E. G.

P. S. I have opened my letter to acknowledge the splendidly large and useful hamper of clothing. It is cap*ital* – thank you all over & over again.

Do you know that you have sent *your riding-habit*? Is not that a mistake? We will not give it to the most starving Lady Godiva even till we have special permission.

"Grove and Baker's"[2] are the best sewing machines tell Mrs. Wedgwood.

---

1   Vernon Lushington (1832–1912), a scholar and radical lawyer who taught at the Working Men's College founded by his father and, among other philanthropic endeavours, supported relief efforts for unemployed factory operatives (*ODNB*).

2   Grove and Baker table top sewing machines dominated the market in the mid-nineteenth century, until they were superseded by Singer in 1870.

Ever yr. most gratefully
Meta Gaskell.
Friday Affn.

Envelope: Miss Effie Wedgwood. 1. Cumberland Place. Regent's Park. London. N.W.

Postmark: Manchester NO 1862 (tear across the date which could be NO 2 or 7)

By Courtesy of the Wedgwood Museum, Staffordshire; W/M 408.

EFFIE WEDGWOOD

Sir B. C. Brodies Bt.,
Augusta House,
Worthing.
Dec. 19th. [1862]

Darling Effie,

You can't be more astonished at this date than I was when I found myself fairly in the train, being whirled away from the "cotton districts", in which I had vowed so often to remain rooted till March – for the last fortnight or so Mama has been extremely unwell. After a week in bed she thought herself recovering, when we received a flying visit from a gentleman who came to Manchester to establish Tonic Solfa singing classes for the factory girls . . . (who are looked upon universally as clay ready to the potter's hand, by every one who has a pet scheme only wanting the human material {necessary} for immediate adoption) . . He of course had the fashionable interest in sewing schools – or rather, for that is a very unfair statement, we have got so absorbed in them that we stretch out and drag any stray comer into the vortex, and this person amongst the rest; and so Mama took him and *did* the schools and kitchens throughout M'Chester. The consequence was, she had a relapse and then last Friday I fairly broke down with overwork, & turned light headed, convincing everyone that I was going to have "the fever" – which one talks about familiarly as part of the Distress, but which, thank God, I believe, is almost a fiction really. At this very time an invite came from Philo[1]

---

1   Wife of Sir Benjamin Brodie the younger (1817–80), formerly Philo Thomson (*Further Letters*, p. 99, n.1). For an account of the situation in Manchester and Philo Brodie's invitation, see Uglow, p. 503.

asking us here; and Papa in*sist*ed on Mama's and my coming. So here we are and hither your letter followed me. The worst of it was, that Mama and I have such elastic health, and change of air and scene does such wonders, that by the time we got here, our railway journey had fattened and rouged us so that Sir B. and Philo very soon gave up any interesting anxiety on our acct. – I am however, sorry to say, that mama is very, very far from strong – however sea-air, and playing with the Baby, and drives in a lemon-coloured chariot, will, I hope, overbalance the fatigue of writing 10 pages \a day/ of the tiresome book that is really a "story without an end".[1] Meanwhile *my* endeavours are to get clean &strong – chiefly the 1st, which I have not been since the Distress began in August – (please tell Catherine). The housemaid here thinks I have a perfect mania for hot baths –

Your letter was such a charming one. I always enjoy your letters exceedingly – Oh would you mind, as I do not want to go thro' a whole letter to Cath. on purpose, saying to her on Sunday that I am afraid that I wrote her a very ungrateful letter on Wednesday; but tell her please that I did not feel so – and that a nemesis has befallen me already; for I have spoilt a drawing, {at} on which I was hard at work for the A. Exhibition. I have done one which all my friends will think a gt. anacronism as it is called "Sunrise" \by M. Gaskell/! – However I *did* see the sunrise from which the [?motivo] is taken, and it was not a vulgar winter sunrise, but one at 5. a.m. – in Sep.

Please tell Snow – tho' it is rather early in the day – that I shld. consider it a particular favour, if she wd. look at it well and send me a severe criticism on it, as it is rather an ambitious attempt in the tulip style – i.e. scarlet & yellows. Oh dear me– I tremble to think of it – & long to forge a "By the Countess Belmingham – Manleverer" or some grand name on the back, to make people think it a powerful work of art.

I always think of you, when I am wicked, Effie, which looks very uncomplimentary as I have put it – as if my associations with you were of wickedness, but in truth it is quite the contrary. I wonder if one is really imperceptibly getting better, so that if one *matched* oneself of the present with oneself of years ago one wd. find the purify-

---

1 A reference to *Sylvia's Lovers* (Uglow, p. 503).

ing that is too slow, I am afraid, to be felt day by day – just as in a gradation from dark to light.

Goodlbye, dearest, dearest Effie. Isn't Eliz'bth Mellor a little darling? with her dimples – I have sent a certain Sarah Davies to Mrs. Wm. Coulson, 1. Chester Terrace – Do you know her? – as servant, née factory-girl.

Ever y. most affc.

M. E. Gaskell.

Envelope: Miss Effie Wedgwood. 1. Cumberland Place. Regent's Park. London. N.W.

Postmark: Worthing Dec 19 62

By Courtesy of the Wedgwood Museum, Staffordshire; W/M 408.

CHARLES ELIOT NORTON

> Hotel d'Allenague
> *Rome.*
> April 17. [1863]

Dear Mr. Norton,

Look at my date! It seems like a dream being here again, like dreaming our old Roman visit over again – with one *great* gap to Mama and me, which not a day passes without our longing to fill up with your presence. She, Florence, Julia and I came here a fortnight ago last Monday (today is Wednesday) under François's charge.[1] I am half afraid lest you should have already heard \of this/ from him; which makes me feel very much ashamed of having delayed so long in writing to you. But our winter at home has been a terribly busy, anxious time, and all our correspondences have suffered very much. It is a long, painful story how spite of all effort, the Lancashire operatives have been "demoralized" as the phrase is, by very injudicious philanthropy, and short-sighted petting and pampering. Lancashire lads & lasses have been the reigning fashion all winter in England, & it {?} \has/ been impossible to hide from such an intelligent, reading class, what thousands of eyes were fixed upon there, and conse-

---

1   See Uglow, pp. 530–34, for an account of this holiday in 1863.

quently they have felt their sudden importance and misused it. There have been many, many exceptions, \and instances/ of the reverse; but the really patient quiet people have been the silent ones, and perhaps we forget their well-doing because it has been negative. There are one or two brave hearts & firm hands at the wheel – Mr Macluse, the hon. Sec. for the Relief Fund for one – or else I think there would be real danger to be feared. As it is these Stalybridge riots sound bad.[1] Our leaving home just now must look, I think, as if we were deserters but Mama, (and we all), got to feel so overworked that when we heard that we were doomed to at least another winter of "distress", she determined that we had better take a good long "piece of change" at once, so as to lay in a fund of fresh energy as soon as possible. So first she and Julia went to Madame Mohl's in Paris for five weeks, where their "change" was very gay indeed, and though pleasant hardly a rest; and then at the end of their visit Florence and I joined them, and we all came straight here by sea as quickly as we could. But before we left England a great event happened in which I know we shall have your unfailing sympathy, on which we always do and shall reckon whenever anything particular befalls us. Florence (whom it seems quite strange to think that you hardly know) got engaged to be married! You must remember her as such a little girl, in the Skelwith Meadows,[2] that you will find it very difficult to fancy such a serious thing having taken place in her life; but she is twenty, and though I think that she looks hardly older than she did six years ago, – her face having kept its childlike curves and \childlike/ movement of feature – yet she has a very decided, formed character, and is quite old enough in mind and heart to meet this great – \this/ *climax* of her life, rightly and wisely. We are all very, very much pleased with her choice; and with Mr. Crompton's having chosen her! He is the eldest son of Judge Crompton, and is himself a very clever young barrister,

---

1   When the Stalybridge Relief Committee found that relief distributed as cash was not always used as it was intended, they announced their decision to replace cash with tickets for food. This announcement led to serious rioting in Stalybridge and surrounding districts, followed by criminal prosecutions and a trial at Chester assizes. It is likely that Meta read reports of these events in the *Manchester Guardian*, 6 April 1863, p. 3, cols. 3–4.

2   Skelwith, two miles from Ambleside in the English Lake District, was a favourite holiday retreat for the Gaskell family (Uglow, pp. 231, 235, 274 and 431).

without happily what are usually considered the typical qualities of a "clever young barrister": flippancy and ambition. Of the latter at least he has just the right amount, – or rather the right *sort*. He is 30, fair, sturdy, bonny-looking, *almost* handsome; very firm and sensible in character, and with a bright, sweet temper, that will make daily sunshine in his home. He is the eldest son of a large family : all very charming in their different ways, & by all of whom he seems dearly loved. Florence is warmly welcomed by them all – There is a funny beginning to the attachment. In a quiet, 19th century sort of way, there has been a *vendetta* between the Cromptons & {Gaskells} \Mama's family/, dating from some past ill-usage – each says on the part of the other of course – And so, though distantly connected, Florence had never met Mr. C – till abt. this time last year – when she went to stay in London. A few weeks previously Mr. Crompton had seen in a stray photograph-book a {carte de visite} \portrait/ of Florence, and been so much struck with it that when he heard she was in London he made gt. efforts to meet her – – – et en voila lefia. Her portrait as *not* a carte-de-visite, or I wd. send you one of her; for I should like you to see her face – and better even in a photograph than not at all – though {another} \the best/ way of seeing it would be if you and Mrs. Charles Norton would come over to Manchester to get to know her. And this reminds me abt. the portrait of Mama. I have never sent you one, just because I have always been hoping to do something better than a copy . . . .

(*April 15th* the anniversary of the day when 6 years ago we started from Rome, as everybody is doing this baskingly-hot day in their heavily packed carriages –) . . of the little portrait you saw; and often when one plans to do something more than one is asked, one fails to do that little. Since beginning this letter to you I have got to feel quite oppressed with thinking how much I want to say to you; and how I shall get hardly any of it said! Writing at such times, in the middle of interruption and plans, one's letter is {?} but a very dull accumulation of scraps, and bears no proper stamp of one's remembrance and thought of the person to whom one writes. You cannot think how constantly & truly we wish for you here; not what a difference it wd. make to us, if we could have you for our companion.

Six years ago it was our greatest pleasure to have your help and knowledge, to which your kindness made us feel always welcome; but now I think, just because we *are* six years older we should value and appreciate your companionship even more. We have your little book, but that gives us but a little bit of you. You would be such a charming guide too; (merely to think of it, in that light) & \you/ wd. fill up all the interstices in that meagre Murray, which alludes in such a tantalizing way to all classical lore which is a sealed book to us who know no Latin.

Mama was so very happy to think that you had been pleased with her dedication. It was such a pleasure to her planning it. I cannot but believe that you will like the book, which I think her chef-d'oeuvre. The days are getting *very* hot here, and we laze in proportion. At first when we came full of what the Times is so fond of calling "*Lancashire energy*", we did a great deal everyday, and got quite formidably "up" in our ruins : then came the Holy Week – which fairly knocked us up. Six years makes a difference in one's view of *that*, at any rate; and I can hardly believe that I ever needed to hear your opinion of R. C. ism. That {?} \there is no temptation to/ look upon those ceremonies as religious, is almost the best thing about them. They are very fine shows, but as homage to God – – –

The Pope looks quite as well as he did six years ago; {?}François says that he hears of a great many assassinations of French soldiers by the Italians; and from everything that one hears, the feeling though suppressed, is growing into something that will soon be irresistible agst. the Papal regime and the French occupation. They have 24,000 soldiers here now. The Storys are very well. Mr. Story's great success last year has made him even more buoyant than before, and taken away the little bitterness of disappointment that there was. Mrs. Story, like the Pope, looks no older; and is so very kind and good to us. With Edie I cannot get on somehow, but, I dare say it is my fault. She is very short and "dumpy"; but certainly handsome, {?} \with/ beautiful long dark eyebrows, her father's eyes, and lovely, mobile, real *coral* lips. The little boys are as pretty as ever, & Mrs. Story contrives their dress so as to make them look doubly picturesque – They have a splendid suite of rooms at the Barberini; of which you will often have heard. They were there last night, and spent a charming evening, that carried one back to the Casa Cabrale. Mr. Dexter was there, & told us some capital stories, abt. the imprisonment of a friend of his – who may be one of your Paul Riviere? – in a Southern prison. This was to take the taste out of our mouths of some lies (I will coolly call them) that \Mama &/ we had been hearing on the other side from a *most* unpleasant Governor Moorhead of Kentucky,[1] the night before, at a party here. The "Roba di Roma"[2] has had a gt. success here and in England; & to Mrs. Story's private friends it is specially interesting for it is such a reflection of himself. If I do anything good in sketching in Italy, I shall send it you; but the chances are few of your getting anything on this condition; for every day I go back in my drawing instead forward, as I do so long to do. I am so ashamed of sending you this letter, dear Mr. Norton – and in return for your most charming one that I got three weeks before leaving home. I looked out for your sad Titian at the Doria gallery[3] with his rosebud & earring. I send you 2 little photographs : one of the steps in the Piazza de Spagnia with the fountain, whose sound you must have heard through the night, in your high room as we do in our corner room – 5th piano! I send you a cyclamen & fern. How I wish that they cd. have been put straight out of my parasol into your hands as we used to give you the flowers after the Pamfilj Doria afternoons. François seems very well and happy, and is *most* loyal to you : but he finds his match {?} in us for that!

Please do not prepay your next letters to us till I am out of your debt for this, which will now be prepaid for greater security, {though} \ for/ it is so dull that it seems hard you should be fined for receiving it. Do please write soon.

Most truly & aff'ly yours
Meta Gaskell

1   Kentucky was a border state during the Civil War, declaring neutrality at the start of the war, though Kentuckians volunteered for both Northern and Southern armies (Keegan, p. 108).
2   William W. Story, *Roba di Roma*, 2 vols (London, 1863). These volumes provide an account of contemporary customs and scenes in Rome, including less savoury aspects than those described by Mrs Gaskell and her daughters in their letters.
3   Doria Pamphilj Gallery, 305 via del Corso, Rome.

Wednesday night – April 17[th.]

P. S. Please, please write soon. I hope that you are stronger.

CHARLES ELIOT NORTON

Plymouth Grove
July 20th [1863]

My dear Mr. Norton,

Last night brought us the news of Genl. Meade's victory on the third of July.[1] We had been quite breathless for further news ever since the last telegram told us of the impending crisis, and I cannot tell you with what deep, though awe-ful, joy we heard of the success of the North. The loss on both sides must have been terrible; but in the North the bereaved people can indeed look on their dead ones as martyrs to a holy cause with certainty that must make them blessed while they mourn. And yet one cannot but think the Confederate army has fought gallantly; although perhaps it is simply as Mr. Shaen[2] (who married a sister of Kate Winkworth's) said, that "they have more devil in them", yet I ought hardly to repeat that when so many are lying dead and dying. It is quite extraordinary how strong the feeling of the middle classes is in favour of the South. Nearly all the really *great* men, however, are for the North : Goldwin Smith, J. Stuart Mill[3] etc. I have just been reading "Our General" in the Atlantic,[4] which shows very startlingly what misrepresentations and consequent false judg-

---

1   General George Gordon Meade, in command of the Army of the Potomac, was instrumental in the defeat of Robert E. Lee's army during the Battle of Gettysburg (1–3 July 1863), thus turning the tide in favour of the North (Keegan, pp. 190–203 and Catton, pp. 248–57). For reports of this event in the British press, see the *Manchester Guardian,* 18 July 1863, p. 5, cols.3–5 and *The Times,* 20 July 1863, p. 9.col.B.

2   William Shaen (1822–87), solicitor and friend of the Gaskell family (*Further Letters,* p. 307).

3   Goldwin Smith (1823–1910), English journalist and historian and staunch supporter of the Northern side in the American Civil War (*ODNB*). John Stuart Mill (1806–73), of Scottish ancestry, author of *On Liberty* (1859); known as a champion of individual freedom (*ODBH*).

4   'Our General', *Atlantic Monthly,* 12 (1863), 104–15.

ments there are made by the enemies of the North.

You will see by the date of this letter that we are back at home again – and very pleasant it is. That is one of the advantages of a foreign tour, that however happy one has been away the return home is the crowning point of all. We had such a very successful tour. We went to Assisi, stopping at all the places where we could see the frescoes of the Perujian school. Who do you think drew up our plan for us, as we could not have you to do it? A very great friend of yours, Mr. Perkins.[1] What a charming person he is! We went to him in gt. distress because we cd. not combine both Assisi & Orvieto within reasonable limits of time and expense : and *your* friend was a fit person to rescue us from a dilemma which was owing to the great wish that your book had given us to see the Cathedral at the latter. He undertook us in our distress most chivalrously and we followed his advice and found it capital. It was quite a pleasure to see his face, even across a bewildering map, and to hear him talk even about scudi and stages. There is something very rare about his direct, *radiant* look. How very beautiful Orvieto is! I think that we cared for the Gior da Pisas more than anything on our journey; and certainly to appreciate them one ought to have your book (as we had) in our hand; and still more surely, to appreciate the truth and insight of your book, one ought to be able to look up from it to the bas-reliefs. The Signorellis[2] are magnificent too. I wish that Murray wd. quote you instead of his favourite idiot, Mr. John Bell. How much of M.Angelo and Raphael is drawn from their masters – When we got to Florence François had a relapse of Syrian fever, and though by no means very seriously ill, returned at Dr. Wilson's recommendation to Paris, to rest there in preparation for another tour, for which he was engaged. It is a thing that one ought *very* seldom to do, to unveil a person's character to a friend who believes too well of him, particularly when that friend is in the position of helper and benefactor; but still Mama and I [were] asking often about it, having determined that it is right to tell you that we had reason to learn to distrust him completely, and to doubt

---

1   A possible reference to Charles C. Perkins (*Norton Letters,* ı. 64 and n.1).

2   Luca Signorelli (c. 1445–1523), known for his fresco at Orvieto depicting a *Last Judgment* (Piper, pp. 116–17).

his honesty. If you would like to hear the full particulars, Mama says I am to tell you that if you wish she will write you out the facts that caused this as accurately as ever she can : and we will most gladly be proved to have judged him on insufficient evidence. *Why* we pain you by telling you, is to save your giving an unqualified recommendation of him.

I do not know how to thank you enough for your constant kind remembrance – The views of Boston are so very interesting to us, who feel a sort of right to Boston citizenship, (which I am afraid you would not recognize) from our love for the dear unknown place; and the stereoscopic views give one most characteristic and beautiful glimpses of the grandeur of your forests. Thank you so much for them all, dear Mr. Norton. You cannot think how pleased Mama was with her pencil. I know she means to write and thank you for it herself; but let me bear witness to her pleasure. For days after she got it, she was constantly fumbling in her pocket to take it out – not to use it – but just to look at it, and ask us if it was not pretty, and if it wasn't kind of you and Mrs. Charles Norton to send it her –

You ask abt. Mr. Rosetti. I have heard nothing of him since last year, when Mama and I saw him at his studio,[1] with a great many fragments on hand. He spoke with an almost strange calmness and familiarity of his wife – I think soon that we shall be seeing a great friend of his, and then I will ask then for more about him, and send you word. When you were in England, did you see any of *Watts*'s paintings?[2] They seem to me almost finer than any; of any time. I should so like to know what you think of them : *please tell me* if you ever have had the opportunity of judging them. I must cross more than I ought to tell you something which you will think very likely "sending coals to Newcastle", as we say, but still I want to let you know that we do sometimes hear some of the things that show the true spirit of the North. Mama went out to dinner here the other night,

---

1   Mrs Gaskell and her daughters were frequent visitors to Rossetti's studio, though there is no record of a visit in the year to which Meta refers here, 1862, which was the year Rossetti's wife died (*Further Letters*, p. 242, n.4).
2   George Frederick Watts (1817–1904), associated with the Pre-Raphaelite Brotherhood and sometimes admired by Ruskin, best known as a portrait painter (Hewison, p. 234).

and putting forward a {?} feeler as to the opinions of her neighbour on American affairs found him as staunch a Northerner as herself : and then he told her that a friend of his a Mr. Russell of New York had gone on to the field of Murfreesburgh,[1] all in the dead of the night after the battle. He had been picking his way along softly and unperceived, when he heard the voice of a poor dying soldier (who turned out afterwards to have been wounded in some *most* awful way) break out into the hymn "Rock of Ages" – and as his voice rose, faint [?yet] full of faith conquering agony, another and another joined in, till it swelled into a great chorus[2] –

    Ever yr. truly affec. friend
    Meta Gaskell

Houghton Library, Harvard University. MS Am 1088 2605.

CHARLES ELIOT NORTON

            Charles Crompton's Esq.
            89. Oxford Terrace,[3]
            Hyde Park.
            W. London.
            Friday Evening
            April 28. [1865]

My dear Mr. Norton,

    It is with the profoundest sympathy & sorrow that I wish to tell \ you/ that we have just received the news of the assassination of the President.[4] Ten days ago I left Manchester to spend a week in the country (at Dumbleton, Thurstan Holland's home);[5] and I packed up

---

1 Murfreesboro (Stones River) Tennessee, scene of a battle fought over three days from 31 December 1862 to 2 January 1863; casualties on both sides were exceptionally high (Keegan, p. 177).'

2 Hymn singing was popular among the soldiers, with 'Rock of Ages' among the favourites (Keegan, pp. 79–80).

3 Meta was writing from her sister Florence's marital home, where she and her mother were staying; see *Gaskell Letters*, pp. 756–57 for Mrs Gaskell's account of this visit.

4 President Lincoln was shot while attending a theatre performance with his wife during the evening of 14 April 1865; he died early next morning, 15 April 1865.

5 The Dumbleton Estate, Gloucestershire, had been in the hands of the Holland

with particular care a little photograph of Mama that I meant to send you, for I felt that I could not keep silence over the glorious news that we had then just heard, & every day I counted amongst the letters that I had to write one to you, to tell you how happy & proud I felt for {America} \the North/ in her great victories, & still more for her Christian bearing under them – But since I have been ill, I cannot write a great many letters at once, & I had so many necessary ones to write first, that this one to you got put off; & now, in this short delay, what an awful change there is – how joy is turned to bitter sorrow & indignation. I had just got such a strong personal feeling for the President, from reading that paper of Goldwin Smith's on him in "MacMillan" & still more from the tone of his message – published in the Times of March 17th., which even the "Saturday" (with its strong Southern tendency) called "sublime in its religious spirit".[1] For his own private sake it seems almost [?] that he should be summoned to receive his crown of glory whilst he was inspired by such noble & sublime feeling as his deeds & words have lately expressed, and when he was so fit to enter the presence of God – but for the nation to have so great a loss, for his wife & friends to pass through so cruel a trial as this has been, seems terrible. The one good is that it has roused the sympathy of people here in an extraordinary way. There is but one voice of lamentation and indignation –

Mrs. Norton's letter came tonight. It was so good of her to write & claim the sympathy that is always ready for you and yours & from your most noble nation, but it was so sad to read it & think how changed was the kind of sympathy that we have to give, & that we are weeping with those who weep instead of rejoicing with those who rejoice.

Your most aff'te

Meta Gaskell.

Please give my love to your wife. Do look at the nice Times arti-

family since 1823, when it was purchased by Swinton Holland, the banker. Following his death, the Estate passed to his son Edward, who was Mrs Gaskell's first cousin, and Marianne's future father-in-law. Edward Holland built a model village and a mansion for himself and his family (*Early Years*, pp. 181–82).

1   Goldwin Smith, 'President Lincoln', *Macmillan's Magazine*, 11 (1865), 301–305. Editorial, *The Times*, 17 March 1865, p. 9, col.b. This article discusses, favourably, the inauguration of President Lincoln for a second term of office.

cle of this morning, (April 29th.)[1] – It is a small compensation for the way in which (as Goldwin Smith says) "it has scattered firebrands amongst the nation".

Houghton Library, Harvard University. MS Am 1088 2606.

MARIANNE GASKELL

[April 1865][2]

Darling M –

Just arrived: & find both Mama *and* F. very much overdone – & "emotional"[3] – \Don't refer to this –/ But I mean to 'save' there as much as I can – I have had a very pleasant visit at Dumbleton indeed –

Ever yr. lov'g
MEG

Torn half sheet without address or date. Watermark: TMAN at foot of page

The Brotherton Collection, Leeds University Library. BC MS 19c Gaskell, MS12.

MARIANNE GASKELL

[April 1865]

My darling Minnie,

Mama is wonderfully better today – Mr. Butler has not yet been, tho' it is 1 o'clock – but I can see, and she feels, a gt. improvement, it has been, however, a very sharp attack of bronchitis. I did not call it that to you before; because I thought it wd. sound more formidable than it was . . . it being only a *very, very* bad cold – with "inflammation of the bronchial tubes".

She *is so much* hurt at Papa's never having written to her – If he is at home tomorrow even'g., when I suppose you will get this letter, do beg him to write by tomorrow evening's post – at once, so that she

1 Special Southern Correspondent, 'The News of the Assassination in New York', *The Times*, 29 April 1865, p. 9, col.e.
2 This date is strongly suggested by Mrs Gaskell's letter to Charles Norton, April 28, 1865 (*Gaskell Letters*, pp. 756–57). She is writing from Florence's London home and refers to Meta's arrival from Dumbleton.
3 A likely reference to the news of President Lincoln's assignation.

may get a letter by Tuesday mid-day post. She says that she thinks he might have written to ask her if she did not want some more money (*which she does*) – I told her to remember how busy Papa was – and she said something abt. his always finding time to read the papers at the Portico[1] – & that she thought he might have written to me, to tell me to get everything money cd. buy – I said ["] it was different from if you had been dangerously ill – tho' even then I think Papa would have *trusted* me to go & get everything necessary" – Whereupon she said she thought she had been dangerously ill – and I cd. only tell her that Mr. Butler had never thought so . . .

Today she seems almost quite well. She says I am to tell you to take *anything you like to* your old women; or to *get* anything they fancy. Often a bit of our home made bread is a treat for them – And you are to please to see abt. [?] dinner with the new Cook – and you are to send Mrs. Horatio Nicholls' character of Sarah M'Clain. (That is because I have never shown her nor told her anything of your letters that came on Thursday, thinking it wd. worry her – but I suppose I must before the time for yr. letter in return to this comes.) And you are another time not to worry yourself abt. such searches as for Caroline's mother; but to get Mr. Rathbone to do it – he employs every Tuesday aftn. in going visiting the Parents of the Children – & it wd. save our time, strength [?] & perhaps get the thing more efficiently done in the end!! I have several letters to write. Do you write to Mama – She does so crave for letters. Perhaps you had better not read Papa all that she said of his not writing; but get him to do so, or to explain in some message why he can't – What a hard day you must have had poor darling – I feel quite cosy about the Tutor's praise of my drawings – especially as I have got all my best with me here – to copy – all in fact except early sketches of a date anterior to the books.

Ever your most loving
M E Gaskell.

No date or address, but content suggests a follow on from the previous letter written in April 1865.

The Brotherton Collection, Leeds University Library. BC MS 19c Gaskell, MS12.

---

1   William Gaskell was a member of the Portico Library, Manchester, for forty years and Chairman for thirty years (Brill, p. 110).

HENRY CROMPTON[1]

Plymouth Grove.
Friday morning.
[17 November 1865]

Dear Harry,

I cannot possibly say to you what my remembrance of your most tender kindness is, – and will be for ever. I am so glad, too, to think that the kindness was given by one who loved my own Mother so dearly, and \of/ whom \she/ spoke {of him} in the lost Crewe letter as "my very dear Harry," if I remember rightly. I want to tell you, Though I think you will think it strange \for me to tell you of it,/ what a certainty of instinctive faith I have in heaven, and in Mama's living on, amongst those whom we call dead, but whom I feel now alone have the true Life. Sometimes when people have died, I have had all sorts of horrible wonders & doubts, about where and how the soul was: but with this utter sorrow comes so clear an instinct of immortality that I want to tell you of it; for if one person knows a thing, it proves it – though a hundred doubt it, and I want to share with you, who have suffered the same grief, this only comfort.   F o r g i v e my having written so to you; and may God bless you for what you have been to us this last week.

Your most truly grateful and affectionate
Meta Gaskell

Black-edged mourning paper and envelope.

Envelope: Henry Crompton 22. Hyde Park Square. W. London.

Postmark: E NO 17 MANCHESTER 1865 30.

© British Library Board. Add Mss. 71701, ff.57–58.

---

1   Son of Judge Crompton and younger brother of Meta's brother-in-law Charles Crompton.

CHARLES ELIOT NORTON

Plymouth Grove.
Nov.24. [1865]

Dearest Mr. Norton,

The papers and a note from Thurstan Holland will have told you of our unutterable loss. I think of you as one of the very first people she would have wished me to write to – and I long to get in answer your words which will speak of the love you have borne her. She was so faithful to you – so unwavering in her affection, not only to you, but to all that she had known through you; in her burning adherence to the side of the North, and her longing for freedom and right to triumph in her "dear America". I remember she wrote to you not long before we went abroad – She and Julia and I went on the 3rd. of Octr. – She had not been well for some time before – but that was only exhaustion from having been a good deal in the bad air of Manchester. We crossed to Dieppe meaning to go on to Switzerland, but she did not feel equal to the long journeys, and she liked Dieppe so much that we stopped there from {from} Wednesday to the Friday fortnight. And in that time she got so well that she said, and we all thought, and she *was*, better than she had been for years and years. Then we went to Rouen – she wanted so to show it Julia & then to Boulogne, and crossed home and we went to Holybourne in Hampshire. I do not know whether she ever told you about her 'heart's desire' of buying a little country house, for Papa to '*retire*' to? She had kept it such a secret from him, and had lavished the most tender pains in making it what he would like, and her last fortnight was thus spent, and in cherishing us {?} with her infinite lovingness –

Charlie Crompton's father died on the 30th of Octr., and he and Florence were to come down to us, *did* come down to us on the 11th. of Novr. Saturday, for a Sunday in the country – \and the Sunday was/ such a happy peaceful day till *that* happened. We talked, and loitered in and out of the lovely garden, and in the aft'n Mama and Florence and Julia went to the little village church, while I went on a walk with Charlie. After church Mama went round the house with a poor widow in the village, to whom she knew it would give pleasure to see the pretty new furniture. Then we had "five o'clock tea" & then again

Mama went and peeped out at her beloved garden with Charlie – Then Florence & Julia and I went upstairs & took our walking things off; and came down into the drawing room. She and Charlie were sitting before the fire, talking about Judge Crompton's death. We took seats near them. Charlie said "Harry wants my mother to go to Rome for a change" – Mama said "I remember at Eardiston, your father saying to me 'I tell Lady Crompton when – \("I am dead" would have been her last words) and she fell forwards dead. By God's mercy I caught her in my arms – I may be, I am, very selfish, but this is such a strange joy to me, to think I held her during her last moment – for but a *moment* it was – though we did not know it till the Doctor came an hour later. We tried everything, with growing terror – Now I know that that look of peace and heavenly rest means Death, but then I only feared it.

Pray for us that we may have God's grace given us to reach her at His Feet, that we may never cease to love her as we do now – beyond everything. Papa is wonderfully calm, & all my sisters are so good and unselfish. Thurstan and Charlie have done everything to help and comfort us. She is laid in Knutsford Chapel yard, by the aunt who was a mother to her. She had always wished for a sudden death. I do so long that we four daughters may love one another as she wished. It was almost like Christ asking his disciples to "love one another", the way she used to beg us to let no differences come in to harden our hearts – God bless you and yours.

    Ever yours aff'ly
    Meta Gaskell.
Write to me some times and help me to keep nearer to God.

Black-edged mourning paper.

Envelope: Charles Eliot Norton, Shady Hill, Cambridge. *Massachusetts* United States of America. p. p. d

Postmark: Manchester 25 NO 65.

Houghton Library, Harvard University. MS Am 1088 2607.

ELLEN NUSSEY[1]

46, Plymouth Grove,
January 22, 1866.

My Dear Miss Nussey,

I am afraid that my delay in answering your kind note of sympathy must have seemed strangely ungrateful; but, indeed, the cause has been very different. For some weeks I have been feeling so ill that I have had to abstain from writing numbers and numbers of letters that I wished to write.

You ask for some particulars of darling Mama's death – We were staying at a small country-house at Holybourne, Hampshire, which she had bought with her own earnings as a present for Papa; hoping in two or three years to make him give up his overstraining work here, and to induce him to live in the country. She had seemed *particularly* well for the last five or six weeks – Before that, she had been ailing – but the doctor said it was merely "want of tone" – and the worst symptoms then were *very* restless nights and great faintness. On Sunday, the 12th November, Charlie Crompton (Florence's husband) and Florence were with us. He had lost his father not a fortnight before, and Mama had persuaded him to come down to Holybourne for fresh air & change from the Saturday till the Monday. He and I had been a walk on the Sunday afternoon, but Mama, Florence, and Julia had been to church, and the clergyman had noticed how particularly well Mama was looking. When we had all come in, we had tea, and then were sitting round the fire in the drawing-room, so cozily and happily (darling Mama talking and planning a most kind plan of lending the house to Lady Crompton, who was very much broken down), when *quite* suddenly, without a moment's warning, in the middle of a sentence, she fell forwards – *dead*. It was disease of the heart. At first we thought she had fainted – next that it was a fit – and Charlie and a servant both ran for a doctor. In three quarters of an hour we knew the truth: It was most fearful the shock – but as we are beginning to recover from that, we do feel God's great mercy in taking our darling

---

1   A long-standing friend of Charlotte Brontë, Ellen Nussey co-operated with Mrs Gaskell when she was researching for her *Life of Charlotte Brontë*, first published 1857.

so painlessly – and before the weariness of failing powers had set in. For me it has changed the face of this world for ever; but thank God one feels every day more sure that this world is but the threshold of the Future, where there will be no more sorrow or parting –

I often have thought lately of the kind, patient help you gave Mama about Miss Brontë's Life. Please let us hear from you sometimes, and do not let us quite *drift apart*. –

> Ever yours affecte.
> Meta Gaskell.

I cannot tell you how beautiful a "sunset" it was – though we did not know it was that at the time; all Mama's last days had been full of loving thought and tender help for others. She *was* so sweet and dear and noble beyond words.

Manuscript, on black-edged mourning paper, on microfilm.

Manchester Libraries, Information and Archives, MF 615 Gaskell Brontë material in the Symington Collection, reel 1.

Published by Clement K. Shorter in *The Sphere*, 25 May 1918, p. 148. In matters of style, i.e. punctuation, paragraphing and enhancements, the transcript here follows the manuscript rather than the printed version.

ELLEN NUSSEY

46 Plymouth Grove,
March 23. [1866]

My dear Miss Nussey,

I need not tell you how very much I should have liked to have accepted your most kind invitation, if it had been possible, but I am afraid that it is not, because I have already promised seven or eight old friends, that if I leave home for any change, I will pay them visits, so that I could not come to you without breaking my word and hurting them.

But I do trust that you will let me consider it only a pleasure deferred, for I should so much like to see you again, dear Miss Nussey.

Thanking both your sister and yourself, I am with much love and best thanks,

Yours ever affly.

Meta Gaskell.

Papa has been very ill with Bronchitis,[1] and is slowly struggling into a recovery which this East wind hinders to the utmost.

Annotation in pencil on back of letter:

Meta Gaskell,
Miss Wooler,
Miss Kemp,
Miss Dixon on Froud & c.

Typed transcript; original with black border is at BPM.

The Brotherton Collection, Leeds University Library. BC MS 19c Brontë C13.

CHARLES ELIOT NORTON

46, Plymouth Grove.
March 27[th.] [1866]

My dear Mr. Norton,

I have been meaning for a long time to write to you; but all through January and February, I suffered so much from the old pain in my head that I had to keep myself from every and any piece of writing, and during this last month dear Papa has been very ill indeed with bronchitis, and complete prostration. He has gone to Hastings now; and the two letters which we have received from him both speak of the great good which he is gaining from the sweet, warm Southern air. I tell you all this to explain my past silence; and I must take the opportunity to say, looking forwards, that if ever in the future you are a long time without a letter, you must *please* believe that it will come from want of time or strength to write, and never from unwillingness or forgetfulness. I think Mama has told you that about two years ago I suffered very much from inflammation of the spine just at the root of the brain, and this very often makes it imprudent for me to write – by threatening to return. I only give you this long story, to prevent your ever doubting my wish to write. I have tried, too, day after day,

---

1   William Gaskell suffered from an attack of bronchitis during the early months of 1866, following the death of his wife the previous autumn. See Meta's letter to Charles Norton dated 27 March 1866.

to copy that portrait rightly, but hitherto failed. I mean to try and try again, and hope so much to succeed. I never copied it before, because it did not – indeed it did not – do Mama anything like justice; and I always meant to make a fresh drawing of her for you – and only at Dieppe this October, there was on a piece of paper, bearing a list of things I meant to do there, a "C.E.N.", standing for the resolution to try and take a likeness of her. It is a broken promise – a piece of dis-obliging neglect – for which I cannot make any excuse. I can only ask you to forgive me. I will continue now to try to copy the portrait – but the photograph that you have is, I think, far the nearest to her of anything.

\(April 6th)/

Mr. Lawrence,[1] whom very likely you know thro' his American connections, took a likeness of her two springs ago, which I saw before the last sitting – and it promised to be very like – though the portrait only told of one side of her character, the nobility and hero-ism, and left all the exquisite tenderness untouched.

It has been a terrible winter for us in some ways. You can under-stand it all, I know; for you fully understood *her*. I do not think that I shall ever get over the longing just to have had one minute in which to ask her to forgive all {?} I had failed in. I had never lost any one very dear or near before; and Death really & truly was a thing unknown to me. I wish I could tell you of so many little things that she said a few weeks before her death, showing how her whole soul was turned to Heaven, though *she* had no more warning than *we* for her that she was so near it. Though I *hate* anything savoring of the doc-trine of a deathbed repentance, and all that follows of giving undue importance to the last words because they *were* the last, yet there is something so beautiful about people dying at their very best, before there is any falling away from their highest life & effort. I remember only at Holybourne, a gentleman telling us of the great aloe at the South Kensington Gardens which had flowered after a hundred years' growth, and died in and through this consummation of its beauty.

---

1   An English portrait painter, not to be confused with the more famous Sir Thomas Lawrence who died in 1830. For Norton's account of Lawrence's visit to America in 1854 see *Norton Letters*, I. 112–13.

At the time I thought of President Lincoln, but now it seems so like Mama – for in everything but health and strength she had seemed more than herself this year – She had never written so easily; nor so well, most people think – and she had done so very, very much for and with others – It gives me a strange feeling of peace having no future happiness in this world to 'carve out' for oneself. I know it is a wrong thing at any time to think of anything so selfish; but it is what one naturally does, till one's whole treasure is in heaven –

I do so wish sometimes that I had a more definite belief. It is so *very* difficult now in England, and it must be the same in America, to know what to believe, when equally good & wise men are ranged on such different sides. Some people end by believing nothing – but I always feel as if I believed too many, and contradictory, things. I want very much to clear up my belief, because I do so hope, if ever I get stronger, that I may work amongst the poor, and for that if you are to call them out of unbelief, you must raise a fixed standard of {hope} belief. For oneself it does not practically signify, I think, do you? what kind of intense union \with God one thinks that/ the "Sonship" of {?} Christ implies, or what view one takes of the Atonement so that it is not the Calvinistic one; but if one has to appeal to the poor, one must know *what* one believes oneself – I feel sometimes so afraid of reading too much on the subject, too; because though of course one would never dread the road to truth, however different to one's wishes truth might be when one reached it, yet so often people start on a course of inquiry which leads them far away from truth. Wasn't it M. Aurelius[1] who said that no harm ever came from the search for truth? But surely it does; for so constantly people believe that they have found it when they have stumbled instead on an error – There are so very many Comtists[2] in England now. Nearly all the best, I mean the *good-est*, young men are led astray by {it} \Comtism./ Mr. Maurice[3] said that he thought it was a reaction,

---

1 Marcus Aurelius, Roman Emperor, early philosopher and author of *Meditations*.
2 Auguste Comte (1798–1857) French philosopher who founded the discipline of Sociology and theory of Positivism. He developed ideas of secular humanism and altruism. *The Philosophy of Comte* was translated and condensed by Harriet Martineau (*OCEL*).
3 (John) Frederick Denison Maurice (1805–72), Christian Socialist, founder of a Working Men's College, known to Charles Kingsley and Alfred Lord Tennyson.

too violent in its direction, from the false dogmas of the church – I hope that I have not said anything 'faithless' about seeking for truth – I do indeed believe that "if with all our hearts we truly seek God, we shall most surely find Him" – but I think, do you not too, with Robertson that "obedience is the organ of spiritual knowledge" – and that doing His will, is the way to learn the nature of God, \& not by speculative enquiry –?/ Have you read "Ecce Homo"? Everybody in England is quite wild about it. There are endless reports about its authorship, which is still a complete secret.[1] A good many people believe that it is the Archbishop of York – Macmillan told some one that it was by one of the highest personages of the realm, which suits this report; and the most intimate friend of the Archbishop's let out by accident that he knew the secret of its authorship. It is curious how everybody sees a reflection of his own views in it: the High Church & Broad Church & Unitarians all seem to find it a ground of meeting. Mr. Maurice says he never knew any book of the kind make such a stir – It has even made people forget Robertson's Life – which was almost like a fresh bit of revelation –

Marianne is at Dumbleton – Thurstan's home. I think that they will be married in August – I often wonder what view you take of political affairs in America – I hope that they are not going in the wrong direction – but I fear it is so. Do not please write when you are busy or tired – I shall never misunderstand your silence.

Ever your truly affectionate friend

Meta Gaskell.

Please give my love to Mrs. Norton, and Mrs. Charles Norton, and to your sisters.

Black-edged mourning paper.

Houghton Library, Harvard University. MS Am 1088 2608.

---

1   Sir John Robert Seeley (1834–95) was the author of *Ecce Homo*, published in London, 1865. Seeley was then professor of Latin at University College London and, in 1869, became professor of modern history at Cambridge (*ODNB*).

CHARLES ELIOT NORTON

Plymouth Grove.
July 5th. 1866.

Dear Mr. Norton,

I need hardly tell you with what *great* joy we accept your proposal; only thank you with our whole hearts for your adding another link to the associations which bind you and yours to darling Mama.

It will be such a very happy thing to think of a little darling child, however far away, who bears her name, and she will always seem to belong to us in a way which you and Mrs. Charles Norton will not grudge – as you will have given us the pleasure of loving her as Mama's namesake as well as for your sakes. How I hope that God may bless her –.

Dear Mr. Norton – thank you again and again – Papa {was} is so pleased to think of your calling your baby by Mama's name – It was exactly – Elizabeth *Cleghorn* – She was called so after the daughter (the only child – "and she was a widow") of a Mrs. Cleghorn who had been very good to Mama's mother; and just as Mama was born this Miss Cleghorn died, and the little baby was called after her – at the poor mother's request.

I want to send this off by the early post, so I will write no more – With much love to Mrs. Charles Norton, ever your truly aff'te. Meta Gaskell –

Black-edged mourning paper and envelope.

Envelope: Charles Eliot Norton, {Shady Hill}, {Cambridge}.Ashfield, Massachusetts, United States of America.

Postmark: Manchester JY 6 66.

Houghton Library, Harvard University. MS Am 1088 2609.

HENRY CROMPTON

Linc. Coll.
Tuesday.
[Oct. 30. 1866]

Dear Harry –

I must thank you for your *most* interesting letter. It was really very good of you to answer my question so fully. I shall keep what you say, as it seems to me conclusive. That is on every point but one; and "infinitely complex" as the whole subject is, that one point is most so – Whether men may take away from a man the life which means in such a case time to repent and retrieve the past. One believes in the perfect justice of God, and that He wd. not punish any one for not having retrieved his sin, when all opportunities were cut off from him; but yet the one limit to God's infinite knowledge must be with regard to what human free-will may or may not do – and to Him even can it be possible to know what a man would had done had he lived? I hope and trust that this is not wrong\ly said./ What I *mean* is not wrong; and you have the power of "taking the right side of one's meaning".

How sad the Blue Book is, as you say. It seems even darker reading it in such a lovely happy house as this – like looking down on a battle from some safe, sunny height. Everything is so beautiful here. Each time I look up I see the old crumbling grey college walls all hung with golden vine-leaves – and the rooms are as lovely as the views through the windows.

We shall not think of "inviting" you to Plymouth Grove. When you are on one of your progresses, send a "command" to us to receive you, as a sovereign does, and you need never doubt a welcome, as you perfectly well know.

I keep remembering what today is to you, Harry.[1] It seems to me oh so sad that you – who deserve it so *much, much* more than I – should not have the comfort that I have; but in Mama's words "It is sometimes the very best that God purifies in the furnace of doubt" – With *her* your goodness to us last year {and} is, & ever will be, most

1   First anniversary of the death of Harry's father, Judge Crompton.

vividly associated.

> Ever your affte
> M. E. Gaskell.

Black-edged mourning paper.

(C) British Library Board. Add Mss. 71701, ff. 60–61.

SUSAN NORTON

> Plymouth Grove.
> Manchester.
> Nov. 9. 1866.

Dearest Mrs. Norton,

I could not have believed when I got your letter that I should have left it so long unanswered; I will not waste time in telling you how busy I have been; but assure you that it has not been from want of loving thought that I have been silent. Indeed, dearest Mrs. Norton, this fresh bond would prevent my [?] forgetting your home, if anything were needed besides my affection for you and Mr. Norton to make me remember it. It seems as if you have given us a little bit of your baby for our own – in letting her bear the name of our very dearest one – and we shall so love her all our lives – I wish that we could look on her little face – May she be called 'Lily'? or would you rather not? That was Mama's name to Papa and her best friends. The meaning – as name of the flower, suggests all purity & nobleness – & a symbol of such beautiful things – It well befitted Mama – and I am quite sure that your little one will, if God spares it, be worthy of it too. Oh why is there such a great gulf fixed between America & England[?] I should so love to see your little child.

I have only just come back from Oxford – and {?} my greatest pleasure there was in hearing Mr. Goldwin Smith talk about America – and particularly in hearing him speak of Mr. Norton with such deep true appreciation, as satisfied even me. He speaks quite confidently of going to America again next autumn, and "wished himself there already". I hope that you will not keep him altogether [as] we could not afford to lose such a man. To me he seems the greatest 'leader' we have – He gathers together all the glimmerings of truth that we have up here in the North of England, & flashes them back like a radiant revelation to the world – and has a faith and wisdom quite beyond our own. His "Civil War in America" I suppose you have seen?[1] If not, I should so like to send you a copy – & please remember in reading it how many now would echo every word in it – I do think that the scales are dropping from people's eyes about America. We are watching the present struggle with the greatest interest – As you say, in some ways it is more terrible than the war. It seems a meaner kind of conflict. But what a noble nation you are! Mr. Goldwin Smith was saying that it was so fine in America to see the way in which every head was busy working at the National problems – and I said carelessly "Is it so even with the common people?" – and he answered quite indignantly "Common people! There *are* no common people in America" – – Would you tell Mr. Norton please that we are so grateful to an unknown somebody who continues to send us the "Nation"; and that we wish so much that we knew whom to thank for it. It does not fall on stony ground – Everything that comes from {across the Atlantic} \the North/ is very dear to us for your sakes \as well as its own/. Has Mr. Norton heard lately from Mr. Ruskin? I saw a letter from him to Lady Brodie when I was at Oxford – It seems as if he were pressed down by the weight of misery that he sees around him in London; and had lost faith in all peace and goodness. It is the failing of a noble mind through its very power of pity – and one cannot help admiring him for the tenderness which makes him so absorbed with the dark suffering side of life; but I think that if Mr. Norton could write him one of his comforting wise letters it might help to rouse him. He refuses to think about Art – overlooking, (as far as I dare judge) one of the best medicines for this sore – one means of leading man into communion with God, and, awakening his heart to the goodness of a Loving Father.

I wonder whether I might ask for the gt. favour of your sending me an autograph of Longfellow's? I know how intimate you are with him –or would not ask. It is for a sad, [?] little girl I know here; whose one

---

1   Goldwin Smith, *The Civil War in America: An Address Read at the Last Meeting of the Manchester Union and Emancipation Society* (London, 1866).

softening interest at present is a passion for autographs.

Thanking you again dearest Mrs. Norton for your letter.

I am your very loving

Meta Gaskell

I have given you no family chronicle! We are all well – Papa, Julia, and I quietly at home – Marianne and Florence living near one another in London & meeting very often – It is such a happiness to know Marianne [is] happy in the marriage which was the end of so many difficulties and anxieties.

Black-edged mourning paper.

Houghton Library, Harvard University. MS Am 1088.1 378.

EFFIE WEDGWOOD

84. Plymouth Grove.
Jan. 12. [1867]

Darling Effie,

We have a day of such deep soft white snow here, that I keep wondering how you are getting on in that grey cold place Paris. I hope you have a fat duvet and a fireplace or you will be frozen : I feel today so very quiet. First there is the silence outside that always comes with snow, & then in the house there is only Papa, locked up in his study, for Julia has been sent off to London – as she "wanted change", an oft recurring necessity to anyone who lives in this climate. I heard of her safe arrival this morning but she tells me no news except that & a few pieces of gossip – one rather scandalous about [?Estella] Hawkshaw's Captain Bennett \which did not come thro' Emily Crompton/. What sort of report has reached you of him? Have you heard (you will not see the connection but there is one) that poor Walter Fletcher has been dismissed from the Brewery for want of energy – i.e. I suppose \for/ being so crossgartered for your cousin.

Marianne got into her house on Monday. They first {?} planned to go up to it from Dumbleton yesterday week, Friday; & Florence left here to have them to dinner with her en route – but fortunately they heard in time that the snow had blocked the line \& that/ their beds & bedding were detained in London so Marianne stopped on at Dumbleton while Thurstan kept to his original plan of going up to Florence's on the Friday; but instead of merely dining, stayed till Monday. Marianne wrote in most bright spirits after "24 hours" in the house, saying that they had already made it look quite snug, and she seems in a most enterprising way to have undertaken all manner of engagements during this past week, (in the thick of her labour of settling into the house,) crowned by having the Thompsons for the day today. She described Lizzy Mellor as warming up to her work capitally. So I think that everything is promising in that direction. I have nothing 'before' me in any way, except (some lectures) of Goldwin Smith. He is going to give 4 lectures here – the first next Monday on [?] – the 2nd. the following Monday on Cromwell & then 2 on Pitt, always a most interesting subject, I think – I am afraid that my ignorance of history will prevent my getting all the pleasure out of them that I might, as I do not know enough of the conflicting historical views. In preparation I am reading John Sterling's play of Strafford.[1] Did you ever read it? It is so uniformly *interesting*; a great thing.

Did I ever tell you that we have got a most charming Skye terrier who plays a most important role in the household now – She is very affectionate, & really seems to understand what one says to her. If there is any strong feeling amongst the people in the room she always seems to try to take her part. If you shld. happen to cry, she does not cease to fawn on you & caress you – trying to pull your hands from your face with her paws – & making a most sympathetic little whine. And if there is any joking or laughter, she jumps round & gives short cheerful barks just as if she entered into the humour. Does your love for cats prevent your liking dogs in the same way? – I *did* so agree with what you said abt. the restful feeling that the simplicity of aim in your present life \must/ give you. It is one of the countless charms that going abroad gives that every morning you wake up with your day's duties as sharply defined for you by Murray as if he were your private confessor –To see as many churches & ruins as lie in the land round you, to taste the vin du pays, to write to your home people [?] is the whole duty of man abroad, & pleasure & duty coincide to

---

1   John Sterling, *Strafford: A Tragedy* (London: Moxon, 1843).

add to one's happiness. Your shorthand does not tease me a bit – in fact I really like it for prolonging the delight of reading your letter through – I suppose you are kept thoroughly up to English news – a Wedgwood who *wasn't* \up/ would be an anomaly – The impeachment of the President is *the* chief topic just now[1] – There seems a *lull* abt. Jamaica – and Mr. Forster of Bradford has, strange to say, made a speech saying that he disapproves of the prosecution. Isabel Thompson says that she thinks it a "shibboleth of unfashionableness" to belong to the Jamaica Committee side of the question.[2] It is so curious how all Manchester is on the *other* side. When people call the advanced school of Liberals the "Manchester School", it does sound so odd to one living here, for of all, Tory society commend me to the rich people here. The Grant-Duffs[3] were staying with Mrs. Shuttleworth a week or two ago, & Mrs. Grant-Duff made just the same remark to me. She said that she had always expected to find a Liberal tone of politics in these parts, but met startlingly the reverse.

How does your French get on? I shall envy you with the whole force of my envious mind, when you come back speaking it as beautifully as I know you will. What a success [?] your visit sounds! When I was at Madame Bein's Mama and I slept together in a large bare room with 2 beds. I remember very little about it – I think that your room must be the one that Isabel Thompson had. How lovely the view out of the side window in the drawing room is, with the spire of the Sainte Chapelle – Does Madame Bein still have "petites soirées

---

1   Andrew Johnson (1805–75), President of USA 1865–69, and former slave-holder, was impeached by the Radical Republicans for his conciliatory approach to the Southern States during the reconstruction period. The Judiciary Committee did not report in favour of impeachment and he was subsequently acquitted. See *Norton Letters*, I. 286–88 and *The Times*, 10 January 1867, p. 9, col.C and 25 February 1867, p. 12, col.A.

2   A likely reference to the indictment of Edward John Eyre (1815–1901), Governor of Jamaica from 1864 to 1865, tried in the U.K. for using excessive force when crushing a rebellion in Jamaica. His case divided opinion in the U.K., with J. Stuart Mill, of the Jamaica Committee, in favour of a charge of murder, while the Eyre Defence Committee, including Thomas Carlyle, defended Eyre's actions (*ODNB*).

3   Mountstuart Elphinstone Grant-Duff (1829–1906) Scottish-born politician and author and his wife Anna Julia. Grant-Duff served as Liberal M.P. for Elgin 1857–1881 (*ODNB*).

musicales"? She had one while we were there; and I can safely say that it was the very longest evening of my life. But I liked Mme. and Mlle. Bein very much; and please give them my kind remembrances. Do you see anything of Madame Mohl? I am so fond of her, for Mama's sake even more than on my own account – but dreadfully frightened of her, in a way – though I think it unjust to her to be so.

I read all my Paris news now, with a squint at you. There was such a *horrid* description of the Opéra Ball Masqué in the Pall Mall.[1] I cd. hardly bear to think that it had taken place in the same town where you were. Forgive this most dull letter, but I cannot spin news out of my body like a spider –

Loving you most truly & dearly, I am ever yours
M. E. G.

Black-edged mourning paper and envelope.

Envelope: Miss Wedgwood. Madame Bein. 49. Boulevant St. Michel. *Paris* France.

Postmark: Manchester JA 12 67.

By Courtesy of the Wedgwood Museum, Staffordshire; W/M 408.

CHARLES ELIOT NORTON

Plymouth Grove.
Sunday Jan. 13. 67.

Dearest Mr. Norton,

I received your letter but a quarter of an hour ago and am beginning at once to answer it, although I can spend but a minute or two in that pleasure before starting for chapel. I think from one or two things that you say, that either a letter which I wrote Mrs. Norton in the autumn must have missed, or else that I did not say one half in it that I meant to do. Perhaps it is more likely that I am fallible than that the post should be. If however my letter did miss, please tell Mrs. Norton that I have not been ungrateful to her for her kind, sweet letter; as from my silence she must have thought.

I remember saying in writing to her how very, very much we cared

---

1   *Pall Mall Gazette* (1865–1923). The article mentioned here has not been found.

for the "Nation"[1] and that though we did not feel sure that it was to *you* that we owed it, yet that we *thought* that it must be you who so kindly sent it. I cannot tell you how much pleasure it gives us. It does much good, too, I am sure, as a fair mirror of American opinion – Not that *I* am in any danger of misjudging the people that Papa sometimes in fun accuses me of loving better than my own countrymen – but it enables one to undo what little of [?the] mischief that the "Times" does, {which} that comes across one. When people try to knock one down in an American discussion by quotations from the "Times", it is delightful to be able to confront them with a passage from the "Nation" because no one can dispute the right of the Americans to know their own affairs best. I am afraid that this will give you a mistaken idea that there are still many battles to be fought for the North, whereas it is curious how nearly all "Southern proclivities" have vanished. Those whose opinion was worth having were, as a rule, Northern from the beginning; & those to whom success is the test of right have slunk round and joined their former foes. There are too those in whom the change comes from gradual conviction that they were mistaken as to the points at issue, and the motives of the North, – (of these Charlie is one) – and I think that the testimony of these is perhaps the most valuable of all, as they are "convinced against their will" – though *not* "of the same opinion still".

Thank you so much, dearest Mr. Norton for telling me of darling little Lily's Christening – I think it must have been in every detail the very best that we could have wished or imagined possible – a Christening service is so beautiful and solemn and such a *glad, happy* thing –. I am going to send Lily a little simple locket with some of Mama's hair in it – which I could give to very few. Do you think that it would be safe to send it by post registered? I do so like to think of the flowers on the table – when little Lily was being Christened – for all lovely bright things seem symbolical of Mama, whose soul seemed to *clasp* all beauty as the gift of God. It is such a pleasant

---

1   *The Nation*, a weekly magazine, published in North America, co-founded by Norton in 1865. He contributed many articles to the *Nation*, often critical of certain aspects of American life, yet defensive of its republican principles (Vanderbilt, pp. 96–100). The *Nation* continues to operate, providing alternative journalism, and claiming British politician Ed Milliband among its class of interns for 1989.

coincidence to me that the words at the beginning of your letter were of the very same thought that I was writing out to a friend *for* – not on – New Year's Day. One does feel as one grows older that the human {?} thirst for happiness is natural and right, but that the only true happiness is in communion with Our Father and in love to Him and His – and that this is within the reach of all, if they would but stretch out their hearts for the true gift.

It is strange too, (& very pleasant to feel that we have so many things in common,) that only about three weeks ago, I was talking of Baron Mackay,[1] to Mr. Grant Duff, who was telling me with high praise how Baron Mackay had broken through the shallow, fashionable society of those diplomats into which his attachéship threw him in London, and found his way into the companionship of the most earnest & thoughtful men we have instead. I remember the night that he dined here perfectly; and I recollect saying to Mama afterwards "I call Baron Mackay almost the truest gentleman in the best meaning of the term, that I ever saw".

(Jan. 16[th.])

I feel quite guilty in never having told you, as you say is the case, of Marianne's wedding. I did not forget you at the time – and meant *fully* to have sent you a piece of her bride cake, (have you that in America?) but it was a time of such great busyness that I did not manage it. We were starting immediately after the wedding for our summer holiday in Wales, & the preparations of the two things *dovetailed* & made one very busy – She and Thurstan got into their new home only last Monday – this day week ago, "1, Sunnyside, Wimbledon, London, S.W." – Did you ever go to Wimbledon?[2] After Richmond it is the

---

1   Donald James (Baron) Mackay (1839–1921) became a lifelong friend of Norton after meeting him in America. His professional life included a spell with the Dutch foreign office, during which time he was attached to the Dutch legation in London (*Norton Letters*, I, 320 and n.1; and *ODNB*).

2   Wimbledon developed as a commuter town after the opening of the local railway station, which, in the 1860s, became a major rail junction providing links to London and the South coast (Milward, pp. 63–64). Marianne and Thurstan's home was, and still is, one of a pair of semi-detached houses situated at the top of Sunnyside, roughly equidistant from both Wimbledon common and the railway station. Today, the house, like its neighbour, appears to be double fronted, but a closer look, especially at the roof-line, makes it clear that the part of the

most lovely of the *satellite* towns that ring London – with a beautiful sandy common, for the non-enclosure of which everybody is fighting sturdily – The Volunteers from all England camp out here in the Summer – Round the common there are beautiful houses – with real forest trees about them. Jenny Lind lives there & W. R. Greg,[1] little horrid man, who has written all sorts of cold blooded things in favour of slavery – Also a very High Church uncle of Thurstan's lives on the Common, who has just naïvely written to offer his house as an asylum to the Pope – These houses round the common are very expensive but behind them lie a great many cheaper but less lovely ones – all pretty [?] and within reach of its beauty and freedom, & some of them with exquisite views over Surrey with its woods and hills \& Marianne's is in the outer circle/ – All I know of Marianne's house \outside/ is that it is semi-detached, has a garden which is to be levelled for a croquet ground, steps up to the door flanked with vases which are to have blue lobelia & scarlet geranium in them in the summer, & that 50 roses from Dumbleton have been planted against the walls. Inside there is at present {only} a small drawing room, but in a month or two the dining room is to be thrown into it, while a fresh dining room is built. The drawing room walls are pale green, the floor varnished, with a dark blue carpet in the middle. \– Upstairs there are 4 or 5 bedrooms – / Thurstan goes off every morning at 9.20 & does not come back until evening. Marianne at present finds plenty to do in arranging her house & household – & when she is less <   >[2] wrong way – not from their mere vehemence, but because they show what great constitutional principles are at stake; & those who wish the hand of those in authority strengthened against the people get roused [?by] these letters to subscribe to the Eyre *Defence* fund. They

---

house to the right of the front entrance was added later. Sunnyside has retained its attractive semi-rural aspect.

1   Jenny Lind (1820–87), Swedish-born opera singer renowned for purity of voice and religious conviction, lived in England from 1858 till her death (*ODNB* and *Grove*); William Rathbone Greg (1809–81), younger brother of Samuel Greg, Unitarian mill owner based in Styal, Cheshire (*Further Letters*, p. 42, nn.8 and 9; and *Early Years*, pp. 139–40).

2   The remainder of this letter is written either in the margins or across the top of the first page; the lack of continuity suggests that one page is missing.

say that it will be a trial as great \as that/ of Warren Hastings[1] – &
the utmost efforts are being made to secure places. – Papa seems
very well, & stands the unusual severity of this weather wonderfully.
Minnie Thackeray, Thackeray's youngest daughter, is just engaged to
Leslie Stephen,[2] a brother of Fitzjames's – a *very* unorthodox clergyman, "unattached".

   With dearest love to Mrs. Charles Norton, ever yours most aff.
   M. E. Gaskell

Black-edged mourning paper.

Houghton Library, Harvard University. MS Am 1088 2611.

CHARLES ELIOT NORTON

Our number has just been changed
84. [Plymouth Grove]
Jan. 30. [1867]

My dear Mr. Norton,

   I have sent you those Manchester Examiners with the reports of
Goldwin Smith's lectures here in them,[3] not in the hope that they
could give you the least idea of what the lectures have been; but
because I wanted you to know that I thought of you each time that I
had the great pleasure of hearing one, and longed that you could have
shared {that} \it/ with me. I do think that Goldwin Smith's is such true
greatness. He is a union of things that one naturally fancies cannot be
'held in solution' together – enthusiasm with judgment, 'broad sympathy with the people {and} \with/ highest mental culture', (as was
said of him after one of the lectures) and, rarest combination of all,

---

1   Warren Hastings (1732–1818) first Governor-General of India was impeached
    for murder and extortion, but acquitted in 1795 after a seven-year trial in England
    (*ODBH*).
2   Editor of *DNB* from 1882 till 1891; his first wife, Minnie, died in 1875. Virginia
    Woolf was a daughter of his second marriage to Julia Duckworth (*OCEL*).
3   *Manchester Examiner and Times*, a daily newspaper priced one penny.
    Throughout January 1867, the *Manchester Examiner* reported on Goldwin
    Smith's lectures, delivered in Manchester and Bradford, on John Pym (1584–
    1643), Oliver Cromwell (1599–1658) and William Pitt (1759–1806). The lec-
    tures were subsequently published as *Three English Statesmen: A Course of
    Lectures on the Political History of England* (London and Manchester 1867).

zeal with charity and toleration. I do not think that I shall ever forget
– I *hope* that I never shall – the deep wisdom of the second lecture, on
Cromwell. It was the least *brilliant* of the three already delivered but
I wish that I could give you any faint idea of the vision that it seemed
to hold out to one, of what a real grand thing national life might be;
men bound together for true service to God – in happy labour and
high unselfish interests. It brought the great awful purpose of life,
and our relation to the 'unseen Realities', almost more vividly before
me than any *words* ever did before. It is indeed his earnest noble faith
in God and Christ that give him such power, more than his genius. It
seems as if his influence and leadership were specially wanted just
now, to show what a truly *Christian Policy* may be. People's minds
are so full of the 'Essays on International Policy', and all the teach-
ings of the Positivists – you get in these, noble theories and ideas,
but without the religious faith that can alone prove a real basis. And
many take these \theories/ to be something that Christianity could
never have produced not seeing that the Comtist theory of 'altruism'
is but the Christian law of self-sacrifice masked under new words;
and that a true development of Christianity would lead to even more
than {they} \the Comtists/ suggest as necessary to right political
aims, and with so much, much higher a meaning and hope. Between
the Comtist political creed, and Goldwin Smith's, there seems to me
just the difference that there is between a beautiful house built on
sand, and one founded upon a Rock! But I cannot put what I mean at
all into right words; and besides I feel how presumptuous it is of me
to "take his measure" in this way – I did so hope that I might have
seen something of him during his stay here; but I have had no chance.
It would have been \but/ little worth his while to dine with us, or else
it has \been/ a great temptation to ask him. There have been many
allusions to America in his lectures, all showing an enthusiastic sympathy for her, which found an echo in my heart, you may be sure.

\Jan. 31./ In the heart of the audience, too; but it is sad sometimes
to feel, how the *general* sympathy of the English has come too late
– how it was withheld from America in her sorest need – Before I
tell you of other things, I must make a confession to you. I do not
think that I have done anything that you will not like; but if I have,

pray forgive me – I would not vex you for the world. I was sending a note on some selfish business to Goldwin Smith a day or two after your letter came, and I enclosed him that sheet of it about the state of affairs in America, and Baron Mackay whom he had introduced to you. { ? }[1] Did I do wrong? Will you forgive me, if I did; and if I did *not*, forgive me for troubling you unnecessarily for absolution?

Julia has not yet come back from London; but I expect her tomorrow or the day following. She has been down twice to see Marianne at Wimbledon, and I hoped much that she would have gone to stay there a short time. I think that very likely when she returns, I shall go to Oxford and London for a short time. Do you see that Ruskin is trying for the Professorship of Poetry at Oxford? His most formidable rival is Sir Francis Doyle[2] – who has just published a volume of poems to support his claims, of which some of the extracts are very good and spirited. I have not seen the book itself. Do you hear from Ruskin often now? I am afraid that the rumours that one hears are partly true, are they not? rumours of his mental ill health – ?. Mr. Waterhouse, the architect of the Assize Courts here, has been staying with us lately, and he was saying that he heard from so many of Ruskin's friends that it was indeed so. It is terrible. Mr. Waterhouse confirmed, too, what I had heard from the Brodies, that he completely repudiated all interest in Art – and even refused to give help and advice to artists who looked to him for it. If it is true that this state of mind comes from his having stared the misery of the London poor in the face till he has become dazed by it, one almost admires him for his madness – though faith might have saved him from such despair. But it is the greatest *strain* on faith of everything, (I think, do not you?) to realize the sufferings of the poor, and their sins – which hardly seem their own choice.

< > busy in that way, she will have time to make friends amongst many of the Wimbledon people whom she already *half*-knows. She will be within reach of Combe Hurst,[3] where Mrs. Clough, I think,

---

1   Several lines have been scribbled out here.
2   Sir Francis H. C. Doyle (1810–88), professor of poetry at Oxford from 1867 to 1877 (*OCEL* and *ODNB*).
3   Combe Hurst, home of Florence Nightingale's uncle and aunt, Mr and Mrs Samuel Smith, whose daughter Blanche had married the poet Arthur Clough,

Charles Eliot Norton, 1827–1908
Photo: NNB.com

almost *lives* now. In the autumn Marianne and Thurstan were in lodgings in London, very near to Florence – Julia is up in London now, staying with the latter – I wish that you knew those two better. I remember so well something that Mama told you on the Grand Canal at Venice, about what an old lady had said to her – Do you remember it? Her prediction was quite true – they are both of them *beautiful* – quite remarkably so – I admire Julia the most – because tho' her physical beauty not being so great as Florence's there are times, when she looks almost plain, yet when she is at her best the radiant expression makes her far the loveliest. And it is no exaggeration to say that she is as good as beautiful.

I wish that you would sometime tell me *what English periodicals you see* – So often there are articles that I should like to send you, and then I wonder whether perhaps you mayn't do so already. Did you see a very good article in December's Fraser?[1] "Why do we want

who died in 1861 (Edward Cook, *The Life of Florence Nightingale*, 2 vols (London, 1913), I, 30, 128 and 342.

1   This is a reference to an unattributed article 'Why We Want a Reform Bill', *Fraser's Magazine*, Nov. 1866, 544–563. Meta is mistaken about the month, but the year confirms the date of the letter.

a Reform Bill?" – It seemed to feel how badly we had behaved & talked abt. the Alabama,[1] with more "national conscientiousness" than most articles. – Every one here is in a great state about Jamaica – I think that parties run as high as about America formerly : only alas, the good are not all on one side now – not on the one that I think right & that I feel sure you would: – the Eyre *Prosecution* side. Mr. Fred \R/ Harrison[2] has written some tremendous letters to the Daily News on the subject, which it is said are turning people just the

Black-edged mourning paper.

Incomplete and unsigned.

Houghton Library, Harvard University. MS Am 1088 2643.

CHARLES ELIOT NORTON

[February 1867]

Papa wished me to ask you, if you know anything of some people of the name of Mr. and Mrs. G. W. Wild, in Boston; and if so, to beg \ you to be/ so very kind as to let us know whether *she* is well. They were very kind to Papa in Rome; and he has written to them several times since. In Mrs. Wild's last letter, she spoke of being extremely delicate; and a short time ago he saw amongst the list of passengers coming by an American steamer the name of Mr. G. W. Wild without his wife. Papa fears lest her illness should have ended fatally – and does not like to write till he hears that this is not the case.

Do you {know} \remember/ that it will very soon be ten years since first we met you? I shall keep the anniversary of that Carnival day when first we saw you at a festa;[3] for I can truly say that your friendship has been one of the greatest pleasures of my life. It is

---

1 *CSS Alabama* was a warship constructed in John Laird's shipyard on the banks of the river Mersey, built for the confederate states of America with the knowledge of the British government. For a full account see David Hollett, *The Alabama Affair: The British Shipyards Conspiracy in the American Civil War* (Wilmslow, 1993).

2 Possibly Frederick Harrison (1831–1923), London barrister (*Further Letters*, p. 239 and n.5).

3 This event and occasion occurred on 24 February 1857 (*Norton Letters* I, 155).

The Sinking of the *CSS Alabama*, built on Merseyside
See pages 120, 180. Photo: pictures-civil-war.com.

sealed now, too, with deep gratitude to you for your faithful affection to Mama, which she prized as highly as she returned it truly. I can see your face and smile now (as distinctly as if I were only just turning away from them) when you caught at some confetti that mama was dangling on a long stick from the balcony – and mama said "Oh look what a charming face" and Mrs. Story (I think it was) said "Oh that's Charles Norton", and then there was a chorus of welcome and bidding you come up –

Goodbye – give my truest love to Mrs. Charles Norton and to little Lily – though she will not know what it means, and believe me

Your most affectionate faithful friend
Meta Gaskell
I want your answer about the locket impatiently.

Incomplete.

Houghton Library, Harvard University. MS Am 1088 2610.

CHARLES ELIOT NORTON

Cowley House,
Oxford.
March 28. 67.

Dearest Mr. Norton,

I have heard this morning from Julia that the locket with darling little Lily's hair has reached home; and I hasten to thank you for it though as yet unseen. It is so kind of you and dear 'Susan' (as she tells me that I may all her) to have thought of this gift for me, and though I could never need anything to remind me of your child and Mama's namesake, I long to have it in my hands and to begin to carry it always with me.

I wish so much that I could see Lily; and it is with quite a pang that I think that perhaps we may never meet –. It is only in looking forwards that I feel how separate our lives are – In the past it has made *no* {real} difference; and every time that I write to you, it seems as if I had only just parted from you – I thank you again and again with all my heart for this gift, dearest Mr. Norton –

If the little locket with Mama's hair in it has reached you, you will perhaps have thought that the lock of hair was clumsily put in; so I wished to tell you how I had not trusted it in the {jewellerr's} jeweller's hands, for fear of its being changed, (which is said often to happen), but our dear old Hearn put it in as neatly as she could.[1] I have so much that I wished to say to you; but I have not time to write it today. I have been away from home for sometime; stopping with Marianne and Florence before I came here. It is so pleasant to see Marianne so perfectly happy as she is. She and Thurstan fit *into one another* wonderfully –

I wish that you were here, to see the exquisite view that stretches before these windows – the trees of the Christ Church broad-walk, like a great Cathedral nave, and then the grey towers and spires of Christ Church, Merton, St. Mary's and Magdalen rising above the nearer elms on the right, with their rich tracery clear in the sunlight. Everything here reminds me so keenly of Mama – it sometimes is terrible the wakening up to days like those that used to be so perfect

---

1   An insertion in a different hand reads '(This locket – now in the Gaskell Mem. Hall at Knutsford.)'

when she shared them, and that now have always such an aching sense of loss in them. I have just read three beautiful sermons of Mr. Llewellyn Davies's[1] – one is on 'thankfulness', and reminds me much of a letter of yours. I do try to be thankful; but sometimes I cannot help feeling *very* lonely – for it was such perfect companionship and fulness of sympathy and love that I felt in Mama's presence, that without that I hardly know how to endure sorrow or welcome happiness. Am I grumbling very wrongly? I must trust that you will not think {?} hardly of me. *You* know what I lost – Will you tell Susan how exceedingly grateful I was for her charming long letter, and for all her sweet loving words. I sent the autographs on at once – they were capital ones – and were greedily prized by the poor little girl for whom I had asked for them. It was so kind of Susan to remember (and grant so much more than) the request. I shall write again soon; for this is not a proper letter.

I am so much interested in every word I hear or read about America just now. I see that the latest telegram speaks of a resolution introduced into the Senate for impeaching the President. Have you time to read much of English news? Reform, Ireland, and the Jamaica Prosecutions are all most interesting \topics/ just now. There are hardly any words strong enough, I think, to characterize Disraeli's conduct about Reform – and it is a national disgrace that he should stand at the helm during such a crisis.[2] Each fresh speech that he makes reveals more clearly his want of principle. – I hope – or rather I feel sure – that you take the right side about Jamaica – (to speak of one's own side as the 'right side' is on the principle of 'orthodoxy being *my* doxy', is it not?) – The prosecution of Eyre began last Monday – and the warrant was granted. When the facts are clearly brought out at the trial, I trust that the indignation of England will

---

1   John Llewellyn Davies (1826–1916), Anglican clergyman; associated with F. D. Maurice, Thomas Hughes, Charles Kingsley and the Working Men's College in London (*ODNB*).

2   Benjamin Disraeli (1804–81), Conservative politician with a reputation for pragmatism. While serving as leader of the Commons in 1867 he made sufficient concession to the demand for political reform to enable his party to remain in office. The Reform Act of 1867 extended Parliamentary representation, but largely through redistribution, thus benefiting large towns at the expense of small boroughs (*ODBH*).

be aroused against the cruelty & injustice that has \hitherto/ been so lightly passed over and condoned, one hopes partly thro' ignorance.

Forgive this stupid letter – and with my best and dearest love to you and Susan, and to little Lily, I am your most affectionate

Meta Gaskell

Do not omit to tell me when you write, please, whether you were vexed or not by my sending on that bit of your letter to Goldwin Smith. I shall not feel quite happy till I hear that you were not – Lady Brodie, with whom I am staying desires to be very kindly remembered to you – She has a very pleasant recollection of meeting you here when you were with Ruskin.[1]

Black-edged mourning paper.

Houghton Library, Harvard University. MS Am 1088 2612.

CHARLES ELIOT NORTON

July 2, 1867.
[Manchester]

Dearest Mr. Norton,

I came home yesterday from a week's visit in the country, to find a most charming greeting in the copy of "May Day"[2] which you have so kindly sent me. I wish you knew the double pleasure that it had given me; both for its own sake, and because anything that comes from you is so truly precious to me. I find in "May Day" a poem of Emerson's, which I had taken very great pains (but all in vain) to recover, after we had lost our copy of the "Atlantic" in which I had seen it – I mean the "Boston Hymn"[3] – Mama thought it so fine. I had, only this winter, written to several people to beg them to give me a copy, if they had one; but I was quite unsuccessful – Just, then, as I had made up my mind that I must not hope to find the Hymn again, I

---

1 A reference to Norton's visit to Ruskin's farmhouse in Cowley, near Oxford, in 1857, when they were joined by Professor and Mrs Brodie (*Norton Letters*, I, 176–77).

2 Ralph Waldo Emerson, *May-Day and Other Pieces* (Boston Mass. and London, 1867).

3 Ralph Waldo Emerson, 'Boston Hymn', the *Atlantic,* February 1863.

receive it – and so much else – in this volume. What beautiful poems these are besides the Hymn! The "Adirondacs"gave me such a real taste of "wild" America[1] – worth hundreds of descriptions by travellers. I am so ignorant about such things that you must not be startled if I ask whether there are traces of people having formerly lived by these wild lakes in America? I fancy that I remember something in Sir C. Lyell's "Antiquity of Man"[2] about American Lake Dwellings; but I like to think that the feeling suggested by the "Adirondacs" is true, of a stillness unbroken from the beginning of the world till invaded by the "ten scholars" or their guides. Thank you again and again for this present. How pretty your American bindings always are! I have seen nothing so pretty as those golden fern-leaves outside "May Day" for a long time.

As I was travelling home in the railway yesterday, I was thinking of you a great deal; and carefully guarding from the dust a copy of the "Star" with an account of the Garrison Breakfast in it,[3] that I might send it you – Has the "Star" a very bad name in America? I should think that it could not have there – because it defends all the great principles on which the Republic is based; but here most people say "that horrid 'Star'" as naturally as possible – Its style is "flashy" – (I really didn't mean a pun, though it looks like it) – and its \exaggerated/ denunciations of Toryism show a want of power to appreciate the grains of good mixed with it, and the temptations to cling to it which beset the upper classes; \that weakens the weight of the "Star"'s influence/ but with all this, (as far as I can judge), it is a high-toned and noble paper – I should like to have heard Bright's speech.[4] Florence was there. I have often since last writing to you remem-

1   Ralph Waldo Emerson "Adirondacs", a descriptive journal in verse, 1858.
2   Sir Charles Lyell (1797–1875) a noted geologist and author of *Geological Evidences of the Antiquity of Man*, first published February 1863 in London by Murray; two further editions appeared in 1863 and one in 1873 (*ODNB*).
3   *The Morning Star*, published in London, carried an eight column account of the public breakfast held at St James's Hall, London, in honour of William Lloyd Garrison, leader of the American anti-slavery party of the United States. See 'Public Breakfast to Mr Garrison', *Morning Star*, 1 July 1867, pp. 2–3.
4   A reference to John Bright, M.P. For a transcript of Bright's speech see *Speeches on Questions of Public Policy by John Bright, M.P.* ed. by J. E. T. Rogers, 2 vols (London, 1868), I, 285–92.

bered with regret, that I never thanked you and "Susan" for her photograph. You would not, I am sure, think from this omission that I did not value it dearly. It was one of those careless omissions that one slips into, and which one cannot retrieve so soon in foreign letters as one would in writing by the everyday penny post here. I think that I quite understand now how *dear* Susan must look, as well as [?] from putting the two portraits of her together – taking the first as giving the spirit, and the second the letter of her face. I was going to say that I knew how I should love her, if I could see her; but I do that already!

If it were not for leaving Papa and Julia, I should really beg you to let me come to you for a month; but that will make it ever quite impossible. Dr. Acland,[1] the other day, at Oxford, was talking so quietly about "running over to finish his sketch of Niagara". It made America sound so charmingly near.

I wonder whether Marianne has yet written to you as she was fully planning to do, to thank you for that lovely broach you sent her. Just supposing that she should have failed to do so, you must not think that either the broach missed reaching her, or that she did not feel most grateful for it : but just now she is getting into sad arrears with her letters, as she is on the sofa a great deal. We are so glad – so delighted – She is going to have a little baby at the end of September. She was with us during nearly the whole of the month of May, and we had charming, cosy long talks with her; and except for the pang of losing her again, it was so happy to have her back. She and Thurstan are at Wimbledon now; and Papa spent last Friday with her, as he was up in London on business. They have been adding a third sitting-room to their house, and this additional space is very pleasant, Marianne says.

While Papa was in London, Julia and I went to stay with some old friends in a lovely part of Derbyshire. We were just in the part so exquisitely described by Lady Verney (Miss Nightingale's sister) in her story of "Stone Edge",[2] which is coming out in the "Cornhill" now – and in the part of the country, too, where the real Dinah Morris (in "Adam Bede") lived and laboured. It is one good of living in a

---

1   Sir Henry Wentworth Acland, Regius Professor of Medicine at Oxford from 1858 and friend of John Ruskin (*Norton Letters*, I, 174 and n.1).
2   Frances Parthenope Verney, *Stone Edge* (London, 1868).

town, and an *ugly* town, that when one goes into the country, it is the intensest delight. The wealth of beauty there, the "Fullness of the earth" makes one understand in a fresh way how good God has been to one. At this house, we came in for all the Midsummer pleasures of hayfields and roses and long lovely twilight walks. It jarred up on one to find all the people of the neighbourhood high Tories – but I am sure I got to make allowances for them. People living in the deep peace of the country cannot understand the cry of suffering that is ever rising in the ears of those who dwell in great towns like Manchester. (In Derbyshire the agricultural labourers have very good wages.) Mama used often to say that the power of sympathy depended on the power of imagination – and I dare say that it is very difficult for the country Tories to realize the sorrows and stress of a town life which might be helped by wiser legislation from a really national House of Commons.

Have you seen what capital caricatures there have been of Disraeli in Punch lately?[1] He is almost {beyond} \beneath/ contempt; but it is most humiliating to find that the House of Commons will be contentedly led by such a man. Into what a ridiculous position he has led his own party! They are now fighting under the colours that they have bespattered with virulent abuse for years. As Punch says, "Dizzie has made the Tories eat their words, and swear they like his cooking".[2] He has thrown all the principles of his party overboard – (he had none of his own to throw) – just to hold light power and place –

Everybody has been reading Mr. Longfellow's Dante here.[3] I heard Professor Nichol of Glasgow say that he thought it the best translation that had ever been made of Dante. I was very much disappointed in it – Do you like it? I cared much the most for the notes. I wish that Mr. Cormington would try his hand at it. He is such a perfect translator to judge by his Aeneid: though I should not think that he had a very Dantesque mind or spirit, if you know what I mean.

---

1   For the cartoons of Disraeli referred to here see *Punch*, 26 May and 15 June 1867.
2   An allusion to 'A Paean for Dizzy', unattributed, *Punch*, 22 June 1867, p. 253, col.3.
3   Dante Alighieri, *The Divine Comedy*, trans. H. W. Longfellow, 3 vols (Leipzig, 1867).

I feel so *doubleminded* about begging you to write to me. It would be the greatest treat to hear from you; but then I know that your hands are so much fuller of work than you have time or strength for, that I must qualify my request for the pleasure of a letter by begging you not to write me one till it will be at no cost to yourself. I have a dread of inflicting "last straws". The "Nation" continues to be the greatest pleasure to us.

I am ever yours and Susan's, most affectionately

M. E. Gaskell.

When – or *if*, – you write soon, please send me a little word of absolution about that bit of your letter that I sent on to Goldwin Smith. It may be quite foolish of me to think you *could* mind, but I should like to be *sure* that you did not mind my having it done it. We are rather people for forwarding letters about. It was, however, the only time I did it with one of yours. How is darling little Lily? I often clasp her locket for a bit of comfort, when I feel sad or worried – It always hangs at my watchchain.

Black-edged mourning paper.

Houghton Library, Harvard University. MS Am 1088 2613.

CHARLES ELIOT NORTON

Augt. 3. 67

Dearest Mr. Norton,

I think that your "winged words" always fly across the Atlantic at the right moment – though at whatever time they came, they would make it seem so. This morning, I was lying down – not very well, and feeling so the aching of the wound which I think sometimes seems all the worse under the *surface healing*, and thinking so longingly of Mama, when a great gleam of sunshine came into my darkness through your unexpected letter. How good of you to write again so soon! And I *am* so glad about your and dearest Susan's new little darling – There will at any rate be *four* New-Englanders to [?turn] to, when America's enemies talk (as they have taken to doing lately) about "the {the} Pilgrim Father race dying out," and "giving place to

Irish hordes". Pray give Susan my tenderest love and heartiest good wishes. I hope that her recovery will be as steady and thorough as possible. What does *our* little Lily say to a baby brother?

I have so much that I want to say to you, and so little time to say it in; for we are very busy putting the final touches to our packing for an autumn journey in Wales, and {to} *swathing* up everything at home for an invasion of painters and plasterers; who, I suppose in America as in England, come in as the family goes out, like buckets in a well. We are going first of all – it is rather an experiment – to a very rough, grey little inn, on one of the shoulders of Snowdon; where we shall be \in a/ literally solitary house – if I remember rightly, without another house in sight. Kingsley in his "Two Years Ago" describes the place.[1] He was staying at this little inn when he wrote the Welsh part of the book.[2] Mama and I first planned to go there. It will be so pleasant to get into the country – into this wild scenery, high up, close to the mountain clouds, after our dusty summer here. We had a break of three days last week, for Julia and I went to Mrs. Nightingale's at Lea Hurst,[3] Florence Nightingale's home. Don't think me presumptuous to send such a bad little sketch so far. I thought you would care for it, because it is a sketch of Florence Nightingale's *window* – curiously enough the only one in the house in which the stone-mullions form a *cross* – {?} The ivy wreathes it and peeps in so lovingly, & the western sunlight lingers there best of all on that side of the house – She will be there when you get this letter – leaving London for a short rest. About going to America. If you only knew how I should delight in it! – But I must not even think of it. I can hardly bear to say why – but when I tell you that I think that every day Papa looks just a little more as if he wanted constant care, you will understand that I could never leave him to go far, and he will not come. Dearest Mr. Norton & Susan, thank you for asking me, but I couldn't leave him. If anything were to happen to him while I was away, it would be so terrible. But I need not say what a *most great* pleasure it

---

1   Charles Kingsley, *Two Years Ago*, first published in 1857.

2   See chapter twenty-two, *Two Years Ago* for Kingsley's description of the Pen-y-Gwryd Inn.

3   Spacious and grand home of the Nightingale family in Matlock, Derbyshire (Uglow, pp. 361–62).

would be to me to come to you – to see *you* once more – and to have seen Susan and the children. In going to America, too, I should feel almost as if I were making a pilgrimage to a Holy Land – for I do supremely reverence the Northerners – Mill[1] well summed up their share in the war by calling it "a *fight for God*" – It always seems to me as if it had been a "sharply defined conflict between the powers of good & evil", and as if in those days, Heaven and Hell must have seemed not the mere names of distant spiritual spheres, but the only true measure of the awful antagonism. Mr. Fitzjames Stephen[2] once told me that it was his amusement whenever he met with great admirers of America to trump their pet prejudices by saying that the day of England was quite past, that America was now foremost etc etc, and then he said these people always shrank back – they could not bear to have England ranked below America : but with all my love and pride for England, I still can feel that you in America are living a much fin*er*, higher life than we are – *at present*. We must hope to catch some of your faith and goodness though as long as the Times reigns here it will be uphill work. Every word you said in your last letter but one about Unitarianism I endorse *most fully*. It is what I have felt for years, only I never could have put it so clearly. It is Papa, not I, who sends you the Herald[3] – and if I may say it without the least disloyalty to him, I sometimes feel it very difficult to sympathize in his interest in the paper, just because it seems, \(I may be misjudging it)/, to *fight for boundaries*, instead of longing to see all barriers of separation removed between good people – \(I am sure that Papa wd. long for that too)/ Robertson is my leader, tho' I'd not felt bound by one of his dogmas – What is Positivism in America? It is making such immense progress here. Half the people I know are Comtists – so good, so *Christian*, in all but name – One longs that they might but see that all they hold (& so much, so *infinitely* more!) is in the New Testament – But I must stop – Goodbye dearest Mr. Norton.

---

1   A likely reference to John Stuart Mill.
2   James Fitzjames Stephen (1829–1894), judge and writer, prodigious contributor to the tendentious *Saturday Review*; friend of Carlyle and known for his willingness to confront opposing notions of thought head on (*ODNB*).
3   The *Unitarian Herald*, founded in 1861 by William Gaskell and John Relly Beard (Uglow, p. 497 and Brill p. 57).

Ever your most aff'ce
M.E. Gaskell

Black-edged mourning paper.

Houghton Library, Harvard University. MS Am 1088 2614.

CHARLES ELIOT NORTON

1. Sunnyside.
Wimbledon.
Oct. 8. [1867]

Dearest Mr. Norton,

I little thought that my dear little nephew would be three weeks and two days old before I wrote to tell you of his and Marianne's well-being, as the paper I sent you only announced the bare fact of his birth. But I have been so busy since I came here that I have never found time for a long letter; and – until today – I was hoping to write you one – Now in despair I am going to send off a short one; on the principle of "half a loaf being better than no bread" – and because I cannot bear you to think that I do not remember you and dearest Susan almost first amongst those whose sympathy I claim, and from whom I care most to receive it.

Marianne seems very well indeed – She says sometimes that she feels stronger than she ever did in her life before – but still she has to be very careful, and not to presume on her strength – and it is acting deputy that has kept me busy. The baby is such a little darling; so sweet and fair and *nestling*, a real little "Bird of God", as some one once called her baby – How Mama would have loved this little treasure – It is to me to so very touching to see it wearing the little nightdresses that she worked with her own dear fingers for one of us – It is registered William Edward – after its two grandfathers – Thurstan pretends to be very *sensible* about his boy, and not to think it very different from all other babies that ever were: but he does not succeed in hiding his true feeling – I hope that you are all well? I have good accounts from home.

Ever your most aff'ce friend

M. E. Gaskell.

Please give my dearest love to Susan. Don't answer this. I do not need any written assurance of your sympathy –

Black-edged mourning paper and envelope.

Envelope: C. E. Norton Esq., Shady Hill, Cambridge, Massachusetts. U. S. of America.

Postmark: London. S. W. OC 12 67.

Houghton Library, Harvard University. MS Am 1088 2615.

CHARLES ELIOT NORTON

84. Plymouth Grove.
Dec. 15. 1867.

Dearest Mr. Norton,

I am sure that you know without my telling you, that nothing but having been very busy would have kept me from sooner writing to you. I have so much to thank you for. First of all, my thanks are due to dear Susan for her charming letter. Does she really mean to hold out to me the hope that you are all perhaps coming to Europe? and why did she ask so – – *wild* a question as to whether or not I should be 'glad'? It would be the greatest pleasure to me possible. The next greatest would be if I could do anything for you on your arrival, besides welcoming you here.

(Dec. 16.) Then I have a letter to thank *you* for, and also the beautiful copy of the Vita Nuova,[1] which it is such a delight to me to have "of my very own", as children say. But how little I deserve it, dear Mr. Norton, after what I said about Mr. Longfellow's Dante! Directly after the letter had gone in which I made those stupid presumptuous remarks, I began to reproach myself for them. When one knows a thing to be of little value, one flings it about recklessly; & it was so with the expression of my opinion. If I had thought it of any {consequence} \weight/ I should not have given it – still I might have

---

1   *Vita Nuova*, by Dante Alighieri, 1295, translated from Italian into English by Norton and published as *The New Life of Dante Alighieri*, Boston 1867. Portions of the translation had previously been published in the *Atlantic Monthly* in 1859 (Vanderbilt, pp. 72 and 173).

spared you the annoyance of hearing the translation depreciated even by such an insignificant critic. I mean to read it again, & "revise my opinion of it"; and if the strongest notion to make me admire \it/ can effect a change in my opinion, I certainly shall learn to do so. Do forgive me. One bad consequence of what I said is, that you will not now care to hear how very beautiful I think your Vita Nuova. I have lost your *good opinion of my opinion* in such matters. Your translation seems to me perfect. How very beautiful some of the passages in the book are. – Thank you, also, (as I like to do every now and then, for it is such a constant pleasure to me) for the "Nation". I have just been reading a number that came today.

Our thoughts here are terribly full of Fenianism.[1] We have boasted so glibly for so long of the peace & prosperity of the country, that it is a fearful shock when suddenly the flames of sedition leap up at 'one's' very feet, betraying a hidden fire of which \one/ can hardly guess the extent. The morning \Dec. 17/ papers on Saturday brought one the news of the Clerkenwell outrage;[2] and since then one has thought of little else. It is a deeply painful subject. I suppose that a misguided patriotism is in great part the root of Fenianism – (whatever people may say about more "Irish-American rowdyism") – and one has profound sympathy with any desire to redeem the Irish from their misery. But how mad a hope it is to think that Fenianism will do so! And when such cruel wicked deeds are perpetrated in its name, (the guilt of which many people insist on laying on the \disaffected/ Irish indiscriminately), one feels that Ireland's so-called friends are her deadliest foes.

It is so painful, too, \to/ feel how much the English are hated; and to remember what centuries of oppression and injustice have bred this hatred.

Papa thinks that the greatest danger for the future is from the spirit

---

1   Fenianism, also known as the Irish Republican Brotherhood, the organization behind the insurrections and uprisings that emerged in the second half of the nineteenth century, which took place in Ireland, and mainland Britain.

2   At Clerkenwell, a district in Central London, a group of Fenians attempted to blow up a prison in order to release one of their leaders. The event was well covered by the press; see, for example, the *Manchester Guardian,* 14 December 1867, p. 5, col.3, and the *Observer,* 15 December 1867, p. 6, col.1.

that is being aroused amongst the English working-classes. The Irish have always been disliked by them, as having flooded the labour-market, and so cheapened labour to their disadvantage. Now this dislike is inflamed by resentment of the Fenian outrages; and in their ignorance \of history/ the poor know little of the claims on our toleration which the unfortunate Irish have. There is constant fear of collision between the two races, whenever – as in the Lancashire manufacturing towns and villages – the Irish are found in large numbers. Manchester is rife with rumours of desperate threats on both sides. The Mayor's "butler" is a detective in disguise; and I know more than one *private* house where there is a barrel of sand kept in the cellar to put out fresh fire, if thrown in. This latter precaution seems to me very unnecessary and \belonging to an/ alarmist view of things: but so it is. I do not know what the political effect will be – whether redress for the Irish grievances, as a sop, or reaction. I should fear the latter. The "comfortable classes" are so apt to think that discontent must be met by more repression. And the Tories may make great capital, when so much fear is excited, by rallying round them those who deny that a fresh government may be a strong government. But you must not take anything that I say about Fenianism as 'correct['].
It is a problem far, far, beyond common judgments.

I saw Baron Mackay when I was at Oxford where I went for a few days after stopping with Marianne and Florence. He gave me many messages of kind and [?grateful] remembrance for you. My talk to him was one long catechism about you and America. Will you soon write & tell me how you & little Rupert are. I trust earnestly quite well.

Marianne & little "William Edward" are very well. She is going to Dumbleton for her Christmas – We shall have Florence and Charlie here. Papa is pretty well but I am afraid that I was wise in refusing to come to you next spring – for he needs constant care.

With dearest love to you and Susan. I am ever your faithful and affecte. friend.

M.E. Gaskell.

I send you all my very best wishes for the New Year.

Back-edged mourning paper.

Houghton Library, Harvard University. MS Am 1088 2616.

CHARLES ELIOT NORTON

84. Plymouth Grove.
Manchester.
April 27. 1868.

Dearest Mr. Norton,

I cannot bear to think that there should have been any delay what-ever in my writing to tell you with what delight I look forward to your all coming to England.[1] But stupidly I waited and waited, think-ing by delay to gain time for a long letter; but I have instead grown rather busier. What *does* make women so busy? If people ask me what I have been doing, I never can name any definite thing; and yet often all day long I have not an uninterrupted half hour.

As far as ever I know, we shall be at home from "between the 15th. to the 28th July", for a fortnight onwards at least, and it would be charming to have you somewhere near us. How I wish that we could expand our house to take you all in! Will you kindly write and tell me what kind of accommodation you would like; what rooms, how near us, how near town; that I may look out in time to secure really desirable ones. I think that you will remember enough of Manchester to recollect that it is like a wheel, with a few great "Roads" as spokes. And I should recommend your having lodgings, or a house somewhere on the Oxford Road, which is the most coun-trylike of the Roads on this side of the town, and the nearest to us. The hotels I should not think desirable for the children, as they are all in the centre of the town, where the air is terribly close. If I knew your plans and wishes by the end of June, I *think* I should not fail to secure you comfortable quarters. I would do my very best; that at any rate I can safely promise. I am so glad to think of seeing Susan face to face. Give her my dear love.

Ever your faithful friend.

---

1   In July 1868 Norton and his family embarked on an ambitious and extended visit to England and mainland Europe. The outward transatlantic sea-voyage meant that the ship docked at Liverpool, making Manchester a convenient destination for the start of their vacation; see the envelope for MS Am 1088 2619 below.

M. E. Gaskell.

CHARLES ELIOT NORTON

July 13.[1868]

Dearest Mr Norton,

You ask for a "Welcome to England" – and I give it you with my whole heart. I have thought of very little else but the great happiness of seeing you and yours for the last few weeks. Only it seems too good to be true! You are so bound up in my mind with Mama that if for no other reason, (and you know what endless other ones there are) I should still be full of most eager & loving delight at your coming.

And now I must tell you what I have done about your quarters; particularly as I have to confess to having not altogether done your bidding! Directly I returned from London, in *June*, I set about the search for what you wanted – "*country-like* lodgings within an easy walk of Plymouth Grove"[.] I have advertised, answered advertisements, and inquired everywhere; but in vain. In fact I feel sure that they are not to be had, for the simple but sad reason that Plymouth Grove and anything "country-like" are not {?tobefound} near together. Well – the alternative you gave me was to engage rooms *at a hotel*; but instead of that I have taken some lodgings near here *in a street*. For these reasons, you say that it would be such a comfort to you to know that there was some place ready prepared for you. Now, at the Queen's, the only really comfortable hotel, they will not *keep* rooms – for I enquired on purpose – without charging the full price. So that either this would have to be paid from the 16th, (and at the Queen's the rooms are very dear) or you would have to take your chance on your arrival, and I always think that if one is tired, one wants to find a rest ready for one to drop into. And though the alternative of "a *week* in *country-like* lodgings" was "*two or three days* in a hotel", yet these lodgings for a week will not be as much, I fancy, as two or three days at the Queen's, so that if you think it best to stay in them only two or three days, they will still be less expensive. They are also in better air, for the Queen's is in the very heart of the town, and they are not so dreadfully far off – from us. In that I *hope* I have done right. If not, I know how kindly you will forgive me.

They are at Miss Aylmer's, 278. Oxford Terrace, Oxford Road : (the last house but one on the right before you come to Ducie Street, for your cabman's information. The fare for each cab from the station is 2s.0d for 2 people, 2s.8d for more; and luggage ought not to be charged extra, though the men will expect something; if they help to carry the boxes *upstairs* :) I have [?seen] some *larger* lodgings just opposite, and where you could have had the front sitting-room upstairs; but these other lodgings were not so clean, or comfortable, – and moreover Miss Aylmer's are on the *shady* side of the street which in this burning weather is an advantage. They are £5 for the week, everything included but the washing of *extra* bed or table linen.

But also, please, dear Mr. Norton, there will be two rooms, \and a dressing room/, waiting \quite ready from the 16th./ for you here to *overflow* into – as you may think best. We would take precious care of the children, if they were trusted to us; or do our best for whoever came – But you may like keeping together; so do just which you fancy most. Only whether you any of you sleep here or not, you must, *please*, spend the "inside" of your days with us.

Papa is looking forward – – – (I was going to say as heartily as I am; but no one can do that *quite*!) – with affectionate eagerness to seeing you all. Julia, I am so sorry to say, is in London.

Hoping that all has gone well with you, \each and all,/ and that you are not quite knocked up.

I am your most affc.

M. E. Gaskell

(P. S. Dr. Gumpert, in this same terrace as Miss Aylmer's, is a famous *children's* doctor.[1] Mr Mellor, a few doors down, is *our* doctor. But I hope you will all arrive quite well.

Houghton Library, Harvard University. MS Am 1088 2618.

---

1   Eduard Gumpert (1834-1893), a German born and trained medical practitioner who worked in Manchester from 1855, specialising in diseases of women and children (*Archives Hub*).

CHARLES ELIOT NORTON

[Manchester]
July 13, 1868.

Dearest Mr. Norton,

I have just written you a long rigmarole to the same address; and this note is merely to tell you, (for the *bare chance* of my letter *missing*), that your lodgings are at

Miss Aylmer's,
278. Oxford Terrace,
Oxford Road.

The last door but one on the right hand side before you come to Ducie Street. The fare to the lodgings from the station is 2s.0d. for a cab with two people, 2.s.8d. for a cab containing more – luggage *not* charged for extra, unless carried upstairs.

Also, there are two bedrooms and a dressing room fully prepared for you here – And the very warmest most affectionate greeting awaiting you.

Ever yours
M. E. Gaskell.

There are some first rate doctors close at hand – Dr. Gumpert for children – Mr. Mellor our own doctor – if you should unhappily arrive in immediate need of one.

Envelope: Charles Eliot Norton Esq., Passenger by the *Scotia*. Care of Messrs. Baring, Bros., & Co. – Liverpool.

Postmark: Manchester, JY 13 1868.

Houghton Library, Harvard University. MS Am 1088 2619.

CHARLES ELIOT NORTON

[Manchester]
July 25. [1868][1]

Dearest Mr. Norton,

How can I let today pass away without thanking you for the happiness of the last week? It was just at this hour that you came – and I cannot put in words what true deep joy it has been to be with you again – And then you took me and (as it were) *gave* me five new friends who will be amongst my dearest all my life – It seems like a great *flash* of happiness having you all here; because though you were so good in staying on longer than we or Manchester deserved, yet to us {it} \your visit/ has been most sadly too short – Still "only to think" you "came and went" will make us always the richer and happier –

I think that I never looked at *you* without a longing that Mama was there : for you know what it would have been to her to see you again.

Please give to each one – to Susan, Mrs. Norton, Jane, Grace and dear Sara,[2] my best and truest love, and accept the same from your most affectionate

M. E. Gaskell

I am "fleshing" my beautiful new pen in this note. I begin to think that I must have very *speaking* eyes – for they seem to have told you the only two things that I most coveted – a glove-box and pen – However, though I call it a glove-box, I do not mean to use it for anything so little precious.

Julia's love and Papa's, – and kisses to the dear little ones –
Excuse the haste of this note, please.

Houghton Library, Harvard University. MS Am 1088 2639.

---

1 Norton's visit to England with his wife, mother, two sisters and his children suggest 1868 as the year of this visit. See Meta's letter to Norton dated July 13 1868 above, and *Ruskin Norton Letters*, p. 108, n.1.
2 These names refer to Norton's wife; mother; two sisters and his eldest daughter.

CHARLES ELIOT NORTON

Aug. 12, 1868.

My dearest Mr. Norton,

I was so much delighted to get a letter yesterday from Sara:[1] not only on account of the great pleasure of hearing from her, but also because it enables me to send you – through her – a letter of most loving farewell before we start for the Continent. We are going to Switzerland \instead of Scotland/; having changed our plans for many reasons – but chiefly on account of health. There is no tonic like going abroad; and I am afraid that *you* will only too readily believe how necessary a tonic is for those who live in Manchester. – There is a great deal keenly painful in going abroad again. It was such a special delight of Mama's to give us and plan our tours; and it seems to bring back the very freshness of one's grief each time that one remembers that she will not be with us.

I shall want so very much to hear of you while we are away – but whether I do or not, my thoughts will constantly be turning to you all. Charlie follows us on Sept. 1st., and any letter addressed to his care at 89. Oxford Terrace, Hyde Park, W., would travel to me in his pocket. But do not trouble yourself to write if you are busy or disinclined.

What a "good time" you must have had at Oxford! It was very interesting hearing of your meetings with all the people one knows there. Mr. Henry Smith and Mr. Harcourt[2] are both very – – *nice*. (I remember that you used eleven years ago, to correct me if I called anyone "nice"; but I have never yet had the wit to discover an equivalent for what I mean by it – (that is *pleasant* and good.) Mr. Henry Smith is very able. I am very fond of his sister; but I think that she is not always rightly understood.

I see in the papers that Mr. Goldwin Smith has accepted the Chair of History at Ithaca;[3] which I fear is putting the seal on his living in

---

1 Sara was the name of Norton's daughter, born in September 1865; it is unlikely, therefore, that she was the sender of the note referred to here. The note is more likely to have come from Norton's wife, Susan.

2 Henry J. S. Smith (1826–83), Professor of Geometry at Oxford and friend of Mrs Gaskell (*Further Letters*, p. 224, n.1); Augustus J. V. Harcourt (1834–1919), assistant to B. C. Brodie at Oxford (*Further Letters*, p. 242, n.3).

3 In November 1868, Goldwin Smith took an honorary academic post at Cornell

America. I think that it is very wrong of people to blame him for leaving England – because of course he knows best what is right – and it is ungrateful to forget \in deploring the future loss,/ what immense service he has already rendered his country. Still, it is a very bitter thing for the people who have felt such earnest loyalty to him as thousands in the North have done, when he leaves them to fight on leaderless. For no one can in the least take his place; do not you think so? No one has the same spirit of fervent faith and devotion – with so much breadth of vision. His \supremely *high and truly*/ philosophical views are wholly different from the ultra-radical rant and mere icon*oclas*m of those to whom I fear many will turn for guidance in his absence. Living in a place like Manchester, one gets the misery of the poor so twisted \in/ with every thought of one's mind; and last winter I saw a great deal of it, having more leisure than usual, and I used often to get a quite desperate feeling about it – as if it would be the greatest *relief* to "go & sell all that one had, and give to the poor". And then, at those times, Mr. Goldwin Smith's words were such a comfort, for one knew, by the way that they made one's own heart burn within one, how they must be rousing others infinitely more capable than oneself, of helping the poor, to true pity and earnest self-sacrificing effort.

I wonder what you think of Mr. Gladstone[1] – ? I never can admire him as much as I wish, and know I ought, to do. He never seems to me to have sufficient trust that if he is fighting for what is really right, he is not fighting alone. You know what I mean – Papa went to Scotland on Monday. It is charming to think of him idling away his days – fishing.

Ever your loving friend

M. E. Gaskell

I do so want to see your "Church of the Future".[2] How can I?

Houghton Library, Harvard University. MS Am 1088 2620.

University, Ithaca, New York (*ODNB*).

1   William Ewart Gladstone (1809–98), distinguished Liberal politician and British Prime Minister from 1868 to 1874 (*ODBH*).

2   For Norton's vision of the future of the Christian Church, see *Norton Letters*, I, 295–96.

CHARLES ELIOT NORTON

Plymouth Grove.
14th. Octr. [1868]

Dearest Mr. Norton,

I have not time to answer your letter properly, but I must thank you for it. One that you wrote me on Aug. 14.[1] was not wasted either – though I only received it on my return, since which I have often read your description of your pretty home, and laughed over your 'disestablishing your Irish rector' –

I am so glad that the wicked London, Chatham and Dover has at length delivered up the trunk. Susan said in her note that she thought it had better be labelled "to be left at the Station till called for", so I put that on it.

And now I am writing in such a hurry that I can't even thank you for your letter as I wish – can only assure you of my delight in having it.

What a "dream" it would be to come to you in France,[2] but I fear too good to come true –

Tell Susan I am only waiting for time to write to her – but neither you nor she must trouble yourselves to answer me.

Your ever faithful and loving friend
M. E. Gaskell.

My truest, tenderest love to you all.

Black-edged mourning paper.

Houghton Library, Harvard University. MS Am 1088 2637.

SUSAN NORTON

84. Plymouth Grove.
Nov. 4. 1868

Dearest Susan,

I shall be less busy next week – and then you shall not have these dreadful hurried scrawls – but this week I can only write such.

---

1   For an extract from this letter, which confirms the year of Meta's letter here, see *Norton Letters*, I, 305.

2   Norton was in Northern France with Ruskin in October 1868 (*Norton Letters,* I, 310).

I want to tell you that Marianne had a little girl at midnight on Sunday – Monday. She and her little [one] are both doing *capitally*.

I have been thinking of you so constantly during all my busy-ness. I am so grieved at the prospect of long-continued weakness for Mr. Norton – and how difficult it must be to know what is best to decide as to your winter plans![1]

Mr. Simon's visit must have been the greatest comfort – How kind of Mr. Ruskin to send him![2] but oh how I envy him being able to do anything for Mr. Norton.

Dear, dear Susan – I think of the strain for you so much – But I know how God will give you all strength and faith even in seeing one so very dear as Mr. Norton suffering.

Ever your own
M.E.G.

Houghton Library, Harvard University. MS Am 1088.1 379.

SUSAN NORTON

84. Plymouth Grove.
19 Nov. 1868.

My dearest Susan,

Day after day I have so fully meant to write to you that nothing but the want of time would have prevented my doing so. (Will the Reformed Parliament,[3] which is to do everything for everybody, give one leisure!). Specially, on the 12th, I longed to write to Mr. Norton – He is always so bound up with Mama to me – and I thought of him so much then – and so lovingly.

I hope and trust that, however slowly, he is surely gaining ground and getting stronger –

Did your house-hunting prosper? Florence does not mention your going to her, as she certainly would have done if you had gone, but

---

1   Norton was staying with his wife and family at Keston Rectory, Kent, when he was taken ill. The winter of 1868–69 was spent in Kent and London. See *Norton Letters*, I, 312.

2   John Simon (1818–1904), Ruskin's medical adviser and personal friend (*Ruskin Norton Letters*, p. 135, n.2).

3   A reference to the Reform Act of 1867.

I hope that it is only a pleasure deferred for a very little for her for she is looking forward so very very much to getting to know you all.

You could not possibly present us with a more really valuable thing than old clothes. I feel a perfect Jew in the winter; and alas! this is to be a "hard" one.

The excitement of the Election here has been intense.[1] I thought \ yesterday/ that nothing could have made Mr. Mitchell Henry's[2] conduct pardonable {yesterday}; but in this morning's paper his speech at the declaration of the poll shows that he has not been devoid of generosity. And I must say, that there is something rather touching in Mr. Birley's efforts to creep into *brotherhood* with his two co-representatives[3] – He says so prettily that he does not doubt that they will "take him into their councils" whenever the good of the town is under discussion, which he is sure that they all three have equally at heart.

Papa took us down on Monday morning to see the nomination – We saw the shameful Tory stone-throwing, and the regular ovation that Ernest Jones had when the proceedings were over[4] – His supporters carried him half across Albert Square on their shoulders – and then when he insisted on getting into a hansom, they crowded tumultuously round it, cheering wildly, & would have taken the horse out, if the police had not interfered. Still, I don't think that he is altogether to be liked – though very fine in many ways. The Salford defeats are a dreadful blow to Liberals here. The coachman of a friend of ours had charge of bringing up some of the Liberal electors; and he has told his mistress that he came across endless instances of bribery and "treating". Yesterday all the church steeples in Salford were flying the blue (Tory) flag!

---

1   The first General Election after the 1867 Reform Act.
2   Mitchell Henry (1826–1910), stood as a moderate Liberal candidate for Manchester in the 1868 General Election and founded the *Manchester Evening News* in the same year. He was defeated in the Election and subsequently sold the *Manchester Evening News* (*ODNB*).
3   Hugh Birley (1817–83), first elected Conservative M. P. for Manchester; he served Manchester with two sitting Liberals, Jacob Bright and Thomas Bazley (*Wik.*).
4   Ernest Jones (1819–69), radical journalist and lawyer, famous for his defence of the Manchester Fenians in 1867, stood, unsuccessfully, as liberal candidate for Manchester 1868 (*ODNB*).

I have sent to try and get the address of the second [?*home*] place; but my friend has not got it. But I will try elsewhere. Baron MacKay called here yesterday; but I was out. I am so sorry – I should have liked so much to see him again. Has he been helping Mr. Roundell? Alas for his defeat! And Mr. Lushington's!

    With dearest love to you all, I am ever yours very, very lovingly
    M. E. Gaskell.

The son of a Tory {candidate} \manufacturer/ in this neighbourhood called the other day to canvass one of his father's work-people for the Tory candidate – and threatened that unless the man voted as directed, he "should never have another day's work at the mill"; "go whoam & tell feyther" the man said, "that an he does na vote for t'Liberals oi'll *niver* work another day for him"! Excuse this untidy letter please.

Houghton Library, Harvard University. MS Am 1088.1 380.

UGHTRED KAY-SHUTTLEWORTH

               Plymouth Grove
               Monday morning.
               [November 1868]

Dear Mr Kay Shuttleworth,

    We are so *truly* sorry at the result of Saturday's election in North East Lancashire,[1] which we have just seen in the papers.

    Pray accept the assurance of our heartfelt regret, for the sake of yourself, your father, and your principles. One can only hope for 'better luck next time', which the large number of those who voted for you makes a most reasonable hope. In great haste, – begging you not to trouble yourself to acknowledge this, – I remain

    Yours very truly
    M. E. Gaskell

Annotation added in pencil at the foot of the letter: U. K. S had stood for the old

---

1   Ughtred Kay-Shuttleworth (1844–1939) was one of two Liberal candidates who represented North East Lancashire in the General Election of November 1868. Neither was successful. Gladstone led the Liberal Party to victory by a substantial majority, but all seats in Lancashire were taken by Conservatives.

Party Division of the N. E. Lancs undivided.

Annotation on archival envelope: Mr Ughtred Kay-Shuttleworth [1868].

Reproduced by courtesy of the University Librarian and Director, The John Rylands Library, The University of Manchester. R129632/N80E7.

SUSAN NORTON

27. Dec. 1868.

Dearest Susan,

How very, very sweet and kind of you to think of sending me Mr. Lowell's poems![1] I shall indeed care for them – And dear little Lily, too – Pray give her endless kisses from me for the fan.[2]

It is so good of you to think of giving me the book, dearest Susan. I am so exceedingly fond of all of Lowell's poetry that I know, that it will indeed be a treat to me to have it.

I am most likely going to Wimbledon on Wednesday next, for Marianne continues very unwell. It is a sudden determination – If I go, I shall so hope to come up some day to see you all again – though I mean to look upon my visit as a purely *nursing* one, and not at any rate at first to be more away from Marianne than I can help. It is a busy sick household –

With my tenderest love,
Ever your most grateful
M.E G.

I am so glad if Mr. Norton keeps better.

Houghton Library, Harvard University. MS Am 1088.1 381.

---

1   James Russell Lowell (1819–91), Harvard-educated scholar, friend of Charles Norton, journalist and poet (*OCEL*).

2   A note added here in different ink reads: L. was named for Mrs. Gaskell.

SUSAN NORTON

Sunday.
Plymouth Grove.
[January 1869]

Dearest Susan,

I have been longing so much every day since your letter came to answer it, but I have been quite "run off my legs", if you know that elegant expression, with business: – And now I am writing in great haste – but I want to tell you Florence's address, and to assure you what *delight* it would give her to see you – Only would not it save you time and trouble if she came down to you?[1] I know that she would so gladly do either – just as suited you – But if you go up to her, let her *know* – that she may not be out. Her house is 89. Oxford Terrace, {W} Hyde Park.

I keep feeling so grieved at the idea of dearest Mr. Norton being delicate all winter – Thank Jane with my truest love for her letter – and believe me your own loving

M. E. G.
Sunday.
Plymouth Grove.

Houghton Library, Harvard University. MS Am 1088.1 384.

CHARLES ELIOT NORTON

[Manchester]
March 23. 1869.

Dearest Mr. Norton,

If you are keeping to your plan of accompanying Mr. Dickens[2] to Liverpool, will you not come to us for a little, or a long, while?

---

1   By New Year's Day 1869, Charles Norton was writing from an address at Queen's Gate Terrace, London. Situated in Kensington, just south of Hyde Park, it was within easy reach of Florence's home on the north side of Hyde Park. Norton and his family remained at this address until May 1869 when they left England for the Continent (*Norton Letters*, I, 312–331).

2   Norton had been the guest of Charles Dickens in Rochester, Kent, during the late summer of 1868 (*Norton Letters*, I, 303–304).

I do not offer to show you anything of what you have not seen in Manchester, or put forward any inducement except that you will give us the very greatest pleasure, because I so entirely want you to come for *our* sakes, and not your own. But if there is anything that you can suggest to us that you would like to do, or anyone that you would like to meet, you have but to say a word, and we will do our utmost \to arrange it./ Trusting that you will grant our earnest petition, believe me ever your faithful, loving

    M. E. Gaskell.

Houghton Library, Harvard University. MS Am 1088 2621.

CHARLES ELIOT NORTON

               Plymouth Grove.
               Manchester.
               April 4, 1869.

My Dearest Mr. Norton,

    I am so *delighted* at the thoughts of your really coming – It seems almost too good to be true: and as for your very *silly* \(though most kind)/ question about my health – why is there any tonic in the world like pleasure? Besides, I am nearly all right again now.

    I am only wondering whether you would not take us *after* instead of *before* Liverpool. I do not mean that your bed and your welcome, will not be as ready for you on Thursday as on Sunday; – but only that this unfortunate engagement for Thursday evening would make such a great hole in the short time that you would spend with us if tied by your banquet on Saturday, whereas, if you came on Sunday, perhaps you would let us keep you prisoner for more than a "brace of days" – unless you were pledged, as I am afraid is only too probable, by some London engagements.

    Our engagement is to a great amateur concert here on behalf of a charity – at which we must "show" – or I would break through it with delight –

    Will you give the enclosed scraps to Susan, please – and {tell her that}\ask her whether/ if she meets with no "second home", she would care to have this [?manse] inspected.

With very truest love to you all, I am ever your loving friend
M. E. Gaskell

Houghton Library, Harvard University. MS Am 1088 2622.

CHARLES ELIOT NORTON

[Manchester]
April 10th. [1869]

Dearest Mr. Norton,

I threatened you with a letter only because I could not *say* what I was so full of, as we parted; and I will not leave you a day to think that it is a letter which will add to those you have to write, by needing a reply.

I wanted so much to thank you for coming to us – (How many companions has Mr. Harcourt in the grudge he must owe us for having taken you from London?) –

It has been the truest, deepest pleasure having you – – I find that I cannot write, any more than say, how great happiness you have given us – but you must have felt what we were feeling.

God bless you –
Ever yours
M.E.G.

Houghton Library, Harvard University. MS Am 1088 2642.

EFFIE WEDGWOOD

84. Plymouth Grove.
6 Feb. 1870.

My own darling Effie,

I will gladly, most gladly, call on Mrs. H. Chichester – & think that I can do so *tomorrow* – I shall be delighted to do it, but I fear that it won't do her much good; for what with my Father being intensely busy & rather shy, our hospitality is becoming very much limited to diminutive luncheons, contrived when he is out for the inside of the day. I wish that you wd. just put Miss Spottiswoode[1] up to the general state of things, for I see that, *just at present*, particularly, there would be no chance of my asking her here to dine – as I should so like to do –

I believe that Lord Acton[2] (late Sir John) is at the bottom of the "Pope & the Council", in fact, I know it almost for a {fact} certainty. I don't use the word *translator*, because I understood that he had something to do with the composition & therefore is more than that.

As to the Fancy Ball – Ours was said to be as brilliant as one cd. possibly be made – people spent *lavishly* on their dresses – up to £2000, & it was very amusing, & I enjoyed it very much – But I should never care to go to another – & in this case I shld. not have thought the game worth the candle, if dear little Florence had not undertaken literally every bit of trouble connected with my dress –

My dress was a "Kabyle woman from the Atlas mountains";[3] & I shld. be *delighted* to lend you any part of it that wasn't borrowed: but there alas! All the characteristic parts *are* that –

I cd. lend you embroidered shoes, the upper (\indian/ red [?lurex]) tunic, & a chain of coins – & the skirt, *without* the border –

I enclose you a letter of Mrs. Lee Bridell's[4] *on* the dress – which please return sometime.

One dress struck me as *very* pretty – I had thought of going as Old Mother Hubbard myself – & then I found a *much* better one than I cd. have been. She had her hair powdered – a little black peaked hat – frilled mob-cap – spectacles – mittens – square cut black silk & sack, red satin petticoat, muslin apron, & of course a stick to beat her dog with.

---

1   Possibly a member of the Spottiswoode family, printers to the Crown (*Gaskell Letters*, p. 237 and *Further Letters*, p. 167, n.5).

2   Lord Acton, 1834–1902, was a scholar and friend of Gladstone. He edited a number of periodicals including the *Rambler* which supported the liberal Catholic movement in England (*ODNB*).

3   Kabyle women belonged to an Algerian tribe, North Africa (*Concise Oxford Dictionary*).

4   Mrs Lee Bridell was formerly Mrs Gaskell's friend Tottie Fox. She married Frederick Lee Bridell, an artist, in Rome in 1859 in the presence of Robert and Elizabeth Browning. An artist in her own right she was a friend of Barbara Bodichon. After becoming a widow in 1863 she married a cousin in 1871, becoming Mrs Fox (*ODNB*).

Striped handkerchief, with string of coins

Necklace without end – amber, – black – & gold

Blue embroidered Turkish sash –

The "Queen of Spades" was very effective – a red satin petticoat – with black satin spades cut out, & sénée round the bottom, (about 6 inches deep, & 3 broad) – bodice to match – and in her hair a tiara of gold spades.

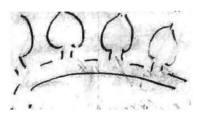

A Vivandiere's dress there was lovely – but every one thought it improper! – "Rouge-et-Noir" was pretty – a skirt made thus –

Old English ladies were in *much* the largest number. That dress is really so like the present that it gives little trouble – just powdering & patching – There was a very pretty "Clair de Lune" sent from Paris – a blue satin skirt with silver stars – short: over it a silver gauze tunic, looped up on one side with a great disk of *silver* – (tinsel on cardboard) – with the moon's face in outline on it. On the head silver stars & a silver crescent. – I heard of a lady who went to a F. Ball at Liverpool as Pride – a violet silk skirt, & fine embroidered linen tunic (for "purple & fine linen") all trimmed with peacock's feathers.

One *very* pretty dress was a Normandy peasant's – the Cauchois [?cap] – gold cross – & red & white striped petticoat. I came to one distinct conclusion, & that was that the most effective dresses, were *peasants'* dresses done in *upper-class* materials – For instance Old *Mother Hubbard's satin* –

I have got to finish my letter on the sofa – my back is very bad, spite of belladonna that I put on yesterday – I have been overworking again – & this is the inevitable result. I have meant so very often lately to write to you – but literally I have been so busy since I came back from abroad that I have written hardly any private letters (not *once* to Philo B. – only once in answer to Louy Jackson.)[1] except in one case where gt. perplexity & distress has given me the opportu-

---

1   Philo B was the wife of Benjamin Brodie (see Meta's letter to Effie, 19 December 1862); Louy Jackson was a long-standing friend of Meta's (*Further Letters*, p. 157, n.4).

nity of trying (not successfully) to be as good a friend as you once were to me when I stood in need of help.

But do trust me just the same, will you not? if I am sometimes for long together silent. I love you so mostly dearly, Effie, that if ever I think that you are ceasing to care for me; or that I have vexed you, it grieves me to the quick – This morning when I got your letter, I fancied you were a little vext. You used to tell me I was fanciful, I wish you wd. write a line very soon, to tell me whether this was fancy or not [&] if it was, I will thankfully accept (in exchange for what I feel now), a good scolding for my folly – And if I was right, pray, pray forgive me – My life now often seems such a hard wearing struggle to keep up to what [?others] require of me – I cd. not bear it, if you ceased to love me – Perhaps it is feeling ill, that makes me think all this! – Pray, don't be vext with me, darling Effie for I do so love you – My Mother loved you too so much – For her sake forgive me, if I have in any way vext you –

Don't say anything to any of my 3 sisters if you see them abt. my being ill – I can bear it better if no one knows & it is easy to hide it from my Father –

 Yr. own devoted
 M. E. G.

Envelope: Miss K. E. Wedgwood 1. Cumberland Place. Regent's Park. London.

Postmark: Manchester 6 FE 70

By Courtesy of the Wedgwood Museum, Staffordshire; W/M 408.

EFFIE WEDGWOOD

       84. Plymouth Grove.
       20. Feb. 1870.

Darling Effie,

Won't you {?have} write to me? If you think that I have \done/ anything wrong, do please tell me – for I am sure that I can explain anything, as I am unconscious of ever having had one moment's disloyalty to you.

I should indeed be ungrateful if I had! –

I am so sorry to say that I have never yet made my way to Mrs. Chichester's – having been very unwell for the last fortnight – and hardly off the sofa.

But on Wednesday or Thursday I *hope* to go. What have you decided about the Fancy Ball? I shall be much interested to know.

With most faithful love.

Ever yours

M. E. G.

Black-edged mourning paper.

By Courtesy of the Wedgwood Museum, Staffordshire; W/M 408.

EFFIE WEDGWOOD

84. Plymouth Grove.
24 Feb. 1870.

Darling Effie,

I have just come in from a (fruitless) call on Mrs. Chichester, and have very little time left before dinner, during which our post always goes out : but I must write you a line – to repeat what I have so often said, that I *will* not be divorced from you!

I think that our natures must be different somehow – for I never feel to change the least however long I am without seeing or hearing from people. I think yours is much the more rational way of the two. I often feel quite pig-headed in my faithfulness – pig-he*art*ed rather –

But I register a solemn resolution to write to you more regularly than I have done – I have just had to give up one great slice of work \ (a sec'yship,)/ & so I shall have more time for single letters.

Will you risk all the horrors of dirt & dulness, and come & stay here in April? I really hardly dare{n't} ask you – things are so bustling & ugly & particularly \dull/ after Mr. Hallé has betaken himself to London.

I very nearly asked you for the last fortnight in Novr., & then when I was wondering about it, came a letter, saying you grudged every day's passing, the end of your natural stay at Caerdeon[1] was coming

1   A likely reference to Plas Caerdeon, a manor house in West Wales between

so near, & I thought that it would be cruel to shorten it by drafting you into this black fog – & yet I thought that your very unselfishness would very likely make you come. As to what you say about your "bad side" – that I consider positive raving, at any rate, I shall never see that bad side, I know, for one – Now, darling Effie, expect a very speedy follower to this letter & don't answer –

Can penitence go further? or rather reg*ret* – for I have not been *able* to write the letters I wished lately.

> Your truly loving
> M. E. Gaskell.

Black-edged mourning paper.

By Courtesy of the Wedgwood Museum, Staffordshire; W/M 408.

EFFIE WEDGWOOD

> S. L. Behrens's Esq.[1]
> Glyn Garth.
> Bangor.
> North Wales.
> 13. March. 1870.

My darling Effie,

Ever since your last letter came, I have been wishing to answer the question with which it ended – – would I "have patience" with you? – You said you would not doubt my answer : and you needn't. My love for you will never fail, & while love lives patience does –

I will say no more – about our 'rapport' – except one word – It has occurred to me lately, that perhaps I have been selfish in stickling so much for the continuance of our friendship. I certainly did it entirely for my own sake – so let me tell you that if ever you really wish me to

---

Barmouth and Dolgellau, overlooking the Mawdach Estuary. Distinguished visitors included Charles Darwin, who spent some time there in 1869 revising *On the Origin of Species* (*Darwin: Life and Letters* III, 106).

1   Solomon Levi Behrens (1788–1873) a Jewish immigrant from Germany, who with other members of his family, made a significant contribution to the Jewish community in nineteenth-century Manchester. The Behrens were friends of the Gaskell family (*Gaskell Letters*, pp. 513 and 784; *Further Letters*, pp. 277 and 302).

do so, I will release you from any bonds of friendship : \in a moment – without a grumble –/ just because I love you so much – not because I am ceasing to do so – *Finis* –

I came here on Wednesday to stay with the Behrenses – whom you have seen in Manchester formerly – Miss Martin's friends – It is a charmingly lazy, luxurious life – with a beautiful view always before \one,/ a pleasant dribbling country society, a very late breakfast – & the great pleasure of being with Georgina & Anna Behrens[1] – two singularly high minded, clever women – Some one said of the former (what is true of both) that she was "the best *Christian* in the world": – being, you know, a Jewess – but in spirit & life – in devotion & unselfishness – truly Christian.

I fancy that you have stayed here in the Schwabes'[2] days – If so, you will know how very lovely the view across the Straits[3] is – Today the mountains are covered with snow – & the trees loaded with great soft lumps of it – One feels \as/ if the calendar had suddenly been reversed, & one had rushed back into Xmas – Yesterday we were watching the opening buds – & talking of spring – & now behold this change! –

I have heard since coming here, in a most round-about {a}way, of the drowning of some cousin of yours – who married the Bishop of Bangor's niece – I hope that it is no one who is very much to you, dearest Effie – But it will be a terrible shock to his own people – Is it one of the Harry Wedgwoods?

Death by accident must have quite peculiar traits & aspects of its own to the survivors. How difficult it is to bear in mind that the one certainty of life is death. Each death one hears of startles one as much as if it were not the common fate of all – only brought to some sooner than to others – And beyond – – I believe that one must have one's very dearest one in Heaven, before one's whole being can be thrilled

---

1   Georgina (1823–71) and Hanna (1829–1904), daughters of Solomon Behrens, and older than Meta by fourteen years and eight years respectively.

2   Manchester industrialists and former owners of Glyn Garth (*Further Letters*, p. 307).

3   Menai Strait, the narrow channel of water separating mainland Wales from the island of Anglesey. Meta's description of the view across the Strait here suggests that Glyn Garth was situated on Anglesey.

with the *reality* of that.

Are you going again to Oxford? I heard through the Thompsons of a party made up by Mr. Sidgwick of Merton of the Hales, Isabel, & you –

Florence & Charlie are keeping Julia company at home – & there is a Barristers' Ball on the [?tapes], which reminds me so much of five years ago –

I wish when you write, you would tell me how Mr. Langton & Edmund are – & the Tollets –

> Ever your devoted
> M. E. Gaskell

Black-edged mourning paper.

By Courtesy of the Wedgwood Museum, Staffordshire; W/M 408.

EFFIE WEDGWOOD

I go home on Saturday next.

> Glyn Garth.

> 24. March. 1870.

Darling Effie,

I left out the very pith of my last letter – I am afraid that I *do* often omit the very 'raison d'être' of my letters –

I wanted to repeat to you, (although not in the form of a troublesome question – please understand that), my invitation for April –

I don't quite know when Florence and Charlie leave – but cd. let you know later on – and towards the end of the month or during the beginning of May, there wd. be no chance of anything \at our end/ preventing my having the [?] pleasure of a visit from you – So if you can come, write and say *when* – But *please* don't trouble yourself to write otherwise.

I hope that your last Oxford visit was a success. What do you think of Mr. Sidgwick? I have heard of your singing – and the delight it gave. How happy your power must make you!

> Ever yours
> M. E. Gaskell.

I have opened my letter to tell you of the only thing abt. your visit in April that makes me not wish for it with all my heart – And that is that April being my month for visiting a certain Hospital in Manchester – I might have to give up two or three afternoons each week to that – I mention this because it might seem to you afterwards as if I ought to have done so.

Black-edged mourning paper and envelope.

Envelope: Miss K. E. Wedgwood. 1. Cumberland Place. Regent's Park. London. N.W.

Postmark: Bangor MR 24 70

By Courtesy of the Wedgwood Museum, Staffordshire; W/M 408.

HENRY CROMPTON

(Cranford)
Knutsford.
July 26. [1870][1]

My dear Harry,

You must not think my congratulations[2] are any the less hearty, because they are of necessity *short* – But pray believe that I am quite delighted at this great piece of good news, & wish you joy from the bottom of my heart.

How I should like to know every detail!

But you will be too busy, with *other* correspondence, to wish for claims on your writing time. So do not even acknowledge this, but only believe me, your very glad,

very affecte
M. E. Gaskell (Meta)[3]

© British Library Board. Add Mss. 71701, ff. 62–63.

---

1 (Cranford) and 1870 have been added in pencil and in a different hand.
2 Probably a reference to the engagement of Henry Crompton to Lucy Henrietta, daughter of John Romilly, first Lord Romilly. They married in November 1870. See Florence Gaskell's letter below, dated 9 December 1870, to Isabella Green, including note 1.
3 (Meta) also added in pencil in a different hand.

CHARLES ELIOT NORTON

84. Plymouth Grove.
Aug. 4. 1870.

My dearest Mr. Norton,

You will tempt me always to misunderstand some little sentence in Grace's[1] letters, if the consequence is that you write one such a charming letter as followed my apology! Thank you a thousand times for it. You don't know what a *great, great* pleasure it was to me.

I am writing to you in a strange dark atmosphere, the air loaded with electricity. We are waiting for a thunderstorm, for which we have been longing for six weeks to clear off the most oppressive heat. We have had many false hopes, but this evening it *must*, I think, come to a storm, and not end, as it has hitherto done, {with} in distant thunder without rain. Since I wrote to you, this most terrible war has broken out.[2] We think and talk of little else. I am glad to see how {willing} \eager/ England has been to commit herself to a declaration of intervention, if Belgium is touched. War "is a fearful thing": but "shamed (national) life a[s] hateful". The country perfectly writhed under Mr. Gladstone's mellifluous ambiguities, and has "risen to its feet" to applaud old Lord Russell's noble speech.[3] There *is* but one path for England, the path of honour.

We hear so much through the German residents here of the suffering and terror on the Rhine. I heard one account the other day of the marching of the reserve out of Frankfurt – all oldish men between 40 & 50, & most of them leaving wives and families. The gentleman who wrote, was standing near a poor woman who had come, with her five little children, to take a last look at her husband. She stood quite still & quiet, and hushed the little things quiet, but her face kept working constantly, and when she caught sight of her husband, she fainted dead away. This gentleman knelt down by her, and tried to revive her, and while he was doing so, a cry broke from the ranks of the reserve,

---

1   One of Norton's three sisters; the others were Louisa and Jane.
2   A reference to the Franco-Prussian War (July 1870–May 1871). One of the most significant outcomes of this conflict was the United German Empire, with William I as Emperor (Davies, pp. 868–69).
3   Lord John Russell (1792–1878), British Prime Minister from 1846 to 1852 and from 1865 to 1866 (*ODBH*).

"[?Muth!] [?Muth!] Wir wollen für das Vaterland sterben!"[1] and the poor woman just opened her eyes, & too weak to speak aloud, yet formed her lips into a heroic echo of the words "Ja – für das Vaterland sterben!". I fear so much lest the war will prevent my October visit. I doubt if my father would let me go on the Continent, but I don't mean to "foreshadow uncertain evils". But to hope that I may have which would be so very great a pleasure.

I am most grievously disappointed about Sara, to whom I have written at Venice. If I understand her places rightly, we must miss each other, I fear. We are going to such tiny quarters in Wales that we spend our days in talking over impossible plans of contriving tents, beds in barns, etc., & are really doubtful whether we can ourselves all get in, so that we cd[.] not possibly squeeze in dear Sara, even if she would forgive being squeezed! There is no house near, & our own house here will be in the hands of the painters, or else I should have come back here to meet her. I am more vexed than I can say, as you will know. I enclose a little tiny picture of Keston,[2] which I asked Snow Wedgwood to do for you. She has been staying near it lately.

I am writing in haste – as you will see.

Please give my best & fondest love to each – to Susan, dear Mrs. Norton, Jane, Grace, Eliot, Sally, Lilly, Rupert and – –!?[3] You have never told me the little one's name!

    Your loving friend
    M. E. Gaskell.

Houghton Library, Harvard University. MS Am 1088 2623.

---

1 'Courage! Courage! We will die for the Fatherland!'.
2 A reference to Keston Common or Keston Bog, near to Bromley, Kent, and to Charles Darwin's home, Down House. Keston was the site of some of Darwin's major research, especially into earthworms (*Wik.*).
3 Susan was Norton's wife. Mrs Norton his mother; the other names mentioned here were various members of his family.

CHARLES ELIOT NORTON

Castell,
Beddgelert.[1]
Sep. 12. 1870.

Though you will hardly believe it, my dearest Mr.Norton, this is the first moment that I have been able to answer your most kind letter. I received it at Wimbledon, where I went on hearing the sad news of the death of Marianne's darling little baby. While I was there, I spent no unnecessary time away from her; and on my journey home I lost my portmanteau, only to recover it this evening. In my portmanteau was my portfolio and in my portfolio the only thin paper suitable for foreign letter-writing. I thought it so specially kind of you writing to assure me of the sympathy, (which, expressed or not, I should never – could never have doubted); and the few words that you said about the death of a child were wonderfully true – how true I could never have known, had I read them elsewhere than in the home of those on whom such a sorrow had fallen. Poor little Sylvia! When she was christened Sylvia, everyone said half sadly, half gaily "and may she have many *Lovers*" [2]– and she lived to be loved by so very few – to be taken back so soon into the shelter of the great Love. Why *does* one speak of the dead as 'poor'? It provokes me in myself to have done it: believing, as I so firmly do, that the true life is never-ending, and is more blessed beyond death than it is here. Marianne bore up very bravely. There is a kind of simplicity in her character and her faith that I think prevented her having that most cruel sorrow that may be felt at such times.

It came like a great shock to us here – the news of this death. We had just settled down into the most perfectly peaceful, bright holiday-life. The words in the Psalm alone seemed to describe it. We had had wings granted us – and had flown away from the wear & tear and clamour of town-life, & had formed a nest built for us in this wil-

---

1   A small town in North Wales, in the foothills of Mount Snowdon; it attracted and continues to attract visitors looking for peaceful surroundings and outstanding natural beauty.
2   A reference to Elizabeth Gaskell's novel *Sylvia's Lovers* published in 1863.

derness where we could be at peace – and amid such great beauty. How often have I longed for you to see it! There is no good trying to describe it. Word-painting of scenery *must* be "blottesque"; and every day that one lives amongst such wonderful beauty the {?} contrast between its *infinitude* of loveliness and one's own finite powers of reproduction becomes more distinct to one. \I feel this in sketching so much./ I will only say that we are on the side of a mountain, facing the great Snowdon range, with the steep valley between filled with rocks, heather, pines, oaks and birches. Our little house is a white-washed farm, with a wing of grey stone added. We have a little ter-raced garden, with crimson [?peustemon], white phlox, and blue [?] making a brilliant foreground to the dark woods & purple craggy mountains.

When it was {once} fixed, \as it was for a time/ for Florence to be the one of us to go up to Marianne, I had fully planned to write and beg dear Sara to come and take possession of the vacant bed; and I had thought out many schemes of showing her well all this *heart* of Wales. (I am so much afraid that the letter I wrote to her from Wimbledon missed. Will you sometime send me her address in America, please.) Our life here is most quiet. We are five miles from a village, and {ten} fourteen from any acquaintance. We do nothing all day but read, and walk – with sketching added for me. Charlie has joined us this last day or two. My father is in Scotland, and is very well.

I am afraid that there will be no chance of my coming to you in October, dearest Mr. Norton. The disappointment of not seeing you is greater than I can say : but everything seems against it. Directly we leave here, at the end of this month, Julia is going to Marianne, so that I could not be away from my father – and besides, I know (so well that I have not even asked him) that he would not for a moment consent to my going abroad during this war. From its first outbreak I have feared and foreseen this. He has an unusual timidity about jour-neys and their chances for us – and would not let us go, I am con-vinced. (I wish that my space was not running short.) I cannot tell you how I regret this – It would have been the greatest happiness to have seen you all again. I feel that the chances are so few – and if my visit could have but been carried out, it would have given me such a delightful time with you all. Jane tells me of dearest Mrs. Norton's illness. Pray give her my tenderest love, & entreat her from me to keep well – How earnestly I hope that she continues better. Jane asks for the names of some novels for her. I have written some on a little slip – not liking to wait till I write to thank Jane for her charming letter.

 Ever yours
 faithfully & lovingly
 M. E. Gaskell.

Houghton Library, Harvard University. MS Am 1088 2624.

EFFIE WEDGWOOD

         Castell, Beddgelert.
         Sep. 28. 70.

My dearest Effie,

 Your 'Mote' sounds so delightful, and if you have the same 'beams' to glorify it that we have on our craggy mountains this morning, you must be very happy. As happy *as one can be* this summer, at least. Don't you find that this awful war prevents one thoroughly enjoying anything? The sharp contrast with the fate of others, is always haunting one, if one's circumstances are very bright & peaceful.

 I am not sure whether this is not morbid – ? Cousin Mary,[1] with whom I was staying during the first outbreak of hostilities, (just when young master was being baptized), said to me very abruptly – "Don't make yourself so unhappy about the war – Have faith in God – " which gave me the feeling of my being very irreligious when I grieved over the wounds, & the torture, & the hearts broken by suspense and news of the dearest – dead. I hope that you continue a good Prussian? So many people have swerved France-wards, because of the heroism of Paris, or because France is governed by a dozen men instead of one. Nought of which changes the bare fact – that France has been for centuries cruelly set on abasing Germany for her own

---

1 Possibly Mary Holland (1792–1877), Mrs Gaskell's cousin (*Further Letters*, pp. 16, n.3 and 209).

glorification, & undertook this wicked war with no higher object.

By the way: *what* a fool Mr. Beesly has been making of himself! It was 'as good as a play', to see poor Florence's face as she read his 'word for France',[1] which Emily innocently sent her. Florence so respectably conservative! and always shrinking from anything outré, in any shape.

I wrote to you last from Wimbledon, I think. I went thence to Dumbleton with Marianne for two days, just to break the arrival there for her. Poor Marianne! I think she felt the going there very much. She is still there waiting for Fanny's wedding, which takes place on the [?11]^{th.} – Captain Ryan was at Dumbleton. What Fanny can have seen {him to make} \in him to have made/ her accept him at the fifth time of seeing him, I cannot conceive. She seems overhead and ears in love – and perfectly content to go out to India – I was so glad to get back here – where we have been living quite quietly, *most* quietly, ever since. Charlie came for a fortnight – and then went off to Ireland.

Florence left us yesterday, for London en route to *Chorley*, where she and *Charlie* met on Saturday – (it sounds a round-about way – !)

Julia and I go home on Tuesday. I don't feel as if I could bear leaving here, and going back to Manchester. It is so very beautiful here, and for a week now we have been having the most perfect weather – each hour bringing some lovely change in the lights & shadows – till the day ends in the 'daffodil sky' of seven o'clock, bringing out a row of pine trees that fringe a hill close at hand, into the blackest yet softest distinctness against it.

I travelled back from Birmingham to Bettws,[2] with a Mrs. Pryce, quite fanatica per la musica, who had been to the Birmingham Festival, about which I got her to tell me everything, that I might fancy how you had been entertained. From her account it must have been most charming. I hope so very much that you enjoyed it as much

1 Edward Spencer Beesly (1831-1915), positivist and historian, sided with France during the Franco-Prussian War (*ODNB*). The 'Word for France' referred to here may be 'Mr Beesly's Good Word for France' in the *Pall Mall Gazette*, 15 September 1870, p. 10.

2 Betws-y-Coed, picturesque village, at the junction of A5 and A470 in North Wales, famous for its natural beauty, especially rivers and waterfalls.

as your last one. Repetitions are such dangerous things that I always want to hear of their success.

It either sub*tracts* from, or multiplies the charms of previous pleasures – instead of leaving them as they were – to try them over again –

I suppose that all your foreign winter plans are quite given up – ? – or do you mean to slink round by Rouen, Tours, etc. – ? Isabel Thompson is careering about Switzerland just as if there were no war – which she never mentions in her letters, I believe! She passed thro' Paris, when it was at fever-heat – just after Wörth – I need not say, dearest Effie, how your relenting has touched me. This stupid letter may make you re*pent of repenting* of your resolve, however!

Ever yours
M. E. G.

Envelope: Miss K. E. Wedgwood The Mote. Ightam. Tunbridge.

Postmark: Carnarvon SP 29 70

By Courtesy of the Wedgwood Museum, Staffordshire; W/M 408.

EFFIE WEDGWOOD

Plymouth Grove.
Oct. 8. 70.

Dearest Effie,

I have just got to feel tolerably settled at home, after two or three days of turning round like a dog does before it lies down – and so now I am writing to you to know when there would be a chance of your coming to us? – The very first days of *Dec*ember being the Assizes[1], but all through November, or during what remains of this month (which after all is three weeks!) there would be no one whatever coming to occupy the spare bed, and it would be so intense a pleasure to me having you.

I shall understand perfectly if you say that you can't come, with-

---

1 Assizes were periodic criminal courts, replaced in 1972 by the single permanent Crown Courts. During their existence Assizes heard the most serious criminal cases referred up by the local County Courts (*Wik.*). The Manchester Assize Court, designed by Alfred Waterhouse, in the Gothic style, was situated near to Strangeways Prison, and completed in 1864.

out expecting a full explanation of the reasons why – things so often inexpressible though none the less real – But *do* come, if you can.

Ever your own loving

M. E. G.

By Courtesy of the Wedgwood Museum, Staffordshire; W/M 408.

EFFIE WEDGWOOD

84. Plymouth Grove.

March 12. [1871]

Darling Effie,

There is no need to say how great a disappointment your letter was to me. I had a strange, deceptive hope that you would come. When next you write, do tell me whether there would by any chance of catching you next autumn. In this next *April* it would suit us beautifully to have you : but that is one of the months that you speak of as impossible. My Father was extremely vext at my having so "mismanaged matters" as not to get you; which I felt was owing to no want of will or wish on my part.

We are now in the thick of the Assizes. They seem like what Mr. Martineau calls "one of the constancies of the universe" – always re-entering at one door of Time just as one has bowed them out at the other. Mr. Bryce, whom formerly they used to bring, & who was certainly one of the pleasantest people belonging to the Northern Circuit, has now gone to the Chancery Bar – so we don't get him – Mr. Fisher, Mr. Cobden's[1] son-in-law, is, I think, the pleasantest man now left. He is a red Republican of the fiercest kind, with a lovely, gentle, saint-like face – He looks like some boy-martyr of the French revolution, in the early days, if there were days early enough, when the revolution *guilded* instead of de*man*ded martyrs.

I shall be so thankful to get a little change of air & *life*. Since we came back from Wales, I have been stationary at home, & very hard at work, without a single break, except for one tiny 3-days visit to

---

1   A likely reference to Richard Cobden (1804–65), radical politician associated with the repeal of the Corn Laws 1846 (*ODBH*).

{Blackborne} \Blackpool/.[1] And I always think that the kind of desultory & yet incessant work that women have becomes very tiring after a time. I do envy men their regular & simple professional work – & their not having to *rest* in the *arena*, as women have \to do./ I mean women rest in the very scene of all their conflicts – & therefore can never really escape from the associations of worry. However "women's work" is too trite a subject to write about, isn't it?

I must congratulate about Madame Viardot's[2] verdict on your singing. She is such a real artist, and consequently a first rate judge. It makes one quite long that you had been born a poor wood-cutter's daughter – Isn't that the sphere of life from which all prima-donnas come? They are heard warbling exquisitely, as they bind faggots, by rich passing travellers, who forthwith adopt them – Isn't that the regulatory career? – What confidence it must give you to know the stamp that Mme. Viardot has set upon you!

My very warmest congratulations.

How interested you must be in the reception of Mr. Darwin's book![3] People seem very full of it here. Have you read it? I hear such diversity of opinion as to whether ladies ought to read it or not.

Write to me soon, dearest Effie, & tell me all about yourself.

   Believe me
   Your loving faithful
   M. E. Gaskell.

Envelope: Miss K. E. Wedgwood. 1. Cumberland Place. Regent's Park. London. N. W.

Postmark: Manchester 12 MR 1871

By Courtesy of the Wedgwood Museum, Staffordshire; W/M 408.

---

1   Blackpool, a resort on the Lancashire coast, famous for its bracing sea air.
2   Mme Pauline Viardot (1821–1910), singer from the distinguished Garcia family of singers, she married Louis Viardot, French theatre director in 1840 and retired from the stage two years later to devote more time to teaching (*Grove*).
3   In 1871 Charles Darwin published his *Descent of Man.*.

EFFIE WEDGWOOD

P. Grove.

Ap. 14. [1871]

Darling Effie,

I have not time to write you a regular letter tonight – but I cannot possibly leave yours without a line of acknowledgment {tonight} by return – For I do not know when I have had such a pleasure as it was – You know you are to me just the very dearest & most charming person in the world – and to get such a letter from you makes me quite *glow* with happiness.

I will write you a proper chronicle of my late doings tomorrow, or Sunday. Meanwhile, take this as a bare "receipt" of a thing too precious to go unacknowledged.

Your most faithful

M. E. Gaskell.

By Courtesy of the Wedgwood Museum, Staffordshire; W/M 408.

EFFIE WEDGWOOD

Plymouth Grove.

Sunday Evening.

[April 17 1871]

My own dear Effie,

Thank you once again for the intense pleasure of your letter. No – I don't think that you need ever fear *my* being fickle. I tried last year to cease to care for you – having the strongest motive, namely your wish, for doing so – and found the task so utterly beyond my powers that I can speak with certainty as to the future. And as to the past – that past to which I have just alluded – this shall be my last reference to it – except to say that I think your apparent – – how shall I put it as I feel it! – your app*arent* soupçon of fickleness is merely a greater degree of sincerity with yourself than {every} most people are gifted with. I think that you have such wonderful insight – and into your own self as well as into others – Hence how can you help seeing the divergence between yourself and your friends, when cir-

cumstances widen that, or \when/ it is done by the natural development of character.

I don't suppose that I have made {?} myself very clear, but shall
trust to your *insights* discovering my meaning – What a trying thing
it must be to be preached at by Snow about me! And oh! How little
worldly wisdom she can have to think that a domestic sermon can
ever have any but a *counteractive* influence! Don't listen to her sermons about me – I beg – or our friendship must indeed come to an
end. – Finis.

I never accepted verbally, tho' of course I did in my heart instantly,
your proposal (to come directly we settled down after our autumn
trips), in answer to my invitation for now or later. It will brighten the
whole summer to look forward to it – darling Effie. I cannot tell you
what a pleasure it will be. And as giving me such months of anticipation, perhaps it is better than \your coming/ now – tho' I must say that
when I heard of your going to Bilbrook,[1] I had a great hope that you
might write and offer to come on here.

Where do you think that I may possibly go this spring? to Venice,
to stay with the Nortons for a month. They have asked me, and my
Father has given his consent, provided that I can hear of a suitable
escort – so perhaps if you hear of any respectable folk going direct &
quickly to N. Italy, on or after May 5th, you would kindly recommend
me as a fellow traveller. If I *don't* go, & I don't look on the journey \
as/ at all certain, there is nothing in this world that I should like \so
well/ as coming to you for a little – Only I object to thrusting my self
in on to you in May or June, when space in London is so precious.

Julia is going up to Florence's for a tiny visit next Thursday. I
wish that you would answer me two questions – which sounds formidable – but {I} \they aren't personal, & I only/ want a trustworthy
opinion. The first is – Did 'London' look upon "Mary James's marrying George Schwabe[2] with horror, as if she had been marrying a
Negro"? \because of his Jewish blood –/ I was told so the other day
by Isabel Thompson – and found that as difficult to believe as the

---

1   Located in Staffordshire, north west of Wolverhampton.
2   Colonel George Schwabe, second son of Salis and Julie Schwabe, married the
     daughter of Mrs Maria James (*Further Letters*, p. 307).

opposite view that [?Mrs] James was so enchanted with her daughter's making such a good marriage! The second question is – What are Mr. Darwin's views, & yours, on women (unmarried), like myself reading his two books? I am particularly anxious for an answer to this question. I remember Catherine's telling me – (you know that I was abroad with her the year in which the 'Origin of Species' was published and read) – that Mr. Darwin was "so much surprised at ladies having read his book". I took this to mean that he thought the subject unfit for them. But as this is all that was said, it is quite possible that I was mistaken in my version, and that all that was meant, was, that Mr. Darwin had not given women credit for sufficient intelligence to be interested in the subject.

Since then I have heard so very many opinions for & against their reading it, that I am fairly puzzled. Do enlighten me.

Your account of your visit to Bilbrook interested me so much. You may imagine how it touched me to hear that Miss Tollet[1] had got any comfort from me, in any shape. How curious it is – the difference that people show in that matter of realization of the other world. It is something so born in them – so of their very nature – I *think* – I never feel very sure what it comes from. I used to believe so completely in Robertson's sermon about 'obedience the organ of faith' – (I am not sure that that is the exact title – but you will remember the one) – and that people's power of realizing God & Heaven depended on their fulfillment of His law. \My own experience proves the contrary –/ But now – tho' of course I believe that people may infinitely increase their spiritual insight by obedience, and fatally – awfully deaden it by disobedience, yet I am not sure that there is the *germ* in every one to develop or kill – I know one girl who is so good & self-sacrificing – and who does so long to believe – and who *can't* – & never has been able to do so – It seems to me that to these poor creatures who have fought so blindly for Christ, without ever having the comfort of beholding the blessed vision, there will come a sudden supreme reward after death – by the film falling from their eyes, and by their beholding Him in the fullness of His glory. I think that this

---

1   A friend of the Gaskell family, she lived at Betley-Hall, Staffordshire (*Gaskell Letters*, pp. 350–51).

girl to whom I am alluding is so noble. She suffers horribly – and has no faith – and yet she devotes herself most unselfishly to others, just as if she had what Wesley would call complete "assurance" – Her virtue is, consequently, extraordinarily disinterested. I was *very* much interested with Snow's Wesley – How capitally it was done. I cannot say that it made one feel Wesley very attractive[.] However, no more does Southey's Life.[1]

I had a very pleasant little progress just lately. First to Lea Hurst, when little Miss Julia Smith[2] and I were alone after the first day, during which my visit dovetailed with a Miss Burnett's[3] – a sister of Mr. Henry Dicy's – Miss Smith was very busy winding up all her philanthropies & friendships & bits of business, as she left by the same train that I did – so I was rather my own mistress – & vastly I enjoyed independent rambles amongst the rocky woods in the sweet 'nimble' Derbyshire air. From there I went to an *old friend's house – the *age having reference solely to the friendship – to a Mrs. Sanders', of Mackworth near Derby – Her husband is land agent to all the gt. Tory squires \of Derbyshire/ – & as bigoted a Tory as you cd. hope to see – so I much enjoyed getting on with him in spite of our intense differences – It is one of those places where everything in the way of society depends on clergymen – and in my five days' visit one individual vicar came to seven meals – so that I felt in the bosom of the Church – I had a charming sight of Mr. Erskine Clarke[4] – as delightful as ever – whom I had not seen since the days when Mr. Bosanquet[5] consulted him as to whether he should rebel against his father's wishes or not – He – Mr. Clarke – is the *roundest* clergyman I ever came across – being Low Church in form of belief –

---

1   John Wesley (1703–91), Methodist preacher and founder of Methodism, was the subject of numerous biographies. By 1888 Snow Wedgwood's biography of Wesley had run to three editions (BHW, p. 330). Robert Southey (1774–1843) had published his *Life of Wesley* in 1820, during the time he was Poet Laureate (*OCEL*).

2   Possibly an Oxford friend; see *Gaskell Letters*, p. 608.

3   Possibly an aspiring writer referred to by Mrs Gaskell in a letter to W. S. Williams (*Gaskell Letters*, p. 641).

4   John Erskine Clarke (1827–1920), British Clergyman whose achievements included the establishment of the *Parish Magazine* in 1859 (*Wik.*).

5   Charles Bosanquet, barrister friend of the Gaskell family (*Gaskell Letters*, pp. 550–53 and 647).

High Church in matters of ritual & Broad Church in spirit & practice. It was a very pleasant *resting* visit at Mackworth – and quite summery with bees & flowers & driving – and Mr. & Mrs. Sanders both intensely kind. From there I went for a week to the Winkworths at Clifton – and a charming week I had. Only Susanna & Kate at home – & every day there was some pleasant plan or other – I saw the Percivals – (he, you know, – the Head Master of the Clifton College, whom many wanted to take Rugby after Dr.Temple) – They are both charming – & have been endlessly kind in accepting on my recommendation a distressed Strasburg widow, whom I have thrust into the niche of their *governess-ship*, humbly hoping that she may prove the right woman in the right place – Mr. Percival is so nice – very pale & delicate & long & languid to look at – but full of wit, wisdom & also quite womanly kindness – with the fire & energy of a *strong* man, which he is not.

I also saw the Hills – the virtuous ones, I mean – who are as racy & delightful as if they were not great philanthropic swells. Also was I taken to see Miss Tuckett – The present *Miss* T., however, is not *the* Miss Tuckett who vo*yag*ed en zig-zag – that one, as you probably know, having gone & married a widowered {?} M. P. – Mr. Fowler – & so the title having descended to the younger sister – who is not known to fame, but is very pleasant – & I suppose figures in the books. I made the dreadful faux pas of "supposing that she had not been abroad last year" – whereupon she said very politely that they had taken a little tour amongst the Dolomites – & it, of course, flashed over me that I had seen a review of a book about this tour, & that I ought to have read it. etc – etc – This Miss T. & her climbing brother are left alone in the house at Frenchay – Such a pretty house – with an upstairs' drawing room – a long room, of which a window at one end looks out on to an ideal village green, with great elm trees – & the window at the other end on to a garden – The walls of the drawing room all hung with beautiful visionary Elijah Walton's[1] \views/ of Swiss peaks rising out of mist & cloud – & all the tables glowing with white & rose azaleas.

---

1   Elijah Walton (1832–80), British-born landscape painter, best known for paintings of Alpine and Egyptian scenery (*ODNB*).

What a tremendous letter! How can you be so foolish & ungrateful as to think of leaving your perfect house!

Ever your loving & faithful

M. E. G.

How aw*fully* snobbish of Caroline Holland! –

Envelope: Miss K. E. Wedgwood. 1. Cumberland Place. Regent's Park. London. N.W.

Postmark: Manchester AP 17 1871

By Courtesy of the Wedgwood Museum, Staffordshire; W/M 408.

SUSAN NORTON

> 84. Plymouth Grove
> Wed. Ap. 26.[1] 71.

My dearest Susan,

As I was putting the finishing touches to my packing this afternoon, \in preparation for starting tomorrow,/ your letter came; and at once on reading it, I felt that I ought not to undertake the journey \ to/ Venice,[2] spite of your most kind welcoming Telegram, and I have therefore sent a messenger to the Cheethams to dissolve our partnership, and with a heavy heart taken everything out of my boxes.

The reasons that brought me to this decision were partly considerations for you and partly for myself. The former, of course, based on a sense of how inconvenient it would be to you to be shackled by any friends' presence at a time when you wanted to have your plans as elastic as possible, and to keep yourselves in 'light, marching order', ready for a start at any time – I don't feel as if, in one way, dearest Mrs. Norton's illness was a reason for my not being with you; because I love her so dearly that I think I could have helped to nurse her rightly, and I should have liked to have helped in that way of all things.

---

1 Though written clearly and apparently in the writer's own hand, this date is not quite consistent with that of the postmarks, suggesting that the letter was written on 23 April.

2 Charles Norton and his family spent part of the summer of 1871 in Venice before moving on to Innsbruck and Dresden (*Norton Letters*, I, 405).

But the sentence in your note that decided me to give up this pleasure was the one in which you bid me "come, if I could so arrange, as to be independent if you were hurried off – " "if I had Hearn," you added, "this could 'be the case.[']".

As the plan with the Cheethams was merely for me to accompany them to Verona, and \as/ I had made no arrangements for a return escort, {and} but was trusting to Fate to provide me with one, I should have been anything but "independent"; and my Father would not have liked my doing anything exc*eptional* – such as travelling part way home alone.[1] If you had been staying longer than "the middle of May or first of June", the chances of my getting a return escort would \have/ been many more than there would have been between the date of my arrival at Venice, (had I gone), probably about the 8$^{th.}$, and the middle of May, supposing that the former of the two times had been the one on which you had finally decided to leave Venice. I am afraid that I am not making my meaning very clear – because I am writing in such haste to catch the post, and also because my head is aching so as to make me feel horribly stupid. But I know how kindly you will disentangle my meaning.

One thing I must try and make clear, though you can hardly need to be told it; and that is how terrible a disappointment it is to me to lose all hope of soon seeing you.

I once tried to plan taking Hearn, as an inseparable escort; but I should not feel it right to deprive both my Father & Julia of her invaluable care and watchfulness.

Give my tenderest love to dear Mrs. Norton. I was bringing her some little medical comforts that I wish I knew how to give to her, & shall perhaps send by the Cheethams.

My very best & truest love to you all – How good you have been to wish for me.

> Your ever loving & grateful
> M.E.Gaskell.

Address: Mrs. Charles E. Norton. Poste Restante. Venice. Italy.

Postmarks: Manchester [?] AP 1871; back of the envelope: London Ap 24 71 and

1   The Franco-Prussian War, which did not end until May 1871, may have contributed to William Gaskell's concern.

Venetia 26 Apr 71.

Houghton Library, Harvard University. MS Am 1088.1 382.

EFFIE WEDGWOOD

3. Morpeth Terrace.[1]

June 26. [1871]

My own darling Effie,

Though I ought to be putting on my things for the Academy (just like last Monday!) I must at any rate begin a line to you. I have thought so constantly of my being with you. I will not épanche – because you have need to reserve all your powers of endurance for that sort of thing – but I must just say how my love & admiration for you grows every time I see you. Pray forbid Snow to preach to you about me – for, spiritual or not spiritual, I {can} \am/ quite incapable of tolerating the idea of your learning to hate me, which you assuredly would if you listened to sermons on that text.

I went to the Abbey twice yesterday – & heard the Dean's very fine elegy on Grote[2] – I liked the idea that he, in common with all great historians, had 'ears to hear the voices of the Dead', as they lifted them up to guide us in the way that they had missed or found – And the analogy between Grote & Herschel,[3] (in allusion to his own sermon on the latter), was very fine – A historian singled out the stars of history, and described the orbits of {his} National Life, etc. Again to the Abbey in the evening, to hear the fat, platitudinarian Archbishop of York, & to see every friend that one ever had! How are your *manners* going on? I still think often of Mr. Jowett's[4] (to my mind) very beautiful sermon –

Affn. – Here I was carried off to the Academy; and after that had

---

1 A row of London townhouses, situated in Westminster, near to Westminster Cathedral and within walking distance of Westminster Abbey.

2 George Grote (1794–1871), banker and historian, best known today for his *History of Greece* (1846–56); see BHW, p. 292 and *ODNB*. Grote's death and elegy suggest the year of this letter.

3 William Herschel (1738–1822), distinguished German born musician and astronomer (*ODNB*).

4 Benjamin Jowett (1817–93), Master of Balliol College, Oxford (*Further Letters*, p. 257, n.3, and *ODNB*).

a most delightful little lunch in Queen Anne St. – topping up with a call on very dull Mrs. Palgrave[1] – who informed me that her husband had thought Mr. Jowett most commonplace, but had liked his Westminster Abbey sermon so much. Which latter Miss Jowett says was so commonplace (I don't know why I should write to you exclusively about sermons.) I felt so inclined to go on to Cumberland after doing Mrs. Palgrave – but I thought that you were sure to be busy or out. And stupidly I omitted asking Hope, of whom I had a glimpse in Gu. A., what your plans might be for the aftn.

How I wonder what your *general* plans are consolidating themselves into. *Nothing* is so wearing as worrying over plans; and then with yours this year there is the special difficulty about the financial part of the business – How I long that I cd. ever take any of your burdens from you! and yet you wd. hardly be – or at any rate – *prove* yourself so noble as you do, if you hadn't them to bear – Mrs. Leslie Stephen[2] & I were gushing over you together on Friday – & saying how handsome you were growing – & she said how good it was for her sister-in-law to have you for a friend – & I said, as I cd. imagine you \might/ wish{?} how much you valued her friendship etc. I *have* read some of the 'Service of the Poor',[3] & A. Dicey[4] himself cannot admire it more. It is most 'able' – and such a beautiful – or rather grand, simple style of thought – *simple* through its candour, I mean –

I have so often thought of all dear Mrs. Wedgwood's kindness to me during my quite delightful visit to you – and the treat of the Opera was gter. than you, who have never had the opportunity of being a

---

1   Possibly wife of Francis Turner Palgrave (1824–97), author of *Golden Treasury of Best Songs and Lyrical Poems in the English Language* (1861), friend of Tennyson and the Pre-Raphaelites.

2   In 1867 Marian Thackeray, the novelist's younger daughter, married Leslie Stephen (1832–1904), first editor of *DNB*, noted Alpinist, friend of Charles Norton and father of Virginia Woolf (*ODNB* and *OCEL*).

3   Caroline Emelia Stephen, *The Service of the Poor, being an inquiry into the reasons for and against the establishment of religious sisterhoods for charitable purposes* (London, 1871). Caroline Stephen (1834–1909) was one of Sir Leslie Stephen's sisters; her correspondence with Florence Nightingale led to her writing *Service of the Poor* (*ODNB*).

4   A possible reference to Albert Venn Dicey (1835–1922), Oxford scholar, lawyer and journalist, whose circle of friends included Algernon Charles Swinburne and Thomas Erskine Holland (*ODNB*).

'country cousin', can imagine.

I enclose stamps for my on-beforwarded letters – with many apologies (the writers ought to apologise, as it was their fault, not mine) for all the trouble given you & Snow.

      Ever your devoted

      M. E. G.

Envelope: Miss K. E. Wedgwood. 1. Cumberland Place. Regent's Park. N. W.

Postmark: London S.W. JU 27 71

By Courtesy of the Wedgwood Museum, Staffordshire; W/M 408.

EFFIE WEDGWOOD

          [Manchester]

          Jul 18 [1871]

My own darling Effie,

Am I not a provoking person – I *had* heard your great piece of news – last night – from Cousin Mary, who is staying near here. But in the most tantalizing fashion – for she could not remember the name of the man to whom H. D. was engaged[1] – Strange to say, I suggested Mr. Litchfield at the fourth guess; and then she accepted it, but in a doubtful, unsatisfactory kind of way – So that I was really *most* grateful when your letter came – which was piquant and interesting beyond description – Spite of my guessing Mr. L's name, I am *intensely* surprised at the news –

I have a very lowminded, Do*wagery* delight in hearing of an engagement – I don't know why – for I have never once sighed for marriage in the abstract. It always makes me very happy, à la Mrs. V. L.,[2] to hear of people being happy in this special fashion. I mean to write to Harriet to congratulate her. How intensely exciting the whole fortnight must have been! And what a capital account you do give – dearest Effie. You are the very queen of letter writers – and I read in your hieroglyphs as prolonging the pleasure of reading what you

---

1   Henrietta (Etty) Darwin (1843–1927) married R. B. Litchfield, founder-member of the working Men's College, after a short engagement in the autumn of 1871 (BHW, p. 299).

2   Mrs Vernon Lushington, at whose home the couple met (BHW, p. 299).

write. It is like chewing prâlines.

Ranger, our lovely cat, is sitting close to me, and wishes to send you a message. In comparing her with recollections of Purley, I fear that I must call her *physically* inferior – no cat, however, can surpass her morally. Purley suggests Mrs. Wilding – – – so at length, her image is superseded in Mr. L's heart. Poor Shepherd – surely she hoped for some one even better for you. I am quite sure *I* do!

You ask about my affairs – I had a very pleasant end to my campaign – and came home, to hardish work with a rather stupid new cook, & general 'setting one's house in order' – which is very hateful work to my mind. Florence came down on Friday – Charlie being away at Durham. The Assizes begin on the 24th·, when he will join her here – I am looking forward much to cracking you up to A. Dicey as the cleverest woman of my acquaintance, because it will make him so feel vicarious coals of fire. I am slowly but happily reading the "Service of the Poor" – It *is* the very slowest reading I ever did. But such perfect *mental workmanship*.

Our plans for abroad are slowly shaping themselves – Mürren, the Faulhorn, and the Ammergau – (Florence told Crompton Hutton[1] the other day that Julia & I are thinking of going to the Passion-play, and he answered indignantly – 'Nay – I won't believe anything so disgusting of your sisters' –). *What* a trouble one's travelling trousseau is! Good gracious, how tired I am of planning skirts and bodies and panniers, each of which is to combine rightly with all the others – And then boots are such a plague! –

Does Mr. Wedgwood go with you after all? And what is your route to be?

I was so much disappointed not to be able to come to Mr. Moore's on the Saturday morning that you left London – I turned it over & over in my mind – but I saw that it would not do. I wish when you write you wd. tell me exactly your opinion of Miss Thackeray. I found her so very charming when I was at the Brookfields' – She seemed so really *sweet* –

---

1   Crompton Hutton was related to the Gaskells through marriage, having married, in 1865, Harriet Sophia Holland, Thurstan Holland's older sister (*Cheshire Records, Hollands of Mobberley*, ed. for the computer by Dorothy Bates).

You cannot think how intensely I enjoyed my visit to you, nor how I am looking forward to having you in Octr., (or either fortnight in November). It will be *most* charming.

Ever your devoted.

By Courtesy of the Wedgwood Museum, Staffordshire; W/M 408.

HENRIETTA LITCHFIELD

[September 1871]

But one would certainly rather have {the} enough tea out of a commonplace kettle, than go thirsty for the sake of an uncommon one.

I have had another urgent appeal from the Brodies about your Father's going to them – so pray pack {up} him up in a brown-paper parcel, & send him off to be delivered immediately. Brockham Warren, Reigate, is their address; & they are devoted to him already.

We start tomorrow. It must be quite superfluous to wish *you* 'bon voyage', for I suppose wedding-tours can't help being perfect – So I can but repeat my heartiest good wishes on your marriage & believe me ever yr. very affect

M. E. Gaskell.

Incomplete. The first page appears to be absent as there is no sender's address The date has been provided by Cambridge University Library.

By permission of the Syndics of Cambridge University Library, MS. DAR. 165.14.

SUSAN NORTON

[Manchester]
Oct 16 [1871]

Dearest Susan,

You must have thought it so very strange that I have not sooner answered your most kind note; but one thing after another has caused delay. First, it did not reach Mürren till after we had left; and had to follow us in our travels. Nextly, everything seemed so uncertain that I waited, hoping to 'see light' – Now that we are settled at home again, it is, I grieve to say, most clear to me that I cannot come to you this winter in Dresden as you so most kindly ask. All the old claims & engagements bind me fast, & new ones rise daily. I tried, whilst abroad, to plan a 'dash' to you at the end, or in the middle, of our tour; but that was equally impracticable. No, as you say, I begin to believe that fate is against our meeting! For the present at least. I could not write lightly of it, if I really feared that we were not sooner or later to look in each other's faces again. Pray tell all and each of those so dear to me how I long for that day to come.

How full your hearts will be of this terrific fire in Chicago[1] – here one talks of little else; and I doubt if their own countrymen can feel more for the people of Chicago than we in England do. Perhaps it will tear down the veil between the two nations – when they know how our hearts bleed for them, they will not care to remember the great wrong of the Alabama so keenly.

We had a delightful tour – ending with the Passions spiel – We came home to find my dear Father looking so strong & well that we are in the best of spirits about him and a week ago I had such a pretty little note from Mrs Shepherd, (of Bolsover St.), enquiring about you all so affectionately. I promised to tell you when I wrote. I trust that Mrs. Norton is stronger, and that Dresden suits her? And how is Grace : and Mr. Norton? and Jane? Would either Grace or Jane write me one of their most charming letters, & tell me all about every one of you? I know that I don't deserve to have my request granted – still I think that I may rely on their kindness to \make them/ do so, though I cannot on my deserts.

Ever your loving
M.E.Gaskell.

Houghton Library, Harvard University. MS Am 1088.1 383.

---

1   This fire, which raged from 8th to 10th October 1871, was widely reported and discussed in British newspapers and journals; see for example *The Times*, 12 October 1871, p. 5, col.B and *Manchester Guardian*, 12 October 1871, p. 6. Meta's reference to this event completes the date of the letter.

EFFIE WEDGWOOD

Nov. 13. [1871]

My own darling Effie,

I seemed to grow quite speechless today when you left: just because I was feeling so many things so deeply. And an *invitation to lunch* to *you*, would not be àpropos.

But *you* would not misunderstand me. You know, I am sure, how intensely I love you, and have enjoyed your visit, and how my heart is set on helping you (if I can) in this most knotty & entangled affair before you.

God guide you right.
Your devoted
M. E. G.

Envelope: Miss K. E. Wedgwood. 1. Cumberland Place. Regent's Park. London. N. W.

Postmark: Manchester 13 NO 71

By Courtesy of the Wedgwood Museum, Staffordshire; W/M 408.

EFFIE WEDGWOOD

Sir B. C. B's –
Brockham Warren.[1]
Reigate.
Nov. 20. [1871]

My own darling Effie,

All last week I kept hugging to myself the prospect of writing you a good long letter in the leisure that I was sure to have here: and now that the leisure comes, I have such a persistent bad headache that I can't enjoy the opportunity a bit. Yesterday I thought that I would wait till today, & that the pain was sure to be gone – But stupidly it isn't.

Your charming bi-value letter was so very great a pleasure to me. Dearest Effie, I am sure that you cannot ever guess the depth of my

---

1   Country home of the Brodie family, situated on the top of Box Hill, near Reigate Surrey (*ODNB*).

devotion to you – nor how I long – just now to have a power quite beyond my own, to help and advise you.

The more I think over your affairs, the more I hope that you will not accept Godfrey[1] – spite of the great sacrifice that it must be to any woman to refuse such a gift as he offers you – spite of the kind of sanction that the past gives to the relation between you – I think that in life, one never regrets playing with – – for? – which does one say? – the highest stake. One may lose – but it has been in a noble game, wherein it is better to have lost than to have won in a more trivial game.

Act, so as not to exclude from your future the chance of the highest & noblest kind of marriage, & I believe that you will never (*in your best & finest moments*) regret it, through whatever deserts of loneliness or dreariness you may have to pass –

But to \have/ taken the marriage vow with anything short of your whole heart & soul, you would shudder to remember when you were face to face with Truth & Reality – with God, in fact. It seems such a hard, cruel doctrine – I think! & one so easily preached by a person not in the thick of such difficulties – But I can assure you that it is real pain to me to write it out – And I may – of course, I may be mistaken. Surely something will turn up soon, to clear up things, & show you which path to follow: & fortunately with you one has no doubt that you will have strength to walk along whichever path is shown to be the right one – however strait & narrow.

Fortunately for you, & for your friends, you are not such weak tea as *some* people.

Did you see Mr. Bryce at Mrs. Grey's meeting? One of the pleasant consequences of my thinking so much about your affairs, is that it has given me a sense of extreme insecurity about my own! As if your catastrophe ten years ago were common & typical! a most ungenerous & disloyal suspicion on my part, I know.

I think Mr. Sidgwick *very* charming.

The girls are improving wonderfully.

---

1 Godfrey Wedgwood, Effie's first cousin, made a proposal of marriage to Effie in 1871 (BHW, p. 302 and Kuper, pp. 133–34). Concern about first cousin marriages formed the basis of much correspondence between Effie and Meta.

Ever your devoted
M. E. G.

After this stupid letter, I don't like to beg for one soon, because I feel as if I didn't deserve it. But I shall want *terribly* to hear how you are going on – dear, dear Effie.

By Courtesy of the Wedgwood Museum, Staffordshire; W/M 408.

EFFIE WEDGWOOD

Brockham Warren.
Reigate.
Nov. 23. [1871]

My own darling Effie,

I keep thinking of you so very much, and wondering how things are going on with you. I feel as if my last letter had been such a hard – almost cruel – one. But it is just because you are so dear to me that I cannot bear to think of you, risking your happiness, and worse than that, risking *yourself* – your highest self – by a marriage which did not fully satisfy your noblest demands.

I do wish that you would write to me here very soon, & tell me about yourself – about the *state of your heart*. Funny – almost idiotic – as those words look, they are the only ones that express what I want to know about you.

Do not think me horridly persistent on one side only – but I must just tell you that the other day Ida Brodie took me here to see a poor idiot-child – & on asking about the causes, I found out that there were epileptic fits in the family – So I said by way of a roundabout inter-rogation that I had never heard of any connection between the two – idiocy & epilepsy – (hardly strictly true) – Whereupon Ida said, 'Oh but I think that there must be, because on the paper sent us from Earlswood[1] that we had to fill up about this child, one of the questions was about Epilepsy in the family'. I quite shuddered for you – & yet, per contra, there was Mr. Mellor's assurance that the risks need not be considered.

1   The Royal Earlswood Asylum for Idiots, Redhill, Surrey, near to Reigate, was the first establishment to cater specifically for people with learning disabilities (*Wik.*).

Do write to me soon, my own darling; & all about *yourself.*
Ever your devoted
M. E. G.

By Courtesy of the Wedgwood Museum, Staffordshire; W/M 408.

EFFIE WEDGWOOD

Nov. 28. [1871]

Darling Effie,

I have read and better read these letters – and literally cannot understand them: both 'absolutely' and 'relatively'! It may be that my brain is going – but they produce no clear impression on me. It is as if they had been written on Talleyrand's[1] celebrated principle.

Perhaps after saying this, it is Irish and inconsistent, to tell you that they do not seem to tally with the truth as at present known. Then comes the question – Which is the truth? My own idea is this – that there has been a horrible complexity of feeling in poor 'Godfrey's' mind – As long as he was under the strong influence of his wife, he thought that the barrier between you rested on the ground he {hints} mentions in these letters – Now, when his old devotion to you returns, he recalls that sad incident of his wife's jealousy, and he makes that the basis of – what I should imagine had really been caused by a freezing consciousness of shockingly weak behaviour on his part.[2]

I wrote *at once* to my Uncle,[3] but told him – knowing that my letter wd. not reach him for two days – to write to me at Plymouth Grove, whither I return on Thursday, sleeping tomorrow night at Florence's. I did not write to you yesterday, because I wished so much to study

1   Charles Maurice Talleyrand (1754–1838), French Diplomat, known for his diplomacy, political pragmatism and even political intrigue (*Wik.*).

2   Godfrey Wedgwood had married Mary Hawkshaw in 1862, though he was fond of Effie. He later confessed to his wife that he was still in love with Effie. He proposed to Effie in 1871, after his wife had died, but after much soul searching Effie declined the offer. He subsequently married Effie's younger sister Hope. Effie married a widower, Thomas Henry Farrer (Kuper, pp. 133–34 and BHW, pp. 302-3).

3   Meta had numerous uncles on her mother's side of the family. If this particular uncle was consulted for medical advice he may have been Henry Holland (1788–1873); see *Further Letters*, p. 16, n.3.

these letters. They have a most curious effect on me – and I will say candidly – not a pleasant one. I think that everything that is strange in Godfrey's conduct *may* be charitably accounted for by attributing to him weakness of will, & a general failure of *self-knowledge*. But then oh, my own dear & most *noble* Effie, is such a man worthy of you? No – I *cannot* think it – My feeling against – – – –

At this moment Isabel Thompson arrived unexpectedly – and everything seems in a whirl – I cannot settle down properly – in this room – where all the congratulations \She is engaged to Mr. Sidgworth/ are going on – and they won't let me leave!

    Your own most devoted
    M. E. G.

By Courtesy of the Wedgwood Museum, Staffordshire; W/M 408.

EFFIE WEDGWOOD

        [84 Plymouth Grove]
        [Manchester]
        Dec. 1. [1871]

My own dear, dear Effie,

Through this weary busy day my thoughts have been continually with you. I long for some *brain-wave* to let me know how you are feeling. Of course you mayn't take my Uncle's evidence as conclusive. (He was *very* frequently consulted, \however,/ on such subjects during his active professional career – & \lunacy &/ idiocy were his specialiti[e]s.

I was wondering whether you wd. like me to go to Dr. Noble here; with the same set of questions – ? or whether Dr. West wd. be better? How I wish I cd. do anything more for you – in that – or any other – way.

I feel as if I cd. but say over & over again, how *tender*ly I love you – [&] how I long for your happiness.

I know so well how it is just when a thing becomes impossible, or is seen clearly to be wrong, that one first feels its full and exceeding value. So I quite expect a great rush of feeling into your heart towards

Godfrey – & then the pain may be very deep – What do you think about Dr. West – ?

Do pray let me hear from you soon. I am so anxious to know about you that I cannot be properly unselfish and tell you not to write. May God help you.

Ever your own devoted
M. E. Gaskell.

Envelope: Miss K. E. Wedgwood. 1. Cumberland Place. Regent's Park. London. N. W.

Postmark: Manchester NO 30 1871

By Courtesy of the Wedgwood Museum, Staffordshire; W/M 408.

EFFIE WEDGWOOD

84. Plymouth Grove.
Dec. 3. [1871]

Darling Effie,

I have been so thinking of you at the Communion just now – It is my afternoon at the school,[1] so I cannot write more than a line – but your silence makes me fear lest things are not well with you. I *thought* of you at the Communion – but, could not, when I tried, *pray* for you; for it seems as if intercession implied that God's Love for you was less than mine – His mercy needing prayers of mine!

Unsigned letter

By Courtesy of the Wedgwood Museum, Staffordshire; W/M 408.

EFFIE WEDGWOOD

Dec. 6. [1871]

Darling Effie,

I must again send you a line of deepest sympathy and love – My thoughts are *perpetually* with you. It seems to me such a sad, dreary

---

1   A likely reference to the Lower Mosley Street Sunday School, where Meta, and her younger sister Julia, taught.

thing your going off alone to Dr. Radcliffe[1] – How I wish that I had been nearer, so as to have gone with you.

It *does* seem to me such a sad thing altogether for you. I *cannot* agree with Hope about want of faith: I feel it such a great deficiency even in a friend – and shld. now never *make* {a} friends with any one who lacked belief in a God – unless they were wonderfully good – this sounds Pharisaical – but I don't mean it so in the least. I simply mean that what I require to charm and attach me in a friend includes real religiousness – and the power of insight into a world beyond this.

I want to tell you two compliments that I have heard paid you – no, *three*. One was from Mr. Bryce, to whom I was giving an account on Sunday of Mr. Walker's speech about women at the Heywoods'[2] – You must know that Mr. Walker is notoriously the most brilliant & clever man possible. I said that Mr. Walker's remarks "had nearly made Miss Wedgwood fire across the table." "Well – if those two ships had come into collision, her ability wd. have sunk his" –

Next, Mr. Bobbins is perfectly *wild* abt. yr. singing – & last night at a ball, Mr. Ward came up to announce solemnly how much "charmed" he had been with you, & how he had been asking & hearing so much about you since. (From *whom*, I wonder?) Please be most careful, tho' of course you will not want a soupçon of what I told you ooze out – about Mr. Bryce.

Ever yr. devoted
M. E. G.

I do so love you. What does Mrs. Clement Wedgwood say?[3]

By Courtesy of the Wedgwood Museum, Staffordshire; W/M 408.

---

1 Dr Charles Bland Radcliffe (1822–89) was a London physician who specialized in diseases of the nervous system, including epilepsy (*ODNB*).

2 A likely reference to the family of James Heywood (1810–97), M. P. , member of Cross Street Chapel and Manchester Athenaeum (*Further Letters*, p. 67, n.3).

3 Mrs Clement Wedgwood, formerly Emily Rendel, who married Clement Wedgwood, brother of Effie's first cousin Godfrey (BHW, p. 291).

EFFIE WEDGWOOD

84 Plymouth Grove.
Manchester.
Dec. 10. [1871]

My own dearest Effie,

I am writing in a great hurry – half in the dark – but write to you by tonight's post, I must. I am so thankful that at any rate you have got your Radcliffe visit over – for it must have been most trying. It is a part of your courage to have undertaken it. I am so glad, too, that you have spoken to Hope, for your heart must have been full to bursting, & expression is such a safety valve. Moreover, it clears up one's thoughts so, *presenting* them to other people.

I cannot waver in my wishes. Let me tell you, (what at present you must breathe to *no* one, since Marianne is not sufficiently recovered to bear it,) that I sent here for a most clever children's doctor – a scientific German, whom Mr. Paget calls the first in Europe, I have heard – & that this Dr. Gumpert told us yesterday, to my horror & grief, that our sweetest little Daisy was deaf & dumb as well as Willy.[1] She has become the very apple of our eyes in this fortnight. And this is entirely, he says, thro' cousins marrying; she quoted two other instances, close here, where the offspring of first cousins were deaf & dumb. I seem to heap up arguments on one side only. But it is not, dear, dear Effie, that I think of that side only; for every day it comes before me more strongly what you wd. be losing in refusing any one so tender-hearted & affecte. as Godfrey. Mrs. C. Wedgwoods' letter seems to me to *glance off* the question a little – It is a sweet, charming letter. My poor Effie. Your words at the end of your letter filled me with intense delight & gratitude. If loving you gives me any claim on your love, I have, indeed, a big one. And even Mr. Wards' *admiration* pales before mine, Madam.

I hardly like saying a word abt. my own affairs in the *presence* of your great, & really tragic kind of sorrow – but still I must ask one question – Have you heard anything of Mr. Bryce flirting with any

---

1   Daisy and Willy were the children of Marianne and Thurstan Holland, second cousins.

one that you speak of being unhappy & anxious abt. me? A great chill struck me when I read those words. Pray tell me soon; & *promise* to tell me of any such thing, shld[.] a rumour of it reach your ears. I like to tell you all – He came down here much earlier than expected – & I was at Brockham – which he didn't know. He was only a week in the North after my return, & then was obliged to hurry for work to London. And 4 days of that week he was obliged to be in L'pool. But everything is quite right between us – I hope & believe – shall fully at least believe, when you tell me that you have heard nothing. I feel as if Miss Stephen must have told you that he was "*carrying on*" with some one! – I don't deny that it is (to me specially) dreadfully trying waiting on & on: but I have the fullest grounds of trust & certainty.

Now – back to your affairs, my own darling – At this point came the doctor to see Marianne's nurse, who has been enlivening this busy week with an attack of dysentery – So I must stop, & before I have said one quarter of what I shld. like – But I never could tell you how I feel for you & love you, my own dearest one.

Your devoted
M. E. G.

Sender's address on writing paper is embossed.

By Courtesy of the Wedgwood Museum, Staffordshire; W/M 408.

EFFIE WEDGWOOD

84. Plymouth Grove.
Dec. 13. [1871]

My own darling Effie,

I was so vext not to be able to write yesterday. You did more than right to tell me openly about Miss Tollemache. I cannot say how I value such frankness, nor what a sense of security "knowing the worst" always gives me. I am not in the least ostrich-like. As long as there is anything left untold, I have always horrible misconceptions of the possible extent and danger. In this case, spite of my being infected with some of your mistrust of men, & spite of the V. L. experience, I *cannot* – simply *cannot* – have the slightest doubt or uncertainty. I hope that I am not copying Miss Tollemache in just telling you briefly the last grounds for this security: that Mr. Bryce last Sunday week loaded his conversation, before Julia, [?] with the broadest doubles entendres – (I hate the word, but know no other) – saying that his real object in coming to Manchester was to see me – etc. & openly that if I was going to Mrs. Leister's ball on the following Tuesday, he wd. go – if I wasn't, he wd.n't – And he went, tho' feeling very unwell. And did everything that was possible in the great crowd, where every word was overheard – & – (to repeat this is very Miss Tollemache-y!) – told me by a clever double entendre that I was "perfect" – & then wrote on leaving Manchester to say that "on leaving it, he felt as if he had hardly been here at all, having had so few chances of seeing friends", & that there were "ever so many things about which he had hoped to speak to me" – And went off very unwell.

Of course I *may* be mistaken – tho' Julia says that it is impossible. And death & illness & estrangement following on misrepresentation, are always possibilities; *and* I find uncertainty (*of the future* only) very, very trying. But otherwise . . .

As to you, Effie; really without pretence, a far more interesting subject to me, I cannot keep my thoughts from perpetual speculations about your decision, which must now be imminent. 'The time draws nigh the birth of Christ'. Each time I think, as I hear how 'near Xmas is', (which people are always saying so tritely), that it is *by* Xmas, that you have to make up your mind.

I quite hate myself, (as if I were another person from myself), for having said so much on the dissuading side. And yet I felt it better to investigate & put before you the full truth on the dark side. If you had felt with me the awful pang last Saturday of hearing Daisy's doom pronounced!

But it is a curious point, in the higher metaphysics I shd. think, what duties you owe to non-existent, & possibly never-existent, beings. I, myself, shld. out of pure selfishness, never undertake a marriage with such possibilities of pain – of ever-gnawing doubt, \even if never jus-tified by fulfilment/ – as wd. be implied in your marrying Godfrey. But then Miss Wynne wd. say, that that, \as every other,/ form of self-ishness wd. be quenched in true love.

Oh my poor, poor Effie – when I think of the long linked past of tenderness on Godfrey's part – of the bond that in one way must be the stronger for having been broken, I cannot bear to think of what lies before you.

But there is a point, I do believe, where one ought to cease wrangling in argument with oneself; & having once yielded up one's will to God's will trust that he will gently show one what that is.

I am so glad that you had Mr. Clark of Taunton – the opportunity of hearing him preach, I mean. You and I are amongst the few specimens extant of sermon-lovers.

Agnes Darbishire[1] is afloat in Manchester again, and is coming to dine with us tonight. Of course I shall be *most* careful : but if anything transpires shall treasure it up. She looks quite well again, I am glad to say.

Ever your devoted & faithful
M. E. G.

By Courtesy of the Wedgwood Museum, Staffordshire; W/M 408.

EFFIE WEDGWOOD

84. Plymouth Grove.
Manchester.
Dec. 22. [1871]

Darling Effie,

You do not know how dreadfully anxious I am getting about you. Every morning when I come down, I feel sure that I shall have a dear yellow letter; & every morning when there isn't one I am oppressed by fears as to what is happening to you. Has Godfrey come up to London? or have you written? or *what*? I do hope that things are going as happily with you as possible – But that is the misery of it, – that I do not see how things can settle either way without very great pain for you; and in my shortsighted *worldly-eyed* way, I should so have longed for . . [I] do so covet happiness – for my precious Effie.

Yet I do believe in things so infinitely beyond human happiness,

---

1   Daughter of Mary and Samuel Dukinfield-Darbishire (Uglow, p. 159).

that I wonder why I crave it so for you. Do you know those lines at the end of Mrs. Browning's 'Isobel's Child' – ? I am so fond of them – (Perhaps you will not like them) –

{'Oh you}   'Oh you,
Earth's tender & impassioned few,
Take courage to entrust your love,
To Him, so-named, who guards above
        Its ends, – & shall fulfil!
Breaking the narrow prayers that may
Befit your narrow hearts, away
        In His broad loving way.'[1]

So he may break my wishes for you, & give you something infinitely better.

I am writing in a great hurry. The days seem dark & dreary just now – with my Father having been seriously, tho' not in the least dangerously, ill with bronchitis; & with this sad, sad doom for our little darlings, twice pronounced here by the best of doctors. – *Marianne knows nothing of it –*

Ever your loving, devoted
M. E. G.
God bless you –

Blue notepaper with sender's address embossed.

By Courtesy of the Wedgwood Museum, Staffordshire; W/M 408.

EFFIE WEDGWOOD

84. Plymouth Grove.
Dec. 29. [1871]

My own darling, darling Efffie,

I have thought of you so constantly – feeling at every moment 'perhaps it is happening now' – And most certainly I should have written

---

1 From Elizabeth Barrett Browning, 'Isobel's Child', a poem consisting of thirty-seven verses, first published in 1838. Meta's quotation here may not be quite accurate. *The Poetical Works of E. B. Browning* (London, 1932), pp. 185–91, gives 'will' instead of 'way' in the last line, and 'and' where Meta uses '&'.

to you, 'on' your Sunday's letter, but that I have been very unwell – When I got your letter this morning, and again when your second came, a minute and a half ago, my heart bled for you. Yes – indeed and indeed you cannot reckon on greater pity than you find in me. It is such cruel pain for you to have gone through. Really you have suffered as much as that poor Godfrey.

My darling Effie – I don't wonder at the remembrance of his 'almost contorted face' haunting you – For a long time you will have recollections that will hurt and wound you piercingly. But I am *sure* that you have done right : quite, quite sure. I had made up my mind never to say another word to you *against* it; feeling that I had said perhaps almost more than I ought to have done.

(One reason that I was so very sorry not to answer your Sunday's letter, was for fear lest it might seem as if I cd. only sympathize with you from the adverse point of view; and as if I might be less hearty in my sympathy when \I had learnt that/ you had not decisively prohibited his meeting you.)

But now it is decided, I do not think that I shall be doing wrong in saying emphatically – – no, perhaps it may pain you *for him* – I can fancy how chivalrously sore you will feel for him. And you know my views. So let me rather just say again and again how I love and pity you for having that worst pain to suffer, – the pain of giving pain – and let me tell you how I grieve with you for him. What a story it is! If it could but be written out clearly, for young men to read, mark, & learn, how mere weakness and indecision may for ever blight their true happiness.–

Darling Effie – I have just re-read your last note – & it comes over me so horribly that you have had, to some extent, great, great pain on your own account, quite independently of your having had to *stab* him. Oh my poor child – how I do love & pity you. When you say that "you think you cd. have been happy with him"–

To throw away such a chance – the world holds nothing bitterer; and when it is a deed of which the wisdom will never be fully known till after death, (when I suppose we *may* learn what wd. have been the issues of deeds that we refrained from), it makes it so much, much harder for you – For you will by wondering whether happiness &

peace & prosperity might not have followed on your choosing the life so tenderly, so fervently offered to you.

I hardly like to say anything of the sort – but oh darling Effie, if ever by any amount of love of another kind I can make up in any tiny degree for the great sacrifice you have made, you know that to me you may always turn for a quite inexhaustible supply of love and admiration – only admiration seems too coarse a word for what I feel for you.

Have just come in before dinner-time – & must end – I can't *tell* you how I feel for you, my own darling: It is *miserable* for you. What are Hope's views?

No signature.

Envelope: Miss K. E. Wedgwood. 1. Cumberland Place. Regent's Park. London. N. W.

Postmark: Manchester DE 29 1871.

By Courtesy of the Wedgwood Museum, Staffordshire; W/M 408.

EFFIE WEDGWOOD

> 84. Plymouth Grove.
> Dec. 31. 1871.
> (for the last time I write it.)

My own darling Effie,

I know that I am selfish, & don't one bit defend my own conduct; still, write to you I *must*, to beg for a bulletin of your dear, dear self – When I got no letter this morning, & felt so dreadfully full of fears of different kinds – I read and re-read your two last letters yesterday – and it seemed to me as if you were in the midst of so much pain that I could hardly bear it for you – Do, dearest, write and tell me of yourself. I know that you are so generous, and will be feeling so much more for him than for yourself, that I cannot repeat one of the reasons that made me so firmly believe that it is right & well for you to have acted as you have. Indeed, I cd. fancy that it would be quite natural, *and right*, for you to hate me if I touched upon that side, just when your heart must be aching so with the remembrance of pain given, and with that longing to staunch instead of deepen the wounds of his poor, broken life. Do write to me, please. Grumble at me, if you like, but write.

I keep wondering whether tomorrow's letter will bid you go to Cannes or not. I think it so good of you to offer to go – though I know how fond you are of Ellinor. Have you heard from, or of, Godfrey? – or from Mrs. Clement Wedgwood? – What do Hope and Mrs. Wedgwood think? – These questions are all real ones, that want answers – God bless you through this next, and each succeeding year.

Yours
M. E. G.

By Courtesy of the Wedgwood Museum, Staffordshire; W/M 408.

EFFIE WEDGWOOD

84. Plymouth Grove.
Manchester.
Jan 18 [1872]

My own precious Effie,

I do so care for hearing from you – only sometimes it gives me such a pang of longing to have you back here – How I *did* enjoy your being here! tho' during your visit, I suffered so for you – dreading a future thro' which you have already passed so bravely & rightly (Are you weary of hearing how I admire you?)

I think that you had told me abt. the arbour talk at Shrewsbury \& the gt. *bond* then felt;/ but never, I am sure, said that you had known instinctively then, how Godfrey was *trying* to speak. I am oh so thankful my very dear Effie, that you are getting over the terrible strain to which you have just been subjected. You say you "feel calm & satisfied", and it does so thoroughly rejoice me to hear it. And *don't* be anxious for me for tho' I admit that it is telling on my health considering (how much of my present weakness may be owing to grief about little Willie, I don't know –), yet I do not, in my *rational* moments, have the tiniest grain of doubt abt. Mr. Bryce. Things, are since *Ober!*/ *A*mmergau,[1] have quite passed out of the debateable realm when you don't know whether it is friendship or not. And he comes to Manchester for a day, at the end of the week after next.

I had a curious confirmation of my opinion the other night, when during a 4 hours talked with Mrs. Robert Darbishire,[2] she volunteered to tell me that Mr. B., when he stayed with her in October, had taken her into his confidence & that he cd. talk to her about nothing but how he ought to propose to some girl he cared for, how he cd. not get the opportunity "& was always asking her, if it was not possible to make a girl understand how he cared for her, tho' he had not been able to speak" – & – it was a long story, & I trust & believe that I did not "turn a hair" – not even when she said, looking hard at me, "I am sure it is not a London girl" – (from something he said) – Thank you *so* much for your full and ample account of the Sunday afternoon's call, you are such an *able* woman, Effie. (No one is "*clever*", nowadays – So I am in the fashion thro' not being so!) – Your letters always strike me as so wonderfully clear & forcible – I wish I were you! –

My Father is getting round again –

I am reading Maine,[3] tell Snow please, with greatest care – both intellectually & with regard to the material book, which I have put into a cover, wash my hands before reading, & never take within 50 years of the fire.

Has your voice come back ? Mrs. Hare is never weary of praising you – & Mrs. Gaddum[4] was another victim – I heard from Isabel today – very *hunting*, à la Sidgwick, & happy. W. Frederic Thompson

---

1 Oberammergau; a village of medieval origin in the Bavarian Alps, best known for the five-hour play performed by villagers in an open-air theatre several times weekly from May to October. The play depicts Jesus's last days on Earth ("Oberammergau." *Encyclopædia Britannica Online Library Edition*).

2 Formerly Harriet Cobb, with whom Mrs Gaskell had a painful misunderstanding (Uglow, p. 275).

3 A likely reference to Henry James Sumner Maine (1822–88), jurist and scholar with a particular interest in legal history. He was founding editor of the *Saturday Review* and author of *Ancient Law* (1861) (*ODNB*).

4 The Gaddums were Manchester textile merchants, known to the Gaskells mainly through their philanthropic works. Marianne Gaskell had supported Sophie Gaddum (1834–89) at the funeral of her father F. E. Gaddum in 1866. Mrs Gaddum, referred to here, would have been Sophie's mother, who lived in Fallowfield until her death in 1893 (*Gaddums Revisited*, pp. 69–70).

is down here, law-lecturing at Owen's college now; but he can tell one nothing interesting about wedding affairs. *What* a trouble brides-maiding is!

Poor Annabel seems driven nearly distracted in trying to grant all the conflicting wishes of the 'troupe' in this case. You darling! How I wish you were here – How is Purley? Ranger is so sweet & lovable. I often grieve over your criticism on her personal appearance –

Ever your faithful, loving

M.E.G.

Sender's address on writing paper is embossed.

Envelope: Miss K. E. Wedgwood 1. Cumberland Place. Regent's Park. London. N.W.

Postmark: Manchester JA 18 1872 Back of envelope: London JA 19 72

By Courtesy of the Wedgwood Museum, Staffordshire; W/M 408.

EFFIE WEDGWOOD

84 Plymouth Grove.
Manchester.
Sunday [Jan 21st][1] [1872]

Darling Effie,

It was *so* kind of you saying that I was not to feel myself in debt to you for your last letter. I am not, however, writing from a sense of obligation, (which I can't easily fancy doing to *you*) but just because I want to tell you, my own precious Effie, how I do feel for you in this *relinquishment*. It is such a peculiar pathetic pang that one feels in throwing back on a person a love offered one – One pities them so acutely, altho' such pity seems \in the abstract/ to imply convic-tion\of one's own worth./ I cannot in the least assent to what you say about the rarity of sympathy between you and men. I know so many who {have} \feel/ such a strong attraction in you. If you had heard Mr. Ward speak about you! – – And he isn't given to enthusiasms. How I long that you cd. keep out of all this ruin just what you wish! But I imagine that it is quite impossible to transmute an affection into a friendship – unless marriage has stepped in to render the former

---

1   This date is added in a different hand in square brackets.

absolutely impossible.

I am conscious that I am writing you such a queer, stiff letter – *so* different to my feelings! But …

Monday. At this moment I am interrupted by a man turning up who had to be entertained. I do so feel for you, darling Effie. It has been so very hard for you. But for him *far* harder – The feeling that all he now craves so intensely for, was once his, if he had but had the courage to hold out his hand & ask. Did you guess nothing of what must have been passing in his mind during your Shrewsbury arbour tête-à-tête?

Alas – it shows how close people may be to their happiness, & blindness prevent them seeing it in each other's faces. Life is very tragic.

Do write to me soon. Have you heard any word about Mr. Bryce? You can't think how trying this 'total eclipse' sometimes becomes – even tho' I *don't*, or rather *oughtn't* to, distrust him for a moment.

Dear, dear Effie – how I do love you.

Ever your devoted

M.E.G.

Sender's address on writing paper is embossed.

This letter is contained in the same envelope as the previous letter to Effie, dated JA 18 1872

By Courtesy of the Wedgwood Museum, Staffordshire; W/M 408.

EFFIE WEDGWOOD

84. Plymouth Grove.
Manchester.
Jan. 28. [1872]

My own darling Effie,

I had been so looking forward to writing you a good long letter today – but I can't get a long one written this affn., and yet must not delay in sending off one, because amongst other things I want to ask you for a piece of information which I think it just possible that you can supply.

I suppose that one will now always be liable to applications for help of the sort that I have just had – now that this dreadful trouble about dearest little Willie, and its cause, is known.

I have been asked to tell, if I know – which I *don't* – and in that case to find out – whether the risk in the marriage of cousins depends upon the *mode* of relationship: it being said that it is dangerous for the children of *brothers* to marry, but not for those of *brother and sister*, or of two *sisters*. Can you tell me of anything that Dr. Radcliffe said on this point? –

The help is wanted for rather a sad case – strangely resembling *yours* in some ways. Did Dr. R. make any inquiry into *how* you were related to Godfrey? or did he, perhaps, speak only of the epilepsy of Mrs. F. W. ?

My heart is so full for you. I cannot bear to hear of your being 'low' – my own dear, dear Effie.

    Ever your most faithful
    M. E. G.

Sender's address on writing paper is embossed.

By Courtesy of the Wedgwood Museum, Staffordshire; W/M 408.

EFFIE WEDGWOOD

        84. Plymouth Grove.
        Feb. 6. 1872.

My own darling Effie,

I should have been writing to you much sooner, but have had endless business notes – (many about this Kitchen meeting) – 'multiplied into' a constant bad pain in my right wrist – I don't know whether it is rheumatism or neuralgia or gout! and is of no consequence, except as making it sometimes impossible to go on writing – I need not say that I have thought of you endlessly – & as ever most lovingly. Can you send me any information abt. the risks run when children *not* of brothers marry? My friend is so unfortunate – & I don't know how to get her this information.

Since writing to you, Brycey has been down here for his one day \

on *Friday.–*/ I do so entreat you never to tell one word of what I have told you. Can you understand how my saying this is perfectly consistent with my entire trust in you? It is as if I were hanging over a precipice, clinging to my Father's hand – I should implore him not to let go, though convinced that it was the last thing he wd. do–

I had a very pleasant little tête à tête with Mr. Boyce, who came when I told him that he wd. find me alone – & things, I *must* repeat, are exactly as if we were definitely bound to one another. (We talked over Miss Tollemache – he beginning & if I had not felt so in honour bound to seem quite ignorant of any special intimacy between them I am sure that I cd. have got even gter satisfaction that I did – For he seemed to think her merely clever, \(this he volunteered)/ to see so much of her, only because she was "the great friend of gt. friends of his" – A. Dicey did not even know her name, I found out yesterday.

Mr. Bryce asked me to write to him, & we have started a correspondence – All this, even with such virtuous young people – or rather middle aged people as we are, would not seem very proper to my mind – & made me sadly uncomfortable – I confess – if Mrs. Darbishire had not again (unintentionally) come to the rescue.

I went to stay with Mrs. Shuttleworth for two nights on Saturday, & found that Mrs. Darbishire had just been calling there – so very full of how Mr. Bryce had confided a 'deep attachment' to her – & 'told her everything but the name' which he seemed to wish her to ask, but which she cd. not screw up courage to inquire about. And – *this* is the comfort – he had said, that tho' he thought he had made his intentions quite clear, he did not feel at liberty to offer \definitely/ yet, because of his means, but that "he was most fidgety & anxious to get on at his profession for the sake of this mysterious *some one*". This is a little different from what I understood as the reason of silence from Mrs. Darbishire – but I was in such a state of trying to look unconcerned when she talked to me about it, that it quite accounts for my missing her meaning. This is a fine dose of egotism, but I reckon more than I can say on your wonderful sympathy.

Have you heard anything of Godfrey? – Pray tell me – I feel as if you must have done, by a sort of brain-wave – (Charlie Darbishire is just engaged to a girl to whom, he says, he has been attached three years! So how about his philandering at Barlaston?)

I am deeply immersed in bridesmaid troubles of dress. Why *can't* people – even sensible people – be married quietly & rationally. By the way – you once gave me leave to offer myself to you in a bold way, whenever I cd. come – As this wedding brings me up to London, might I come to you sometime after it (it is on March 14th.) –? For it, itself I am with Miss Ewart.

Of course, you will be as frankly open in refusing, if inconvenient, as I am in offering.

Ever your devoted
M. E. G.

Envelope: Miss K. E. Wedgwood.1 Cumberland Place. Regent's Park. London. N.W.

Postmark: Manchester 6 FE 72; reverse: London N.W. Fe 7 72

By Courtesy of the Wedgwood Museum, Staffordshire; W/M 408.

CHARLES ELIOT NORTON

[Manchester]
Feb. 20. 1872.

My dearest Mr. Norton,

No words can tell you how most deeply I feel for you in this awful trial. Our hearts bleed for you. I feel quite overwhelmed by it. It seems to me quite impossible to conceive anything more cruel, more terribly sad, than that our darling Susan should thus have been taken from you.[1] Dearest Mr. Norton, you will *know* how I am feeling for you – It is a bitter sorrow for every one who loved her; but for you it is the utmost of human suffering. And yet as I write those words, I feel how untrue they are and rebel against them – for your blessedness is great in proportion to your grief – the blessedness of remembering how that "beautiful soul" has been yours for all these years, and what a wealth of devotion has been given by you to her, and by her to you – and how you will meet again in the presence of God for

---

1   Norton's wife Susan died in Dresden in February 1872, within a few days of giving birth to their youngest son Richard (*Norton Letters*, ı, 415).

endless unbroken communion of love.

My heart aches for you – I cannot tell you how we all are feeling for you, dear, dear Mr. Norton. Don't think of our trouble – for that is so little in comparison –

Every moment some fresh sweetness and unselfishness of darling Susan's rises to my mind. Oh how will you bear the loss of her tender, sweet presence! The little darling children will help you – and your dear Mother and sisters will be doing their utmost for you, and if sympathy can be any consolation to you, you will have more of it than anyone can say. But beyond this, I pray so earnestly that you may have what is above and beyond all other solace – and I am sure that in this bitterest hour God will not leave you without comfort. Jane[1] says that you are bearing it with such wonderful courage and unselfishness. Who [?that] knows you could doubt it! God help you is the prayer of your most deeply sympathizing & loving

M. E. Gaskell

Houghton Library, Harvard University. MS Am 1088 2625.

CHARLES ELIOT NORTON

84 Plymouth Grove
28 December 1876

Dearest Mr. Norton,

I wish that you could know *half* the pleasure that your lovely present has given me, and then I am sure that you would be very glad. It has only just come, and I feel in such a state of impatience to thank you that I am not waiting to read it before I do so; but the *glimpses* that I have had – just peeping between the pages – convince me that a real treat of reading lies before me, and makes me long to begin it. I always like Lowell[2] exceedingly.

But even if it were *not* a present that I cared about for its own sake, it would still have given me vivid pleasure – as a proof of your think-

---

1   Norton's older sister by three years.
2   James Russell Lowell (1819–91), American writer and personal friend of Norton's. See Vanderbilt, *passim*; *OCEL*; and, for a comprehensive selection of his writings, *Poems of James Russell Lowell* (London, 1912).

ing of me just now, at this Christmas time, when somehow every gift seems to have a double value from association.

Dear me! how I wish that there was not this dreadful, wide Atlantic between Shady Hill and Plymouth Grove! How delightful it would be to run in and thank you face to face, instead of writing cold, dead words that never seem one bit to explain what one means.

Someone from Shady Hill will, I do hope, write to me soon; for I want very, very much to hear about you all.

Here everything has made our Christmas a very bright one, for all our dear ones are quite well, and – just think! – we have no cloud whatever of anxiety hanging over us at present. How few grown-up people can say that.

We are at fever point about the Eastern question, however.[1] Ld. Beaconsfield[2] was forbidden by the Queen to leave London even for Christmas Day, and many people believe that "scarlet fever near Osborne"[3] is a mere excuse for keeping her close to her ministers at Windsor. England is divided into two hostile camps of opinion – and to be "Russian" or "Turkish" means to enter into a social conflict as bitter as to be "Northern" or "Southern" in the days of your War then involved.

Everyone is busy reading Kingsley's Life.[4] It is *the* book this Christmas. There is something so inescapably pathetic in *her*, \Mrs Kingsley's/ having survived to write *his* life – when he caught his last illness in his efforts to rescue her from the death that then seemed so imminent for her – I hear that she is painfully anxious about the verdict, not on her work, but on his life as recorded in it. His daughters found it necessary to make her promise to read no critiques for fear of agitation. You know that it is a heart complaint that she suffers from.

Marianne & Thurstan are (today) removing back again to their beloved Wimbledon, their exile from which, into the modern

---

1 The Eastern Question involved a power struggle between Russia and Turkey in Eastern Europe (*ODBH*).
2 Benjamin Disraeli (1804–81), Prime Minister 1874–80, Lord Beaconsfield from 1876; he supported Turkey in her struggle against Russia (*ODNB* and *ODBH*).
3 Osborne House was Queen Victoria's private home on the Isle of Wight (*ODBH*).
4 *Charles Kingsley: His Letters and Memories of His Life,* F. E. Kingsley ed. (London, 1876). Charles Kingsley had died the previous year, 23 January 1875, after nursing his wife, Fanny, through a long illness (*ODNB*).

Babylon, has been to them as the exile of the Israelites into the Ancient Babylon. It has struck us repeatedly this resemblance – for they have never ceased mourning for the delights of their old home –

   With renewed most hearty thanks,

   Ever your aff'te

   M. E. Gaskell.

My best, best love to all who are so very dear to me at Shady Hill.

Envelope: Charles Eliot Norton Esq., Shady Hill. Cambridge. Massachusetts. U.S.A.; United States of America along the top.

Postmark: Manchester DE 29 76; back of envelope: New York, Jan 12.

Houghton Library, Harvard University. MS Am 1088 2626.

MR SMITH[1]

12 Aug. 1878.

My dear Mr. Smith,

   I never thanked you for your most kind note that I received at Buxton,[2] solely because I wished to spare you the trouble of reading an unnecessary one.

   I write now, because we are going abroad on Friday, to prevent your writing to me after that date in case you *should* by any happy chance succeed in finding a place for that boy about whom I wrote to you, as you said was just possible; for there might be endless delay, if you wrote to me. *If* you did {do} \succeed in finding him a place/, and would send *him* a note, I would answer for his betaking himself promptly to any place you might name, & I will leave everything that is necessary at his disposal here – I mean so that you will have no trouble about fare or outfit – (of course.) Outfit reminds me of trousseaux – & do you know I haven't an idea of what Dolly was "married in" or "went off in" – (so very important to the feminine mind!) – nor who were her bridesmaids, nor where she is gone for

---

1   Either George Murray Smith, or Reginald Smith a reader for Smith Elder the publishers.

2   A Derbyshire town noted for its fine architecture and beautiful surrounding countryside. Its Spa waters made it especially popular with visitors hoping to improve their health.

her wedding-tour! I have so longed for some details : & tho' of course
I couldn't ask you for them, yet if you could suggest to Ethel how
much I should care for an account of the wedding I should be more
than ever yours gratefully
    M. E. Gaskell.

CHARLES ELIOT NORTON

                        Plymouth Grove.
                        Manchester.
                        Oct. 5. 1879

Dearest Mr. Norton,
    You cannot think what a pleasure it was to find your most kind
letter here on our return a few days ago from Venice. It seemed to
have come just at the right time – (not that it could have come at a
wrong one!) – for I had been thinking so constantly of you in Venice;
and if your spoken words had not seemed still echoing in certain
places, before certain pictures, I should all the same have had you
often brought before me there, through our daily use of the copy of
the Guida di Venezia which you gave us, and in which there are your
notes – written most truly "in a fair Italian hand".
    How I should like to have a long talk with you over all we saw!
One comes away with a terrible ache in one's heart – for Venice
"in her decay" was not half so sad as Venice in her present prosperity. The Ducal palace[1] is being restored – (and it did not need
Mr. Bunny to tell us *how* badly, tho' his account of the constitution
of the Committee \for the restoration,/ of its parsimony and ignorance, explained the causes) – the Piazzetta and Riva are become the
starting-place of numberless steamers that pollute and desecrate the
quiet waters with rush of steam and smoke, and noise of screws and

---

1   Also known as the Doge's palace, constructed in the fourteenth century in the
    Gothic style, one of the city's most famous landmark buildings, formerly used as
    a centre of government; it is now preserved as a museum in which many Italian
    paintings, especially those by Titian, are hung.

engines – and all Venetian joy expresses itself now-a-days \only/ in Bengal lights of magenta \red/ and emerald green, which, however typical of Italian unity, are only a hideous repetition of the "Crystal Palace pyrotechnical fêtes.["]

Everywhere the old Venetian beauty is passing away – it is a dream already half-fled – and yet what is left is so *very* exquisite that one cannot be wholly sad. The *sunsets* no one can touch! and we had such magnificent ones – some rose and purple – with storm clouds, others all gold & scarlet – & perhaps best of all the quiet ones, without a single bar of cloud, but with the veil of gold drawn over blue – making that heavenly glow of \palest/ green that Cima uses for his backgrounds.

And then the Cimas and Bellinis![1] We went back and back and back to our favourites. – *Carpaccio*[2] it is the fashion to exalt above every one else at present, on account of what Mr. Ruskin has written about him; but except for his St. Ursula's Dream, I cannot imagine putting him on a level with Cima and Bellini. – The great Bellini in S. Giovanni [?Cistostomo] (oh dear! I have forgotten to put the 'h' in) struck me profoundly this time. Do you remember it well? St Jerome sitting on a 'mount', high up in the middle – (like the mount for the Sermon on the Mount, or for the Sacrifice of Isaac) – deeply occupied in reading his own Translation, and St. Christo*pher*, with the child, on one side, standing, & St. Augustine on the other. I didn't care for St. Jerome a bit – but the other two are most deeply beautiful. It cannot be *fancy* that they represent \St. Augustine['s]/ meditation over Evil, over the problem of Evil as an abstract mystery, and \St. Christopher/ the *practical* effort to help and overcome it; and what I think is so wonderful is Bellini's just sympathy with *both*. One is not made nobler than the other. In St Christopher's face, uplifted to the helpless tiny child, one sees the tender, wistful, earnest longing to help and shelter and {?} save, and one thinks nothing *can* be higher. And then one turns to St. Augustine – and it thrills thro' and thro' one,

---

1   Giovanni Bellini (c. 1430–1516), Italian painter of the High Renaissance; Cima da Conegliano (c. 1459–1518), influenced by Bellini and famous for altarpieces depicting the Virgin and Child (*Oxford Art Online*).

2   Vittore Carpaccio (c. 1460–1525), painter of the Venetian school (*Oxford Art Online*).

the grandeur of his faith; {?} \which seems, as one looks at him, to be reaching/ its final triumph in that celebrated sentence in the 'City of God' – I cannot remember the words, but you know which I mean, about the trust in a loving god conquering and transcending one's knowledge of the sin and suffering in this world – I like *that* Bellini, and the San Zaccania one, and the St. John the Baptist of Cima, and Cima's "Doubt of Thomas", his Baptism, and his [?] *much* better than Carpaccio's Presentation : and yet Mr. Ruskin tells you that you are to stand or fall in your own estimation, as well as, in his, by your preference of the latter to – I think *all*, other pictures at Venice. *How do you rank them*?

To turn to other things – I have been thinking so constantly of Grace[1] all this year. If I have not written, it has been that I have been so broken down in health. But I am so much stronger just now and I do hope to keep well, and tell her that I am meaning to write to her very, very soon. *Her* life seems to me a blending of St. Augustine and St. Christopher. Every day one lives, one admires such a life as hers more & more.

My father has come home from his Scotch visits much stronger, and all is going well with us. I *think* the gloom that is overhanging the country is very terrible – bad government, bad trade, a bad harvest. Here the employers are getting so embittered against the work people, (who are persisting in their strikes spite of the vast trade difficulties) and are threatening to withhold the relief this winter that they gave so generously last winter. This is answered by counter-threats. Meanwhile the outlook in the East is very dark – and the Afghan[2] difficulty is very serious. Ld. Beaconsfield (he has given up the futile attempt to get it called Beckonsfield, as he wished) still flourishes like a green bay tree, and is said to be more potent at Court than ever.

---

1   Grace Norton, one of Norton's sisters. The indications are that she remained unmarried and devoted herself to caring for her mother, who died in 1879, and to Charles Norton's children following the death of their mother.

2   Afghanistan was a troubled part of the world throughout the nineteenth century, subjected to Russian and British interests. In 1878 Britain launched its second military intervention which concluded without success in 1881 (*ODBH*). The area has continued to be politically unstable.

Ever your very affectionate
M. E. Gaskell.

Houghton Library, Harvard University. MS Am 1088 2627.

CHARLES ELIOT NORTON

Plymouth Grove.
16 Oct. 1880.

Dearest Mr. Norton,

I have just received your book[1] – I cannot tell you how delighted I am to have it; not only as a proof of your kind thought of me, but also because I see it treats of the very things of which our hearts are fullest at present. (We are only just home from Venice) and I know that in your treatment of them we shall find not only our own impressions crystallized into beautiful brilliant words, but we shall find endless *more* than we have been able to see or feel or think, and yet all so delightfully in the very same direction as the present current of our thoughts. The book looks quite delightful. I feel that it will open up a hundred points that I shall have to write to you about again. I had no notion you were writing a book; and I always think that whatever people may say of the pleasures of anticipation, it is best of all to get a present quite, quite unexpectedly – like a rose thrown suddenly in your lap. Thank you a *thousand, thousand* times.

We have so often been blessing you in our hearts lately; for at Venice we profited so much by undimmed recollections of your knowledge of critical remarks – I should like if I had time, (which I *haven't* you will see how hurriedly I am writing), to tell you of our hunting out the Titian S. Christopher on the staircase in the Ducal Palace, owing to our remembrance of you and it, and of Cav. Fabris' wonder at any strangers knowing of it – and of how thro' this incident we came to see the most splendid Georgione[2] in this old Cavaliese's[3] collection.

---

1   Charles Eliot Norton, *Historical Studies of Church Building in the Middle Ages: Venice, Siena, Florence* (New York, 1880).
2   Georgione (1477–1510), Italian High Renaissance painter who studied under Bellini (*Art Cyclopedia*).
3   A possible reference to Cavalese, a former medieval commune in Northern Italy, now a ski resort.

I was so startled to find that Lily[1] was in England. Her letter had awaited me here, and hence I received it and the news of her arrival together. She must not leave England without coming to us for a visit; and I hope that nothing may prevent this.

I know of so many people who would 'give their ears' to have your book. I am indeed lucky. I hope that I shall be as generous as I ought to be about lending it. But at present I don't feel as if I should *ever* be inclined to part with it; even when I had read & re-read it!

Give my dearest love to Grace – I think of her so often –

Ever yours affe. and *most* faithful

M. E. Gaskell

Houghton Library, Harvard University. MS Am 1088 2628.

MISS TOLLET

Rome
April 6[th.] [1881]

My dearest Miss Tollet,

You can fancy with what a welcome I greeted "Country Conversations"[2] – I have re-read nearly the whole of the book, and think it even more wonderfully entertaining than \I did/ when I was hearing it – or reading it in M.S. – I like the binding and printing very much indeed. It may be but the "Guinea's stamp" – yet I do think *outsides* matters of gt. importance. I was so pleased that when Julia began to read "Mrs. Harland", she exclaimed almost at once why – how like George Eliot it is! – Of course I made her notice the earlier date.

Mr. Bright's address is:–

Ashfield,

Knotty Ash,

Liverpool.[3]

---

1 Norton's second daughter, now aged approximately fourteen years, was named after Mrs Gaskell (*Norton Letters*, I, 155, n.1).

2 *Country Conversations*, by Georgine Tollet, first published London, 1881, comprising a collection of recollected conversations by the narrator with various country people.

3 Henry Arthur Bright built Ashfield at Knotty Ash in 1869, as a grand family home.

I shall feel so much interested to know what people think of the "Conversations". Do keep any interesting letters that you may have about the book.

There are so many people that I am planning to lend it to – if I can trust the precious volume out of my hands. It is so very good of you to let me have a copy, dearest Miss Tollet; and I thank you most heartily.

I am so very much grieved to hear about your having been so ill. I think that a "feverish influenza" is *the* most utterly wretched form of illness. How I wish that I lived near you! & cd. often call in & see you – or at any rate enquire about you! You have had a dreadful winter of suffering – and this quite dreadful east wind as a finale too. After this we really may expect some proper weather. I wonder *what* you think of the Transvaal![1] A clear & direct *Christian* act, I think the Peace – tho' it was the first thing that \ever/ stirred the Jingo within me – When people say that it is bad policy, dangerous, & so on, I think of what Mrs. Huxley sd. to Effie – "All the present trouble in the world comes from people having followed the *foolish* [?] *precept* of turning the left cheek" –

Ever your grateful & loving
M.E. Gaskell.

Shropshire Archives, 4629/1/1881/29.

PORTICO LIBRARY

Plymouth Grove.
2, July, 1884.

Dear Sir,

Will you offer to the Committee of the Portico Library the heart-felt thanks of my Sisters and myself for the Resolution passed at the

---

Visitors included the American author Nathaniel Hawthorne. The house was subsequently renamed Thingwall House and bequeathed by the Bright family to Liverpool Corporation (*Wik.*).

1   Annexed by Britain in 1877, the Transvaal regained internal autonomy in 1881, though it continued to be a trouble spot, featuring in the Boer War of 1899, until it became part of the Union of South Africa in 1910 (*ODBH*).

meeting on June 12th. – [1]

The kindness of the Committee in sending us such an expression of their sympathy has touched us most deeply.

My Father's interest in the Portico grew year by year during his long connection with the Institution; and the exceeding kindness always shown to him within its walls, and the most generous recognition of his services in Oct. 1878 deepened his feelings towards its members into a really affectionate gratitude.[2]

Manuscript of this letter to the Portico Library
(showing the above paragraph).

1   Portico Library Archives. The Minute Book records a Resolution in which the Committee unanimously records an expression of sorrow for the death of the Reverend William Gaskell, Chairman for thirty-six years; and profound sympathy with the family of Mr Gaskell. He had died aged seventy-nine.

2   This year marked William Gaskell's forty years service as a proprietor of the Portico Library and thirty years as Chairman. To mark the occasion, a bust and a portrait were commissioned. The bust, by G.W. Swynnerton, was placed on a pedestal in the Library; the portrait by Miss A. L. Robinson was presented to William as a personal gift (Brill, p. 110).

I cannot end without saying that though every day since we received it, we have learnt to take a keener pleasure in the most beautiful and life-like portrait of my Father presented to us in Oct. 1878,[1] yet that it is only since his death that we have been able to realize how priceless a gift it was to us – one for which no possible expressions of gratitude would now seem to us in the least adequate.

 With the deepest respect, I beg to remain yours truly,
 M. E. Gaskell.

Black-edged mourning paper, archived between marble boards.

Portico Library, LETTER-GASKELL 1884.

CHARLES ELIOT NORTON

Plymouth Grove –
Sunday –
13. VII. 1884.

My dear Mr. Norton,

 I did not answer your letter at once, because I was hoping so fully to plead with you for one half-hour of your precious time, as you were passing so near.

 But such presumption has been thwarted, as on Friday I feared that it might be, by \my/ being again too weak for any such pleasure – and I dare say that you could not have given it me – anyhow.

 Still it seems quite dreadful to me that a second visit to England on your part should pass without my having one glimpse of you.[2]

 I am an unfortunately faithful person!

---

1 The portrait may now be seen in the Manchester gallery of Manchester City Art Gallery; it is reproduced in Brill, p. 111.

2 Norton spent part of the summer of 1884 in England, fulfilling engagements at Emmanuel College, Cambridge, where he was awarded an honorary degree. During his stay he also made a tour of the Cathedral towns in the south east of England and visited Ruskin at Coniston. He was accompanied by members of his own family and the artist Burne-Jones's daughter, Margaret (*Norton Letters*, II, 159–62). Earlier visits to England, referred to here by Meta, included a spell in the summer of the previous year 1883 when, accompanied by his oldest son, he stayed with Ruskin, en route to the Continent and again on his return to England, before returning to America (*Norton Letters*, II, 148–50).

Your words of sympathy were so very consoling to both Julia and myself. We have felt my darling Father's death *fearfully*. I cd. not have imagined it possible beforehand that a death so "in the course of Nature", & for which we were through that fact somewhat "prepared" could have fallen with such cruel force of intense suffering – and *that*, notwithstanding such endless blessings in connection with his life & death.

My father has left us the most wonderful example – "a lovely ideal of Xian piety and duty" to quote a line out of the epitaph chosen by his Congregation for an inscribed brass at Cross St. Chapel that they are putting up to his memory. His sweet tenderness, patience and unselfish humility grew day by day more and more beautiful – and a heroic death crowned his almost perfect life.

I don't call myself "unfortunately *faith*ful," (as I have just done in one respect), as regards my still being able to cling firmly to the Xian faith, tho' I have shirked – shrunk from – *no* writing on the other side. I have suffered so terribly of late years that I at any rate can uphold my testimony 'de profundis' –

Will you put on this card the name of your Liverpool hotel,[1] in case I can carry out my intention of sending you there a little gift for dear Lily.

Ever, with Julia's love, your very affectionate friend
M.E. Gaskell.

Black-edged mourning paper and envelope.

Envelope: Charles Eliot Norton Esq. 3. Bolton Street. Piccadilly. London. W.

Postscript (on reverse side): Wd. you also most kindly put on the card your Sister's address at Cambridge U.S.A.

Postmark: Manchester JY 13 84; on reverse side: London JY 14 84.

Houghton Library, Harvard University. MS Am 1088 2629.

---

1   A letter from Norton to his oldest daughter, written on 16 July, 1884, indicates that he was staying at the city's grandest hotel, the Adelphi (*Norton Letters*, ɪɪ, 164).

MANCHESTER DISTRICT
SUNDAY SCHOOL ASSOCIATION

Plymouth Grove,
Manchester,
5 Aug. 1884

The daughters of the Revd William Gaskell beg to acknowledge with the deepest gratitude the most kind Resolution passed by the Committee of the Manchester District Sunday School Association on July 8th.

They value most truly this expression of sorrow at their Fathers' loss, and sympathy with themselves in this terrible bereavement and they will always keep the copy of the Resolution that has been so kindly sent to them.

Typescript taken from the Minute Book of Manchester District Sunday School Association.

Reproduced by courtesy of the University Librarian and Director, The John Rylands Library, The University of Manchester.

WILLIAM E. A. AXON

84 Plymouth Grove
Oct 22. [1885][1]

Dear Mr. Axon,

Would you and Miss Axon come to tea with us on Friday next at four, or a little after?

We have just settled down at home again; and getting to know your daughter was one of the pleasures that we promised ourselves on our return from the Continent.

Yours very sincerely
M. E. Gaskell.

Black-edged mourning paper.

Reproduced by courtesy of the University Librarian and Director, The John Rylands

---

1   In letters from the Axon Archives, dates given in square brackets are taken from archive records. Dates without brackets are given in the letters themselves.

Library, The University of Manchester. Axon Archive.

CHARLES ELIOT NORTON

84. Plymouth Grove.
28 October, 1886.

Dearest Mr. Norton,

I can hardly tell you what an intense pleasure it was to me to receive a copy of your "Early Letters of Thomas Carlyle" this morning.[1] It came as such a bit of brightness to me when I was ill in bed; for last Saturday when I thought myself quite well, the *gout-fiend* sprang out of his ambush, and I have lain in his clutches ever since – with a bad kind of internal gout, not a good honest big toe gout.

The only rift in the lute[2] of my pleasure in your gift consists in my not having yet written to you or Lily to say how keenly I had enjoyed and appreciated your article in the New Princeton Review,[3] but I will not let this stab of self-reproach interfere with my delight – especially as my silence has been due to great pressure of business and not in the least to ingratitude.

What a lovely book it is that you have sent me! The etching at the beginning of the first volume of Carlyle's mother is most exquisite, and every detail of type and binding is worthy of your taste. But even if the book were less precious in itself, I should value it most deeply as coming from you – After all, there is nothing to compare with one's early friendships – the sense of security is so great – and they strike their roots down into soil enriched with so many memories. When Julia took off the brown paper coverings of the parcel by my bedside this morning, and I saw from whom the books came, in an instant there flashed across me unbidden, the remembrance of your face as you smiled up at my Mother and grasped at what she was dangling from the Corso balcony in the merriment of the 1857

---

1   *Early Letters of Thomas Carlyle*, ed. by Charles Eliot Norton, 2 vols (London, 1886).
2   See Tennyson, *Vivien*, 240 'It is the little rift within the lute'; 'lute' here meaning clay or cement.
3   "Recollections of Carlyle", in *New Princeton Review*, July 1886 (*Norton Letters*, I, 434).

Carnival[1] – That smile seemed like an earnest[2] of all the sweet brightness that was to come into her life and ours through our friendship
with you and yours –

   Ever your grateful and affe.

   M. E. Gaskell.

Houghton Library, Harvard University. MS Am 1088 2630.

WILLIAM E. A. AXON

Plymouth Grove.
July 21. [1888]

Dear Mr. Axon,

   When your beautiful flowers and still more beautiful poem came
to us from St. Leonards,[3] uncertainty about your address there made
me think it better to wait before writing to thank you – and, like
all delays, nearly, this has proved longer than it was either meant or
ought to have been.

   Julia and I have a perfect passion for flowers so that your gift filled
us with a vivid gratitude. Our room was sweet and scented and beautiful with the roses you sent for nearly a fortnight.

   As to your poem – its drawback is that it makes one cry every time
one reads it –! It wrings one's heart quite with its exquisite pathos.
Sunt lacrimae rerum in Manchester with a vengeance.

   Yours most sincerely

   M. E. Gaskell.

   I wonder whether you would ever care to come & lunch quietly
with us.

Letterhead: a bird, possibly a stork, embossed.

Reproduced by courtesy of the University Librarian and Director, The John Rylands
Library, The University of Manchester. Axon Archive.

---

1   A reference to the first meeting between Meta Gaskell, in the company of her
    mother, and Charles Norton in Rome.
2   See Wordsworth, 1814, *Excursion,* 1, 815, 'When on its sunny bank the prim-
    rose flower | Peeped forth, to give an earnest of the Spring.'; 'earnest' here
    meaning foretaste.
3   A resort town near to Hastings on the south coast of England.

WILLIAM E. A. AXON

84 Plymouth Grove.
Sept. 5. [1888]

Dear Mr. Axon,

On returning home for a few days, I have found your kind invitation to the meeting about Liberia[1] which, owing to a servant's mistake, was not forwarded to me as it ought to have been.

I must thank you for it now – although so late in the day – and say how sincerely I hope that the meeting was a success.

Would a guinea be of any use?

It seems such a drop in the ocean of African needs that I hardly dare offer it!

 Yours most truly
 M. E. Gaskell.

Reproduced by courtesy of the University Librarian and Director, The John Rylands Library, The University of Manchester. Axon Archive.

WILLIAM E. A. AXON

84 Plymouth Grove.
Saturday. [Jan. 1889]

My dear Mr. Axon,

No words can rightly say how deeply Julia and I feel for you.

It is indeed *terrible* for you. However firmly one believes in the Love of God, and in a Future of reunion with those one loves, yet the pang – the agony of parting is indescribable.

Altho' it is 25 years since my mother's death, I cannot yet think calmly of it – my brain quite *reels* each time I have to recal the suffering it brought me[2] –

---

1 A public meeting was held at Manchester Town Hall on 20 August 1888 to promote support for the education of girls in Liberia. Axon had drawn attention to this event by writing to the *Manchester Guardian* on 18 August. The event was reported in the same paper on 21 August.

2 Mrs Gaskell's death in November 1865 suggests that this letter was written in 1890, rather than 1889 as attributed by the Axon archive, but the *ODNB* entry on W. E. A. Axon gives 1889 as the year his wife died. Meta's sympathy here

So that I know, I fully understand what you must be enduring.

One can but say, "May God help you to endure bravely". I felt such sympathy for your daughter, because of what she wrote about my mother. Do give her our grateful love. We had to go into town this morning, and we saw some grapes and a few flowers that we thought might be right for a sick-room, so we had them sent off –

How little we thought yesterday, as just at this time we sat expecting you, how *terribly* sad a reason was preventing your coming!

    Yours sincerely

    M. E. Gaskell.

Black-edged mourning paper.

Reproduced by courtesy of the University Librarian and Director, The John Rylands Library, The University of Manchester. Axon Archive.

KATE AXON

                84, Plymouth Grove,

                Manchester.

                April 30. [1890]

Dear Miss Axon,[1]

My sister and I are so grateful to you for letting us see your charming notice of my dearest Mother.

It is so curious that two remarks that you make, (one about the most powerful scene in "Mary Barton["], the other about "Sylvia's Lovers") precisely agree with opinions that I have often felt and expressed. This gives me a feeling of very great sympathy with you.

I do so trust that you will soon get stronger. With very kind regards,

    Yours very truly

    M. E. Gaskell.

Sender's address is embossed diagonally across left hand corner of writing paper.

---

may have been a little excessive since in 1892 Axon married again to Miss Setta Lüft, who bore him a daughter. She died in 1910, three years before Axon himself died (*ODNB* and *Manchester Guardian*, 29 December 1913, p. 5, col.1).

1   William Axon had two daughters, Sophie and Katherine, and a son, from his first marriage (*ODNB*). It may be assumed that this letter was meant for Katherine.

WILLIAM E. A. AXON

> Plymouth Grove.
> Thurs. [?SOS]
> [23 November 1890]

My dear Mr. Axon,

What a lovely face!

"Of such are the Kingdom of Heaven". Those words *rushed* into my mind directly I saw the face –

We have thought of you so very often – and sympathized with you most deeply; but until I *saw* this photograph I had no idea *what* your loss had been –

The face tells what was the spirit within, as a flame shines through a lovely lamp. She was too good for this world –

But oh *how* sad for you to have lost so enchanting a companion as she must have been![1]

Forgive great haste. I could not leave such a gift a post unacknowledged.

> Yours most truly
> M. E. Gaskell.

Black-edged mourning paper.

---

1 Axon's daughter Katherine died in October 1890.

WILLIAM E. A. AXON

84 Plymouth Grove
Jan. 9. [1891]

My dear Mr. Axon,

"The Tenants of Johnson's Court" came this morning,[1] which happened to be a specially busy morning. But having just glanced into the book, I found that I could not lay it down until I had read to the end! Everything else was forgotten.

What a *wonderful* life! What extraordinary powers! How I wish that we had ever had the privilege of seeing her!

You must have moments, amidst all your sorrow, when you are glad that this young Saint has reached the only place fit for her – Heaven.

We notice the reference to my Mother.[2]

In greatest haste,
Yours, with truest thanks,
M. E. Gaskell.

Letterhead: a bird, possibly a stork, embossed.

Reproduced by courtesy of the University Librarian and Director, The John Rylands Library, The University of Manchester. Axon Archive.

---

1   Janet Armytage, *The Tenants of Johnson's Court: And Other Tales* (London and Manchester, 1890). Katherine Janet Armytage Axon, daughter of William Axon and his first wife, born in Rusholme 1872, died from consumption at her father's home in Bowdon in 1890. This volume comprises prose tales of humble life, many of them set in the poorest quarters of nineteenth-century Manchester. Illustrations include a photograph of Katherine Axon, taken in 1884.
2   In her Introduction to *Tenants of Johnson's Court*, Beatrice Lindsay notes that the author's favourite novelists included Elizabeth Gaskell.

CHARLES ELIOT NORTON

[Plymouth Grove
Manchester]
Oct. 29. 1893

Dearest and most kind Mr. Norton,

Did my good fairy whisper to you how I was *longing* to see the Lowell letters,[1] (without ever the tiniest expectancy of having a copy of my very own)?

It was perfectly enchanting when the fat brown-paper parcel was opened yesterday – and both Julia and I went wild with delight. Of course I ought to have written at once to thank you, instead of leaving a day's delay. But I rashly peeped into the book, and became so absorbed in it that I *could* not put it down even to thank the generous giver.

I must tell you one curious little coincidence – as I "took the fences" first of all, my eye was caught by a letter to dearest Jane in 1848, which led me on to read several of that date – and I said to myself – "Surely Lowell is at his very best here – this is the perfect bloom of power and wit and feeling"; and then in reading the book "steadily", I came upon your remark to the same effect at page 61 –! – It made me feel so as if we had been talking together –

And the whole book seems to bring *you* so vividly before me – for in those old Roman days do you remember how you used to say poems of Lowell's to us? "I only know she came and went",[2] and others almost as lovely.

I was thinking of you so much the other day in Venice; to which Julia and I went for 4 days, with your copy of the "Guida" in our hands. We went to see the Titian Tobias,[3] which you had taken us to see in '57 – and I told her of that attempt of mine to talk Italian with your learned priest, which I am sure that you have courteously

---

1 *Letters of James Russell Lowell*, ed. by Charles E Norton, 2 vols (New York, 1893).

2 From 'She Came and Went', *Poems of James Russell Lowell*, Oxford Edition (London, 1912), p. 125.

3 A likely reference to Titian's *Tobias and the Angel* (1470–75), now believed to have been painted by one of Titian's pupils, to conceal an earlier, incomplete work by Titian (*Daily Telegraph*, 17 September 2005).

forgotten.

These "Letters" will be a most precious possession to me all my life; and they come at such an opportune moment – I am rather out of health, though ever so much better than last winter, and consequently I am very dependent on books – and then, too, we are living under such a pall of gloom here in the North, owing to this fearful coal-strike[1] – All industry is paralysed, and the bitterness of feeling is, if possible, worse than the material suffering – So that anything that brightens life is doubly welcome just now; and what *can* brighten life like a most charming gift from a faithful friend –

Ever your grateful and affectionate
M. E. Gaskell.

Houghton Library, Harvard University. MS Am 1088 2631.

WILLIAM E. A. AXON

Plymouth Grove
6 Jan. 94.

Dear Mr. Axon,

An autumn of hard and anxious work, varied only by "bouts" of illness, have prevented *my* giving *our*selves the pleasure of asking you to come here some day to talk over the Bibliography.[2] But I do hope that when we return home – we are just leaving Manc[r]. for a few weeks – you will fulfil your kind promise of coming here.

I write in bed – out of reach of *unhalved* paper[3] – Pray forgive.

I enclose a *donation* for your Temperence Society.[4]

We have been so grieved to hear of the great sorrow that befell you

---

1 The strike, which was widely reported in national newspapers, originated in the South Wales coalfields, when hauliers demanded higher wages, thus disrupting supplies of coal to industry. For detailed accounts of this dispute see the *Observer*, 27 August 1893, p. 7, col.5, and, for the end of the strike, the *Observer*, 19 November 1893, p. 5, col.5.

2 Meta and her sister Julia co-operated with Axon on his Bibliography of Elizabeth and William Gaskell's published works.

3 This letter is written on a small semi-stiff piece of paper.

4 Temperance societies were a feature of nineteenth-century Manchester.

last year.[1] It makes me wonder whether or not I ought to send you and Mrs. Axon[2] wishes for a happy New Year – But there are worse sorrows than even those that Death brings.

Yours very truly
M. E. Gaskell.

WILLIAM E. A. AXON

84, Plymouth Grove,
Manchester.
12 Nov. 94.

Dear Mr. Axon,

We have been away from home again, and on our return I found your pretty "Ancoats Skylark" awaiting me.[3] "It brightened all the room". It is so pleasant to receive a gift and a token of good will.

I would not write to thank you until I had read the Poems; feeling sure that in this case the prudent plan of writing before reading was unnecessary!

They touch me to the quick.

Do you think that the Poor suffer as much as the Rich do in remembering their misery? I *don't*.

"Wee Jessie" is a terrible tragedy[4] – But many of them are beautiful –

Yours most truly
M. E. Gaskell.

Sender's address embossed on right-hand side of small semi-stiff piece of paper.

---

1   This event has not been traced.
2   A reference to the second Mrs Axon.
3   William E. A. Axon, *The Ancoats Skylark and Other Verses*, Original and Translated. (Manchester and London, 1894).
4   *Ancoats Skylark*, pp. 39–43. 'Wee Jessie' carries echoes of some of William Gaskell's poetry, since it focuses on alcohol abuse and the brutal killing of a child by her drunken father.

Library, The University of Manchester. Axon Archive.

WILLIAM E. A. AXON

The Sheiling.
Silverdale.
Carnforth.
1 June, 1895.

Dear Mr. Axon,

We are most grateful to you – We should like 50 copies, and I will send you *or* Heywood[1] the 10/6 as most suitable – if you will kindly let me have a card to say to *which* –

We have a copy of Beard's Hymnal[2] at home; but we do not think that the maid left there could find it – so I am writing to Mr. Steinthal,[3] asking him to send you on loan *his* copy.

Mr. and Mrs. Hawke were speaking so charmingly of you and Mrs. Axon the other day that I must *betray* them!

Yours very sincerely
M. E. Gaskell.

Sender's address embossed in capitals on right-hand side of notepaper.

Reproduced by courtesy of the University Librarian and Director, The John Rylands Library, The University of Manchester. Axon Archive.

---

1 Heywood was a well-known Manchester publisher of the time. The price quoted here is approximately fifty pence in decimal currency.

2 *A Collection of Hymns for Public and Private Worship*, compiled by John R. Beard (London and Manchester, 1837). Beard (1800–76) was a Unitarian Minister at Salford and friend of William Gaskell (*Early Years*, p. 410). The hymns in this collection were compiled as an alternative to Trinitarian and Calvinistic psalmody. William Gaskell contributed more than seventy hymns to this collection.

3 Unitarian minister at Cross Street Chapel; he had conducted William Gaskell's funeral service in 1884 (Brill, pp. 112 and 117, and Payne, p. 123).

WILLIAM E. A. AXON

> The Sheiling,
> Silverdale,
> Carnforth.
> June 26. [1895]

My dear Mr. Axon,

Julia and I send you the enclosed £15, as our promised contribution to the collection of my dearest Mother's books, etc., for the Moss Side Library.[1]

> Yours most truly
> M. E. Gaskell.

Written on a small piece of semi-stiff paper, with sender's address handwritten.

Reproduced by courtesy of the University Librarian and Director, The John Rylands Library, The University of Manchester. Axon Archive.

WILLIAM E. A. AXON

> 84, Plymouth Grove,
> Manchester.
> 2 April, 96.

Mr dear Mr. Axon,

After *great* searching of heart, we have decided *against* Moss Side; but literally no words can say how touched my sister and I have been by your *most* kind thought and plan of commemorating my darling Mother –

We have asked the opinion of two representative men, on whose judgment we can rely – And they have most strongly advised us, if we can*not* get a place in the Whitworth Gallery,[2] to have a "museum" in some more central place, either attached to the (central) Free Library, or in some little independent habitation.

We *do* feel so grateful to you, dear Mr. Axon! As the older of the

---

1   This was the forerunner of what came to be known as The Gaskell Collection, subsequently kept at Manchester City Reference Library. See Christine Lingard, 'The Gaskell Collection in Manchester Central Library', *GSJ*, 2 (1988), 59–75.

2   Whitworth Art Gallery, on Oxford Road, near to Manchester University.

two men we consulted said, "If you could *always* have a Mr. Axon, it would be different" – But later on, – Heaven grant many years hence! – the management might be all so changed – –

We shall hope still to help you about the Library, dear Mr. Axon. Shall we make ourselves responsible for all first editions? or would you like a fixt sum?

I write with a bad headache – Pray forgive any stupidities or inadequacies.

With kindest regards to Mrs. Axon from us both[.]

Yours most gratefully

M. E. Gaskell.

Sender's address embossed on right-hand side of small semi-stiff piece of paper.

Reproduced by courtesy of the University Librarian and Director, The John Rylands Library, The University of Manchester. Axon Archive.

WILLIAM E. A. AXON

84, Plymouth Grove.
Monday, 23rd. [1896]

Dear Mr. Axon,

Would it be possible for you to come next Monday or Tuesday about noon, for that talk? and would you most kindly bring some plans of the building with you?

It would not signify *how* rough.

Yours most truly

M. E. Gaskell.

Reproduced by courtesy of the University Librarian and Director, The John Rylands Library, The University of Manchester. Axon Archive.

WILLIAM E. A. AXON

Silverdale –
Carnforth.
July 6. [1898]

My dear Mr. Axon,

This postal order has been waiting \to go to you/ for sometime – but I hoped to see the books first, and that seems impossible just at present.

No words can say how grateful both Julia and I feel to you for what you have done.

It will be what all our lives we shall owe you a great debt for.

Yours most truly
M. E. Gaskell.

Reproduced by courtesy of the University Librarian and Director, The John Rylands Library, The University of Manchester. Axon Archive.

CHARLES ELIOT NORTON

84. Plymouth Grove,
Manchester.
15 Nov. 1898.

My dear Mr. Norton,

I thought it just possible that you might care to see the enclosed, which appeared yesterday in the very widely-circulated "*Manchester Guardian*".[1] I am also directing to be sent you – straight from the photographer's – a photograph taken from a Della Robbia[2] plaque which

---

1   Our own correspondent, 'Professor C. E. Norton on the "New America"', *Manchester Guardian*, 14 November 1898, p. 10, col.1. This is a report of an address Norton gave to the Harvard Graduates' Club in Cambridge, Massachusetts, in which he endorsed his country's need for increased military power in the light of war with Spain. War had been declared between the United States and Spain in April that year, ostensibly to relieve Cuba from a corrupt Spanish rule. Norton had initially seen this war as unjust and had advised young men against enlisting, bringing upon himself charges of traitorous behaviour. For reports of this episode in Norton's life see *Norton Letters*, ii, especially 259–61; 266; 270–73 and 457–59.

2   Luca della Robbia (1400–82) founded a family workshop in Florence famous for

Julia and I picked up . . . (do you say *picked up* when you have given a large sum for it in a well known shop!) . . . this spring at Venice; and which we have "presented" to the Whitworth Institute here.

Though I assure you I do not write for that reason, it would be a *great* satisfaction to me to know whether you think it a Luca, an Andrea, or a Giovanni.[1] There has been a great discussion amongst experts –

Marianne has been terribly ill for three months this year; but she is recovering – Julia and I are so happy together that we felt it quite strange that such a dark shadow should fall on us!

Are you never coming to Europe again? Oh *what* a welcome we would give you here, if you would ever enter these doors again.

Your most faithful and affecte. old friend,
M. E. Gaskell.

Houghton Library, Harvard University. MS Am 1088 2632.

WILIAM E. A. AXON

84, Plymouth Grove,
Manchester.
Feb. 27. [1899]

NO![2]
Dear Mr. Axon,
Could you possibly tell me who the "Miss Tyler of cleanly memory" was, referred to in "*Cranford*" in one of the first pages?
I should be *so* grateful to you, if you could.
Yours most truly
M. E. Gaskell.

Sender's address embossed on writing paper.

Reproduced by courtesy of the University Librarian and Director, The John Rylands Library, The University of Manchester. Axon Archive.

---

its terra cotta sculptures (*Oxford Art Online*).
1 Andrea was Luca della Robbia's nephew; Giovanni was his grand-nephew (*Oxford Art Online*).
2 This appears to be a later annotation, and not in Meta's hand.

CHARLES ELIOT NORTON

[Manchester]
April 26. [1900]
Miss Gaskell.[1]

My dear Mr. Norton,

To think that you are coming once more to England! It is too delightful.

My pleasure is an unselfish one, for I have so little hope that you will be able to spare any time away from Brantwood and London – (I know the sacred errand on which you come).[2]

Still perhaps I might catch a glimpse of you at some railway station or on some landing-stage; and I feel as if I would travel anywhere just to look once more on the face that smiled up at my mother – on the Corso balcony – *43* years ago![3]

We have so many memories in common. At any rate whether I and Julia see you or not, this is a heart-felt "welcome to England". You come at such a terrible time for us – the Indian famine and the war[4] make a fearfully dark background to one's life.

Ever your affectionate old friend
M. E. Gaskell.

This needs no answer – You will be overwhelmed with writing.

Envelope: T*o await arrival*. Charles Eliot Norton Esq. L.L.D. c/o A. Severn Esq. Brantwood, Coniston. R.S.O.

Postmark: AP 26 [19]00

Houghton Library, Harvard University. MS Am 1088 2633.

---

1 Written in a hand other than Meta's.
2 Norton was coming to England to carry out his duties as literary executor to John Ruskin, who had died in January that year. For Norton's account of this visit see *Norton Letters,* ii, 291 and 293–95.
3 A reference to the Italian holiday when Meta first met Charles Norton.
4 Famine was a recurring feature of life in India during the eighteenth and nine-teenth centuries; the one referred to here lasted from the summer of 1899 to the end of 1900 and resulted in more than a million fatalities in British prov-inces (*Wik.*). The war referred to here would have been between the British Government and the Boers in Africa, lasting from October 1899 to May 1902 (*ODBH*).

CHARLES ELIOT NORTON

[Manchester]
13, June 1900.

Miss Gaskell.[1]

My dear Mr. Norton,

How can I thank you enough for your 'lovely' note; which will be the best consolation for me, if I do *not* see you.

I should have written before to thank you for it; but I have been ill again with a fresh *fierce* attack of influenza – It has been a regular plague in Manchester this year, and we have lost one or two friends by it.

We are going away on Friday; but *three days' notice* would bring us hurrying back to receive you and Sally[2] –

If she does not come this time, please beg her to let us have a visit from her when next she is in England.

I am so delighted that Oxford is going to make you a D. C. L.[3] – It will honour itself as well as you by so doing –

With heartfelt thanks for your kind words, I am ever your grateful and affectionate friend,

M. E. Gaskell.

Envelope: C. E. Norton Esq. Brantwood, Coniston Lake. R.S.O.

Postmark: (partly obliterated):13 [19]00

Houghton Library, Harvard University. MS Am 1088 2634.

---

1   Written in a hand other than Meta's.
2   Norton's eldest daughter, Sara Grace, often referred to as Sally, born September 1865.
3   Norton was awarded an honorary degree from Oxford University in 1900.

HENRY GUPPY[1]

The Sheiling,
Silverdale,
Carnforth
Sept 21st [1901]

Dear Mr Guppy,

Miss Norton,[2] a daughter of Professor Charles Eliot Norton of Harvard, is coming to us next week, and we were wondering whether you would care to come and meet her at luncheon next Saturday, at 1.30?

There would be no one else. She is very bright, like all American girls, and "knows" everyone.

You have twice over been so *very* kind in showing our friends the treasures over which you reign – but Miss Norton will not have time, unfortunately, to visit the John Rylands Library.

Yours very sincerely,
M.E. Gaskell.

It is, of course, at our Manchester home – 84 Plymouth Grove – that we hope to have the pleasure of seeing you.

Reproduced by courtesy of the University Librarian and Director, The John Rylands Library, The University of Manchester. JRL/1901/178.

WILLIAM E. A. AXON

84, Plymouth Grove.
New Year's Eve. [1901]

My dear Mr. Axon,

I am afraid that you will have thought us very ungrateful for not having yet acknowledged your beautiful Christmas gift of the Treasury of Translations.[3] But the truth is that I waited to thank you

1 Henry Guppy (1861–1948) was Librarian at the John Rylands Library, Manchester, from 1900 to 1948.
2 Probably Norton's eldest daughter. She was by now aged thirty-six, but as late as 1899 she was still addressed as 'Miss' (*Norton Letters,* II, 280).
3 W. E. A. Axon and Albert Broadbent, *A Treasury of Translations. Verse*; published in Manchester; reprinted 1903. I am grateful to Christine Lingard for this information.

for it until I could at the same time fix a date for meeting you at the Moss Side Library.

It is literally the case that only a quarter of an hour ago did our plans clear themselves sufficiently for me to name a morning – would Monday next, at 11.30, suit you? Please send just a post-card with a 'yes' or 'no' on it.

We are looking forward very much indeed to looking at the Collection with you. It is very kind indeed of you to have proposed it.

How beautiful your translations are, dear Mr. Axon, and what a wonderful man you are to be able to do so much so perfectly!

With our united best New Year greetings to you and Mrs. Axon, I am ever yours sincerely

M. E. Gaskell.

WILLIAM E. A. AXON

84, Plymouth Grove,
Manchester.
[19 Aug. 1902]

My dear Mr. Axon,

Your report of the Moss Side Public Library is *most* interesting.

Should Julia and I send you a little more money to spend on the Gaskell Colln.?

It would be a real pleasure to us.

In gt. haste,
Yours most truly
M. E. Gaskell.

Sender's address embossed on right hand side.

WILLIAM E. A. AXON

84, Plymouth Grove,
Manchester.
Aug. 25. 1902.

Thank you, dear Mr. Axon, for your very kind note. I enclose £10 from my sister Julia, and £10 from myself.

Please be so very good as to send one word of acknowledgment of safe receipt to the
Euston Hotel,
London.

We are just going abroad. On our return (in Septr.) we should be delighted to go with you to the Moss Side Library.
Yours most truly
M. E. Gaskell.

Written on a half sheet, with sender's address embossed on the right-hand side.

Reproduced by courtesy of the University Librarian and Director, The John Rylands Library, The University of Manchester. Axon Archive.

WILLIAM E. A. AXON

84, Plymouth Grove.
13 Feb. 1903.[1]

My dear Mr. Axon,

Miss Hallé, Sir Charles's daughter and biographer, is extremely anxious for literary reasons to find out something about a Marchera Campana dei Cavelli, and it struck us that of all living people you would be able to *procure* the information. Even you, I fancy, would hardly know without seeking!

Miss Hallé has tried to find out what she wants at the John Rylands Library, the British Museum and in Paris and Florence – in vain! *Rome* is still unsearched.

I put over the page what she has written out for us.[2] You will earn

---

1   Address and date written in Meta's hand across the top of the page.

2   "Marchera Campana dei Cavelli, who, in 1871, published 'Les Dermiers Stuarts

her keenest gratitude (as well as ours), if you can help her.

> Yours most truly
> *M. E. Gaskell*

Reproduced by courtesy of the University Librarian and Director, The John Rylands Library, The University of Manchester. Axon Archive.

WILLIAM E. A. AXON

> 84, Plymouth Grove,
> Manchester.
> Wednesday Night
> [18 Feb 1903][1]

My dear Mr. Axon,

You are as kind as you are clever!

You sound to have thought of an excellent source of information, and I am forwarding your card to Miss Hallé in Paris.

I know how grateful she will be for the trouble that you are so kindly taking, whether it is eventually successful or not.

> Yours most sincerely
> M. E. Gaskell.

Sender's address embossed to the right hand side.

Reproduced by courtesy of the University Librarian and Director, The John Rylands Library, The University of Manchester. Axon Archive.

---

a Saint-Germain-en-Laye' Is she still alive? and where? If she is no longer living, who and where are her heirs 'or representatives'? She was an Englishwoman by birth, as she says in her preface, but does not give her maiden name".

1 The Axon archive gives 13 Feb for this date, but 18 Feb makes more sense since it follows on from the previous letter dated 13 February by Meta.

WILLIAM E. A. AXON

> S. Juan les Pius
> 23 March, 1903.
> but just going on to the
> Hôtel Bella Vista,
> Bordighera,
> Italy.

My dear Mr. Axon,

The above address will explain the delay in my thanking you for your most kind help for Miss Hallé. I am *most* grateful to you for it – and am at once forwarding your letter and Contessa Venniti's to Miss Hallé in Paris.

I am sure that it will be of the greatest assistance to her to know that Marchera Campana is *dead*. For in spite of all her researches, she has hitherto failed to discover that very important point.

As we are just starting for the train, I have to write with great curtness, but must assure you once more of the warm gratitude that I feel, and which I am sure that Miss Hallé must most heartily join in.

> Most truly yours
> M. E. Gaskell.

CLEMENT KING SHORTER

> 84, Plymouth Grove,
> Manchester.
> April 28 [1903][1]

Dear Mr. Shorter,

We got back from Italy late last night; and we looked at once among the letters waiting for us, hoping to find one that would tell us on which day you were coming down to Manchester.

I think that I {had} said in my last note – (which perhaps has not

---

1   Meta and Julia were in Italy in March 1903, see letter to W. E. A. Axon dated 23rd March 1903.

reached you) – that the 13th., 14th., 15th., or 16th. of May would suit us –

But I dare say that your engagements make one of those dates impossible for you – in which case, we would try and arrange a later day, although one of those would be the most convenient to us –

You referred to our Stevenson forbears – we can tell you one rather interesting thing about them, which has never yet been published –

Pray forgive my troubling you with this inquiry as to the date of your visit.

> Yours very truly
> M. E. Gaskell –

I am still reeling with the fatigue of our long journey; but I *hope* that I have written clearly, though I am not sure.

The Brotherton Collection. Leeds University Library. BC MS 19c Gaskell, MS 16.

WILLIAM E. A. AXON

> The Sheiling,
> Silverdale,
> Carnforth.
> May 23. 03

My dear Mr. Axon,

Can you out of your infinite kindness and knowledge tell me *where* "Mr Harrison's Confessions" first appeared?[1] i.e. what are "the other sources" referred to in your Bibliography?

Do not take any trouble about it – whatever – Only if you *already* know, most kindly send a post-card to "the above address", which here ought to read "on the other side".[2]

> Most sincerely yours
> M. E. Gaskell.

Please forgive an epidemic of *blots!*

---

1   'Mr Harrison's Confessions', by Elizabeth Gaskell, first appeared in *The Ladies Companion and Monthly Magazine*, III, 1851 (Sharps, p. 113 and n.1).

2   This was written on a postcard with the Silverdale address printed on the right-hand side.

WILLIAM E. A. AXON

The Sheiling,
Silverdale,
Carnforth.
May 26 [1903]

My dear Mr. Axon,

Thank you most warmly for your kindness abt. "Mr Harrison's Confessions".

We came down here last Friday –

We are so sorry to have missed seeing you and Mrs Axon –

We should have liked so much to hear whether you already *had* been, or were going – *when* you were – to Italy – And we should have been so glad to know that you were better – Are you?

We have suffered ourselves so much from weakness after influenza that we can indeed sympathize with you.

With heartiest thanks for your help, and kindest regards to Mrs. Axon, I am,

Yours most truly
M. E. Gaskell.

Reproduced by courtesy of the University Librarian and Director, The John Rylands Library, The University of Manchester. Axon Archive.

WILLIAM E. A. AXON

The Sheiling,
Silverdale,
Carnforth.
3 June, 1903.

My dear Mr. Axon,

Julia and I are getting rather anxious about your health.

Pray do not run the risk of working on too long.

In our own experience we know of more than one case where such heroism has been *punished* instead of rewarded.

I feel very guilty to have troubled you at all. Peccavi.[1]

---

1   'I have sinned'.

I do not *remember* my Mother's having written an article on the Civil War in America;[1] but there is no inherent improbability, as her sympathies for the North were most keen, and fostered by our dear American friends who were all on that side.

Yours most truly

M. E. Gaskell.

Do take to heart my words about your health and work.

Reproduced by courtesy of the University Librarian and Director, The John Rylands Library, The University of Manchester. Axon Archive.

JOHN ALBERT GREEN

August 14th 1903.

Dear Mr. Green

I cannot tell you how very grateful we are to you for your kindness in sending us a copy of the Handlist of the Gaskell Collection at the Moss Side Library.[2] Nor can I say how very carefully and beautifully I think that you have compiled it. Pray accept our very heartiest thanks for the care and pains that you have bestowed on it.[3]

. . . .

I am, yours very truly

M. E. Gaskell.

Taken from a handwritten transcription in the Gaskell Collection, Manchester, with the following annotation: Extract from a letter to J. A. Green from Miss M. E. Gaskell.

Manchester Libraries, Information and Archives, Gaskell Collection, Box 3 File 3C.

---

1   The article in question may have been Mrs Gaskell's obituary for Robert Gould Shaw, son of a wealthy Federal family who gave his life fighting for the Northern cause. The obituary was published in *Macmillan's Magazine*, December 1863 (Sharps, p. 445–6 and nn.1–8).

2   *A Hand-List of the Gaskell Collection*, compiled by J. A. Green, Librarian. Published at the Library, Corner of Bradshaw Street, Moss Side. Manchester. 1903. William Donkin Jnr. Printer.

3   The *Hand-List* is a comprehensive catalogue of all works published by Elizabeth Gaskell and by William Gaskell, together with titles of associated biographical and critical material. A copy in the Gaskell Collection, Manchester, is bound in blue boards, with *Moss Side Gaskell Collection* in gold letters on the spine.

LUCY HENRIETTA CROMPTON[1]

84. Plymouth Grove,
Manchester.
May 31. [1905]

My dear Mrs. Crompton,

It was exceedingly kind of you to write to me, and to send us dear Harry's "Criminal Justice."[2] I should have certainly written before now to thank you, had I not had to deal with a great mass of rather anxious business-correspondence, which made it quite necessary for me to take on no extra-writing, as my right-arm is so weak that often for months together I have been unable to use a pen.

Please forgive this long explanation! It is only to account for the delay in my writing – which, at the same time, I am *sure* that you would never have attributed to ingratitude –

The delay has been enabled me to read the pamphlet, and I cannot tell you how deeply it has impressed me. It gives one such an insight into the underlying principles of Law – It is so philosophical and logical, and yet put in such terse, pithy sentences that there can be no one incapable of understanding it.

Reading it has so carried me back to the days when Harry and my Mother had such long talks together; and when his friendship was such a pleasure in her life.

It would have given us such great happiness to have seen Paul once more.[3]

London is a most tantalizing place – holding within it so many people and things that one wants to see; but so many out of reach at the right moment.

I could hardly believe in Paul's *four* babies! Do please give him our love when you next write to him, and with the same to yourself, believe me to be,

---

1   Née Lucy Henrietta Romilly.
2   *Our Criminal Justice*, republished with an introduction by Sir Kenelm Digby (London, 1905).
3   Paul Crompton (1871–1915), son of Henry and Lucy Henrietta Crompton, married Gladys Schwabe in 1900. The couple had six children, all of whom perished with their parents and nurse in the sinking of the SS Lusitania in 1915 (http://www.jjhc.info/cromptonpaul1915.htm).

Ever very sincerely yours,
M. E. Gaskell.

© British Library Board. Add Mss. 71701, ff.64–67.

WILLIAM E. A. AXON

Switzerland.
Sept. 20. [05]

We have just received your note here, with its *invaluable* information.

I dare not on a card put all that we feel of sympathy (*and more*) for you on your "retirement". How we shall miss your writings in the columns of the Manr. Guardian! – I shall write fully soon.

M. E. Gaskell.

Postcard.

Address: W. E. A. Axon Esq., 6. Cecil St., Green Heys, MANCHESTER. ENGLAND.

Postmarks: [R.H. corner] Luzern 20. IX. 05 – 4 BRF. AUFG. [L.H. corner] GRAND HOTEL GÖSCHENEN [L.H.corner] MANCHESTER 11.30 pm SP. 21 05 20.

Reproduced by courtesy of the University Librarian and Director, The John Rylands Library, The University of Manchester. Axon Archive.

THOMAS SECCOMBE

The Sheiling
Silverdale
Carnforth
Sept 9 [?1906]

Please return Mrs Clifford's letter – and most kindly let me know whether or not you mean to interpolate those words of mine about Mrs Lumb – ? in your "Sylvia's Lovers".

I hear praise from so many people of your Bookman article.[1]

Unsigned, written on a card (no border on card) in a black-edged envelope.

---

1   A possible reference to *The Bookman*, September 1906, pp. 76–78.

Address: Thomas Seccombe. 18 Perryn Road, Acton, London. W

Postmark: Carnforth PM SP 9

Reproduced by courtesy of the University Librarian and Director, The John Rylands Library, The University of Manchester. Sharps Collection.

CHARLES GREEN[1]

The Sheiling
Silverdale
Carnforth
14. 1X. 06

From the two Miss Gaskells – (we hate "the Mi*sses* G."!)

You will receive copies of all the volumes of the New Edition from us, for the Library; *but please don't think it necessary* to acknowledge each volume[.]

Postcard with black and white engraving of the Sheiling (shown above) in the top right-hand corner of the card.

Address: Charles Green Esq., Moss Side Free Library, Moss Side, Manchester.

Postmark: Carnforth 9.30. pm SP 14 06

Manchester Libraries, Information and Archives, Gaskell Collection, Box 4.

---

1   Charles Green has not been identified. The content and date of this letter suggest that it was meant for John Albert Green, Moss Side librarian from 1897 and subsequently Librarian for Special Collections Manchester Public Library (*Manchester Public Free Libraries List of Librarians, Assistants, etc*). See also Julia Gaskell's letter to J. A. Green, postmark July 10 1906.

LADY RITCHIE[1]

84. Plymouth Grove,
Manchester.
11 Nov. 1907.

Dear Madam,

I beg to enclose you £5.00 for the Memorial to dear Mr. George Murray Smith.

Please let me say, as emphatically as I can, what *real* pleasure it would give me to send more, if needed later on.

Yours very faithfully
M. E. Gaskell.

© British Library Board. Millar Bequest f.47.

CLEMENT KING SHORTER

84, Plymouth Grove,
Manchester.
17 March, '08.

Dear Mr. Shorter,

I am still so weak after a very bad attack of influenza that it is with some difficulty that I answer your letter – But I want at once to let you know that you may keep the Holland[2] book until you have finished with it; when, of course, we should require it back, as it is not to be bought.

We shall always be glad to answer definite questions; but we know nothing whatever about the first meeting /(with his future wife,[)]\ or the subsequent "wooing" of my Grandfather, Mr. Stevenson –

Very probably, he went from Dobb Lane to preach at Knutsford,

---

1   Anne Isabella Thackeray Ritchie (1837–1919). Oldest surviving daughter of novelist Wm. M. Thackeray, she married her cousin Richmond Ritchie in 1877, becoming Lady Ritchie following her husband's knighthood in 1907 (*ODNB*). The British Library attributes this letter to Lady Ritchie, but there is no envelope.
2   'Holland' was the maiden name of Elizabeth Gaskell's mother, before she married William Stevenson. The Holland book referred to here may be a history of the Holland family which was privately printed in Edinburgh in 1902 (*Early Years*, p. 439).

and was invited to stay at the Hollands' – We are starting for the South early on Friday; but any letters would be forwarded to us.

Yours very faithfully

M. E. Gaskell.

The Brotherton Collection, Leeds University Library. BC MS 19c Gaskell, MS 16.

CHARLES ELIOT NORTON

The Sheiling.
[Silverdale]
Aug. 5. [?1908]

Forgive *haste.* [1]

I cannot wait one single post without thanking you for your *most delightful* letter. [2]

What immense pleasure you have brought into my life! I once thought of coming over to America to see you!! Marks of astonishment are all right there, as the doctor has *quite* forbidden such a venture.

M. E. G.

(view from the Sheiling Drawing room)

Photocopy of this document indicates that the message is started on one side of a Post Card and continued on a plain card. The view of the drawing room may be on the reverse side of the first Card. Neither card bears an address; nor is there an envelope.

Houghton Library, Harvard University. MS Am 1088 2638.

---

1   This line is written across the left hand corner of the postcard, probably added as a postscript.
2   This may refer to a letter dated 24 July 1908, in which Norton looks back to their first meeting in Rome in 1857 (*Norton Letters*, ii, 409–13).

CHARLES ELIOT NORTON

Miss Gaskell[1]

84, Plymouth Grove,
Manchester.
Oct. 18. 1908.

My dearest Mr. Norton,

My thoughts are so constantly with you that I must send you another line of deep, deep sympathy in your suffering and illness –

I hear that you bear all the weariness and weakness with such extraordinary patience and courage; and this seems to put the crown on your wonderful life –

You have given such untold joy and help to others that it is no wonder that so many are watching with you in most grateful solicitude.[2]

God bless you –
Ever yours
M. E. Gaskell.
Julia's most sympathizing love –

Envelope: C. E. Norton Esq. D.S.L., Shady Hill, Cambridge, Massachusetts, U.S. of America.

Postmark: Manchester 8.30 pm OCT 18 08

Houghton Library, Harvard University. MS Am 1088 2635.

WILLIAM E. A. AXON

84. Plymouth Grove –
3. XII. 08.

My dear Mr. Axon,

Your words of kindest sympathy came so swiftly that it must have seemed very strange to you that they \have/ remained so long unanswered – but I am sure that you will attribute this delay to anything but ingratitude.

I had a bad accident which made the doctor forbid me to write for some weeks; and this has been the cause of so many of the letters that

---

1 Written in a hand other than Meta's.
2 Charles Norton died on 21 October 1908 (*Norton Letters*, II, 423).

I cared for most even having had no acknowledgment.

My darling Sister was curiously like my Mother in many ways – She was a "creature of delight", so beautiful and sweet and out-wardly, and within extraordinarily good and noble –

She is spared some things that she much dreaded – and she was taken[1] before any power or quality had been dimmed by age –

For me the loss is quite beyond words –

There is left for me \in this life/ only "endless sorrow" – but I believe in the Life Eternal, and in the Mercy of God – and {?} in a blessed reunion.

Please thank Mrs. Axon for her messages, and believe me ever gratefully yours

M. E. Gaskell.

Back edged mourning paper.

Reproduced by courtesy of the University Librarian and Director, The John Rylands Library, The University of Manchester. Axon Archive.

JOHN ALBERT GREEN

The Sheiling,
Silverdale,
Carnforth.
Sept. 13. [1909]

I have not read the book to which you refer; but from what I have heard of it I do not think I should care to give it to the Library.

I shall be delighted to see you in Octr. –

M. E. Gaskell.

Postcard.

Address: J. A. Green Esq., Moss Side Free Library, Manchester.

1   Julia Bradford Gaskell, Meta's sister, and the youngest of William and Elizabeth Gaskell's children, died peacefully in her sleep on the 23rd of October 1908, just two days after the death of Charles Norton, causing a double sorrow for Meta. Julia was buried at Brook Street Chapel, Knutsford. Meta was unable to attend the funeral service because of the accident referred to in this letter. For accounts of Julia's death and funeral see the *Manchester Guardian,* 26 October 1908, p. 14, col.2; 27 October 1908, p. 14, col.2 and 28 October 1908, p. 14, col.3.

Postmark: Carnforth 1.pm SP 13, 09.

Manchester Libraries, Information and Archives, Gaskell Collection, Box 4.

CLEMENT KING SHORTER

dictated

84 Plymouth Grove.
Nov. 25[th.] 1909.

Dear Mr Shorter.

Thank you for your kind enquiries. I am sorry to say that I am not at all well, & therefore have to write by dictation.

I am trusting to your promise to let me read over your manuscript of the English Men of Letters book before it is put into type, as this might possibly save some erroneous statement. I feel specially keen about this because of a mistake made in Mr. Seccombe's introduction. In that he says that after her Father's death my Mother was sent out into the world to earn her own living, & that she went to Mr. Turner of Newcastle in order to do so. The fact was that her aunt Mrs Lumb's house was always a real home to her, & that she returned to live there like a daughter to her aunt. The relation between my Mother & her aunt was really of the closest & tenderest nature – Her stay in Newcastle in two successive winters was just the ordinary visit of a girl to her connections – Visits in those days were very long when journies were so tedious. In each case she went on to pay visits to friends of her Father's & Mother's in Edinburgh. Except for the above fact I have nothing different to say.

I was so deeply touched by a few words to your introduction to "Cranford".[1]

> With kind remembrances to Mrs. Shorter, believe me
> Yours very sincerely
> M. E. Gaskell
> by E.G.N.

Black-edged mourning paper.

---

1   Clement Shorter, 'Introduction', Elizabeth C. Gaskell, *Cranford, The Cage at Cranford, The Moorland Cottage*, The World's Classics, III (London, 1907).

The Brotherton Collection, Leeds University Library. BC MS 19c Gaskell, MS 16.

WILLIAM E. A. AXON

From Miss Gaskell
84, Plymouth Grove,
Manchester.[1]
Sept. 1, [1910]

Mr dear Mr. Axon,

As ever, I was in such a great hurry when I wrote to you yesterday that, tho' I didn't forget your great kindness about the sermons, I *literally* had not time to thank you – But I had put your name down on my list of (important) letters for today. I now thank you *most* heartily.

It may be "morbid" of Mrs. Bridgeman; but as my own experience tells me, one must not consider *what* others think of one – but only try to carry out the wishes of the Dead, to whom one has been so devoted.

What an imaginative man Laycock must have been to write an Ode to the Sun in Lancashire![2] Shall I – when less busy, write and ask Mrs. Bridgeman? I owe her a letter.

Black-edged envelope delivered by hand (no postage stamp).

Address: W. E. A. Axon Esq, 191. Plymouth Grove. Do not wait.

On reverse of envelope is written: Just starting for The Sheiling, Silverdale, Carnforth.

Annotation on envelope: answr'd Sept 8.

Envelope contains a small card unsigned, and a slip of paper containing the following notes:
Snow
LL. Davies –
Miss Halstan –
Axon –) Documentary evidence
Green –) that I was meaning to write to you anyhow today.

---

1 The address block is printed in black across the top of the card except for 'Miss' which is added in ink.
2 A reference to 'Ode to th'Sun' composed in 1862 by the Lancashire dialect poet Samuel Laycock (1826–93). See *Lancashire Songs, Poems, Tales, and Recitations* by Samuel Laycock (Manchester, 1886).

WILLIAM E. A. AXON

Sept. 5. 1910.

Dear Mr. Axon,

Forgive a most hurried note, please – just to say that I do *trust* that you won't carry out your intention of writing an article on "Country Conversations", as the family quite *hate* any public notice of it.

All I told you about Miss Georgiana (pronounced "Georgina")[1] Tollet, too, was meant in perfect confidence.

Very truly yours
M. E. Gaskell.

Black-edged mourning paper.

CLEMENT KING SHORTER

From M. E. Gaskell,
84 Plymouth Grove,
Manchester.
Sept. 6. [1910]
just leaving for
The Sheiling,
Silverdale
Carnforth.

The birthplace has only been discovered within the last month – *I* thought by Mrs. Tooley.

My sister and I paid a large sum to an "Expert in such things", as he was called, for a search for the exact house – because there was only a tradition as to its being "in Cheyne Walk" before that.

I am so little "assisting Mrs. Chadwick" that I first heard of her

---

1　Words in parenthesis may not be in Meta's hand, and are written in different ink.

proposed book[1] through the newspaper advertisement! In great haste,
    Yours very truly
    M. E. Gaskell.
I refused her request for help in a biography, of course.

One of two cards in black-edged envelope marked *Private*. Printed address with M.E. in ink.

Address: Clement Shorter Esq. Office of the "Sphere", Great New Street, Fetter Lane, London. E.C.

Postmark: Carnforth 9.30 am, SP 12 10.

The Brotherton Collection, Leeds University Library. BC Shorter Correspondence.

CLEMENT KING SHORTER

The Sheiling,
Silverdale
Carnforth.
[12 September 1910]

PRIVATE
    The mistakes in that book are simply *innumerable*.
    The spirit is kindly and sympathetic; but the letter . . .!
    I wish that if she had determined to trawl our private accounts out to the public gaze she wd. have mentioned the £400, or £500 a year that my Father had inherited from Mrs. Holbrook Gaskell, some years before we moved into Plymouth Grove[2] – I think that my Mother was *very* brave* in facing life in such a large house on 10 or 11 hundred pounds a year – but not idiotically rash!
    The mistakes of every kind are *endless*. (*'specially brave, as we daughters were \in turn/ at expensive boarding-schools.[ )]

---

1   Mrs Ellis H. Chadwick, *Mrs Gaskell: Homes, Haunts, and Stories* (London, 1910), advertised as 'The First Biography of a Famous English Novelist' in the *Manchester Guardian*, 29 September 1910, p. 9, cols.6–7. This publication caused Meta a great deal of annoyance. A second, revised, edition, published in 1913, addressed many criticisms and is considerably shorter.
2   Mrs Chadwick only mentions Mrs Gaskell's legacies from her side of the family, Mrs Lumb and Miss Abigail Holland, together with her earnings from her writing (Chadwick, 1910, p. 253). In the revised edition (1913, p. 173), she refers to William Gaskell's income derived from the proceeds of his father's sail-making business.

Second of two cards in black-edged envelope marked *Private*. Printed address with M.E. in ink; unsigned and undated.

Address: Clement Shorter Esq. Office of the "Sphere", Great New Street, Fetter Lane, London. E.C.

Postmark: Carnforth 9.30 pm, SP 12 10.

The Brotherton Collection, Leeds University Library. BC Shorter Correspondence.

WILLIAM E. A. AXON

Silverdale,
Carnforth.
12. IX. 10.

My dear Mr. Axon,

I must begin by saying how much I hope that you are really better. I return the proofs, which seem to me admirable.

I am very much upset with the terrible inaccuracy of Mrs. Chadwick's book –

I wonder whether you would most kindly read through the enclosed note. to Mr. Barber[1] – You will see my economy of strength and writing-power – in my asking you to read it first, and {lastly} planning for it to go to Mr Reginald Smith[2] afterwards.

Your letter was most interesting.

Very truly yours, with best wishes;
M. E. Gaskell.

Reproduced by courtesy of the University Librarian and Director, The John Rylands Library, The University of Manchester. Axon Archive.

---

1   This enclosure has not survived with the letter.
2   Reginald John Smith (1857–1916), a reader for Smith Elder and son-in-law of George Murray Smith, he formed lasting friendships with families of successful writers, including Elizabeth Gaskell (*ODNB*).

WILLIAM E. A. AXON

The Sheiling,
Silverdale,
Carnforth,
Sept. 14. [1910]

I think this admirable – My rt. Hand is giving out!

Brown envelope containing a card with sender's address printed at the right hand side; no signature.

Address: W. E. Axon Esq. 191, Plymouth Grove Manchester

Postmark: Carnforth 2 pm SPT. 14 10

On reverse of envelope is written: Would you kindly *give me the enclosed*[1] after you have done with it?

Reproduced by courtesy of the University Librarian and Director, The John Rylands Library, The University of Manchester. Axon Archive.

THOMAS SECCOMBE

The Sheiling
Silverdale
Carnforth
18 Sept 1910

Dear Mr Seccombe,

Thank you for your charming letter.

How I envy you being able to lead Jupiter by the nose!

Mrs Chadwick's book is a perfect monument of inaccuracy; as well as of industry, it must be said. It would be impossible to copy out and correct all the mistakes.

There is the compressive error of "riding to death the autobiographical element", as Mr Axon writes to me this morning; making her writings chiefly compilations of experience. Nothing could have been further from the truth.

Then Mrs Chadwick tries to make out that each *character* was a

---

1 This enclosure has not survived with the letter.

photograph of some living person. – Quite false again. She makes out that Margaret Hale[1] was meant for my mother; and so on –

As to the errors of fact, they are *endless* – on some pages 3 or 4. If Mrs Chadwick had had your courtesy, she would have let me look through her proofs, and then I could have corrected these, but she even concealed from me that she was writing this book! Knowing how earnestly I had tried to persuade her to respect my mother's wish that no biography should be written of her – and, as Mr Shorter writes me, this is practically a "Life" –.

I will put on a separate sheet or two some of the worst errors – and the correct versions.

As to the literary judgments, they are beneath contempt. Fancy comparing \page 390/ that sweet Molly with sour Philip Hepburn![2] In any way.

Then her criticism on Sylvia's Lovers! I have always loved that book the best of my Mother's works.

Quite, quite privately, when she was writing Sylvia's Lovers, she and I were staying with the Brodies, and she *was ill* and rather exhausted – (there were other guests, etc) –and one morning she wrote that scene of Kinraid's reappearance and Sylvia's meeting him. She asked me what I thought of it? To my death, I shall remember the next few moments. To tell her that it might be better, I knew would not only give her a *pang*, but would force her to re-write some pages.

The *beautiful* humility with which she accepted my opinion, when I advised the scene's being re-written, was most characteristic of her – and the second version justified my *cruelty*, – as I felt it to be at the time. I chose the motto.

I strongly belong to the *anti – Cranford – supreme party*; and so did my blessed Julia. Mrs Chadwick's touching words about her go far to redeem the book in my eyes! Indeed throughout, the *spirit* is very kind and sympathetic; and I feel rather a brute for thinking so much of her mistakes – when she has taken such pains and written [?usually] with such deep appreciation of my beloved Mother.

Always yours

---

1   A fictional character in Elizabeth Gaskell, *North and South*.
2   A reference to characters in Gaskell's *Wives and Daughters* and *Sylvia's Lovers*.

Very sincerely
M. E. Gaskell

Black-edged mourning paper.

Reproduced by courtesy of the University Librarian and Director, The John Rylands Library, The University of Manchester. R 1484384.

THOMAS SECCOMBE

> 84 Plymouth Grove
> Manchester
> 25. IX. 10.

Dear Mr Seccombe,

As I was coming back yesterday from Silverdale, the motor – for the first time in my experience of it – suddenly *stuck*, and refused to work.

This made my return late; and in a hurry – (how foolish women are! Which remark will show you that I am not a suffragist!) – in my hurry I scurried off notes to "the Times" and "Morning Post" – and no sooner had they gone, than I realized the full drift of your most kind card, and that you would have been so very good as to revise whatever I wrote to those papers.

It is too late now to take advantage of your kindness, but not too late to send you my heartiest thanks for it, \and for your opinion about writing./

> Ever yours gratefully
> M. E. Gaskell

Black-edged mourning paper and envelope.

Address: Thomas Seccombe Esq 18 Perryn Road, Acton, London. W.

Postmark: Manchester 8.30 pm SEP 25 10

Reproduced by courtesy of the University Librarian and Director, The John Rylands Library, The University of Manchester. Sharps Collection.

THE GUARDIAN[1]

84, Plymouth Grove,
Manchester
Sept 30 1910

MRS GASKELL'S LIFE

Sir – Might I beg you kindly to grant me a little space in your columns in which to correct a mistake in your review of Mrs Chadwick's book, *Mrs Gaskell: Haunts, Homes and Stories*?[2]

Instead of my having "co-operated" with Mrs Chadwick in writing the book, I have urged her most earnestly, on the only three occasions when I have seen her, to respect my mother's wish that no biography should be written of her. This book, whatever entitled, is practically a "Life". I was so convinced that Mrs Chadwick had yielded to my mother's wish that I talked to her the last time that I saw her perhaps a little too openly of the past; and the few things that I mentioned in what I believed to be private conversation now appear in this book in a very inaccurate form.

M. E. GASKELL

The letter here has been transcribed from printed material.

Manchester Libraries, Information and Archives F205 G1

THOMAS SECCOMBE

84 Plymouth Grove
Friday Morning
[October ?1910]

My dear, kind Mr Seccombe

I am just starting off from home; but I could not leave without writing to thank you most warmly for the beautiful "Sylvia's Lovers" – lovely from the lining to that most pathetic, *exquisite* picture of poor

---

1   *The Guardian Newspaper;* a church paper, weekly 1d, not to be confused with the daily *Manchester Guardian*.
2   See *The Guardian*, 16 September 1910, cols.1–2 for this review.

Sylvia's head against the dying Philip – [1]

I shall reach Alfrick[2] after the post has gone out today; but tomorrow I hope to write again –

Most gratefully

M. E. Gaskell

Black-edged mourning paper and envelope.

Address: Thomas Seccombe Esq 18 Perryn Road, Acton, London. W.

Postmark: Manchester 3.45 pm OCT

Reproduced by courtesy of the University Librarian and Director, The John Rylands Library, The University of Manchester. Sharps Collection.

WILLIAM E. A. AXON

From M. E. Gaskell
{84, Plymouth Grove,
Manchester.}[3]
Oct. 16. [1910]

I am so glad about this. You would, I am sure, secure the rights of your article, (so as to prevent its being reproduced in England) and \ would/ *not* mention the name of the place of the writer.

Kind regards.

No signature

Reproduced by courtesy of the University Librarian and Director, The John Rylands Library, The University of Manchester. Axon Archive.

WILLIAM E. A. AXON

84, Plymouth Grove.
9 Dec. 10. [1910]

---

1   Seccombe wrote an introduction for an edition of *Sylvia's Lovers* published in London by G. Bell, in 1910, with illustrations by M. V. Wheelhouse.
2   Alfrick Court, Worcester, her sister Marianne's home from 1884.
3   Name and address printed in one line across the top of a small card, but with the Manchester address crossed out in ink.

My dear Dr. Axon,[1]

I do hope that you are better – Strength I fear that you cannot regain during this weather.

I write in bed, rather overdone with all the writing and arranging that I have had to do lately –

I found yesterday that those letters from Paris that my Mother wrote to the Pall Mall[2] during its frail infancy, must have been written between March 7th. And April 20th., 1865.

Could you tell me of any one who can decipher Doddridge's shorthand,[3] please? I have a copy \(of a letter of Charlotte Brontë's)/ in my Father's hand – half shorthand – which I want copied out in ordinary writing.

The letter is of such value that I should not like to part with it for more than a few hours.

Would there be a book in any Library that would enable me to do it: please?

    Yours very sincerely

    M. E. Gaskell.

1 Axon was awarded an honorary doctorate by Wilberforce University, Ohio, in 1899 (*ODNB*). This is the first time Meta uses the title Dr. rather than Mr.

2 See 'Columns of Gossip from Paris in *The Pall Mall Gazette* (1865)' in Sharps, pp. 527–29, including nn.1–10.

3 Philip Doddridge (1702–51), non-conformist minister, developed a system of shorthand devised by Jeremy Rich, 'A Brief and Easy System of Short-hand: first invented by Jeremiah Rich, and improved by Dr Doddridge, 1799' (*DNB*). This work is not included in the entry for Doddridge in the later *ODNB*.

MISS NINA LOUISE KAY-SHUTTLEWORTH

84 Plymouth Grove
Manchester
17 Dec. 1910

Dear Miss Kay-Shuttleworth,

My beloved sister Julia and I had always such a great admiration for you that it would be a real pleasure to me if you would accept a copy of the very first Edition of the "Life of Charlotte Bronte", which I am sending by this post.

It is a very rare book; and as "original boards" are supposed to be more *correct* than the most sumptuous new bindings, I have resisted the temptation to have it rebound!

My mother first met Charlotte Brontë at your Grandfather's. Hence the friendship between the two, and "The Life", owed their existence to your forbears.

I have been reading with very great interest high praise of your biography of Sir Woodbine Parish.[1]

With heartfelt wishes for you in your new life, and kindest remembrances to Lord and Lady Shuttleworth, I am ever yours sincerely

M. E. Gaskell

Please do not trouble to write to me, as your last days before your marriage must be so very full and busy.

Sender's addressed embossed on head of writing paper. The letter was donated to the John Rylands Library with the edition of *Life of Charlotte Brontë* referred to here.

Reproduced by courtesy of the University Librarian and Director, The John Rylands Library, The University of Manchester. R129632 N80E7.

---

1   Nina L. Kay-Shuttleworth, *A Life of Sir Woodbine Parish (1796–1882)* (London, 1910). Woodbine-Parish was a Diplomat and historian (*ODNB*).

SARA NORTON

[1910][1]

(Miss) M. E. Gaskell[2]

We reached Rome late at night on 23 Feb., 1857, and drove thro' the dark, strange streets to the Casa Cabrale where the Storys were living, who had so kindly invited us &, next morning it was all brilliant sunshine and colour & \wild/ gaiety. We were taken down by the Storys to a balcony in the Corso, from which we were to see the great day of the Carnival – \Shrove Tuesday./ The narrow street was filled with a boisterous crowd of Romans, half mad with excitement at the confetti-throwing & horse-racing. Suddenly against this turbulent back-ground there stood out the figure of a young man just below the balcony, smiling up at my Mother, whom he knew he was to see there, & whom he easily {recognized} \distinguished/ from the others.

It is 53 years since that day,[3] & yet even now I can vividly recall the beautiful, sweet, welcoming expression on the \radiant/ face. When brought on to the balcony, he and my mother greeted one another with little expectation that until her death they were to be most true & intimate friends – {For}\During/ the 7 weeks that we were in Rome, we saw him constantly. He came to the famous breakfasts at the C. C. where Manning and Aubrey de Vere[4] were nearly always to be found. Every time he came he brought {some} \a/ beautiful bouquet of flowers, with the true American generosity and courtesy. He constantly joined us in our sight seeing, and we learnt from him more \ vividly/ than {from} any book on art cd. teach, all the deep principles of painting & sculpture –

On the 15th Ap. We joined forces with Mr. Norton, and travelled vetturino to Florence, sleeping in half-barbarous places on the road – At F. we stayed till April 23rd, and then drove on to Venice – and

---

1   The date is a Houghton Library annotation.
2   '(Miss) M. E. Gaskell' has been added by another hand at the top of the first page.
3   This fixes the year of this letter as 1910.
4   Both men, as well as being friends, were converts to Catholicism, partly through the influence of Cardinal Newman (*ODNB*).

stayed at Danieli's, where Mr. Norton held quite levées of distinguished writers and artists. At V. he discovered & bought the first copy of my Mother's "Life of C. Brontë" that she had seen \and brought it to show her/. –

We parted at V. on May 6, but he came to stay with us at P. G. in July – to see the famous Art Treasures Ex^n.

Incomplete letter and unsigned.

Houghton Library, Harvard University. MS Am 1088.1 809.

THOMAS SECCOMBE

84 Plymouth Grove
16 Jan. 1911

Dear Mr Seccombe

Please burn the enclosed, when read; without troubling to acknowledge it.

I think that I have given away two dozen copies of "Sylvia's Lovers", and every one in to whom I have sent a copy, is loud in praise of your Introduction.[1]

Durrant furnishes me with most laudatory press-notices too.

In haste
Yours most sincerely
M. E. Gaskell

Reproduced by courtesy of the University Librarian and Director, The John Rylands Library, The University of Manchester. Sharps Collection.

---

1   Elizabeth Gaskell, *Sylvia's Lovers*, with a Preface by Thomas Seccombe and illustrations by M. V. Wheelhouse (London: Bell, 1910). Thomas Seccombe (1866–1923) was a literary biographer, who contributed to the *DNB* and to the *'Bookman' History of English Literature*. He also edited, with his own introductions, reprints of Elizabeth Gaskell's novels. His introduction to this edition of *Sylvia's Lovers*, pp. ix–xlvii, includes a few basic facts about Gaskell's life; compares Gaskell favourably with other nineteenth-century novelists including Austen and Dickens; and rates *Sylvia's Lovers* as one of her finest achievements.

THOMAS SECCOMBE

84 Plymouth Grove
24 Jan. 1911

My dear Mr Seccombe

I sent off that note of Mrs Toller's[1] in great haste so didn't refer to your most kind note of Nov. 14.

I need not say that I have read and re-read it often; but each time that I did so, I more completely realized how impossible it was for me to add anything to what has already been printed about "Wives and Daughters".

My Mother never talked about the end; except to imply that the story would end happily. And that is quite obvious.

There were really so few pages left for her still to write.

The fullest truth is: that I know nothing whatever about her intentions with regard to the happy meeting of Roger and Molly as the close of the story.

I would *gladly* tell you, if I did; for I feel sincerely grateful to you for the "Sylvia's Lovers'" Introduction. If there is a new edition of that, – as I am sure that there ought to be soon – may I just point out that the "tea" in the drawing-room at Holybourne, on 12 Nov. 65, is a mistake.[2]

There was none in the room (Mrs Chadwick amplifies the mistake.)[3] of course it is a most trifling error; and I would not mention it to you, if I did not want your Introduction to be flawless.

Ever yours most sincerely

M. E. Gaskell.

I write in bed – very weak – so kindly forgive mistakes.

1 Possibly Edith Toller (1854–1935) wife of T. N. Toller, professor of English at Manchester University and associate of Adolphus Ward (*ODNB*).

2 There are indications that Meta's memory is playing her false here, for she had previously claimed that they were taking '5 o'clock tea' when her mother died. See her letters, above, to Norton dated 24 November 1865 and to Miss Nussey dated 22 January 1866.

3 Mrs Chadwick merely reiterated Meta's account of the event by stating that Mrs Gaskell was taking tea in the drawing room at Holybourne, with three of her daughters and son-in-law, when she suddenly died (Chadwick, 1910, p. 437). In her revised edition, perhaps to mollify Meta, she claimed the event took place 'just before tea' (Chadwick, 1913, p. 306).

WILLIAM E. A. AXON

> 84 Plymouth Grove
> Manchester
> Feby. 14th./ 11.

Dear Mr. Axon,

I am sorry not to write to you in my own hand but I'm sure you will kindly forgive my not doing so.

Your explanation of "The Face" story is very ingenious, but there are two facts against it, first that I remember distinctly my Mother's conviction that it was Dickens who himself used the plot.

Secondly, that she met Mrs. Lynn Linton[1] only once and that was before my Mother had heard the story. Still of course Mrs. Linton may have heard a second or third hand version of of [*sic*] it.

I hope that you feel as indignant as I do about the treatment meted out to Richter[2] lately, it injures the reputation of Manchester, but not of Richter.

I hope you are keeping better.
Yours very sincerely
M. E. Gaskell.

Dictated.

Manchester Libraries, Information and Archives, Gaskell Collection, Box 4.

1 Eliza Lynn Linton (1822–1898), English novelist and journalist, valued by Dickens for her numerous contributions to his journals (Lohrli, pp. 343–46).
2 Hans Richter (1843–1916) had conducted the Hallé Orchestra in Manchester since 1899. He retired in 1911 with one year of his contract still to run. See the *Manchester Guardian,* 9 February 1911, p. 4. col.3 and *Manchester Evening News*, 13 February 1911, p. 3. col.3.

WILLIAM E. A. AXON

> From Miss Gaskell,
> 84, Plymouth Grove,
> Manchester.
> But *just* leaving for
> Silverdale Carnforth.
> 13. VI. II

Dear Dr. Axon,

I dare say that you didn't hear how very ill I was thro' April and part of May – 3 weeks kept in bed by the doctor, and 5 in my bed-room, with "heart-trouble" – It has left me so weak that often I have not strength to get through my very large correspondence – which I feel *very* annoying.

This is the reason why I have not yet thanked you for your really *most* interesting article on "the Wayside Inn".[1] I longed after reading it to send it to Miss Norton, who is at Cambridge – (Mass) but I felt so selfishly unwilling to let it out of my hands that I am keeping it for to read until her return to Europe next autumn. Wd. you most kindly put a reply to the question on the card that I enclose.

Best regards

Written on a small card with printed address across the top; no signature.

Reproduced by courtesy of the University Librarian and Director, The John Rylands Library, The University of Manchester. Axon Archive.

WILLIAM E. A. AXON

> The Sheiling,
> Silverdale,
> Carnforth.
> [17th June 1911]

Dear Dr. Axon,

Please let me know in very good time about your and Miss Axon's

---

1   Possibly a reference to 'Tales of a Wayside Inn' by Henry W. Longfellow (1807–82) (London, 1864).

being at Arnside[1] – so that I may have the pleasure of seeing you here.

Is it the wife of the Librarian of the Public Library in King St. who is just dead? If so, please forward the enclosed most kindly. If *not*, then please burn it, and "swallow" the stamp! – a dangerous dose, as one is warned not even to lick stamps by those who spend their lives in deadly bacilli! For *you* to talk of lacking energy! Gentle idea!

Unsigned note on a small card with pre-printed address.

Reproduced by courtesy of the University Librarian and Director, The John Rylands Library, The University of Manchester. Axon Archive.

WILLIAM E. A. AXON

The Sheiling
4. VII. 1911.

Dear Dr. Axon,

I am feeling horribly weak again today – so please forgive curtness; but I must just thank you for your beautiful article –

The pathos of that passage you quote from "Cranford" – – always fills *my* eyes with tears, just as you once told me that it had always done your eyes and your beloved wife's –

I *am* so sorry to find that I shall not be here when you are at Arnside

I leave here on the 24[th.] of this month, and do not return till early in Septr. –

There is only a *very* little that I can tell you about the Tower-house here. I will write that soon to you.

Please keep Mrs. Bridgeman entirely to yourself – all of it.

The name Tollet had better never be used again in connection with "C. C."

There is only one final T – It was printed with 2 in "Coke of Norfolk",[2] & Miss Julia Wedgwood wrote indignantly to the biographer! a small error, certainly, but Mr. T. was one of the first landlords

---

1   A small town on the edge of Morecambe Bay, two or three miles from Silverdale.

2   A reference to Thomas William Coke (1754–1842), Norfolk landowner, pioneer and populariser of improved agricultural methods. The biographer referred to here may have been A. M. W. Stirling (1865–1965), author of *Coke of Norfolk and His Friends*, first published 1908, new edn 1912 (*ODNB*).

to establish schools for his tenants, [?] –
>Most truly yours
>M. E. Gaskell.

WILLIAM E. A. AXON

>Silverdale,
>Carnforth.
>Sept. 21. [1911]

My dear Mr. Axon,

Thank you for your *wonderfully* interesting article in "The Inquirer"[1] – which I should not otherwise have seen.

It was very good of you to send it me.

I never forgot about Gibralter and the Tower House[2] – but I felt that there was very little to say.

If you go to Arnside again, I will hunt up some references to the two out of the *privately-printed* Winkworth Memorials.[3]

I have just come here to find the country more delightful than ever – and such splendid skies!

It is "cloudland" {at} \round/ this cottage, as our architect said.

>Most sincerely yours
>M. E. Gaskell.

---

1   William E. A. Axon, 'Sir John Bowring and the Athanasian Creed', *The Inquirer*, 16 September 1911, pp. 588–89.
2   Gibralter Farm in Silverdale is situated on top of a rocky eminence, overlooking the sea. Nearby Lindeth Tower, built as a 'folly', became a favourite summer retreat for Mrs Gaskell, where she found much needed peace and quiet for her writing (David Peter, pp. 19–21).
3   *Letters and Memorials of Catherine Winkworth*, ed. Susanna Winkworth and Margaret J. Shaen, 2 vols (Clifton, 1883–86).

JOHN ALBERT GREEN

84. Plymouth Grove.
8 Oct. 1911.

My dear Mr. Green,

I admit, frankly and unreservedly, that I was wrong to write so sharply; but I thought that you were "in collusion" with Mrs. C. – I see how entirely mistaken I was; and can only express sincerest regret.

Pray forgive me.
Yours very sincerely
M. E. Gaskell.
Of course I shan't *change anything*.

Manchester Libraries, Information and Archives, Gaskell Collection, Box 4.

WILLIAM E. A. AXON

[Manchester]
[9 October 1911]

Of course, I was a brute! Please forgive
M. E. G.

Postcard with half-penny stamp; no signature.

Address: Dr. W. E. A. Axon, Plymouth Grove, M/C.

Postmark: Manchester 10 am OCT 9 11

Reproduced by courtesy of the University Librarian and Director, The John Rylands Library, The University of Manchester. Axon Archive.

WILLIAM E. A. AXON

84. P. G.
Oct. 12. [1911]

My dear Dr. Axon,

"In my wrath" I thought that you and Mr. Green had been "in collusion" with Mrs. C. [hadwick].[1]

---

1 Letters inserted in pencil by another hand confirm this reference to Mrs. Chadwick.

And now I have a kind of "Gelert" feeling.[1]

You will understand what I mean – that murder of the faithful dog! *What* a tragedy!

I write in bed, being rather worn out with 3 hard days – and the doctors' remedy is a quiet day in bed for me –

But tomorrow I shall have to be up –

So will you and Miss Axon come and lunch with me – (alone) – at 1.30.? It would be such a pleasure to me if you would –

> Yours sincerely,
> & penitently, and
> gratefully
> M. E. Gaskell.

Reproduced by courtesy of the University Librarian and Director, The John Rylands Library, The University of Manchester. Axon Archive.

WILLIAM E. A. AXON

84. Plymouth Grove.
Dec. 26.[1911]

I am very sorry that I am not a subscriber to the Devonshire Hospital[2] – The Corporation is "bleeding" me for these drains to the amount of £450!! So I am "pinching" myself at every turn, or I would buy her an order.

Unsigned postcard with half-penny stamp.

Address: Dr. W. E. A. Axon, [191][3] Plymouth Grove, M/C.

Postmark: 15 Dec. pm [1911]

Reproduced by courtesy of the University Librarian and Director, The John Rylands Library, The University of Manchester. Axon Archive.

---

1   A reference to the legend of Beddgelert in which a faithful dog was killed and buried in the village of that name in North Wales.
2   Located in Buxton, a former stable block belonging to the Devonshire family, it was converted and extended from 1859 onwards to become a charity hospital for the sick poor in the manufacturing towns in Lancashire and Yorkshire. Substantial funding came from the Cotton Districts Convalescence Fund. In 1934 it became known as the Royal Devonshire Hospital. The building now forms part of Derby University (*Wik.*).
3   The street number is in a different ink, so presumed to be added later.

WILLIAM E. A. AXON

84. Plymouth Grove.
Jan. 20. [1912]

Dear Dr. Axon,

I have been waiting to answer your note in the expectation of receiving back from my sister, Mrs. Holland, an extract that I sent her from "The Musical Standard"[1] – but I will delay no longer.

I will, however, order the Editor to forward you a copy of the number of Jan. 13th., which contains an interesting account of the Burnetts' coming to Manchester.[2]

Mrs. B. was Dickens's sister. (Mrs. Holland had lessons from Mr. Burnett in singing[ )].

My only recollection of seeing Dickens here is when he once called, rather flashily dressed. *Please* don't *mention that.*

I found amongst my Mother's papers the original play-bill of "The frozen deep"[3] – (Wasn't that the title?) and all his life my Father liked to talk of a delightful party after one of the performances, to which he and my Mother went – at which *Mark Lemon* was so {de} charmingly humo{u}rous –

I gave the programme to the Brazenose Club (through Judge Parry.)[4] Please forgive a most untidy note.

Very sincerely yours
M. E. Gaskell.

The following note has been added in a different hand: no date on env. Addressed to 191 Plymouth Grove 1 1912

---

1 *The Musical Standard: A Newspaper for Musicians, Professional and Amateur,* price 2 pence weekly, established 1862.
2 The number for 13 January 1912 included an account of recent concerts in Manchester; the article on the Burnetts in Manchester appeared in the number for 6 January and not 13 January as stated here by Meta.
3 *The Frozen Deep,* a play written by Wilkie Collins with help from Charles Dickens, was first performed publicly in 1857, running in London and Manchester that year. Mark Lemon, journalist, actor and, for a while, a personal friend of Dickens, played the part of Lieutenant Crayford (*Companion to Dickens*).
4 Judge Parry, a successful Manchester barrister, and friend of Meta and Julia Gaskell, was a frequent guest at 84 Plymouth Grove. For Parry's account of the Brasenose Club and similar Manchester institutions, see Parry, pp. 236–37; for his account of hospitality at Plymouth Grove see pp. 116–18.

WILLIAM E. A. AXON

March 4. [1912]

You, who know about *everything* literary, will perhaps kindly tell me (for a friend) who wrote a novel, called "Charles Auchester["]?[1] It is an *old* one –

I do so like Mr. Seccombe's introduction to the Everyman "Mary Barton".[2]

Unsigned postcard with half-penny stamp.

Address: Dr. W. E. A. Axon, 191. Plymouth Grove, Manchester.

Postmark: Manchester 11.30 AM 4 MAR 12

WILLIAM E. A. AXON

84. Plymouth Grove.
April 19. [1912]

Dear Mr. Axon,[3]

I am afraid that I am a dreadful trouble to you! and sometimes I must *appear* ungrateful, tho' indeed I never am so.

I have never, however, thanked you for your most kind information about the writer of "Charles Auchester"! Forgive me, please; and accept my belated thanks.

---

1   A reference to *Charles Auchester: A Memorial,* 3 vols (London: Hurst and Blackett, 1853; repr. 1911 and 1928 by Everyman.) The first edition was published anonymously and sometimes wrongly attributed. The author was Elizabeth Sarah Sheppard, who also wrote under the name E. Berger.

2   Elizabeth Gaskell, *Mary Barton* With an Introduction by Thomas Seccombe, Everyman's Library (London, 1912). In his introduction, Seccombe praises *Mary Barton* for its fidelity to truth and to nature, placing it in the front rank of English novels, before giving a few biographical details of the author's life.

3   Meta reverts to the title Mr, although in the body of the letter she uses the title Dr.

You will think that my gratitude shows a hope of "favours to come", when I ask you if you would once more help me by telling me if you know anything of the children of Frank Smedley, about whom Mr. Ellis asks in the enclosed.[1]

I hope that you are better than when I last heard of you, dear Dr. Axon –

Yours most sincerely

M. E. Gaskell.

Notepaper with embossed monogram: MEG.

Reproduced by courtesy of the University Librarian and Director, The John Rylands Library, The University of Manchester. Axon Archive.

WILLIAM E. A. AXON

84. Plymouth Grove.
April 24. [1912]

My dear Dr. Axon,

I had heard nothing of your illness, or I should have sent to inquire. It distresses me *very* much –

And oh how guilty I feel at having troubled you, when you are ill! – But you have such extraordinary power of helping others that no wonder that you are so often applied to in dilemmas –

Please send just a *verbal* report of how you are this morning.

Yours with sincerest wishes for your recovery,

most gratefully

M. E. Gaskell.

Reproduced by courtesy of the University Librarian and Director, The John Rylands Library, The University of Manchester. Axon Archive.

---

1   No enclosure was included with this manuscript.

WILLIAM E. A. AXON

THE SHEILING,
SILVERDALE,
CARNFORTH.
May 16, 1912

My dear Dr. Axon,

I had often been wondering how you were going on, so I was delighted to get some news of you this morning – and I am delighted that you are a little better.

After such a very serious illness as bronchial pneumonia, the progress must, I fear, inevitably be slow.

(Anch'io have been rather 'bad',[1] as poor people say, {also} – but this delicious air is curing me.)

It was so specially good of you to take the trouble to copy me out those admirable remarks on "Mary Barton", when you must still be feeling so weak.

But you have not done it in vain, for it has given me very great pleasure to read them, I can assure you.

My darling Julia saw a great deal of Miss Fox,[2] when she was staying with some friends at Falmouth – and the latter told me how charmed with my Sister Miss Fox had been – and Julia spoke enthusiastically of the kindness and hospitality of Miss Fox –

With very heartiest good wishes for your *complete* recovery,

I am gratefully yours
M. E. Gaskell.

Sender's address embossed in black, in block capitals.

Reproduced by courtesy of the University Librarian and Director, The John Rylands Library, The University of Manchester. Axon Archive.

---

1   'Also I have been rather bad'. I am grateful to Emma Marigliano, Portico Librarian, for help with this translation.
2   See *Further Letters*, p. 269 for Mrs Gaskell's reference to the 'Foxs of Cornwall'.

WILLIAM E. A. AXON

[22nd July. 1912]

Dear Dr. Axon,

I am so sorry to say that I know nothing about a Brontë room in the Cove at Silverdale.[1] I believe that Major Saunders, who lives there, is very nice and kind; but I don't know him.[2]

I should advise your writing straight to him, *without mentioning my name*, or to the

Revd W. Sleigh,

The Vicarage,

Silverdale,

Carnforth,

to whom you *can* mention that I advised you to write.

We did not call on any of the newcomers, as we wanted quiet at the Sheiling; so did not call on Mrs. Saunders.

Please return the enclosed hymns after choosing one –

In haste,

Very sincerely yours

M. E. Gaskell

Annotation across corner of page: *July 22* thanked & MSS returned after copying "Gethsemane".

Reproduced by courtesy of the University Librarian and Director, The John Rylands Library, The University of Manchester. Axon Archive.

---

1   A reference to Cove House, at one time the home of the Revd Carus Wilson of Cowan Bridge School, where the Brontë sisters were taught for a time (David Peter, p. 45). Mrs Chadwick suggests that Charlotte Brontë stayed at Cove House as a child (Chadwick, 1910, p. 333), but there is no firm evidence for this claim.
2   Major Morley Saunders lived at Cove House from 1900 to 1918 (David Peter, p. 45).

WILLIAM E. A. AXON

Silverdale,
Carnforth.
July 18. [1913]

My dear Dr. Axon,

I am so much afraid from your message that you have been ill –

I can only assure you that in my own long-continuing illness, I have been so much out of the world that I had not heard of it, or I should have *most certainly* sent to inquire after you –

I have had a letter from Mr. Clement Shorter, wanting to know where my Mother's story of "The Half-brothers" first appeared.[1]

If any one would know, it would be you; but it is not in your most highly-prized Bibliography, for I have looked.

Pray take no trouble whatever about the matter: not even replying to this if you *don't* know, and if you *do*, sending me a mere word on the enclosed card –

Yours most sincerely
M. E. Gaskell.

Reproduced by courtesy of the University Librarian and Director, The John Rylands Library, The University of Manchester. Axon Archive.

WILLIAM E. A. AXON

The Sheiling.
July 22. [1913]

My dear Dr. Axon,

It is *infinitely* good of you to have taken so much trouble for me; and I feel most grateful to you.

I am so shocked to hear how very, very ill you have been.

An operation of any kind must be a *dreadful* thing to face, and when it is of such a very severe nature as colostomy, true courage must indeed be needed.

But that – *and Faith* – I know that you have.

---

1   According to Sharps, p. 307, n.3, this tale first appeared in *My Lady Ludlow and Other Tales*, 2 vols (London: Smith Elder, 1859).

What a beautiful hand your Daughter writes! And what a comfort to have such a secretary!

Yours most gratefully

M. E. Gaskell.

Reproduced by courtesy of the University Librarian and Director, The John Rylands Library, The University of Manchester. Axon Archive.

CLEMENT KING SHORTER

[?November 1913]

I will undertake very carefully to revise your proofs, but I am sorry to say that there are no more letters that I can send you. I am precluded from doing that by my mother's wish. So few people nowadays respect the wishes of the beloved dead that I daresay my trying to carry out her two solemn bequests may appear to many people morbid, but I hope not to you.

Extract from letter to Clement King Shorter; reproduced in *The Sphere*, 8 November 1913. Date letter was first written remains uncertain.

Manchester Libraries, Information and Archives.

CLEMENT KING SHORTER

[?November 1913]

I have come quite unexpectedly on a letter of Mr Brontë's to my mother in which he says that the part of her life of Charlotte Brontë that he likes best is that referring to his unfortunate son and his abominable seducer.[1]

Extract from letter to Clement King Shorter; reproduced in *The Sphere* 8 November 1913. Date letter was first written remains uncertain.

Manchester Libraries, Information and Archives.

---

1   See *The Letters of the Reverend Patrick Brontë*, ed. by Dudley Green (Stroud, 2005), pp. 251–52 and n.3.

CLEMENT KING SHORTER

[?November 1913]

I do not quite understand the question of the copyright of letters as now fixed, but we are prepared to waive any question of copyright; that is, not to restrain publication of any of my mother's letters that you may possess as well as to lend you material on condition that allowing us to see the proofs of your book you will promise to obey our veto on any particular passage to which we may object.

Extract from letter to Clement King Shorter; reproduced in *The Sphere* 8 November 1913. Date letter was first written remains uncertain.

Manchester Libraries, Information and Archives.

~~~~~~~~~~~~

UNDATED LETTERS FROM M. E. GASKELL

MR SMITH

Plymouth Grove.
Sept. 29 – birthday.

My dear Mr. Smith,

It is always delightful to receive a present of game but the flavour of the birds certainly varies with one's feelings towards the giver.

Hence I am quite sure that these, coming from you and dear Isabel, will taste *most* delicious.

Two brace, also, are so very much more than double *one* – contrary to arithmetic as that may be – It is a case where the generosity of the giver clashes with one's justice of judgment.

I hear from Ethel – in a most charming letter – that you are (more or less) at Thrums – and perhaps that mysterious "Cuk" refers to something classical that I ought not to have forgotten –

Do you know that for two or three days round the 12th., we sat fixt to our chairs at the Sheiling,[1] in hopes that you might suddenly appear from Mr. Willink's – as you did one year, just after you had been to see Mr. Nicholls in Ireland.[2] How *wonderfully* successful your and Mrs. Smith's goodness has been in warding off from us what we dreaded so acutely. No words ever seem in the *very least* to express what we feel about it.

Ravenous à nos "birrds" – I remember Mr. Henry Bright saying that he received an invitation at Boston (U.S.A.) "to meet a few souls at Tea", and that he replied that he must refuse, "as he was engaged to meet a few stomachs at dinner" – Well – (if ladies have stomachs, or anything so inelegant) – I should like to say that we thank you for the grouse {both} \from/ our stomachs as well as \ from/our hearts.

With best love to Isabel,

---

1   The Sheiling was the property in Silverdale, on the Lancashire coast, where members of the Gaskell family spent many of their holidays.

2   Arthur Bell Nicholls, Charlotte Brontë's husband, who returned to Ireland following the death of the Revd Patrick Brontë. The publishing house Smith Elder had been the first publisher of Mrs Gaskell's *Life of Charlotte Brontë*.

Ever yours truly
M. E. Gaskell.

EFFIE WEDGWOOD

Oak Hill Lodge
June 21.

Darling Effie,

I have literally only one moment before being carried off to the Handel – but I must send a line to thank you – to beg you thank Mrs. Wedgwood, too, – for my most delightful perfect visit to Cumberland.[1] Perhaps it is as well that I have not time to tell you all that I feel for you, & how I love & admire you – or you might say that I was a horrid humbug, which is always the kind view you take of my worship. I trust the wind is in the S. – & that your plans are shaping themselves happily. I cd.n't help being a bad shilling yesterday. –

Ever your own
M. E. G.

CHARLES ELIOT NORTON

[Manchester]
Oct. 22.

Dearest Mr. Norton,

When I wrote to you last I said nothing in reply to your most kind invitation for me to come to you in November – and I think that it may have seemed strange to you. But I could not bear to cut away my chance of coming by a refusal before I was quite certain of the impossibility; and yet I did not see my way to making it possible. And now I am afraid that it is positively certain that I *can't*: – so I am writing to

---

1   A probable reference to the Wedgwoods' London home at Cumberland Place, Regent's Park.

send you the thanks for the invitation – for your kind wish to have me – which {?} you must have known from the first are most lovingly yours. I have got dreadfully busy –

Somehow it is such a whirl here – when everyone is settling down for the winter, and work of all kinds is begun – And I have got involved in much which will keep me fast here for some months. I often think of an expression you used in one of your letters – about "putting the drag on to one's life" – I wish that one could do it on to life in general – for things seem to me going at a dangerous pace – and an ever-increasing one. I doubt if the next generation will feel as grateful to Watts and Sir Rowland Hill[1] as we do – !

I wonder what you all have been doing latterly – How lovely your trees must be looking now! Julia is at the Lakes for a few days with Florence and speaks so much of the beauty of the autumn tints – Here our poor shrivelled leaves have not much "glory" to boast of –

Ever your loving faithful friend

M. E. Gaskell.

Houghton Library, Harvard University. MS Am 1088 2636.

THOMAS SECCOMBE

Alfrick Court
Worcester
Friday Evening

My dear Mr. Seccombe,

I have a few minutes before the post leaves this out-of-the-way place, and I want to assure you of my deep, deep sympathy in the great sorrow of your beloved Aunt's having passed away.

I know so well what such partings mean – the terrible, aching long-ing to be with the lost ones, which only the thought of reunion in Heaven can assuage.

I can realize from all that my mother said of her feeling for Aunt

---

1   Rowland Hill (1795–1879) was responsible for postal reform; John Watts (1818–87) was a social reformer associated with the development of public parks and technical education (*ODNB*). Meta may have been thinking of James Watt (1736–1819), since he was associated with steam power (*ODBH*).

Lumb, what the intense, tender bond has been between you and your own dear, dear Aunt.

And thank you ever so much for telling me about her interest in your beautiful Edition of "Sylvia's Lovers".

I shall always link her name with it – and shall remember so gratefully that she, like you, appreciated it so much.

> God help and keep you!
> Ever Yours
> M. E. G.

Top left hand corner gives the following information:

Telegrams: Alfrick

Parcels: Knightwick Station, G.W.R.

Black-edged envelope.

Address: Thomas Seccombe Esq 18 Perryn Road, Acton, London. W.

Reproduced by courtesy of the University Librarian and Director, The John Rylands Library, The University of Manchester. Sharps Collection.

[No Addressee]

Monday Morning.

The Times critique of last Friday,[1] and the one in the Mancr. *Courier* are far the best hitherto.

There is no picture of the Tower[2] here, where much (of Ruth and others) was written.

We have no "proofs" – of illustrations – but we will send you a photograph of the Laurence portrait[3] – when it is taken! There will be an excellent portrait of my Father – in Vol. Lv.

> M. E. Gaskell

---

1 A search through *The Times Digital Archive* reveals only one likely entry for a Friday. This is a discussion of the discovery of four letters from Charlotte Brontë to Professor Heger, together with a reference to Mrs Gaskell's *Life of Charlotte Brontë* (*The Times*, Friday, 17 October 1913, p. 11, cols.3–4). The *Manchester Courier* article has not been found.

2 Lindeth Tower, Silverdale, where Mrs Gaskell did much of her writing.

3 A likely reference to the pastel portrait by Samuel Laurence, 1854. See Uglow between pp. 338 and 339 for a reproduction.

The above note is written on two separate pieces of paper, each the same size and colour, with neither date, address, nor name of addressee.

Manchester Libraries, Information and Archives, Gaskell Collection, Box 4.

CLEMENT KING SHORTER

The only times that Mrs. Gaskell stayed in Germany were, during a short tour in Rhine-land with her husband, in 1839 or 1840; and during a long visit to Heidelberg, in the winter \late autumn/ of 1858–{9}, with two of her daughters – I think the visit lasted 13 weeks –

She went down the Rhine in going there; and "Six Weeks at Heppenheim" was planned and, I fancy, written at Heidelberg. While there, she saw a great deal of both poor and rich residents – amongst the latter were the Bunsens (Baron Bunsen's people – not the great Chemists) – and the Robert von Mohls, one of whom afterwards became Madame Helmholts[1] – and was a special favourite of Mrs Gaskell's.

She paid more visits to France – than to Germany. In 1853, we went a tour in Normandy – she, my Father, and her two eldest girls. In 1854, she and her eldest daughter paid a winter visit to Paris, staying there with Mrs. Salis Schwabe, at whose house she first got to know Mme. Mohl and the (American) Storys –

In 1855, she and her second daughter paid about a month's visit to Madame Mohl –

In 1857, she and her two eldest daughters stayed for \a/ few nights, with Madame Mohl on their way to Rome –

In 1858, she and her second and third daughters stayed for a few nights with Madame Mohl on their way back from Heidelberg.

In 1862, she and Mrs. (William) Sidgwick and Mrs. Gaskell's second daughter made a tour in Normandy and Brittany \after a short stay in Paris/. In 1863, ({?}), she and her youngest daughter stayed with Madame Mohl, on the way to Rome, whither the second and third daughters accompanied them – On the journey South, they

---

1   A likely reference to Hermann L. F. von Helmholz (1821–94), who married R. von Mohl's daughter in 1861 (*Further Letters,* p. 225, n.4).

Incomplete, no date, address, or signature.[1]

The Brotherton Collection, Leeds University Library. BC MS 19c Gaskell, MS 16.

CLEMENT KING SHORTER

84, Plymouth Grove,
MANCHESTER

The second letter is one of the very sweetest, tenderest I ever read. It is from Marianne Lumb, Mrs Lumb's only child – who was terribly crippled.

As a little wee child; she suddenly leapt out of her nurse's arms, thro' an open window, in her joy at seeing her mother coming up the garden-path and in her eagerness to reach her. She fell on the hard ground, and was maimed for life! It has always been said that Aunt Lumb conceived the idea of adopting little Elizabeth for the sake of Marianne – But this letter, to her mother in London, shows that the first thought was Marianne's.

She pleads in the most touching way to be allowed to have the little motherless Elizabeth to live with them at Knutsford, and mentions all the sacrifices of time and pleasure and money that she will make, if only her mother will grant her request.

The *third* letter[2] is from the second Mrs. Stevenson, who writes to Mrs. Lumb to say how beautifully my Mother had behaved whilst nursing her father during his last illness.

It is the highest praise. You shall have the exact words –

Yours very truly
M.E. Gaskell.

Sender's address embossed; no date.

The Brotherton Collection, Leeds University Library. BC MS 19c Gaskell, MS 16.

---

1   For background information on this letter, see Sharps, p. 343, n.3. Sharps claims that dates given in this letter were not entirely accurate, Meta's memory having become less than perfect.

2   Copies of extracts of these letters are filed with this one at the Brotherton Library, Leeds.

FLORENCE ELIZABETH GASKELL

(1842–1881)

Elizabeth and William Gaskell's third surviving daughter,
'loving & generous' (*Gaskell Letters*, p. 725).

Family names included 'Flora' and 'Flossie'.

The first of the Gaskell daughters to marry, Florence married Charles
Crompton, son of Judge Crompton, in 1863. Following their wedding, Florence and Charles set up home in London; she died, childless, in 1881.

CHARLES ELIOT NORTON

Monday Morning.
July 19th. [1863]

My dear Mr. Norton

I am afraid you will have thought me very ungrateful, never to have written to thank you for your pretty present. It was so very kind of you to send it me. I always think of you as a friend of mine though I never saw you but that one time at the Lakes, \just/ six years ago,[1] yet I have heard so much about you from Mama and my sisters, that I quite feel to know you. I hope when you{come} and Mrs. Norton come to England, you will remember that you have some friends in London, who will be nearly if not quite as anxious to see you, and make Mrs. Norton's acquaintance as your Manchester friends. We had such a delightful time in Italy, this spring. It was very unfortunate, that François was obliged by his illness to go back to Paris.[2]

Again. thanking you very much believe me dear Mr. Norton

Yr affectionate & grateful
Florence Gaskell.

Houghton Library, Harvard University, MS Am 1088 1490.

Brantwood, Coniston. See pp 229, 230

---

1   Florence spent a month in the English Lake District, with her sister Julia, in the summer of 1857, during a time when Norton was in England (*Gaskell Letters*, p. 455).

2   For an account of this holiday in 1863 see Uglow, pp. 534-5 and *Gaskell Letters*, pp. 932-3.

ISABELLA GREEN

89 Oxford Terrace.[1]
Hyde Park.
Wednesday
[20 April 1864]

My dear Isabella,

Shall you think me, the most changeable person of your acquaint-ance, if I ask you if you will mind {?} coming to us on Monday the 23rd instead of Friday the 20th? The reason is this, I intended to have gone to Manchester last week, but Papa's unexpected return to England upset all my plans, I had kept that week clear of engage-ments, and now I am so complicated with various engagements, that I cannot possibly get away before the 13th. Now you understand my difficulty. If it is in the least inconvenient to you, please, tell me, and I will try and manage some other way. It will be so pleasant having you dear Isabella, only I feel very much afraid of my hostess capa-bilities, and that you will find it dull. Can't Mrs. Green come to[o], it would be such a great pleasure to us both if she could.[2] I am almost afraid that she will not like to leave Miss Brandreth, but I am sure the change would be so good for her after all her anxiety and sorrow. Please dear Mrs. Green think of this plan, you should be as quiet as ever you liked, and I would try my best to make it pleasant for you. I hope you will all make this your town house, and treat it as if it

1   Oxford Terrace was the name of a row of houses dating from about 1840, in what is now called Sussex Gardens. The houses comprise six stories including base-ment and attic, and balcony to the first floor at the front. The nearby Bathhurst Mews, now gentrified, but formerly providing accommodation for carriage and horse, suggest a high degree of opulence. The terrace is fronted with its own pri-vate road together with garden and hedge to provide separation from the main thoroughfare. Number 89 was Florence's first marital home. Mrs Gaskell wrote from this address on a number of occasions when visiting her daughter, refer-ring to it, on one occasion, as 'the Crompton's roof' (*Gaskell Letters*, p. 756). For a young married couple's first home it was both substantial and prestigious, but Mrs Gaskell does stress her son in law's professional success and prosper-ity (*Gaskell Letters*, p. 725). Wilkie Collins had lived at 85 Oxford Terrace as a young man. See http://www.web40571.clarahost.co.uk/wilkie/Homes/85O.htm for excellent photographs of Oxford Terrace.
2   Isabella's mother, wife of Henry Green, Unitarian Minister at Knutsford. Before marriage she was a Miss Brandreth (*Further Letters*, p. 305).

were "The Crompton Arms", write and order yours beds, and the time you would like dinner etc. etc. I want to know if you will bring up your "Illustrated Hymns in Prose", I have heard so much about them, and I should so like to see them. Our doctor is a nephew of Mrs Barbauld's.[1] London is a great hurry and bustle just now, and we are out nearly every evening, which is rather hard work.

Tomorrow there is to be a grand breakfast at the Reform Club, given to Garibaldi.[2] Mama and Meta had 5.o'clock tea with him yesterday at Mr. Seely's. I was very sorry I was unable to go, but I had another engagement. I hope Julia's back is better, and that she is not going to be troubled with a weak back, like some members of the family[.] Please excuse this untidy note, written in a great hurry, and believe me, with much love[.]

    Yours affectionately

    F. E. Crompton

First page embossed with FEC monogram.

Reproduced by courtesy of the University Librarian and Director, The John Rylands Library, The University of Manchester. Green Jamison Archive.

ISABELLA GREEN

        89 Oxford Terrace.

        Hyde Park.

        Wednesday

        May 3[rd.] [1865]

My dear Isabel,

    Only this morning have we heard of your dear little nephew's

---

1 Anna Laetitia Barbauld (1743–1825), wife of dissenting Minister Rochemont Barbauld, and a prolific writer of prose and poetry (*Women's Writing of the Romantic Period, 1789–1836: An Anthology*, ed. by Harriet Devine Jump, Edinburgh, 1997, p. 220).

2 Garibaldi spent twelve days in London, in 1864, arriving on 11 April to an enthusiastic welcome. During his visit he was entertained at the Reform Club. See Derek Beales, 'Garibaldi in England: The Politics of Italian Enthusiasm' in Davis and Ginsborg, pp. 184–216 (pp. 185-93). He was also a guest at Mr Seely's home (*Manchester Guardian*, 22 April 1864, p. 3, cols.3–4). The Reform Club was founded in 1836 as a centre for the Liberal Party (*ODBH*).

death.[1] I am so very sorry for you all – it must be such a terrible loss. We heard sometime ago (from Manchester) that he had scalded himself badly, but then we heard that he was so much better, and that it was not as bad as you had at first feared it would be. Was it from the effects of the scald that he died? or was he ill in some other way? When you can and will, I shall so like to hear from you, anything you will tell me, you know how interested I shall be to hear it. I don't even know when he died. Poor Annie she will hardly be able to realize her sad loss yet. Is she still at Southport,[2] or had they come home? It must be such hard work going on with the lesson, in the midst of all your sorrow. You were at Southport for some time were you not? Dear Isabel don't {?} feel obliged to write until you are quite inclined.

> Ever with much love to you all,
> Yours affectionately
> Florence Crompton.

First page embossed with FEC monogram.

Reproduced by courtesy of the University Librarian and Director, The John Rylands Library, The University of Manchester. Green Jamison Archive.

ISABELLA GREEN

Wednesday.
May 17[th.] [1865]

My dear Isabel.

Thank you so much for your letter telling me all about your little darling's illness.[3] Poor dear Annie it must be such a terrible blank for her. I cannot tell you how very very glad I was, to hear from Ellen's[4] letter to Mama, that there is another little one coming – it will be such a great comfort to her and Mr. Falcon[5] – they will almost feel as if

---

1   A reference to Isabella's nephew who died from scalds, in 1865, aged only seventeen months (*Gaskell Letters*, p. 761).
2   A popular, genteel resort on the Lancashire coast.
3   See Florence's letter to Isabella dated May 3rd 1865 and note 1.
4   Mary Ellen Green, Isabella's younger sister (*Further Letters*, p. 305).
5   Charles Falcon was Annie's husband; they had married in February 1863 (*Further Letters*, p. 261, n.1).

Max's spirit had come back to them in another form. I am so glad to think that the trial of going home is over – and that she has become a little used to the quietness of the house. What has become of the poor nurse? I feel so terribly sorry for her – for however careless {?} she may, indeed must have been, yet the dreadful remorse must be an awful punishment – and she can never forget the sad end of her carelessness. I am glad the little boy is buried at Knutsford.

Ever yours very affectionately

F. E. C.

May I have Emily and Ellen's photographs?

First page embossed with FEC monogram.

Reproduced by courtesy of the University Librarian and Director, The John Rylands Library, The University of Manchester. Green Jamison Archive.

ISABELLA GREEN

The White Heart

Sevenoaks.[1]

Friday Evening.

July 1[st.] [?1865][2]

My dear Isabella –

I have been intending to write to you, ever since you left London, to tell you how shocked and grieved I was, to hear that, after all my good advice & warning, you had joined the E. R. A. Well all I can say is that I hope you will have plenty of fines to pay – though I think you will soon find the society punishment enough. Have you repented yet, of your what shall I say *act of folly*? Charlie and I were astonished to hear you had joined, I could hardly believe it until I heard it from you – I thought you disliked it nearly as much as I did. Carry[3] and I

---

1 Now a commuter town for London, Sevenoaks would then have been a rural or semi-rural location.

2 Florence became Florence Crompton in September 1863 and as her mother, to whom she refers in this letter, died in November 1865 this letter would have been written in either 1864 or 1865.

3 Probably one of Judge Crompton's daughters, born 1837. Named Caroline, after her mother, the familiar 'Carrie' suggests reference to the daughter rather than Lady Crompton.

came down here yesterday, and we all go home on Monday, it is very pleasant getting out of London for a few days – We have had to give up all our parties on account of the death of Lady Cromptons aunt. The two garden parties, were the two parties I wanted to go to more than any this year, it is a pity. I saw Mama at Hampstead yesterday, I don't think she is looking well. I am glad Thomas found you a car-riage with ladies – he is always very good about managing those sort of things – This is such a charming place – I don't know if you know it at all – I never saw such splendid trees as these are in the Parks near. Please don't forget that I am to have one of your photographs –

> With love to Mrs. Green and Emily, believe me
> Yours affec'ately
> F. E. Crompton.

First page embossed with FEC monogram.

Black-edged mourning paper.

Reproduced by courtesy of the University Librarian and Director, The John Rylands Library, The University of Manchester. Green Jamison Archive.

ISABELLA GREEN

89 Oxford Terrace
Hyde Park W.
Thursday.
November 10$^{th.}$ [1865]

My dear Isabel.

Thank you for your kind note. It has been indeed a terrible loss to us all[1] – and though we had known for some time that he could not recover, yet the blow was none the less severe. It was all so quiet and peaceful at the end, that even Mr. Aiken hardly knew when it was all over. Yet I cannot realize, that we shall never again see his dear face, and almost expect to see him come in.

He is buried at Willesden one of the few really country church-yards left near London. It was a place he was so fond of, and often used to go there with Lady Crompton. It is such a blessing that he had

---

1   Florence's father-in-law, Judge Crompton, died on October 30th, 1865.

no pain – and that his sons were able to nurse him to the end, more
tender or devoted nurses I never saw. Dear Lady Crompton is wonderfully well, and so calm and good, thinking always of others loss,
before her own.

> Ever with love,
> Yours very affectionately
> Florence Crompton.

First page embossed with FEC monogram.

Black-edged mourning paper.

Reproduced by courtesy of the University Librarian and Director, The John Rylands
Library, The University of Manchester. Green Jamison Archive.

ISABELLA GREEN

Sunday Evening
February 24[th.] [1867]

My dearest Isabel.

I am quite ashamed to have been so long in answering your letter –
but the days seem to slip away so fast, that I have hardly time for anything. Julia was here for sometime and I missed her dreadfully when
she left. I am expecting Meta on Wednesday, which I am looking forward to, very much, it is so long since she has been here – at present
she is with Marianne. I have not yet got over my disappointment at
the E. T. Hollands[1] not living in this neighbourhood, as I had hoped
they would, it is quite a journey to get down to Wimbledon from here
– if it were only on the Great Western line that would be much better.
I envy you having heard Goldwin Smith's lectures – I should so like
to have heard him deliver them, though there was a great deal in them
that I disliked so much.

I suppose we shall be coming to Manchester in about a fortnight,
and I believe Marianne is going to Church House[2] about the same

---

1 Edward Thurstan and his wife Marianne, Florence's sister.
2 Church House, Knutsford, was at one time the home of Peter Holland (1766–
   1855), surgeon, and Mrs Gaskell's maternal uncle (Payne, pp. 36–37). The
   property may have remained in the Holland family.

time. I wonder if you have made many changes at Heathfield,[1] now that you have the house to yourselves – have you still your same bedrooms? I envy you have so much space, we are so cramped in this tiny house.[2] I suppose you have hung your curtains – I thought they were so very beautiful. I went about three weeks ago, to see the designs for the new Law Courts – and am sorry to say I like Scotts so much better than Mr. Waterhouse's.[3] It was very awkward we met Mrs. Waterhouse there, and of course she would ask what we thought of all the designs which was a most difficult question to answer. Everyone says however, that the interior of Mr. Waterhouse's design is much better than any of the others – and I fancy he will get it – though he himself thinks not. We went to see the Reform Demonstration on the 11th – which was the most tawdry affair I ever saw[4] – and very inferior to the former one – I believe even the most ardent Reformers consider the last to have been a complete failure. By way of a different sight, I went the week before to see the Queen open Parliament which was a grand show. We had a window close to Westminster, and saw the procession capitally. As the Queen came back there was a distinct hiss – and I never saw her so badly received.[5] Poor Sir Richard [?Magee] was regularly hissed whenever he rode past, which was very hard on him, as he is a great Liberal, and disliked so very much the part

---

1   A letter from Mrs Gaskell to her daughter Marianne, dated 1851, suggests that Heathfield was the Knutsford home of the Revd Green and his family (*Gaskell Letters*, p. 165). The Brook Street Chapel Website states that the Revd Green's boarding school was at Heathfield and that in 1851 seventeen pupils boarded there.
2   This comment is puzzling if it refers to her home in London, but no address is given here.
3   Royal Court of Justice in London. Competition was severe for this commission, which went to George E Street (1824–81) in 1868 (*ODNB*).
4   Organized by the Council for Reform League, delegates from towns throughout England, Ireland and Scotland took part in this event. The procession started at Trafalgar Square and concluded at the Agricultural Hall, Islington. Fifteen to eighteen thousand people were estimated to have taken part, but there were reports of poor management, falling off of numbers and straggling (*Manchester Guardian*, 12 February 1867, p. 5, col.4).
5   Queen Victoria arrived in London, from the Isle of Wight, where she had been staying, to officially open Parliament on 5 February. See *Manchester Guardian*, 6 February 1867, p. 3, col.3 for reports of enthusiastic crowds but no mention of hissing.

he had to take in the Hyde Park riots[1] – but of course was obliged to obey his orders, and now has to bear a great deal of the odium of it. Please forgive this dull letter, but I feel very stupid this evening.

> With love to you all
> Ever yr. very affec'*ate*
> Florence E. Crompton.

First page embossed with FEC monogram.

Black-edged mourning paper.

Reproduced by courtesy of the University Librarian and Director, The John Rylands Library, The University of Manchester. Green Jamison Archive.

ISABELLA GREEN

> 1. Sunnyside.[2]
> Wimbledon.
> Sunday
> July 21*st.* [1867]

My dear Isabel.

I hope the petticoat came all rightly, and was what you wanted[.] As I was away from town, I was not able to choose it myself, and so do not quite know what patterns they still have. I could not remember if yours had one or two flounces, but told them to send Annie's with two. I believe the price is 5/9.[3] at least that is what I paid for mine. I am beginning to be in despair about my dress as I cannot get them to send it home, and they have had it eight weeks – and all my repeated letters, seem to make no impression on her. If I had known how long she would have been I should not have bought my dress until I came home in the autumn. I was so glad to hear of Catherine Holt's little girl. I went to the breakfast to Mr. Garrison, and enjoyed some of the speeches very much, particularly Mills',[4] which I thought was

1 The Reform League (1865–69), which pressed for increased manhood suffrage, called a meeting at Hyde Park on 23 July 1866. When the crowd found the Park closed, they broke down the railings and clashed with the police (*ODBH*).
2 Marital home of Florence's sister Marianne.
3 Five shillings and ninepence in sterling; approximately thirty pence in today's decimal money.
4 John Stuart Mill was a guest at the Garrison Breakfast. See Meta's letter of 2

quite beautiful – Mr. Garrisons I disliked very much, it was so full of puns and little jokes, which were quite unsuited to such a serious affair. What a very odd mistake it was of the Inquirer to say that Mr. Beesley was *not* Mr. Beesley – for *he* it was at Exeter Hall. He seems very proud of that performance and delighted with all the notice he has had. Did you see Mr. Harrison's letter about it in the "Pall Mall"?[1] Have you heard any thing more about Emily Aspland's engagement.[2] I was very much interested to hear of it. I am sure you cannot wish half so much as I do, that I were with in reach of your strawberries – they sound most tempting. I have been down here for the last week, while Charlie has been off at Durham and Newcastle but leave Wimbledon tomorrow. It seems very odd being here, for never having slept here before – I have never quite realized that Marianne has a house of her own. We have not seen very much of the Volunteers owing to the bad weather – but one day we managed to get to the camp. You have no idea what a pretty sight it is, and so different to everything else – which of course made one think it looked foreign. The place was swarming with Belgians. Yesterday we saw far away in the distance a man with a *fez*? on a white horse, who we were told was the Sultan so I suppose we can say we have seen him, but that is all. I am going to Chorley for a few days next week, \be/fore joining Charlie at Manchester. Then Papa Meta, Julia, and I are going to Pen-y-gwrud [*sic*], at the top of the pass of Llanberis, for a few weeks, What Charlie and I shall do afterwards I have not an idea. I wonder if you have heard how Philip likes the plate – or is it to soon? I hope Mrs. Brandreth[3] is better than she was when you wrote, and that you are less anxious about her. Will you remind Annie that she promised me a photograph of Emma –

    With love,

    believe me dear Isabel

July 1867 for her account of this event.

1 Frederick Harrison, 'Mr. Beesly and his Censors', *Pall Mall Gazette*, 12 July 1867, correspondence, pp. 3–4. The letter is a defence of Edward Spencer Beesly who had spoken on the subject of Trade Unionism.

2 The Asplands were Unitarian friends of the Gaskell family (*Further Letters*, p. 109, n.3 and *Early Years*, p. 413).

3 Isabella's maternal grandmother.

Yours affec'*ly*
Florence Crompton.

First page embossed with FEC monogram.

Black-edged mourning paper.

Reproduced by courtesy of the University Librarian and Director, The John Rylands Library, The University of Manchester. Green Jamison Archive.

CHARLES ELIOT NORTON

84 Plymouth Grove
August 4th. [1867]

My dear Mr. Norton.

I have so much wished to send your little Lillie a present – and I remember being so fond of a scrap book myself that I have made one for her – which I hope will amuse her – it has been such a very great pleasure making it for her – I have so often wished to tell you how much touched and pleased we were at her being called after our darling mother – and I like so much to think of your little girl bearing *her* name I should dearly like to see her – but I am afraid there is no chance of that for some time to come – I am writing in a great hurry as we are going into Wales tomorrow and I want to send off this book before we go[1] – We were so much interested to hear of the birth of your little boy –

Please forgive this stupid letter, which does not say half what I wish, and believe me dear Mr. Norton,

Ever yours most sincerely& truly
Florence Crompton.

Black-edged mourning paper and envelope.

Address: Charles Norton Esq. Shady Hill. Cambridge. No stamp or postmark.

Houghton Library, Harvard University, MS Am 1088 1491.

---

1   See Meta's letter of 3 August 1867 and Florence's letter above dated 21 July 1867, both of which suggest the year of this letter.

ISABELLA GREEN

> Chorley
> Bridgenorth
> October 12th.
> Monday [1868]

My dear Isabel

Thank you so much for your charming long letter. I am so sorry that I don't know any one living on the Mediterranean, the only people I know living in that region, live at Constantinople, which I am afraid will be no use. I was so surprised when I got your letter telling me the news. I think it is so spirited of them going off, but what a hurry they must so be in. It will be most delightful, I only hope they are good sailors – are they going to provide themselves with Dr. Chapman's ice-bags. I am most interested in the expedition – do send me news of them. I wonder if the three doubtful ones will go. I suppose the children will be with you while Annie is away. I had no idea you had been in London again. I suppose it was quite lately? Madam Craven's new book is "Anne Sèverins".[1] I am in the middle of it and *rather* like it. I have not read the Curid-Ars but have heard it so much praised, and also so much *dis*-praised, that I am most curious to read it.[2] I was very much amused with "The odds on the race", it is very clever, particularly the end. We are all very much interested in Dr. Sandwith's election for Marylebone,[3] though I am not sure if I wish him to get in – I dislike him so much, though he did behave so well at Kars. I must stop now, with very best wishes to them all for a pleasant and calm voyage.

> Ever yours affec'ly
> F. E. C.

First page embossed with FEC monogram.

---

1   *Anne Sèverin*, by Mme Augustus Craven (Paris, 1868), translated into English by Lady G. C. Fullerton (London, 1869).
2   Possible reference to the 'Curé d'Ars', St John Vianney (1786-1859); accounts of his life were published during the years following his death.
3   Dr Humphry Sandwith (1822–81), Chief Military Officer for British and Turkish Forces at Kars during the war between Russia and Turkey, stood unsuccessfully as Liberal Candidate for Marylebone in 1868 (*ODNB*).

ISABELLA GREEN

Thursday
November 5th [1868]

My dearest Isabel

I was so very glad to get your letter and to hear your great piece of news, which was a great surprise to me. And now I want to know a great deal more about it all – if I may. How your family must envy you having seen Miss Herbert. I have only seen Mr. Herbert twice, when he was painting at the Houses of Parliament,[1] and did not even know he was married, they live somewhere in St John's Wood don't they? What news for Emily and Annie, would they hear at Malta. I am so much interested for you all. It is so pleasant that you know and like her, please give Philip my warmest congratulations. Will they be married before he goes back, but I dare say I am asking questions I had better leave alone, so don't answer any you don't like. What a pretty name she has, is she as pretty as her name? How could you begin your letter with anything else? I am so glad you have such good accounts from your travellers. I fancied the children were at Heathfield. Marianne is going on wonderfully, I am going down this afternoon to be introduced to my small niece.

Ever dear Isabel with
love to Ellen
Yours ever affec'ly
F. E. C.

First page embossed with FEC monogram.

---

1   John Rogers Herbert (1810–90), painter, known for his frescoes at the Palace of Westminster (*ODNB*).

ISABELLA GREEN

Erdiston House[1]
Tenbury.
Thursday Evening.
September 7[th.] [1870]

Dear Isabel.

I have been a long time in answering your letter. I think the brides-maids' dresses sound very pretty. I always think, a thin grenadine or muslin look so well over self coloured muslin. Is the wedding on the 19th or 20th. I hope you will have a fine warm day. We have had splendid weather here, for the last week, and have almost lived out of doors. There is rather a pleasant river almost at the bottom of the garden, and it is delightful to be on it. We stay here until Wednesday or Thursday, when the Swiss party come home. Charlie and I are going abroad on Friday or Saturday.

Geneva is as far as we have fixed at present, as so much will then depend on the state of the mountains. We shall get there next Sunday, and if you are kindly disposed, a letter there will be most welcome. I hope we shall have fine weather, and not *too* warm. My only draw-back, is that I know we shall meet so many friends, as all the barris-ters are loose. Charlie has such a great love for his friends, that he rushes up and greets every acquaintance, that he sees, which is very trying to my feelings. When we have fixed our plans, I shall send you a further direction, as I shall be so anxious to hear how Annie goes on.[2]

Thursday Evening. I came up to London yesterday to get endless odds and ends, that one wants for a journey. I never felt anything like the heat here – it is almost impossible to read even, and one wan-ders over the house in a hopeless way, trying in vain, to find a cool-*ish* place. We have given up Geneva, and are going to Thun 12th Sep. Leukerbad, Brig 18th. Baveno, and Lugano 22nd where I shall hope for news of Annie.

---

1 Erdiston House, located in Tenbury Worcester, was Judge Crompton's tempo-rary home for two years (*Gaskell Letters*, p. 741).
2 Reference to Annie Green's circumstances place this letter in the same year as the one following, dated 9 December 1870.

Ever with much love
Yours very affectionately
Florence Crompton.

First page embossed with FEC monogram.

Reproduced by courtesy of the University Librarian and Director, The John Rylands Library, The University of Manchester. Green Jamison Archive.

ISABELLA GREEN

84 Plymouth Grove.
Manchester.
Friday Evening
Dec. 9th. [1870]

My dearest Isabel –

I am so sorry not to have answered your letter before this – but I have been so very busy – I do hope dear Annie is better, and the nurse also – I was so very sorry to hear how ill Annie was – I have seen so many cases in the Hospital, and they always seem to suffer so dreadfully. I hope she is better than when you wrote. You have so often, all of you, been in my thoughts – and I have so often wondered how Annie was. Only the day before I heard from you, I {was} had such a strong feeling that some of you were ill. How glad you must have been when the Knutsford nurse came – you must have been nearly knocked up. I hope you were fortunate in having a good doctor – I am afraid \the change/ will not have done either you or Mrs. Green much good – but now I hope you will have some quiet, and that Annie will get quickly well. Harry's wedding went off very well, though we had not a very good day, rather a fog. Lucy looked particularly pretty, I did not fancy the white would have suited her, as she has rather a dark complexion, but it did. She was dressed in a very rich white silk, with a deep lace flounce, the dress cut square filled up with a tulle handkerchief, round her neck a beautiful ruby ornament – a tulle veil, with a quite a small spray of white flowers – & ruby ear rings. I think I never saw such a pretty bride – At times I admire her almost more than any one I have ever seen – she has such splendid eyes – five or six times the size of most people's eyes – It is curious at times I think her quite plain, [?the] changes make it a most interesting face to watch, & I am never tired of looking at her. She had four brides-maids, Carry, Sophie Romilly & two little nieces. Their dresses were deep pink silk \skirts/, with white muslin tunics, tulle veils, a[nd] a spray of pink flowers. We were rather unlucky and did not get to church until they had begun the service, so the Romilly's[1] clocks were all wrong, and they got to church much too early. Every body got through very well, and we had no crying. It seemed very odd their driving off to their own home at once. I have only just seen Harry since then, Today is Mary James'[2] wedding day, rather a wretched day if the weather is anything like what we have had here. I have been very much interested about Miss Garrett's election to the School Board – I think she will be such a capital person for it, so practical – and so much sound strength. It was a great triumph both for her, and Emily Davies, their coming in at the head of the Poll.[3] With love to your mother –

Ever dear Isabel
Yours very affec'ly
F. E. Crompton.

First page embossed with FEC monogram.

Reproduced by courtesy of the University Librarian and Director, The John Rylands Library, The University of Manchester. Green Jamison Archive.

1   See *Gaskell Letters*, p. 298 and *Further Letters*, p. 150, n.6 for references to this distinguished family who were known to the Gaskells. John Romilly (1802–74) was a judge and politician (*ODNB*). His daughter, Lucy Henrietta, married Henry Crompton (Florence's brother-in-law), in 1870 (www.jjhc.info/crompton-henry1904.htm).
2   Possibly daughter of Sir William M. James (1807–81), judge and friend of William Gaskell; she married a member of the Schwabe family, who were also known to the Gaskells (*Further Letters*, pp. 47 and 49, n.4 and *ODNB*).
3   Elizabeth Garrett (1836–1917), was one of the first women in Britain to qualify in medicine; her election to the London School Board for Marylebone in 1870 (ODNB) dates this letter. Emily Davies (1830–1921) was a suffragist, remembered as co-founder of Girton College for Women, Cambridge (*ODNB*).

ISABELLA GREEN

Wednesday. [1872]

My dearest Isabel.

How you have taken my breath away! but how very delightful – few people have such [?plums] in their lives – I will gladly do what I can for you – but it seems to me it would be a far better plan, if you would come and do your own shopping – If you came up on Saturday or Monday, by which time you would have seen Harriet, & stopped till the 2nd, I think I am more likely to have a chance of getting you by asking you for a short time, also I believe Meta is coming then. Do think of the advantages of my plan, to begin with the charity of it – Charlie is on circuit and I find it very dull all alone, and should delight in having you – then think how much better & cheaper things are in London, and the much greater choice you have – then there are the Old Masters still open, a capital collection at the Dudley Gallery, Burne-Jones, Solomons,[1] etc etc – The Duke of Edinburgh's collection at South Kensington[2] – and I am sure by hook or by crook I could get orders for the house – then on Sunday afternoon Mrs. Fawcett[3] is giving a lecture on Women's Education – this is only half of what we will do if you will only come – Then doubtless Philip will be in town before he goes & you would have another sight of him. Please write and tell me. I may expect you, I am sure it will really take you very little more from Heathfield than having to go to M'chester a dozen times for one thing –

I am writing in most frantic haste, so please forgive the scrawl – from
Your very affec'^{ate}
F.E.C.

Reproduced by courtesy of the University Librarian and Director, The John Rylands Library, The University of Manchester. Green Jamison Archive.

---

1 The Dudley Art Gallery, London, was founded in 1864; its first exhibition opened in April 1865 (*Victorian Web*). The artists referred to are Edward Burne-Jones (1833–98) and, probably, Abraham Solomon (1823–62) (*ODNB*).
2 This event provides the year of this letter, and suggests either February or March as the month. See Florence's letter dated Feb. 4th. [1872].
3 Millicent Garrett Fawcett (1847–1929), a suffragist, who in 1871 co-founded Newnham College, Cambridge (*ODNB*).

ISABELLA GREEN

Sunday Evening.
Feb. 4*th.* [1872]

My dearest Isabel,

Thank you very much for your capital long letter – Do come home from Torquay via London, it would be so pleasant to have you – if only we have a house – but I feel as if any day the perfect house we have so long looked for in vain might turn up – or rather that we shall have to give up our ideal house, and content ourselves with an uninteresting one. Agnes Berry[1] arrived about ten days ago – and we all like her very much indeed – which is fortunate for she might have been anything but nice – She is not, to my mind, at all pretty but has a very bright intelligent face – constantly changing, which is pleasant to watch – She is only five and twenty but seems a good deal older, and looks so. Mr. Berry was a merchant, & married his second wife within eight months of the death of Agnes' mother – I believe the step-mother was not at all a nice person, and got so much power over Mr. Berry that he left all his money to her, and so his daughters had to go out as governesses. It was as a governess that Agnes went to Alexandria, where she was for nine months. They will live in Egypt for five or six years after they are married, till Edward has finished the docks, that the Viceroy is building near Alexandria.[2] They had a most fearful passage home – and were several days late – I fancy some friends of Ellen's came over in the same ship. Did she not know a Capt. & Mrs. Monroe in Bombay? I fancy I remember seeing a photograph of a Mrs. Monroe when I was at Heathfield, on hearing Ellen mention her. I wondered as soon as Agnes spoke of them if they were friends of Ellens, and she said they told her a young lady a friend of theirs who had been with her brother in Bombay had come home about nine months ago, and was very musical – all of which facts, I thought, fitted on to Ellen – I am so sorry to hear that Philip is going back to India so soon, and that Mrs. Philip Green will not be well

---

1   Agnes Mary Berry, wife of Edward Crompton, brother of Charles Crompton, Florence's husband (*www.jjhc.info/cromptoncharles1865.htm*).
2   Egypt's largest seaport, Alexandria had become an important trading centre especially in connection with Egyptian cotton (*Wik.*).

enough to go with him. Do they think she will ever be well enough to go back to India – or is the climate too trying for her? It must be a great trial for her not to be able to go with Philip, but I do hope it will not make her worse. I hope you think she is better than she was when I was at Heathfield. It was Harry that read the paper at Nottingham – I thought it read very well in the papers, and I believe it was very much liked by the men – I am amused to hear of a Bachelors Ball at Knutsford – I hope it went off well – Carry and I are very busy going to lectures at University College – She is more active than I am as she goes to six a week, while I content myself with four, two on psychology, and two on physiology & hygiene – I like the physiology ones much the best – as the others are so very metaphysical – The lectures on physiology are most interesting, and very well delivered. I find that with all the reading for them and the getting there, that it takes up a great deal of time, and I doubt if in future I shall ever undertake more than two a week. We have been out a great deal lately, so that with society & learning I seem to have had very little time for letter writing – or reading. I have only had time to go once to the Old Masters[1] – From the glance I had then I did not think it looked nearly such a good collection as the other two have been – there are a great many Dutch pictures and I do not care much for them. I intend to go down some day to South Kensington to see the Duke of Edinburgh's things[2] – The account of them in the newspapers sounded very interesting – only I know they will make me so envious – I always have such a longing for queer quaint foreign things. I wonder if you have heard that the Albert Cromptons are going to live in Liverpool. Albert has got some place, I am not clear what, in the Holt's shipping business.[3] It was only finally fixed last Saturday, yesterday week, and he

---

1   The Royal Academy hosted an Old Masters exhibition most winters, from December to February. Although the events in 1870 and 1871 were well reported in the press there is no report for 1872.

2   The Duke of Edinburgh's Collection of artefacts and paintings was on public display at South Kensington from 25 January 1872 for approximately two months (*The Times*, 24 January 1872, p. 5, col.D). The Duke was Queen Victoria's second son, Prince Alfred (1844–1900). After pursuing a successful Naval career he made his home in Coburg, but maintained Clarence House where his Collection was housed after the exhibition closed (*ODNB*).

3   Albert Crompton, another of Charles's brothers, became a manager at Alfred

has already found & taken a house, and they expect to be settled there in less than three weeks – It seems such quick work at last, to be off so soon. I think he will like the work, and he has always hated law, and so I think would never get on in it.

I am afraid now that even Marianne and Thurstan, have given up all hope of Willie hearing – It does seem so very sad for the poor little fellow – he is such a bright loving little child – I suppose really they are very happy, and after all it is not like the loss of a sense \ once had/ – It seems so wonderful being able to {tell} teach them to talk – I had a long conversation the other day (in German so not our natural language either of us) with a young Dutch gentleman, who was born deaf and dumb – He understood everything I said, and there was only one word of his that I could not make out, "Seeds" which he called "Erst" – I so far forgot that he was a deaf mute, that at the end, I thought how rude and unpleasant it was of him, never to take his eyes off my face – quite forgetting it was his only way of understanding what I said. I am sure you will long before this be quite tired of this endless letter – Please forgive the horrid writing but my hand is quite stiff with the number of letters I have had to write today – With a great deal of love to you all

Ever yours very affec'ly

F. E. Crompton.

The tea is very good. Do write soon.

Holt and Company in 1882 (Hyde, p. 80 and n.1). It is not clear when he first joined the company, but Florence's reference to her nephew Willie's impaired hearing in her ensuing paragraph suggests 1872 as the date of this letter, since that was the year Meta first mentioned the condition, in which case 1872 is the year Albert Crompton first moved to Liverpool.

ISABELLA GREEN

Wednesday Evening
March 27th. [1872]
[89 Oxford Terrace]

My dearest Isabel –

I really think I must be getting into my second child-hood – for never from the time you left Oxford Terrace till yesterday, did I remember the recipe for the egg. I am so sorry, and I cannot say how very stupid I think myself – Shall I, when I go back to town, send the recipe to Heathfield? I am so glad you like the law pens – I think them so very nice, and easy to write with. It seems so strange to think that this day week you will be well started on your journey. I do hope you will have a good journey, and no drawbacks. We met Harriet Long[1] yesterday in town, very much puzzled what books to get – she said Mr. Holt was taking a great stock – and after all such things are to be had in America. One is so apt to start on a journey, with the belief that one will not be able to supply, or, replace anything till one returns. I shall feel such an interest in hearing if all your dresses are right – for I feel to have stood god-mother to them. We are all so disappointed, that owing to some squabble between the Egypt people & Mr. [?Fowler] that Edward will not be able to get off this month, and will now I fancy not be able to come till the late summer. I am sorry for Agnes,[2] for it is so wretched for her waiting on at the Cromptons – She has been very ill with bronchitis, and unfortunately the news of the delay in Edward's return came just when she was so very ill, and has kept her back very much. We are all very anxious about Llewelyn Davies' election for the school-board which takes place tomorrow.[3]

---

1 See *Further Letters*, p. 30 and p. 31, n.3 for references to Harriet and other members of the Long family.
2 Florence's sister-in-law; see Florence's letter above dated 4 February 1872 and n.1.
3 John Llewelyn Davies (1826–1916), friend of F. D. Maurice, Thomas Hughes and Charles Kingsley, was involved in the establishment of the Working Men's College in London in 1854, and in the promotion of higher education for women. (*ODNB*). He was related by marriage to Florence's husband (*Gaskell Letters*, p. 706). He was successful in his bid to become a member of the London School Board in March 1872 (*The Times*, 29 March 1872, p. 3, col.2).

He had a capital chance at first, and was in very good spirits about it, but quite late in the day Prof. Sylvester[1] came into the {field} field, and all the Jews, who had promised to vote for Llewelyn deserted to their own man. I shall be so very sorry if Llewelyn does not get in, as I think he would be such a good man, and it makes it harder, that he was so very much pressed to stand, and all his friends said he was so sure to be returned. We were so sorry that we were engaged the day you came over to Manchester – I should dearly have liked another sight of you before we have to "think a great deal of you". I am so very glad that you find Mrs. Philip Green[2] so much better – I suppose Philip will be nearly back at Bombay by this time.

> Ever with a great deal of love,
> Yours very affec'ly
> Florence Crompton.

Reproduced by courtesy of the University Librarian and Director, The John Rylands Library, The University of Manchester. Green Jamison Archive.

ISABELLA GREEN

13 Cromwell Place.[3]
South Kensington.
Saturday
April 18th 1874.

Dearest Isabel –

I am so glad to hear (from Ellen)[4] such delightful accounts of your goings on – How fortunate you were to get rooms and servants so

---

1   James Joseph Sylvester (1814–1897), a distinguished mathematician, who added the name Sylvester to his family name; a highly gifted man, he also wrote and published poetry (*ODNB*).
2   Isabella's sister-in-law, since John Philip was her brother.
3   Cromwell Place is another row of substantial terrace houses, each comprising six stories including basement and attic, and balcony at the front. Unlike Oxford Terrace, there is no evidence to suggest the existence of a former garden or private road, but each house has its own balconied portico entrance. The nearby Cromwell Mews again suggest accommodation for horse and carriage. Number thirteen is now a language school; a blue plaque indicates that number seven has been home to a number of artists including John E. Millais.
4   Probably Isabella's sister (*Further Letters*, p. 305).

quickly in Rome. I hope you still like them – We have been having such bright weather here, and if you have at all the same it must be quite delicious. Does Rome come up to what you expected? I hope you have been to all the villa gardens near, for I think they and the country round Rome, are almost as delightful as Rome itself. How do you find your Italian [?]? I saw Signor Volpe in the street the other day, I do not know if he was coming from Prince Leopold,[1] but we doubt he was. We have only just come back from the North, and seem hardly settled into our London life – The Ainsworths[2] have a house in town for two months, but I have not yet seen them – Dr. Morgan's marriage has just come off – I believe it is not yet three months since she and Dr. *Hoggan* (such a name) first met.[3] He is a great deal older than she is, and has retired from practice, so I suppose he is a sort of consulting partner in the firm. They had the courage to be married on the first of April – want no wedding tour, but went and dined at Richmond – quite a unique way of passing your wedding-day. They sent the most peculiar wedding cards "Dr. George & Dr. Frances Hoggan". I have not seen her since the marriage but Marianne has, and says she looks most bright and happy. The other strong-minded marriage has come to a most terrible end – I mean Miss Cook's. The wedding was to have been last Tuesday – Mrs. Scott had come up for it, and on Sunday her friends believed that all was going on (so that I do not quite know if it was [?over] on Sunday or Monday) but on one of these days he went out of his mind, and late on Monday evening they sent to tell their friends that the wedding was put off – I fancy he has never been very strong, and that he has had a good deal to try him in this engagement – for I think her friends were more anxious for it than she was – and certainly she did not look at all happy since she was engaged, but quite wretched – Is not it a dreadfully sad

---

1   Prince Leopold (1853–84) was Queen Victoria's fourth and youngest son. Fond of European travel, he became President of the Royal Society of Literature in 1878 and Vice-President of the Society of Arts the following year (*ODNB*). Signor Volpe was Professor of Italian at University College London and teacher of Italian to Prince Leopold (*Observer*, 7 June 1868, p. 3 col.5).

2   Possibly Peter and Elizabeth Ainsworth (see *Further Letters*, p. 244, n.2, and *Gaskell Letters*, p. 637).

3   Frances Morgan (1843–1927), one of the first women in Britain qualified to practice medicine, married Dr George Hoggan in 1874 (*ODNB*).

story? It seems so sad, when at last Mr. Scott *had* got what he had been longing and trying for, for so long that at the very last moment it should be lost. He has "gone away" for several months – I do not know where to, or anything beyond the vague fact of his being gone – We are expecting the Edward Crompton's back in England very soon – a horrid change I should think from Egypt to Liverpool – they however seem thankful to leave Alexandria – I hope this letter will get to Rome before you leave. Have you seen anything of the Storys?

    Ever yr. very affec'*te*

    F. E. C.

First page embossed with FEC monogram.

Reproduced by courtesy of the University Librarian and Director, The John Rylands Library, The University of Manchester. Green Jamison Archive.

ISABELLA GREEN

84 Plymouth Grove

December 14*th* [1889]

My dearest Isabel –

Papa brought us today the sad news of the Long's terrible loss.[1] I am so very very sorry for you all. It seems too terrible to be true – and one cannot realize that it is – I saw him and Mrs. Long only last week on my way down here – and he looked so bright and well – Dearest Isabel I do so wish I could do anything for any of you – at these times one feels so sadly useless – but I do so think of you all – One's words seem so poor & inexpressive, but you have never been out of my thoughts since I heard of it – We have only heard the bare fact – and do not even know when it was. I am so very very sorry – Please believe how I feel for you thought [*sic*] I cannot say it.

    Ever dear Isabel

    Yours very affectionately

    Florence Crompton.

---

1 The Longs were Knutsford acquaintances of the Gaskells (*Gaskell Letters*, p. 17). John Long was one of Brook Street Chapel's Trustees; his death in 1889 provides the year of this letter and the one following dated December 30th (*Brook Street Chapel Website*).

ISABELLA GREEN

> 84 Plymouth Grove.
> Sunday
> December 30th [1889]

My dear Isabel –

You are all of you so much in our thoughts, that it seems the natural thing to write to you – We do hope Mrs. Green will not write before she feels inclined, letters are I know, at such times so difficult to write, in fact almost impossible. It must be so difficult to believe that it is true, and not some terrible dream. I do so hope that Mr. & Mrs. Alfred Holt[1] will be able to stay for some time, at Grove House,[2] or at any rate that she will stay. It does as you say seem such a large house, for only Mrs. Long and Louisa – I do hope dear Annie is not worse for the sad news, and that it has not undone the good {?} of the change to Bournemouth – Had she left before the accident? How very glad you must be, to be at liberty, and able to go to Grove House often.

> Ever dear Isabel
> Your affec'ate
> F. E. Crompton

---

1   Alfred Holt, whose shipping company, based in Liverpool, owned the Blue Funnel Line, first registered as Ocean Steamship Company in 1865. As a son of Unitarian parents he attended the Revd Green's school in Knutsford from 1838 to 1844 (Hyde, p. 1 and n.1 and pp. 9–10). Holt married into the Long family twice, in 1865 to Catherine and, after her death, to her cousin Frances in 1871 (*Brook Street Chapel Website*).

2   Grove House, adjacent to Brook Street Chapel, was the home of the Long family (*Brook Street Chapel Website*).

JULIA BRADFORD GASKELL

(1846–1908)

Elizabeth and William Gaskell's fourth and youngest surviving daughter, 'that dear but dangerous little person – Julia'
(*Letters of Charlotte Brontë,* II, 677).

Julia Bradford Gaskell
from *Manchester Portraits* (1910) by Will Rothenstein

After Marianne and Florence had married and set up home in London,
Julia, who never married, shared her life with Meta. The two women
became known as the Miss Gaskells, leading the kind of independent
lives that their mother would have admired and respected.

AUNT ANN[1]

[February 1859][2]

My dear Aunt Ann,

Thank you so very much for getting such nice presents. I am going to have the box of soap and the cotton. I was so very sorry to hear that you had been so ill. If Florence was at home I am sure she would write and thank you but she may not write to anybody but us.[3]

I remain your affecate niece

Julia B. Gaskell

Give my best love to Willie.

No date or sender's address.

Manchester Libraries, Information and Archives, MF 615 Gaskell-Brontë Material in the Symington Collection Reel 1. Microfilm (*COPY*)

ISABELLA GREEN

46 Plymouth Grove
Manchester
Sept. 21[st.] 1866.

My dearest Isabel.

Thank you so very much for remembering yr. promise about the photograph, which I think is charming, I do so like it, don't you?. thank you for it so very much. You ask me for mine, but I am sorry I can't send you one, I have not been taken again except by Fred Schwabe,[4] and though he took 13 of me they are none of them good, or else I wd. send you one, I think I never shall take well, but I think some time I shall be tempted to try "Bibo" his always seem so satisfactory, and there is a new mode now of taking photographs called "Wathlotype" (at least that is what it sounded to me like) which

1 Probably Anne Robson, William Gaskell's sister with whom Elizabeth Gaskell kept up a regular correspondence.

2 See *Gaskell Letters* p. 529–530, in which Elizabeth Gaskell thanks her sister-in-law for presents sent to her daughters.

3 Florence is at school in Knutsford (*Gaskell Letters* pp. 530 and 537).

4 Frederick Schwabe, third son of Salis and Julie Schwabe, whose considerable wealth was derived from calico printing (*Further Letters*, p. 307 and Uglow p. 161).

makes it look as if done from a picture, I want somebody to try it, and see if it answers, I believe there is a man in Regent Street who does [?this] sort. You can't think how very glad we were to hear that you had a better account of Ellen, I do hope so much that she will go on improving. We feel already Manchester air making us feel stupid, it always seems so heavy and unhealthy, it makes one feel so sleepy. I think we shall be at home for some time, but we have been asked to go to Pendyffryn and Glyn Garth,[1] but I don't think we shall, we have only just come from Wales, which was so lovely that it has made us feel "out of sorts" with Manchester. I suppose Manchester will be very busy with the Social Science, {wl} which begins on Wednesday week,[2] Is Mrs. Green coming over for it? or any of you? Marianne was so sorry to miss seeing more of you. She and Thurstan left us on Thursday, and go today to Dumbleton, we thought they were both of them looking so well, it seems so odd Meta and I being the only two at home, we seem somehow very busy having been away from home for some time, and also there being so few. I have taken Marianne's kitchen on, which makes me busy. We went to the pictures here the other day, seeing a very good account of them in "the Guardian" but we were much disappointed with them,[3] there were very few good ones and what there were, were mixed with some such horrid ones. Are not the Totnes revelations shameful.? We are so sorry for *Mrs*. Pender, I think she will feel it so very much people seem to think that Mr. Pender[4] will

---

1 Glyn Garth was the country home of the Schwabe family on the Anglesey coast, facing Snowdonia. There is a Pendyffryn on the North Wales coast and also in Pembrokeshire, South Wales; it is not certain which is referred to here.

2 The National Association for the Promotion of Social Science held its Annual Meeting in 1866 in Manchester, starting on 3 October. This event was widely advertised in the national and regional press; see the *Observer*, 2 September 1866, p. 3, col.2; *Manchester Guardian*, 8 September 1866, p. 1, col.5; and *Manchester Guardian,* 29 September 1866, p. 1, col.5. Distinguished speakers included James Kay-Shuttleworth and John Stuart Mill.

3 See *Manchester Guardian*, 14 September 1866, p. 2, col.7, for a report of the Exhibition of Pictures at the Royal Institution, Manchester.

4 Sir John Pender (1816–96), Manchester Textile merchant, born in Dumbarton, served as Liberal member for Totnes 1862–66 but was unseated on petition. He was associated with the successful laying of the Transatlantic Cable 1866 and knighted in 1888 (*ODNB*). The revelations referred to here followed investigations into corrupt practices in which Pender, and others, were found guilty of

very likely be imprisoned. Did you see that Miss Agnes Crum was dead, she died at Malvern, she has been delicate for so long, but it must be so lonely for Miss Polly Crum now, Miss Louisa Fletcher is much worse as perhaps you have heard, it must be so sad for Miss Fletcher, and indeed for all her sisters, poor Lady Crompton it seems as if she had had so much sorrow lately.[1]

We are very full of a Sky dog that is coming to us next week "Irving" by name and from all accounts the most charming little thing. I had the offer of a most beautiful dog, but it was a very large one and we thought it was better not to have a large one in a town, We did so enjoy Barmouth, it was quite lovely, we had a charming little house with a lovely view from it, and by just going round the corner a lovely view of Cader[2] and all the hills near Dolgelly. I don't know if you know this part of Wales, it is so beautiful, we had great fun coaching we went from Carnarven to Barmouth, and from Dolgelly to Beddgelert, and on to Corwen on the outside getting wet through and through, the most tremendous showers, but the lights on the hills between them was lovely. I saw Jessie Mackie's marriage in the paper, do you know where they are going to? I can't fancy Jessie married can you?. She is going to live very near here I believe, I am afraid I have written a long letter but I wish you ever, all of you could know how I love you all[.] Home does seem so sad now, I think that each day is worse than the one before, I can now begin to realize everything, which before somehow I did not do fully. But though each day is sadder it is such a comfort that time does really go, and that each day is one day nearer Mama, it does feel as if one can now go on living without her. I am sorry to have written this to you but if you knew what it was to be or seem to be always cheerful you wd. know how one does so want somebody to vent all one's sorrow to: for I can't bear to add to their grief, which is indeed almost more than we can bear.

---

bribing potential voters. Reports of the Election Commissioners featured in the press throughout 1866 and 1867; see, for example, *Manchester Guardian*, 26 February 1867, p. 7, col.5.

1   Lady Crompton was Miss Caroline Fletcher before her marriage. Her husband Sir Charles Crompton had died in 1865 (*ODNB*).

2   Cader Idris, a mountain range in North Wales.

Ever dear dear Isabel
Yr loving
JBG

Black-edged mourning paper.

Reproduced by courtesy of the University Librarian and Director, The John Rylands Library, The University of Manchester. Green Jamison Archive.

ISABELLA GREEN

46 Plymouth Grove
Manchester
Oct 7th 1866

My dearest Isabel

Thank you so very much for your letter I was so very much obliged to you for it – dear Isabel – we have been so busy or else I should have answered your letter before, however though late, they are none the less hearty. We have been so busy with the Social Science, we have gone, I every day & Meta all but one, we feel so tired, we set off from here at 9 and sometimes did not get back until nearly 6, some of the papers were so very interesting, I enjoyed Mr. Roundels on "Jamaica" and Sir James K. Shuttleworth's address the most I think,[1] Madame Bodichon's paper on "Female Suffrage" was also very good, *if* you took her side,[2] I dare say you will have heard all about it from the Longs, and about Dr. Marie Walker the little American who wore a bloomer costume, I thought she was horridly indecent, and I disliked her so very much[.] The Courts[3] looked splendid, so lovely full of flowers and bright people, I was so glad that [?] Waterhouse, and Mr Theodore[4] & Mrs Waterhouse were all there, when the Courts were

---

1   Mr Roundell was Secretary of the Jamaica Commission during the Eyre trial (*Observer*, 24 February 1867, p. 6, col.5 and *Manchester Guardian,* 28 March 1867, p. 4, col.3).
2   Barbara Bodichon, née Leigh Smith. Mrs Gaskell had signed her petition to amend the law on married Women's property in 1856 (Uglow, pp. 396–97).
3   Manchester Assize Courts, completed in 1864, designed by Alfred Waterhouse (1830–1905), described in the *Manchester Guardian* as a 'palace of justice' (*Manchester Guardian*, 30 July 1864, p. 6, col.2).
4   Theodore Waterhouse, Alfred Waterhouse's younger brother (*ODNB*).

so much praised, it was so sad to see Mr. Fawcett feeling them as much as he could, it is wonderful how quickly he knows people, we were talking to him, and he said "is Mrs Crompton there" – Florence and Harry stayed here, and Miss Julia Smith-Cave for one night, she is aunt of Madame Bodichon's & Miss Florence Nightingale and a charming little old lady, Madame Bodichon is a great friend of Mrs. Lewes and she told Madam Bodichon the other day that Shakespeare heroines were trumpery after the heroine she had been reading about, (in the Greek plays.) We saw some such pleasant people that came here, and some such odd ones, we saw a good deal of several strong minded ones Miss B Parkes, Mrs Knox (née Isa Craig) Miss Emily Davies,[1] and we also saw a great deal of Dr. Elizabeth [?Caucett], she is so charming, we quite fell in love with her she is so perfectly feminine with it all – Florence left today to join Charlie, we have very good accounts of Marianne, she and Thurstan are at Dumbleton, they go to London on or about the 22nd, Meta and I are going away on Monday with Mrs Shuttleworth to Aberystwith,[2] it will be so odd going back there so soon, but our drains are going to be done when we are away – I don't know if we shall stay long at Aberystwith or whether we shall travel about, after a week or 10 days we shall leave Mrs Shuttleworth, and we shall go on to Oxford to stay with Dr. & Mrs. Pattison,[3] he is rector of Lincoln, and the "Essays Reviews" man and perhaps, I shd. think, we may go on to the Brodies, then we are coming home for some time I think.

Our new little dog "Irving" is such fun, he's a constant subject of fun, but we are getting so very fond of him – I do so hope that Ellen is better, Papa has gone down tonight to Owens College, we went

1   Bessie Parkes (1829–1925), grand-daughter of Joseph Priestley, involved in women's suffrage and promoter of education for women, she married Louis Belloc, becoming, through one of her children, grandmother to Hillaire Belloc; Isabella Craig (1831–1903), social reformer, women's rights activist and writer of prose and poetry, married a cousin John Knox; Emily Davies (1830–1921) suffragist and co-founder of Girton College, Cambridge (*ODNB*).
2   Aberystwyth is a resort on Cardigan Bay on the west coast of Wales.
3   Mark Pattison (1813–84), appointed Rector of Lincoln college Oxford in 1861; a noted scholar, he contributed an essay on religious thought in eighteenth-century England to *Essays and Reviews*, a theological volume published in 1860. His wife, Emilia, was a keen student of French Art History (*ODNB*).

the other day to hear Mr. Ward's speech he is the new professor & such a clever person, he writes some of the historical reviews in the "Saturday".[1]

Meta said I was to ask you if you ever could give us any cuttings of that little rose that grows before the drawing room {bed} window a very pretty red one, we do so want to try & make roses do here, I am almost afraid its hopeless, Are not you sorry about Mr. Ruskin, I am very *anti* Eyre, and the paper on Jamaica & the talk afterwards the other day only strengthened me.

I wish you cd. have heard Mr Roundel's paper it was so very good, and clear, he was strongly against Eyre & more {predictably} if possible against the young officers [?]

I have today had such a number of fresh photographs sent me of various people we knew in Paris, some of them I like so much, but some others are not good ones. I have amongst them Guizot[,] Montalembert,[2] Prerot Parodol, Tulor Simon – which are the best I think – I am so sleepy I must stop.

> Ever with much dear love to you all
> Your loving and affectionate
> Julia B Gaskell.

Black-edged mourning paper with sender's address embossed.

Reproduced by courtesy of the University Librarian and Director, The John Rylands Library, The University of Manchester. Green Jamison Archive.

---

1   Ward contributed regularly to the *Saturday Review* from 1863 to 1887. The speech referred to here is probably 'National Self-Knowledge'. Lecture delivered in the Town Hall, Manchester, October, 2. [1866] Introductory of the Session of Owens College, Manchester (Bartholomew, *passim* and p. 5).

2   See *Further Letters*, p. 271 for Mrs Gaskell's account of Guizot and Montalembert in Paris in March 1865.

ISABELLA GREEN

46 Plymouth Grove
Manchester
Jan 5*th* [1867]

My dear Isabel,

It will be quite right about the money, I am going up to town on Thursday, and will take it to Florence. I am so sorry that I shall miss your coming here, I wished very much that you could have come before I go, but everyday next week is quite full, with various engagements, indeed I don't know how I am to get through all I have to do before leaving home. I am so glad that Annie is looking better, than when she left. I am so glad that baby remembered her. I think that I never felt anything like this dreadful weather, its quite wonderful if anybody is well, Florence went up this morning, when we got down to the station yesterday (Friday) morning it was so dark, with a thick fog that the men advised her not to go, so we came back again. This morning was quite clear & bright. We feel such a small party now, after having had F & C so long with us. And I am afraid that it will be lonely for Meta next week, I hope that when I come back that she will go to London for some time, we had a great temptation in another invitation to Oxford which it would have been charming to have accepted, but we are not going now, but I hope may do so sometime soon. I hope so much that Mr & Miss Long are pretty well, you can't think how often we think of you all, I think that each day their sorrow must become worse, as they get to realize it. I do so hope that Mr. Green is better indeed that you all are, I believe that Mr. Green will be here tomorrow, only unfortunately we shall not see him, as we are going out to lunch. Are you as much as interested as I am (which without yr. knowing, how much that is, is difficult for you to tell) in Jamaica?[1]

I don't know what I can do on Wednesday evening as we are going to the Grundys and Fred Grundy was out in Jamaica at the time in Colonel Hobbs[2] regiment and takes for Eyres side; Herbert Thompson

---

1   A likely reference to the Jamaica Prosecutions which were held in 1867 and which, therefore, suggest the year this letter was written.

2   Colonel Hobbs ordered the execution of a local rebel Arthur Wellington

(a brother of Isabel & Anabel Thompsons) went out to Jamaica just after with his regiment and he is the only person, only officer I mean, that I have heard speak properly about it. I am so sorry to think that I shall miss Mr. Greens visit here next week. Papa was so sorry to hear that he could not come tomorrow though of course he could so well understand the cause. I have been so busy with my kitchen,[1] bringing out the new report, and I was in great fear lest I should not get through the winter, however now I shall quite.

I am always so glad to hear from you if ever you feel inclined to write letters. I don't know if you hate writing them as much as I do. I suppose you don't think of coming over to Mr. Goldwin Smith's lectures. I *must* be home for the two last.

> Ever with much dear love to you all from
> Yrs. affectionately
> Julia B Gaskell

Black-edged mourning paper with sender's address embossed.

Reproduced by courtesy of the University Librarian and Director, The John Rylands Library, The University of Manchester. Green Jamison Archive.

ISABELLA GREEN

> Pen-y-gwryd Hotel.
> Llanberis.
> North Wales.
> [August 1867][2]

My dearest Isabel.

You can't think how glad we were to get your letter, particularly glad in this place, one feels to depend a good deal upon letters. We are so happy here – the only drawback is that one can't *quite* forget that one has to go back to Manchester and people. Its so wild and grand, we are quite up in the middle of the hills, we feel to be quite in he heart of them – we are just at the point, where the roads from Capel

---

(*Manchester Guardian*, 28 February 1867. p. 3, col.5).

1   A likely reference to one of the soup kitchens in Manchester that helped the poorest people.

2   Meta's letter of August 3 1867 confirms the date of this letter.

Curig, Beddgelert and Llanberis meet – Snowdon is quite close –[1] We have got now very fond of this little inn, at first our rooms seemed so tiny as if we could hardly turn round. Now that we have got used to them they seem quite spacious – one of the sitting rooms has two windows, from both of which you have a perfect view, it makes one very lazy, for one is very much tempted to do nothing but look out of them. Writing is difficult for another reason – we have only two little tables the larger of which is covered with books, so we have to write on our knees or on one [of] the chairs. We meant to get so much reading done, and thought we should have so much time, but somehow we have hardly done anything, for one thing we are out nearly all day, and though one does take a book out, one does not read much. I suppose you have read Carlyle's absurd article in Macmillan[.] I wonder if you have read Mr. Sidgwick's in that, a much better one I think, its so extremely clever I think, and I am so glad that it cuts up Mathew Arnolds lecture on Culture that was in the Cornhill.[2]

This inn is so elastic, it seems to hold so many people, though nearly every night they have to turn away a great number – nearly every night there are people on the coffee room floor. Its most amusing watching all the people one gets to feel so interested in them – There have been a good many people here we know – The Crompton boys and a friend of theirs who are on a walking tour, have been here – and perhaps come back today. The people that come are young men who come to fish and sketch, it's rather I think too rough (or thought to be so for ladies to come) it reminds us very much of a little Swiss mountain inn. There is nearly always a car or coach going past, and its most amusing watching the people, Wales always seems to swarm with brides and bridegrooms.

The Owens the people to whom the inn belongs are such nice people,[3] they have 8 children (one "Owen Owen") and down to the

---

1   For a detailed account of the Pen y Gwryd Hotel, its situation and history, see the less than aptly titled *A Scrapbook of Snowdonia*, by Vernon Hall (Ilfracombe: Stockwell, 1982; repr. 2004).

2   Thomas Carlyle, 'Shooting Niagara: And After?', *MacMillan's Magazine*, August 1867, pp. 319–36; Henry Sidgwick, 'The Prophet of Culture', *MacMillan's Magazine*, August 1867, pp. 271–80 and Matthew Arnold, 'Culture and its Enemies' *Cornhill Magazine*, July 1867, pp. 36–53.

3   See Hall, especially chapter two.

youngest boy but one are all so useful – that boy (the youngest but one) who is only five cleans down the carriages and sees after the horses, its most amusing to watch him. They have such Welsh names like "Griffiths". I think that we shall stay here until the beginning of Sept. when we shall probably go home – after a little Meta will go to Wimbledon[1] and I shall stay with Papa at Manchester. Its so hard for Charlie[2] being at Liverpool we hope that he and a friend of his a barrister will come over here for next Sunday but it seems such a long way to come just for the one day. I wonder how yr. picture has gone on – it must be very difficult to get in the sun – Meta has been drawing a good deal here.

I am quite dreading leaving this place, If you should want any more information about the lectures I shall be so glad to be of any use. I don't know who they will have for Political Economy, perhaps I shd. think Mr. Fawcett[3] – hes so much in favour of womans rights that I shd. think he wd. be willing to come and make them worthy to have a vote, by improving them.

Florence had a letter from Annie, I was so glad to hear a better account of Emma. I should like to see the photographs of her very much. Annie mentioned that Emily was perhaps going with Cousin Mary into Wales. I hope if she does go, she will be as fortunate as we are in our choice of place. Are you going away any where? Papa has just gone off fishing, he does so enjoy it, and I think it does him a great deal of good.

Have you ever read Kingsley's "Two Years Ago"?[4] in that there is a long account of this place and the inn and Owens – he wrote a long piece of poetry, he, Tom Taylor, & Mr. Hughes, in the visitors book, and some one has taken them, it does seem such a shame –[5] Meta has

---

1   A reference to her sister Marianne's marital home.

2   Charlie Crompton, Julia's brother-in-law, husband of her sister Florence.

3   Henry Fawcett (1833–1884), distinguished Economist and Politician; in 1867 he married Millicent Garret (1847–1929) the noted suffragist (*ODNB*).

4   Charles Kingsley, *Two Years Ago*, first published in 1857, reprinted numerous times throughout the nineteenth century, though not much read today. For an account of the background to this novel see Colloms, especially pp. 217–23.

5   An entry in the Hotel's Visitor's Book for 1864–1868 reads as follows: 'Henry [?] Rawlins – Working Men's College, London[.] Disappointed in not finding some verses by Professor Kingsley – Thomas Hughes & Tom Taylor inserted by them

written to him for them – and he has promised to send them.

We went the other night to the theatre when Miss Kate Terry, Mrs Watts, Tom Taylor, Tenniel, Du Maurier, Mark Lemon, Hal Power, and a great many more of the Punch staff, acted for the family of Bennett, it was such a capital performance – I did so enjoy it. We are going out a long drive this afternoon, which will be very pleasant. Does Emily Aspland seem very happy? how young they both are to be married, particularly Mr. Lang hes only 23, is he? Papa is going soon to stay with Rupert Potho, who has taken a Rectory in Derbyshire – I envy him rather his going to Derbyshire it's so lovely. Meta and I have been there twice this summer, the second time to Lea Hurst and the country about there is so pretty.

Ever with much love to you all

Yrs. aff.

J.B.G.

Black-edged mourning paper.

Reproduced by courtesy of the University Librarian and Director, The John Rylands Library, The University of Manchester. Green Jamison Archive.

ISABELLA GREEN

84 P. G.

[?November 1867]

My dearest Isabel.

Thank you so much for your letter – I am so sorry that you will not be able to come over, I should have liked it so much – but I know how difficult it is to form plans beforehand. I think that as thats the case that I had better give up coming to you for the ball – as I am afraid I can't fix – so please fill up my place – I did not go down to the Fenian

---

in the book kept at this Inn in 1856. Sep 26. 1868.' A note at the foot of the page to the left of this entry reads: 'The said verses were *stolen* in the autumn of 1866. H. B. B.' A further note in different writing adds 'New copy rec – from Rev. C. K. OCT 1868. These verses by Kingsley, Hughes and Taylor may now be read in the appendix of Hall, pp. 278–280, and in the appendix of this volume. Photographs of the three men are framed and displayed on a wall in one of the public rooms in the Pen y Gwryd.

trials.[1] Ladies did go, and James Mellor is one of the marshals,[2] but I *cdn't* bear to go down and hear it – I hate to make a sight of the thing, I think another trial is different, though morally I object to giving way though my practice is quite contrary. I have had a great many discussions about these Fenians with many people – I can't quite make out my own mind – I am trying to reason out for myself the real truth, the philosophy of it – its so difficult not to take up a thing in a party spirit – I do feel very strongly about it – though I think the Fenian movement[3] itself a fearful mistake yet I admire the people (however mistaken I think them and their cause) who are willing to give up their liberty and lives for the sake of what they believe to be the right way of helping Ireland – what are these uneducated people to do? They can't alter the land laws or the church grievances – and yet whatever one says one sees the arguments on the other side – My sympathies are all for the Fenians and Ireland generally – \not that they are synonymous/ – but my sense – I condemn this movement – I have had such battles. I know every argument and its answer on both sides, and yet I am puzzled. Mr. Jack with whom I chiefly talk and write on such subjects, and who though "[?]" I think against Ireland, owing to his being Scotch – says – and says truly I think that "seriously I disagreed with Mr. Bright[4] and his petitioners most heartily (I, J B. G didn't) I believe Ireland has been

1   The Manchester Fenian trials opened on 28 October 1867, for the trial of twenty-six prisoners charged with the murder of Police Sergeant Brett on 18 September, during an attempted rescue of two Fenian prisoners from a prison van. Three men, Allen, Larkin, and O'Brien, were executed on Saturday morning, 23 November 1867 (Messinger, p. 177 and the *Observer*, 6 October 1867, p. 2, cols.1–3). The trial was covered by the *Manchester Guardian*, national newspapers and the American press. The three executed men became known as the 'Manchester Martyrs'. For a full account of these events and their repercussions, see Paul Rose, *The Manchester Martyrs: The Story of a Fenian Tragedy* (London 1970).

2   A Marshall was an official who accompanied the judge, providing administrative support. The judges on this occasion were Mr Justice Blackburne and Mr Justice Mellor (*Manchester Martyrs*, p. 52).

3   The Fenian movement, also known as the Irish Republican Brotherhood, was a secret society responsible for a series of insurrections in Ireland and Britain during the nineteenth and twentieth centuries. Its aims included independence for Ireland and the use of violence, if necessary (*ODBH*).

4   John Bright (1811–89), radical politician with a keen interest in Irish affairs; he was in favour of land reform in Ireland and supported a lenient approach to Fenian prisoners (*ODNB*).

shamefully used – she has still great wrongs, and every legal power of remedy is open to her, But if I catch people attempting a hopeless rebellion in even a modestly just cause – wickedly {working} rework-ing all the blasting lightnings of civil war on their country, for no end but to make dis-peace – especially if I catch a good ringleader, I shall have no hesitation about shooting or hanging – He may be a most hon-orable man – but he has committed an offence worthy of death. And if another person shoots down an innocent policeman, I, (calling myself the law and not myself) have no choice and should never hesitate – the (alien) against whom I have no moral indignation, has committed a crime which (as the law) I should never dream of not punishing" – that's what he thought[.] I trust that I have modified his views some-what since then, the case against McGuire[1] seems to me extremely weak how the jury cd. convict him on that evidence is surprising – I think however that there is such a very strong feeling that his alibi was a true one that hes almost sure to receive a pardon.

I am afraid I may have bored you – I didn't know if really it's a subject that you feel very deeply about, if it is – you may have cared for this, if not – well it cant be helped now. I have been reading lately one or two such interesting books. I wish that one had more time for reading – I haven't often had so many callers and calls as in the last month or so – and that does take up so much time –

Lucy Roscoe[2] and I are having German lessons together, and are working hard at that, I am afraid that we shall find it rather diffi-cult to be regular with it – but our present intention is to let nothing come in the way. I am very low just at present[.] I have a [?debt] of 23£ to begin the winter with. I see that that's what I never overdraw

---

1   A reference to Thomas Maguire, a private in the Royal Marines, who was included in the list of principal offenders along with Allen, Larkin, O'Brien and Condon but was given a free pardon on the grounds of mistaken identity. Maguire was subsequently discharged from the Marines, on the grounds of redundancy, but later recalled for service. Condon, helped by his American citizenship, was given penal servitude, initially for life, but later reduced to eleven years (Rose, pp. 52, 63, 65, 67 and 88–89). Michael McGuire, whose surname Julia has confused with Maguire, though one of the original prisoners, was not one of the principal offenders and was released without charge (Rose, pp. 43, 52 and 63).

2   Probably the wife of Henry Roscoe (1833–1915), distinguished chemist at Owens College, Manchester, from a Liverpool Unitarian family (*ODNB*).

my bankers book for – and of course winter is the very time that the dinners at the kitchen are most needed. I am going to write an urgent appeal to the Guardian. I have such an objection to people giving to a charity – either that they don't approve of – (and some people don't do so often kitchen), or else from a sense of it being the polite thing to do – Meta sounds so very happy in London she will be away until sometime longer – and as thats the case I can't fix my plans etc – so I consider I have quite given up on Knutsford Balls, I hope it will go off *very* well – and that you will enjoy – [it.] I *am* sorry that you can't come over. You don't feel inclined for 3 historical lectures on Germany "Germany before 1815" – "The German Confederation" – and the German Federal States – they are to begin next Wednesday the 13th. at 3 o'clock, *3{?}s for all 3* not much – they are going to be given by Professor Ward, one of the Professors here – and will be, I wd. think very able – he writes all the German reviews in the Saturday, and "knows German better than any Englishman" his father is the ambassador out at Hamburg – they are *not* to be for the Higher Education of Women – or the men – (the Higher Education I mean for men) and no examinations either – If you wd. like them I will get you tickets "The money to go to some Manchester Charity" – Alice Wimbush who was here the other day, she sounded to have enjoyed being at Forest Hay so much – Have you seen the Saint Pauls home office articles particularly in the first number strike me as good – the trades union ones, and the "leap in the dark" – the 2d. number I thought poor. I really must stop I have written in a great hurry as I ought to go out. Papa the last day or two has not been well I am sorry to say, nothing serious but its so wretched for a man to be unwell.

I am feeling very stupid as I have been all day at the "Clothing", acting shop woman and its very tiring work – I had the calico and very hard work I found it – Lucy Roscoe had stockings which I thought much nicer as she hadn't to add up 13 ¼ yds. at 53/4 or whatever it was, so I feel stupid – Do write to me I do so want letters and I feel so lonely at times – at any rate at any time ones glad of them

In haste with love

Yrs. J.B.G.

Black-edged mourning paper.

ISABELLA GREEN

84 Plymouth Grove,
Sunday.
[1867]

My dearest Isabel,

I feel so guilty as if I had written a cross letter, which was far from my intention – forgive me if I seemed so –

I am only writing a line to tell you how grieved I am to think that I wrote in the way I did – I was feeling rather overdone & at the same time rather "low" – and also I feel now that I shall be doing my duty by getting rid of these papers[,] I have had such numbers and what am I to do with them? all the ladies in Manchester have had them sent – I think I shall send all my superfluous copies to gentleman. They want their lectures just as much – I am setting up a rival set after these are finished for the higher "Education of Men" the committee being

Miss J B Gaskell

Mrs & ~~Professor~~ Jack[1] –

I forgot we are to have only ladies on *our* committee.

Will you[,] do you feel able to give a lecture {on} no 4 on "The application of the sewing machine in conjunction with the other ~~sewing appliances~~[2] \branches of domestic management,/ skirts, bodies and piques –" really why shd. not men be taught something useful – The introductory lecture on "the Laws of Cooking, or \household management/" will be given by Meta.

Excuse the nonsense I am writing but I have written already (and I am thankful to say this is the last) about 30 letters – the lecture next Wednesday Mrs [?Gogh] says will be "very good" –

---

1   The word 'professor' has been scored through, but not deleted. William Jack was appointed professor of Physical Science at Owens College Manchester in 1867; his inaugural lecture had focussed on the history of electricity (*Manchester Guardian*, 8 October 1867, p. 6, col.2).

2   Again, scored through, but not deleted, the intention apparently being to make the change of mind clear to the reader.

Dearest love to you all
Given in haste
Yours J.B.G.

Black-edged mourning paper.

Reproduced by courtesy of the University Librarian and Director, The John Rylands Library, The University of Manchester. Green Jamison Archive.

ISABELLA GREEN

> 84 Plymouth Grove
> Manchester
> June 23. 1868.

Dearest Isabel,

You can't think how glad I was to see yr. writing this morning, and to find a good long letter from you, and such a charming one too – The elections are extremely exciting to look forward to – I am not much interested in our local one – Ernest Jones means to get in, and so does Jacob Bright – and Mr. Matthew Arnold does not seem to have crushed our "butter spoiled" i.e. Mr. Bazley[1] – he was awarded with the Beehive idea of an examination, I have had such a quantity of liberal talk lately that I have got rather satiated. I don't know whether you heard of Meta and my going to Oxford? We were there just 3 weeks, I don't know when I have enjoyed anything more – it was quite ideal, everything perfect of its kind, and I never saw Oxford looking so lovely, all the roses out and the trees so green and fresh and the coleges a more tender gray than recollected – there were nightingales and all sorts of delightful things – then May is *the* time there – one got almost too much agreeable talk, one wanted to get hold of some stupid person who you need not think when you talked to – on the Saturdays numbers of people came down from London,

---

1 Ernest Jones (1819–69), who had acted for the defence in the Fenian Trials, stood, unsuccessfully, as Liberal Member of Parliament; Jacob Bright (1821–99) younger brother of John Bright, was Liberal M.P. for Manchester 1867–74; Thomas Bazley, MP for Manchester 1858–80, was regarded by Matthew Arnold as a philistine (*ODNB*). At the General Election in November 1868 Manchester returned one Conservative Member of Parliament, Hugh Birley, and two Liberals, Bright and Bazley (*Manchester Guardian*, 19 November 1868, p. 6, col.1).

numbers of M.P. s , we used to have such busy days, lectures in the mornings, a great many of the professors now allow ladies to attend the lectures, in the afternoons we used to go out great boating parties, coming home to go off to the boat races which were going on \ during/ the time we were there, they were most exciting, and it was so pretty as a sight, all the banks of the rivers covered with crowds that race along the side of the boats and on the barges any amount of smartly dressed people, and each barge with its flag flying. We used to go out most evenings we went to some most pleasant parties at Balliol, one of Mr. Jowetts was particularly pleasant,[1] I never saw such a collection of "somebodies", even the undergraduates were sons of somebody great – Browning, Mr. Lowe, {Grant Duff} some too pleasant people, and all the nicest Oxford ones too, the Grant Duffs, and Leslie Stephens and Miss Thackerey were down there a good deal.[2] We had a great many pleasant college parties, which are so unlike anything else, and its so quaint going through the meads in evening dress, and then up little narrow staircases, where only one can go up at the same time. We came in for some very pleasant lectures with Goldwin Smith giving the Brodies and Liddells,[3] we had some of them out in the garden, they were most enjoyable, he was so briliant over them and so epigram\m/atical, they were perfect of their kind, then we heard him give another "[?]" a sort of fourth "English Statesman" series[4] –

I am straight home from Oxford, and Manchester did look so dirty

---

1 Benjamin Jowett (1817–93), appointed Master of Balliol 1870; he became known for his controversial essays (*Further Letters*, p. 257, n.3 and *ODNB*).

2 Robert Browning (1812–89), poet and honorary fellow of Balliol (*ODNB*); Robert Lowe (1811–1892), politician and administrator, who developed competitive examinations for the Civil Service; Sir Mountstuart Elphinstone Grant-Duff (1829–1906), politician and author (*ODNB*), Leslie Stephens (1832–1904), distinguished writer, editor of the *Cornhill* 1871–82 and, from 1882–91, the *DNB* (*OCEL*); Anne Thackeray (1837–1919), writer and eldest daughter of W. M. Thackeray (*ODNB*).

3 Dean and Mrs Liddell, of Christ Church College (*Further Letters*, pp. 275 and 319).

4 A likely reference to Goldwin Smith's *Three English Statesmen: A Course of Lectures on the Political History of England* (London, 1867) which focused on William Pitt (1759–1806), Oliver Cromwell (1599–1658) and John Pym (1584–1643).

and colourless after it – we stayed with the Brodies all the time, their house is perfectly lovely, they have built a new drawing room, without exception the most beautiful room I ever saw, one side is one large window looking right over the Ch.Ch. meadows and Oxford. I can't tell you the pleasure it was, there seemed nothing hardly to wish for. They wanted us to stay for [?], but we could not, I hope we shall go there soon again – I am so glad that you had so good a time in London, it must have been most pleasant – I am going up there at the beginning of July for a month, to Florences and perhaps the Waterhouses. I hope so much that Mrs.Brandate[1] is better, I did so want to have some [?time] talk to Mr. Green the other night; but it seemed such a rush – the Nortons our American friends are coming over here in July how charming Americans are! Are not they – I liked Mr. Bellons very much, though he was not quite American enough for us. I am glad your concert went off well, did you pay your debt? I hope you will enjoy your visit to Wales, I didn't think *her* \(cousin Lucy's)/ part nearly so pretty as our part; – Pennygwryd, but then I like a very wild place, and she does not. I wonder if you will have much coaching its such a pleasant way of travelling I think, don't you? I am sorry that Mr. & Miss Long have been obliged to miss Italy, I do hope so much that it may do them good – I shall be so glad to hear from you again – I go to Flo' on the 1st I think, I don't know if you will write there or not I always hate writing to *two* sisters so to speak, it is such a mental squint. [?] about the waitress, we have heard of one, a Moravian!

    With best and dearest love to you all
    Ever yours affectionately
    Julia B. Gaskell.

P. S. You will no doubt of heard of Albert Cromptons engagement to the 2d. Miss Aikin, I hope shes worthy of him, hes such a charming lad – We have got a waitress now – I have kept this letter some time, but haven't had time to direct an envelope.

Sender's address embossed.

Reproduced by courtesy of the University Librarian and Director, The John Rylands Library, The University of Manchester. Green Jamison Archive.

---

1 Brandate: a possible mis-spelling of Brandreth, Isabella's maternal grandmother.

ISABELLA GREEN

84 Plymouth Grove
Manchester
March 14: 73.

Dearest Isabel,

I enclose a 1/s for the telegram –, which I took with me to the concert and fully intended to give you at leaving – p*lease* say no more about it, as I quite think and consider the telegram my affair – I was grieved I didn't see you into the hands of the Knutsford people, I trust you met quite safely – ? and didn't think me rude not to come with you – the truth was – I felt almost stunned with the music, and as if ones everyday life, of catching trains etc were quite forgotten. My adventures were rather I fear 'American' as I came out with the sorry tale, however, (I felt ashamed of it) I kept looking and smiling at an imaginary chaperone in the far distance and I think they only thought I got separated from her by the crowd – I did so enjoy having even that peep at you – My brains are rather excited by a wonderfully able exalting sort of lecture on Mathematics from wh. I've just returned home – [?] a life of music in mathematics and no everyday duties, such as finding kitchen maids etc [???]

Your loving
J. B. Gaskell.

Sender's address embossed.

Reproduced by courtesy of the University Librarian and Director, The John Rylands Library, The University of Manchester. Green Jamison Archive.

ISABELLA GREEN

Clapham Inn.
Aug 11[th.] [1873][1]

Dearest Isabel,

Our hearts are full of the deepest sorrow and sympathy for you, and also for ourselves in this great grief – we were so startled when we had your letter this morning and can hardly believe that so dear

1   The Revd Henry Green's death in 1873 dates this letter.

a friend has been taken from us, though one feels what perfect happiness it will be for him to be with the one he loved so dearly – I always think that dear Mr. Green was so intensely pure and humble, quite like a child in the way he never thought ill of anyone[.] I feel one ought to be so much better for knowing a nature like his; I felt he always was so ready for Heaven – I do feel dear Isabel so very sad for you all, tho' it must be a great comfort to you to feel that Mr. Green was spared pain and you the pain of watching his suffering. You must feel so lonely and dreary without him, I can only pray that God will comfort you as he alone can do, and if warmest tenderest sympathy can help you you have it dear dear Isabel from us all – My Father will I know mourn this loss very deeply, indeed, everyone that knew Mr. Green will do so

    With much love to you all
    Your most loving
    Julia Gaskell.

Sender's address embossed.

Reproduced by courtesy of the University Librarian and Director, The John Rylands Library, The University of Manchester. Green Jamison Archive.

WILLIAM E. A. AXON

84 Plymouth Grove
Manchester
Jan. 7th. [1903]

My dear Mr Axon,

Thank you very cordially for sending me Mr. Morley's speech,[1] and also for your thought in writing to him to point out the mistake.

My sister, I am thankful to say, is *very* much better.

I enjoyed my morning on Monday so very much and I must thank you for sparing so much of your time to show me the most interest-

---

1 John Morley (1838–1923), Liberal politician, writer and newspaper editor; a supporter of English Literature as a degree subject, he became Chancellor of Manchester University in 1908. The speech referred to here may have been one given to the National Liberal Club, London, the previous November (*Manchester Guardian*, 22 November 1902, p. 7, cols.1–2).

ing collection.

In haste

Very sincerely yours

Julia Gaskell.

Sender's address embossed.

Reproduced by courtesy of the University Librarian and Director, The John Rylands Library, The University of Manchester. Axon Archive.

JOHN ALBERT GREEN

The Sheiling –
Silverdale
Lanc
July 10th. [1906]

Thanks so much for the book safely received; which shall be returned as soon as possible.

J. B. Gaskell.

Picture postcard with photograph of the Sheiling on one side.

Address: J. A. Green Esq. Free Library. Moss Side Manchester

Postmark: Carnforth, 9.30 pm, July 10 06.

Manchester Libraries, Information and Archives, Gaskell Collection, Box 4.

~~~~~~~~~~~~

Appendices

BOSTON HYMN

The word of the Lord by night
To the watching Pilgrims came,
As they sat by the sea-side,
And filled their hearts with flame.

God said, — I am tired of kings,
I suffer them no more;
Up to my ear the morning brings
The outrage of the poor.

Think ye I made this ball
A field of havoc and war,
Where tyrants great and tyrants small
Might harry the weak and poor?

My angel, — his name is Freedom,
Choose him to be your king;
He shall cut pathways east and west.
And fend you with his wing.

Lo! I uncover the land
Which I hid of old time in the West,
As the sculptor uncovers his statue,
When he has wrought his best.

I show Columbia, of the rocks
Which dip their foot in the seas
And soar to the air-borne flocks
Of clouds, and the boreal fleece.

I will divide my goods,
Call in the wretch and slave:
None shall rule but the humble,
And none but Toil shall have.

I will have never a noble,
No lineage counted great:
Fishers and choppers and ploughmen
Shall constitute a State.

Go, cut down trees in the forest,
And trim the straightest boughs;
Cut down trees in the forest,
And build me a wooden house.

Call the people together,
The young men and the sires,
The digger in the harvest-field,
Hireling, and him that hires.

And here in a pine state-house;
They shall choose men to rule
In every needful faculty,
In church, and state, and school.

Lo, now! if these poor men
Can govern the land and sea,
And make just laws below the sun,
As planets faithful be.

And ye shall succor men;
'T is nobleness to serve;
Help them who cannot help again;
Beware from right to swerve.

I break your bonds and masterships,

And I unchain the slave:
Free be his heart and hand henceforth,
As wind and wandering wave.

I cause from every creature
His proper good to flow:
As much as he is and doeth,
So much he shall bestow.

But, laying hands on another
To coin his labor and sweat,
He goes in pawn to his victim
For eternal years in debt.

Pay ransom to the owner,
And fill the bag to the brim.
Who is the owner? The slave is owner,
And ever was. Pay him.

O North! give him beauty for rags,
And honor, 0 South! for his shame;
Nevada! coin thy golden crags
With Freedom's image and name.

Up! and the dusky race
That sat in darkness long,—
Be swift their feet as antelopes,
And as behemoth strong.,

Come, East, and West, and North,
By races, as snow-flakes,
And carry my purpose forth,
Which neither halts nor shakes.

My will fulfilled shall be,
For, in daylight or in dark,

My thunderbolt has eyes to see
His way home to the mark.

Ralph Waldo Emerson, 'Boston Hymn' (*Atlantic Monthly*, February 1863).

THE ANCOATS SKYLARK

The day was hot, the summer sun
    Pierced through the city gloom;
It touched the teacher's anxious face,
    It brightened all the room.
Around him children of the poor,
    Ill fed, with clothing scant,
The flotsam of the social wreck,
    The heirs of work and want.
The sunlight glorified their rags
    As he essayed to tell
The wonders of the country side,
    Of clough, and burn, and fell.
For, as he spoke, the schoolroom walls
    Kept fading from his sight.
He stood upon his native hills,
    All bathed in golden light.
Once more he heard the skylark sing,
    Sing right at heaven's door,
And fill the span of earth beneath
    With music from its store.
A summer cloud sailed o'er the sky,
    The sunlight passed away,
The teacher saw his puny boys
    With city grime all grey.
"And which of you has heard a lark,
    "Or seen its fluttering wings,
"As o'er the hills of Lancashire
    "It rises and it sings?
"Ah, no, the hills are far away,
"From Ancoats' toil and stress.

"The skylark, have you heard its song
   "Or seen its homely dress?"
A silence fell upon the class,
   On all the listening ring,
Then one said, "Sir, I've seen a lark,
   "And heard him loudly sing."
"And where, my little Ancoats lad,
   "Did you the layrock see?"
"'Twas in a wooden cage that hung
   "Outside the 'Cotton Tree.'"
Alas, poor bird! chained thus amidst
   The city's smoke and gloom,
No more for thee the sunny sky,
   The wild flower's sweet perfume.
Alas, poor cagéd Ancoats boy!
   That freedom's song ne'er heard
Trilled o'er the fells of Lancashire
   By this bright poet-bird.
Alas the teacher, who of hills
   The dear delight has known,
And, now amidst the city slums,
   Is bound by walls of stone.
And yet the teacher finds it joy
   To help the laddish throng;
The boy is blithe, and strong of heart,
   The bird ne'er fails in song.
So may the teacher's magic art,
   The bird's melodious ditty,
The sunshine of the boyish heart,
   Ne'er fade from out the city.
Until the time once more shall come,
   When free from bars and ties,
The bonny layrock's song shall thrill
   Through all the Ancoats skies.

W. E. A. Axon, *The Ancoats Skylark and Other Verses*
(Manchester 1894, pp. 9–11).

REMINISCENCES

TT   I came to Pen y Gwryd with colours armed and pencils
But found no use whatever for any such utensils
So in default of them I took to using knives and forks
And made successful drawings – of Mrs Owen's corks.

CK   I came to Pen y Gwryd with frantic hopes of slaying
Grilse, salmon 3 lb red fleshed trout, and what else there's
no saying
But bitter cold and lashing rain and black nor'eastern
skies, sir
Drove men from fish to botany, a sadder man and wiser.

TH   I came to Pen y Gwryd a larking with my betters
A mad wag and a mad poet, both of them men of letters,
Which two ungrateful parties, after all the care I've took
Of them, made me write verses in Harry Owen's book.

TT   We've been mist-soaked on Snowdon, mist-soaked on
Glyder Fawr,
We've been wet through on average every day three times
an hour,
We've walked the upper leather from the sole of our
balmorals
And as sketchers and as fishers with the weather had our
quarrels.

CK   But think just of the plants which stuff'd our box – (Old
Yarrels gift) –
And of those who might have stuff'd it, if the clouds had
given a lift
Of tramping bogs, and climbing cliffs, and shoving down
stone fences
For spiderwort, saussurea and woodsia ilvensis.

TH   Oh, my dear namesake's breeches, you never see the like,
He burst them all so frightful a'crossing of a dyke
But Mrs Owen patched them as carefully as mother
With flannel of three colours – she hadn't got no other.

TT   But can we say enough of those legs of mountain muttons

And that onion sauce lies in our souls, for it made of us
three gluttons
And the Dublin stout is genuine, and so's the Burton beer
And the apple tarts they've won our hearts, and think of
soufflets here.

CK Resembling that old woman that never could be quiet,
Though victuals (says the child's song) and drink formed all
their diet.
My love for plants and scrambling shared empire with my
dinner
And who says it wasn't good must be a most fastidious
sinner.

TH Now all I've got to say is, you can't be better treated,
Order pancakes and you'll find they're the best you'd ever
eated.
If you scramble o'er the mountains you should bring an
ordnance map
I endorse all as previous gen't have said about the tap.

TT Pen y Gwryd, when wet and worn, has kept a warm fireside
for us,
Sock, boots and never-mention-'ems, Mrs Owen has dried
for us;
With host and hostess, fare and bill, so pleased we are, that,
going,
We feel, for all their kindness, 'tis we, not they, are 'Owen'.

TH Nos tres in uno juncti hos fesimus versiculos

TT Tomas piscator pisces qui non cepi sed pisciculos

CK Tomas sciagraphus qui non feci ridiculos
Herbarious Carolus montes qui lustravi operpendiculos,

TH There's a big trout, I hear, in Edno, likewise in Gwynent
lake
The governor and black alder are the flies that they will
take.
Also the cockabundy, but I can only say
If you think to catch big fishes, I only hope you may.

TT I have come in for more of mountain gloom than mountain
glory

But I've seen old Snowdon rear his head with storm-tossed
    mist wreaths hoary
I stood in the fight of mountain winds upon
    Bwlch-Cwm-y-llan
And I go back, an unsketching, but a better-minded man.
CK And I too have another debt to pay another way
For kindness shown to those good souls to one whose far
    away
Even to this old collie dog, who tracked the mountains o'er.
For one who seeks strange birds and flowers on far
    Australia's shore.

Charles Kingsley, Tom Hughes and Tom Taylor; 1856
reprinted in Hall, *Scrapbook of Snowdonia*, 1982 and 2004)

See pages 317-18 above

APPENDIX II: BIOGRAPHICAL INDEX

William Edward Armytage Axon (1846–1913), a true Manchester man, born out of wedlock to a young servant girl; he received little formal education yet became a noted librarian, antiquarian and poet. As a Manchester Unitarian, he would have worshipped at Cross Street Chapel. He became a member of the Manchester Literary Club and was founder member of the Lancashire and Cheshire Antiquarian Society. He and his first wife had two daughters, Sophie and Katherine, and a son. Following the death of his first wife in 1889 he married for a second time, a third daughter, Dorothy, being the issue of this marriage (*ODNB*).

Henry Arthur Bright (1830–84), Liverpool Unitarian and shipping magnate. Literary connections included Richard Monckton Milnes, to whom he was related, and Nathaniel Hawthorne, who was a regular visitor to his home in Liverpool (*ODNB*).

John Bright M.P. (1811–89), born in Rochdale from a religious Dissenting background. As a prominent member of the Liberal party, he was a noted orator. He successively represented Durham, Manchester and Birmingham. Jacob Bright, his younger brother, was also a Liberal politician (*ODBH* and *ODNB*).

Ellis H. Chadwick. Although Mrs Chadwick features so prominently in Meta Gaskell's later correspondence, little is known about her background. Her biography of Elizabeth Gaskell, although still consulted today, is regarded by scholars as amateurish.

Crompton family. Sir Charles Crompton (1797–1865), Justice of the Court of Queen's Bench, was descended from an old Lancashire puritan family. He married Caroline Fletcher in 1832. One of their sons, Charles (1833–90), married Florence Gaskell. Another son Henry Crompton (1836–1904) married Lucy Henrietta Romilly; their son Paul (1871–1915) perished with all his family in the sinking of SS Lusitania 1915 (*ODNB* and Derby Local History Library).

Henry Green, Revd (1801–73), graduated from Glasgow with William Gaskell in 1825 before becoming Unitarian minister at

Brook Street Chapel Knutsford from 1827 to 1872, during which time he established a successful boarding school in Knutsford. His wife Mary Green was one of Elizabeth Gaskell's closest friends and a long-term friendship was established between the Green children, especially Isabella, and the Gaskell daughters (*ODNB*).

John Albert Green, Manchester Librarian and bibliographer associated with the early Moss Side Library. He was the author of *A Hand-List of the Gaskell Collection* (1903) and *A Bibliographical Guide to the Gaskell Collection in the Moss Side Library* (1911).

Norton family. One of the most important and enduring friendships enjoyed by the Gaskell family with another Unitarian family. Charles Eliot Norton (1827–1908) was the only surviving son of Andrews Norton and his wife Catherine Eliot. Andrews Norton was descended from Dissenting English settlers who established a public House of Worship in New England in the late-seventeenth century. Charles Norton grew up in Massachusetts with three sisters, two older than himself and one younger. He was denied the company of a younger brother when another boy, born in 1833, died at the age of three. There was also another girl who died in infancy in 1834. After graduating from Harvard in 1846, Charles Norton took a post in a counting-house and concurrently established a night school, the first of its kind in Cambridge Mass. Teaching, rather than commerce, proved to be more suited to his natural gifts. When he joined Mrs Gaskell with her two older daughters, Marianne and Meta, in Rome in 1857, his ability to share his knowledge and understanding of art with his companions formed the basis of a life-long friendship between the two families. During the remainder of her life, until she died in 1865, Mrs Gaskell exchanged letters with Charles Norton, sometimes with a postscript from Meta. After 1865 Meta built on this friendship, writing to Norton until the end of his life. Following Norton's marriage to Susan Sedgwick in 1862, Meta established a friendship with Norton's wife and, later on, made friends with their daughter Sara. In 1874, two years after the death of his wife, Norton became Professor of History of Art at Harvard University. He made several visits to mainland Europe and to England where he received an honorary degree from Oxford. A close friend of John Ruskin for many years, he acted as Ruskin's literary executor (*Norton Letters*).

Thomas Seccombe (1866–1923), an Oxford graduate and scholar, assistant editor of the *DNB* from 1891 to 1900 and major contributor. He held senior academic positions in universities in this country and abroad. He wrote introductory prefaces for reprints of several well-known authors including Elizabeth Gaskell (*ODNB*).

Clement King Shorter (1857–1926), journalist, civil servant and editor; he founded the *Sphere* in 1900 and the *Tatler* in 1901. His publications included several studies of the Brontés (*ODNB*).

Effie and Snow Wedgwood, daughters of Hensleigh Wedgwood (1803–91), who was a grandson of Josiah Wedgwood (1730–95) founder of Wedgwood Potteries in Staffordshire. Frances Julia (Snow) (1833–1913) was the most intellectual of the two sisters; Katherine Ephemia (Effie) (1839–1934) became one of Meta's closest friends. The Wedgwood family were prominent Unitarians with links to other well-known Unitarian families, including the Darwins, and Gaskells (BHW).

APPENDIX III: TABLE OF LETTERS

Marianne Gaskell

Charles Eliot Norton	1857	21
Charles Eliot Norton	1857	22
Charles Eliot Norton	26 June 1857	22
Charles Eliot Norton	9 July 1857	24
Charles Eliot Norton	8 September 1857	25
Charles Eliot Norton	25 January 1858	28
Effie Wedgwood	22 April 1858	32
Charles Eliot Norton	5 July 1858	33
Charles Eliot Norton	13 October 1859	37
Charles Eliot Norton	30 October 1859	41
Charles Eliot Norton	21 April 1862	42
Charles Eliot Norton	3 March 1865	44
Susan Norton	10 September 1867	45
Isabella Green	1870	47
Clement King Shorter	10 December 1914	47

Margaret Emily Gaskell

Snow Wedgwood	8 November 1856	50
Charles Eliot Norton	1857	52
Charles Eliot Norton	27 January 1859	53
Charles Eliot Norton	9 May 1859	54
Charles Eliot Norton	20 September 1860	58
Charles Eliot Norton	19 April 1861	62
Charles Eliot Norton	28 August 1861	64
Effie Wedgwood	7 January 1862	66
Effie Wedgwood	19 January 1862	68
Effie Wedgwood	25 January 1862	70
Effie Wedgwood	28 January 1862	74
Charles Eliot Norton	20 April 1862	75

Florence Elizabeth Gaskell

Julia Bradford Gaskell

LOCATIONS AND ACKNOWLEDGMENTS

Alphabetical list of individuals and institutions who have made this volume possible:

Birmingham City Library
British Library at Collindale and St Pancras, London
Brotherton Collection, Leeds University Library
Cambridge University Library
Easson, Professor Angus
Greater Manchester County Record Office
Houghton Library, Harvard University
Knutsford Library
Lingard, Christine
John Rylands Library, University of Manchester
Joy, Dr Christine
Manchester Central Library
Marigliano, Emma
National Library of Scotland
Portico Library and Gallery, Manchester
Prince, Mrs Sarah
Shelston, Alan
Shropshire Archives, Shrewsbury
Uglow, Jenny; FRSL, OBE
Wedgwood Museum Staffordshire
Weyant, Professor Nancy
Wiltshire, Eur Ing Gerald Sidney.
If any names have been omitted, I apologise sincerely.

GENERAL INDEX

Names given in bold indicate correspondents. Page numbers for correspondents are also given in bold.

Literary Titles from Humanities-Ebooks

John Beer, *Coleridge the Visionary*

John Beer, *Blake's Humanism*

Richard Gravil, *Wordsworth and Helen Maria Williams; or, the Perils of Sensibility* †

Richard Gravil and Molly Lefebure, eds, *The Coleridge Connection: Essays for Thomas McFarland*

John K. Hale, *Milton as Multilingual*

Simon Hull, ed., *The British Periodical Text, 1796–1832*

W. J. B. Owen, *Understanding The Prelude*

Pamela Perkins, ed., *Francis Jeffrey: Unpublished Tours.*†

Keith Sagar, *D. H. Lawrence: Poet* †

Wordsworth Editions

The Cornell Wordsworth: a Supplement, edited by Jared Curtis ††

The Fenwick Notes of William Wordsworth, edited by Jared Curtis, revised and corrected †

The Poems of William Wordsworth: Collected Reading Texts from the Cornell Wordsworth, edited by Jared Curtis, *3 volumes* †

The Prose Works of William Wordsworth, Volume 1, edited by W. J. B. Owen and Jane Worthington Smyser †

Wordsworth's Convention of Cintra, a Bicentennial Critical Edition, edited by W. J. B Owen, with a critical symposium by Simon Bainbridge, David Bromwich, Richard Gravil, Timothy Michael and Patrick Vincent †

Wordsworth's Political Writings, edited by W. J. B. Owen and Jane Worthington Smyser. †

† Also available in paperback, †† in hardback

http://www.humanities-ebooks.co.uk

All HEB titles are available to libraries from MyiLibrary.com, EBSCO and Ebrary